Born in 1965, Jeremy Dronfield grew up in South Wales. He was educated (eventually) at the universities of Southampton and Cambridge, where he took degrees in Archaeology. This is his first novel.

The Locust Farm

Jeremy Dronfield

HEADLINE
FEATURE

First published in Great Britain in 1998
by HEADLINE BOOK PUBLISHING

First published in paperback in 1998
by HEADLINE BOOK PUBLISHING

A HEADLINE FEATURE paperback

10

ISBN 0 7472 5947 X

Printed and bound in Great Britain by
Mackays of Chatham plc, Chatham, Kent

HEADLINE BOOK PUBLISHING
A division of Hodder Headline PLC
338 Euston Road
London NW1 3BH

For Kate

The Locust
Farm

Rain . . .

Imagine it; all you can see around you in the deep darkness is rain, a world of sheeting points of water blowing, blinding, blattering, streaming and teeming in your face, stinging your eyes, sweat-salted in your mouth, runnelling cold down the back of your neck. Look behind; rain. Look all around you; black darkness shimmering with rain. Ahead, a puddled road winding across the blacked-out moorland.

Ignore the cold wetness and the pain; concentrate on the fear and keep running, stumbling onwards. Limping, trudging, one foot squelching in mud, one foot juddering on tarmac, both splashing and surging through hard-bottomed water, wandering, veering, dragging – Lungs ache – Breathe in hard, and the drops ride on the inrushing air, trickling around your lips, cold pinpricks on your tongue. Summon up the dregs of effort and will and surge onwards, trying to break the grip of the empty darkness behind; a vast black space with its single invisible occupant. Through the cold and wet and noise and aching exhaustion you can sense him out there, pursuing you.

—Legs keep trudging – vacuous inertia dragging at the drained muscles. Keep them pumping, left-right, flex, extend, up-down and onward – No . . . can't go on – *Keep going! Work those legs!* – Yes, work them, up-down-onward . . . no, can't. Too empty, too painful, no more resources, all spent, all wasted – *He's behind you!* – Where? – *Right there, in your head; he lives in your head. You can't escape him; you can run, but—*

1

There! There on the left. A track, a farm. A small twist of hope and relief draws out the last trickle of energy, fuelling your legs to carry you down the narrow track to the farmyard. Everywhere blank and dead, except for one light; a solitary square of curtain-coloured light in an upstairs window. You press the doorbell; a long, loud, raw jangling ring. There is a long pause before a sliver of light flicks through the gap under the door, reflecting on the rubber mat at your feet. The sound of a bolt sliding back and a chain-rattle.

A woman's face, a dark curtain of hair across her brow; a fearful face bisected by the curve of the door chain. You wipe the rain from your face and smile. You're lost, you need a bed for the night would she be kind enough to – Her wide eyes rake you from feet to face, and she frowns. *Who are you?* – You're lost, you need somewhere to shelter. Now that you have stopped moving, you can feel the intense wet cold filling the vacuum left behind by your dissipating body heat, shivers excoriating your torso and spreading outwards to your limbs and lips – She doesn't understand your cold, your desperate need. *This isn't a guest house* – You know that, but you need shelter. You can pay; look – She glances at the notes fumbled from your pockets, already damp and limp, and shakes her head. *Sorry, you can't come in* – But you can pay! There must be – what, fifty, sixty pounds here, just for a bed for the night. The notes are getting soaked as you hold them out, drooping sadly from your rain-glossed fingers – The door starts to close, chain slackening, light narrowing, face drawing away. *Sorry* – You start to beg, but too late; the lock snaps shut and the light is gone. You press the doorbell again ... Please, for God's sake ...

It's no use; she is alone in the house, alone in the dark on a storm-drenched night, miles from the nearest neighbour, and you have scared the living shit out of

2

her. You try to call through the door. You're lost, you've got nowhere to go. Please help . . .

The door opens a crack once more, and a grin of relief stretches your mouth wide.

Go away.

Slam, rattle, the bolt sliding firmly home, and you are left dripping desolately in the yard.

Part I

Mutatis Mutandis

1

The alarm clock's insistent jittering tore Carole from sleep with the dream still unfurling in her mind.

She was lying prone, her face squashed into the pillow and her left arm crushed crooked under her body, gradually growing deader and deader. Her jaw worked erratically up and down, forcing out amorphous moans and dragging her parted lips back and forth across the slithery patch of drool on the pillowcase cotton. She gasped hoarsely as the staccato bleating cut through the layers of unconsciousness, jerking her to the edge of the bed in a spasm of alarm. She tried to lift herself up, but her deadened, paralysed arm wouldn't move. Snaking her body, she struggled over onto her back and sat upright. At last, she could reach out with her still-living right arm, chopping her palm down heavily on top of the clock.

Silence.

She sat on the edge of the bed in the dark with the clock's luminous green hands jumping sporadically between her fluttering, gummed eyelids.

Light on; click.

In the yellow bath of the bedside lamplight, she examined her left arm, holding up the limp, insensate sausage with her right hand. It interested her, how heavy just one little arm could become when the muscles inside it stopped working; even more interesting to realise how much work those muscles must be doing even when you thought they were relaxed. She pulled up the sleeve of her nightshirt and looked at her bare arm. The white skin was deeply impressed with a welted red map of the sleeve's intricate folds; ridged and pink-furrowed arabesques like braille tattoos.

She let go of the arm, allowing it to flop into her lap, and looked at the clock. Five-thirty, and still dark out. After her first few days here, she had learned to place her alarm clock out of reach, so that she was compelled to get out of bed to switch it off. Otherwise, she would never be able to haul herself up to the surface in the numb silence of a rural dawn.

As she dressed and her arm began to tingle and ache with returning life, fragments of the interrupted dream replayed themselves in her mind.

She stripped off her nightshirt and threw it on the bed, then straightened the duvet over it. *Rain.* Fresh pants and a bra; she clipped it backwards under her breasts and swivelled it round her ribs, stretching the elastic straps up over her arms and settling her heavy flesh into its cups. *Running, breathing hard, running through rain from ... something ... someone behind her ...* When her deodorant had dried, she put on a T-shirt, thick oatmeal jumper and work jeans. In the bathroom, she sat on the toilet listening to the echoing trickle below her and letting the images flicker past. *Running – Raining – Running on exhausted in another person's body ...*

A quick cup of instant coffee and a cigarette, sitting shivering at the kitchen table; proper breakfast would come later, after the dawn shift. She drew slowly and deliberately on the cigarette, gazing at the mug of coffee and trying to order the recurring fractured, frayed-edge fragments of her dream. It was a familiar dream, so she was able to supply the missing pieces from deeper memory. *Running ...* She was always running in the dream. Running, stumbling, staggering in a blinding night storm in someone else's body ... Something else had been there, though, something not of the usual pattern. She searched for the oddity, and found it:

A face.

There had never been a face before. That was what usually made the dream so fearful; that feeling of desolate isolation. She could always feel the silent presence of people like watchers on the far side by a two-way mirror, and that one person behind her, pursuing her relentlessly and invisibly. Always fleeing; the faceless threat closing in from behind as she forced her faltering borrowed legs onwards. But now a face . . . and not just *a* face; *her own* face. That was right . . . closing the door on herself because she was in another body and couldn't recognise her self-image on her own doorstep.

A familiar dream. She had experienced it periodically ever since leaving her old life behind, but seeing herself in the dream was a new feature. She would have to give that some thought, to work out what it might mean. The rest was clear; her subconscious obsession with running away but never really escaping. Even here, even in this remote place, she could not hide from her own mind.

The coffee in her mug was growing tepid. She sipped at it, spinning it out while she finished a second cigarette. Dawn was emerging outside, its blue-grey light beginning to dilute the reflection of the white-lit kitchen in the age-rippled window panes. She stubbed out her cigarette, drained the cold dregs of coffee, and stood up.

She put on her wellies and stepped out into the mud-puddled yard. There was a lot of work to be done this morning: turning the soil in the kitchen garden ready for the seed potatoes, mending the fence in Randall's field and tending to the livestock, all to be finished in time to drive over to Haworth by late afternoon.

The first job was quickly struck off the list after she had walked over the field and inspected the soil. The heavy rain in the night had saturated the already wet earth, and was standing in shallow puddles in the ruts.

9

Running the rotavator over it would churn it into a quagmire and, even if she could get the seed potatoes in, they would start rotting before they could shoot. She made a note to get something done about the drainage, then sighed and headed back to the yard. There was still the fence to be mended.

She took a roll of wire and a bundle of baling twine from the shed, then went to the old cow byre. The cattle stalls had long since been removed, and the byre now served as her garage and workshop, the cobwebbed limewashed walls lined with shelves and tool racks. Parked on the cobbled floor astride the drainage gully was the only artefact of her old life (aside from her Alfred Wallis and her grandfather's cigarette case) to have stayed with her; the red Morris Minor pick-up bought by her father for her twenty-first birthday. She had intended to get rid of it along with all the other detritus associated with the old her, as soon as it had completed its last task of bringing her here, but somehow she had never seemed to get around to it. Anyway, that was so long ago that all its accreted memories had been shunted aside by a host of new ones. She no longer associated the old Morris with that time; it was now as much a part of the farm as the ancient stone buildings, the machinery, the rich, thick wet soil and the thin wind that coursed over the moors.

Propped aslant on its stand beside the pick-up was her only other vehicle, the fluorescent green Suzuki 125. Like the Morris, the land had left its imprint on the motorbike's scraped paintwork, the soil working in and lodging itself in the deep criss-cross valleys of the tyre treads and caked along the grey undersurfaces of the engine.

Looping the wire around her body and stuffing the twine into her belt, Carole kicked up the bike's stand and wheeled it out into the yard. The engine fired on the second pump of the kickstart and rasped out a billow of blue smoke. Nudging it into gear, she revved raucously across the yard towards the open fields beyond.

The sun climbed slowly as she worked, dissolving the high haze of cloud left behind by the night's storm, and by the time she returned to the yard at eight o'clock, the rain-dripped buildings were glittering brightly and clothed in sharp shadows. She rode the bike straight in through the open byre door and parked it, then headed back towards the house for breakfast.

That was when something strange happened. She was walking past the barn door when she was overcome by a prickling sensation up the back of her neck, spreading down over her chest. She stopped walking and stood motionless, head tilted slightly to one side like a bird, listening to the sounds around her and within her; crows cawing as they rose from the bare branches of the ash beside the house, the muttering of a distant diesel engine, her own breathing welling and ebbing, heart pulsing, bumping in her chest, faster than it should be ... and something else ... some other subliminal sound that had induced the prickle; a noise that should not have been there, had no place in the accustomed spectrum of the yard. She turned her head from side to side, folding her hair back behind her ears, but the sound had gone. She replayed it in her head, trying to find its form and source in her memory imprint ...

The barn. The sound – something between a grunt and a gasp – had come from beyond the barn doorway.

The realisation triggered a sequence of associations which led back again to last night's dream ... *Rain – Running – Her own face shutting her out, looking fearfully back over her shoulder as the doorway light vanished ...*

Yes, the barn: *Go away*, she had told herself, and she had trudged away towards the barn.

She smiled and shook her head; she had just imagined the sound, a little auditory hallucination popped out by her subconscious as it quietly processed the dream. She was getting jittery, she thought, letting the dreams prey on her. Perhaps it would be best to get away for a couple of days. Rosalind would always put her up in Haworth if she wanted. And now that the tilling had had to be put back, she could afford to take a bit of time off. She decided to ring Ros after breakfast and sound her out about the idea. Satisfied, she set off again towards the house.

Then stopped.

She had heard it again; a distinct grunt and a sigh this time, from inside the barn. Her eyes widened as she looked back over her shoulder. The noise came again, and she stepped softly over to the open doorway and peered into the gloom; probably just one of old Willis's pigs escaped again, she told herself. The right-hand end of the barn was closed off by a large green tarpaulin suspended from the roof-beams, behind which she kept her sacks of feed and manure. She crept along, staying close to the wall, footsteps silenced on the straw-softened mud floor, and lifted aside the edge of the tarpaulin.

The piled plastic sacks were alone and untouched; no sign of pigs in here. She let the tarpaulin swing back, and turned round. Then she saw it. At the far end, protruding from behind a rank of old milk churns were some straw bales, and jutting out from the top of the nearest bale was a shoe; a scuffed and chewed black trainer with a grey-socked ankle and a flap of denim trouser leg.

Carole didn't pause for a closer look. She sidled back to the doorway, then ran across the yard and into the house, bolting the door behind her. She had seen those feet before; last night, in the dream, they had carried her

12

across the rainswept moor . . . and earlier . . . yes, before that, they had stood on her doorstep and begged for shelter. The tangle unravelled in her head, and she remembered his face and his voice, indistinct in the fuddle of late-night fatigue; the insistent knocking and jangling bell pulling her back from bed and sleep . . .

In the parlour, she unlocked the heavy wooden cabinet bolted to the wall beside the dresser and took down the shotgun and a box of cartridges. Cracking open the breech, she slotted in two cartridges and snapped it closed, then hurried through the kitchen to the back door. Halfway across the yard, she hesitated, glancing down at the gun's barrels. *Relax*, she whispered. *Don't panic; be cool*. She broke the breech again and slung the shotgun casually in the crook of her arm, barrels pointing to the ground and the shiny brass discs of the cartridges gazing up at the sky. After all, the gun was just a precaution; she didn't want a confrontation, just a psychological crutch. If her dreams were going to begin entangling themselves with reality and manifesting themselves as flesh before her eyes, she didn't want to face up to them without the might of firepower on her side.

She strode confidently into the barn, turned left and walked along to where the bales and churns were. She opened her mouth to speak, then stopped abruptly, her jaw hanging slack . . . There was nobody there.

2

When he woke, the rain had stopped and he was back on the road; a narrow, tree-tunnelled hollow-way cutting along the valley side. Thick cloud blacked out the stars, and all around him was impermeable darkness.

He had only been walking for a few minutes – stepping forward cautiously, arms stretched forward into the ink – when he heard the sound; a thin metallic buzzing in the far distance. A motorbike. He remembered hearing it earlier – the very same sound, receding – but he had only been dreaming then.

Soon the sound was joined by light; a diamond pinpoint on black-bed velvet, strobing between the trees. The pinpoint grew brighter as it approached, the dazzling apex of a broad cone of gradated night blue. He felt a perfect calm as the motorbike cleared the tangential point of the curve ahead and came screaming towards him. He stepped aside and pressed his back against the thick bole of a tree at the edge of the road.

And remained standing in the motorbike's path.

He stared at himself; he could feel the tree's rough, ridged bark against his back, but his vision gave him two superimposed images. He could see himself in profile, brightly lit in the growing headlamp wash, standing impassively, face calm as the roaring machine fractioned its distance second by split second. And behind this stark image, he could see the orb of light at the centre of a milling, swirling annulus of blue-white, expanding, enveloping, swallowing him in a vortex of sound and light.

Then it was upon him.

The engine roar wowed, the light flared, and the motorbike scythed through his body and dissipated like a spent sky-rocket, vanishing, leaving its dying echoes hurtling around the hollow, bouncing in receding waves from the invisible tree trunks as darkness slumped back into the void . . .

—and he woke.

The bed felt familiar, but it took some time to work out where it was. Then it came back; he was sitting up, shivering despite the hot weight of the blankets and Dad's old army greatcoat, in the bed he shared with his big brother Tim. Tim was sitting up too; his eyes, wide with fear, shone in the crack of streetlight seeping in through the curtains. As they looked into each other's eyes, they knew they had both been woken by the same thing; a presence in the room, a dense black shadow stooping over the foot of the bed, watching them in silent malediction.

They could still sense it, even in waking; an accretion of dull red surrounding and shaping the amorphous coalescence.

Tim moved first, bolting from the bed and racing across the room. Paralysed, he could hear Tim panting and fumbling for the light switch, and he waited desperately for the click and the feeble yellow light from the little bulb to annihilate the malevolent presence . . .

—and he woke again, gasping.

The presence had gone, leaving him lying there with something prickling the back of his neck . . . Straw; he was lying on a straw bale next to some milk churns, staring up at the thick, dusty Chinese-checker grid of a barn's roof beams and listening to a noise; a distant susurrant humming which at first he took for machinery – a generator or something. But is was too erratic, lulling and wowing irregularly. He sat up, easing his aching joints and hugging himself against the cold. The hessian sacks which he had wrapped around his body, and which had felt so cosy in the rain-soaked chill of the night, were now damp from his wet clothes, and their thick manurey smell made his empty stomach gripe with nausea.

He stood up slowly, letting the sacks fall to the floor, and walked over to the open doorway. There was no sign of anybody in the yard, and no sounds of activity from any of the other outbuildings. Except for that humming. There was a large, windowless breeze-block annexe built on to the end of the old stone barn, and the sound was coming from there. The door was secured by a heavy padlock. He pressed an ear to it. The sound became clearer – deep and throbbing – but he still couldn't interpret it.

His nausea was growing, so he went across to the front door of the house. Perhaps he would be able to beg some breakfast and get his clothes dried before moving on. He was about to press the doorbell when he heard a door slam at the back of the house. *As one door closes*, he thought to himself . . .

As he turned the corner, he saw a woman with a dark helmet of glossy hair – the very same woman who had refused him shelter the night before – walk in through the barn door, a shotgun slung casually over her arm. He hesitated a moment, then followed her.

Heart thumping, Carole grasped the twin barrels in her left hand and snapped the breech closed, then thumbed the safety catch off.

She had certainly not imagined the shoe, just a few minutes earlier, and here was proof. Rumpled over the straw bale in front of her were some old pieces of sacking she had left folded in the corner a few days ago. She prodded them with the muzzle tips; they looked slightly damp, even though everything else in the barn was dust-dry.

'Hrrmmph!'

The guttural, wet-throated noise behind her made her gasp and flinch; she spun round, muscles tightening, lips parting and eyes widening. Her fists squeezed involuntarily around the wooden stock and steel tubes, and she snapped a momentary glimpse of a dark man-shape against the bright rectangle of the doorway before both barrels detonated, vomiting parallel fountains of sparkled white smoke with a concussive double slamming, dense with instant echoes off the stone walls. The gun was only half-raised to aim, and the double-powered recoil flung the heavy wooden stock hard against her shoulder, tipping her off balance, sending her staggering back against the bale and down amongst the clattering hollow churns.

She knew she had hit him – she had seen his arm flung out and his body pivot under the impact before he fell – and she felt panic rise up instantly from her stomach to her throat. It surprised her, replaying the scene later, to realise that her mind had rehearsed two sides of a moral debate about whether to inform the police or not, concluded that secrecy would be safest and evaluated several possibilities for disposing of the body, all within the few seconds it took to scramble to her feet and run to the door.

She crouched over his body, the shotgun still cradled in her arms, and hastily examined him. He was alive; his eyes were closed and he was limp, but she could see his lids flickering and his chest swelling and contracting erratically. She loosened his damp, grimy blue puffer jacket. Its shoulder was raggedly spattered with holes, some blackened and curl-edged where spits of hot wadding had melted the thin nylon. Underneath the jacket, he was wearing a thick, marl grey cotton sweatshirt, which was rumpled across his chest and yellowed under the armpits. Its shoulder had a corresponding pattern of holes, soaked in an expanding patch of red.

. . . The fourth time he woke, he felt sure he was passing into another layer of dreams, a layer in which everything was a dense, swirling mass of red. He felt himself jostled by invisible hands, and heard a voice speaking.

He lay still for a few moments, believing he was eaves-dropping blindly on one half of a conversation, before realising that the voice was addressing him.

Come on, it said. *Open your eyes.*

He opened his eyes obediently, the livid red lava flow dissipating into blurred white dazzlement. His right shoulder ached and his arm was numb.

Can you hear me?

He could hear all right. It was a woman's voice, and beneath its panicked urgency, he could discern a deep, dark smoothness of tone. It was a voice he liked; he could spend a lot of time listening to this voice, if only it would calm down. He would like it to tell him stories or read poetry or sing to him ... He felt his cheeks slapped, and a shadow loomed into the white blur.

Can you hear? Just nod.

He nodded.

Look, said the shadow with the alluring voice, a little more calmly now that he had decided to collude with the dream, *I'm going to get you to hospital. I'll have to leave you a minute while I bring the car over, okay?*

He nodded again, but the shadow had gone; quick footsteps receding. Hospital? Why hospital? That was for ill people. True, his arm was numb and unresponsive, but that was all. He'd wake up properly in a minute, then he'd just roll over in bed and let the blood-flow resume. That would sort it out.

The white blur flooded again with oozing red.

Carole was through the byre door before she remembered that the car key was still on the hook in the kitchen. She ran again, the shotgun still clutched like a baton in her hand, around the side of the house. She discarded the gun on the kitchen table and grabbed the key. Back in the byre, panting frantically and sweating, she turned the key in the Morris's ignition.

Thrrrrrrrr—

She tried again.

Thrererrerreerr—

She stared at the dashboard. The fuel gauge set into the speedometer dial was reading three-quarters full.

Threhreehhrreeehhrreeehhrrrrr—

The engine churned and wheezed slower and slower under the whining twist of the dying starter motor, until it finally gasped and gave up, leaving just the hollow *tchnk* of the solenoid at each futile turn of the key.

'Fuck it!' she shouted, slamming the heels of her hands on the steering wheel. 'Fuck, fuck, fuck! Of all the bloody fucking times . . .'

Leaving the car key in its dead socket, she left the byre and hurried back to the wounded man. He was completely motionless now, not even twitching. She crouched over him and listened for his breathing – hoarse and weak – then his heartbeat, which was faint and erratic.

'Right,' she whispered, 'last resorts.'

Grasping his intact arm, she managed, with a great deal of hauling, grunting, readjusting and scuffling, to raise his body into an awkward, staggering fireman's lift. As she carried him to the house, she could feel his head bumping heavily against her shoulder blades, and his limp arm swinging, the hand brushing her buttocks. With each jolt, he wheezed and grunted in his unconsciousness.

In the kitchen, she laid him out on the rough wooden table, removed the shotgun and went to collect the items she would need. The bathroom cabinet yielded a bottle of surgical spirit and a pair of long, narrow-nosed tweezers. Back in the kitchen, ransacking cupboards and drawers produced bandages, wound dressings, a soup bowl and a pair of heavy duty scissors. Working quickly and dexterously, she removed his jacket and cut away the sweatshirt, sweeping through the fabric in long, bold slices from hem to neck and neck to cuff, then pulled it away from his bare torso. His shoulder was thickly glossed with viscous red, stained darker, almost black, where the pellets had pierced. The blood was still trickling, dripping from his skin onto the scarred oak tabletop.

She tipped half the bottle of spirit into the bowl and soaked a wad of paper towels, with which she wiped the blood from his shoulder, arm, chest and back. Now she could assess the size of her task. He had been lucky, and so had she, she supposed. He had only caught the fringe of the pellets' spread. If the barrels had swung round just a few millimetres more before going off, the force of both barrels at that range would have torn his body in half. She wiped away the ooze of fresh blood and counted: one, two, three... twelve entry holes scattered over the hard bulb of his shoulder and the soft muscle of his upper arm. Raising him slightly and peering underneath, she could see four exit holes, where the pellets had torn through skin, fat, muscle, fat and another layer of skin, tunnelling the yielding flesh from end to end and departing. That left eight still inside; eight little lead balls butted against hard bone and trapped.

She sterilised the tweezers in the bowl of spirit and probed the shallowest hole until she could feel the tweezer tips grate on lead. She squeezed, gripped and withdrew, and the first distorted, flattened pellet dropped onto the table. The second had buried itself much more deeply, and the tweezers sank in more than an inch, their widening shafts stretching the lips of the wound wide before the ball was snicked between their tips. She worked on for nearly an hour, penetrating, probing and pulling, until all eight pellets lay on the table beside his head, gummed in a congealing, purpling smear. Then she swabbed the wounds again, dressed them and wrapped his upper arm and shoulder in swathes of coarse, cream-coloured bandage.

Throughout the improvised operation, she had monitored his breathing and consciousness. Although his respiration had begun to liven up as the sharp vapours of surgical spirit drifted into his nostrils, he remained unconscious, not even twitching when she caught and twisted a thread of tendon with the tweezers. She had felt it scrape and spring away, and the beaded sweat on her forehead dribbled in sympathy, making her eyes sting, but he didn't move.

She decided to leave him where he was for now, at least until she felt strong enough to lift him again. She fetched a pillow and some blankets, removed the last of his damp, dirty clothes, and made him as comfortable as she could on the hard wood. Then, with weariness creeping over her, she sat down on the settle in the corner and began to watch over him.

From where she sat, his face and chest were profiled against the window and the greying sky. The blankets rose and fell steadily and his pale, waxy face twitched from time to time as he slept. Cut loose at last from the exigence of panic, she began to wonder about his identity and provenance. From what she could remember of his accent the previous night (trying to tease apart the true memory and the dream), he was certainly from down south, like her; London maybe. Obviously homeless, to judge from the state of him and the manner of his arrival, but what was a London vagrant doing wandering in the depths of Yorkshire?

Her stomach gurgled and her throat contracted with hunger; it was past ten o'clock now, and she still hadn't had breakfast. She got up again and cut some bread, which she spread with butter and honey. As she stood chewing, she took her first proper look at her patient.

21

He was tall; long-boned and lean, but it was an unnatural leanness, a gaunt wastedness of the kind that comes from stress and hardship and malnourishment. His features were strong and symmetrically structured under his unkempt, overgrown beard, but the cheeks and eye-sockets were hollow, sunken and dark. As for his age, he could be anywhere between late twenties and early forties.

Finishing off her bread and honey and standing back, she noticed his shredded jacket lying where she had dropped it, twisted against the table leg like a half-flayed animal. She eyed it for a few moments, then picked it up and searched the pockets. She found a small bundle of soggy ten- and twenty-pound notes, as well as some loose change in his trouser pocket, but there was nothing to indicate who he was or where he came from. The jacket, though, had a label inside the collar with something written on it. She angled it to the window to catch the light. The blue ink was blurred and faded by damp and wear, but she could make out the ghost of a name; 'S' something – possibly Steven or Simon – and 'Gold' something. She adjusted the angle. Gold*cliff*? Steven, she decided, was likeliest, Steven Goldcliff.

She put the jacket down and looked at him again. 'Well, Steven,' she said quietly to his sleeping face, 'I don't know where you've come from, but you're lucky to be alive.'

The Strand Scourer

Nigel sat on the walled edge of one of the raised flowerbeds in John Frost Square and waited for the clock to mark the hour. As the hands moved closer to eleven, a small audience – mostly mothers with push-chairs and struggling toddlers – gathered around to wait with him. The clock-face itself was relatively small and insignificant in comparison with its setting, a twenty-foot high mockery of a classical portico heavily engineered from what looked to Nigel like galvanised steel or distressed aluminium. They waited two minutes more, as the minute-hand moved to vertical and the clock's mechanism whirred alive. Fissures appeared around the columns and across the pediment, widening and gaping as the whole structure began to collapse inwards, steam hissing from the gaps. Square portals flapped open in the columns and horned devils leaned out, leering and rotating their heads. Under the roof of the ruptured pediment, wire-mounted creatures and pedalling mannequins tracked from side to side, flapping and trailing steam to a chiming, grinding, whirring accompaniment while children laughed and clapped and adults grinned, *ooh*ing and *aah*ing. The performance lasted a few minutes, then the devils disappeared and, with grinding gears, the portico slowly reassembled itself, a few last wisps of vapour escaping from the cracks as they closed.

Still smiling distantly, Nigel stood up and went on his way. He wanted to get a haircut on the way home, and Fred closed up at twelve-thirty on Saturday afternoons.

★ ★ ★

Fred Wright's barber shop stood in Bacon Road, one of the gridded warren of streets which clung like a net mantle over the shoulders of Stow Hill, clasped in a loop around the throat of St Woolos Cathedral and ending in slate-grey folds at the fringe of Commercial Street. Bacon Road was about halfway up the steep hill, and Fred's shop stood about halfway along it, sandwiched between the Carpenter's Arms and the United News shop.

Despite the chilly October weather, Nigel was sweating slightly by the time he had climbed to Bacon Road. He bought some cigarettes from the newsagent, then pushed open the door to another time, a vanished world. Little had altered in Fred's shop in nearly fifty years of proprietorship: Fred did not like things to change. Nigel had only recently moved to Newport, and the first time he had walked into Fred's shop, it had been for the simple sake of a cheap haircut, but he had returned (far oftener than he really needed to) for the pleasure of the experience, of stepping into the little cabinet of anachronism and dustily forlorn forgottenness. Every time, as he stood up to pay, brushing the prickles of cut hair from his collar, he half expected to walk out of the door and find that he had passed through a time warp into a street choked with black Morris Eights, Ford Populars and short-trousered boys with grimy knees and lumpy leather footballs; a world that was withering in the white heat of change before Nigel had even been born.

As he walked into the shop, Fred was peeling the white sheet from old Dai Davies's neck, whip-cracking the thin linen over the floor to eject a teeming cloud of hair trimmings. He looked up at the sound of the bell above the door, peering a little to penetrate the obstruction of his incipient cataracts.

24

'Morning, Nigel,' he said, his tone displaying more confidence than was evident in most of his greetings; Nigel was one of the few customers Fred always recognised at first glance, probably because he was the only one young enough to possess a full head of dark hair. 'And how are you today?'

'Fine, thanks,' said Nigel. 'All the better for a shave and a haircut, though.'

He looked around. Aside from Dai Davies, there were two other customers in the shop; old men seated on worn bentwood chairs beside a coffee table piled high with last week's newspapers and old copies of *Reader's Digest*. They both looked up and nodded as he approached. The cash register jangled and slammed shut. 'Next please,' Fred called. Nigel looked at the two men, but they shook their heads. 'Already been sheared, butt,' said one of them; Bill Morgan, a retired metalwork teacher from Croesyceiliog. He was a large, lumpy man with an almost geometrically cubic back to his head which was covered with a thin grizzle of silvering cropped hair. The story was that Bill had been a great boxer in his youth, and had once laid a man flat and dead in the first round. It affected him so badly, they said, that he had put away his gloves and was ever after more easily provoked to bitter, blubbering tears than to violence.

'Looks like it's you, Nige,' said Fred, flicking out the sheet again and standing expectantly by his solitary pneumatic barber-chair.

Nigel eased himself comfortably into the chair's elderly cracked and buckled leather, slippery as ice from decades of buffing from a thousand slackly-trousered buttocks.

'What'll it be today, then?' Fred asked as he swept the sheet over Nigel's body from knees to neck, tucking the rough linen neatly under the collar.

25

'Five-bobber and a scrape, please.'

As Fred went to work with his hand-operated clippers, Nigel's gaze wandered over the collection of artefacts arrayed before him; the neatly arranged row of scissors and open razors (he tried not to think of them as 'cut-throat' since starting to entrust his stubble to their tender attentions), the thick leather strop hanging from its brass hook, the mock tortoiseshell combs, and the faded advertisements for Brylcreem and Vitalis bordering the large mirror, the silvering of which was patinated and dulling with age.

In all the decades of his proprietorship, the only major change Fred had tolerated within his shop had been his own name, and that had been way back at the beginning when he was still keen to gather favour from his customers. When he came home from Burma in 1946 as Leading Aircraftsman John Williams, he took a job working on the railways. In 1948, after a brief courtship, he married Gwyneth Rhys, whose father was station-master at Cwmbran. They moved to Newport, where John used his savings and a loan from Mr Rhys to buy old Fred Wright's business. John had learned the rudiments of barbering in the RAF, and could turn out as neat a short-back-and-sides and Friday night shave as any man living. For the sake of good will and continuity, he decided to keep the black-and-gold painted sign above the window saying 'F. WRIGHT, BARBER'. The customers all called him Young Fred, and the name stuck. (Nowadays, the older ones still called him Young Fred, even though he was within spitting distance of seventy-five). For the first twenty years of their marriage, the Williamses lived austerely in the little flat above the shop. There were no children. Gwyneth complained often about his refusal to follow the times and put up his prices so that they could improve the flat or move somewhere bigger and start a family, but he liked being where he was, and he hated things to change. By 1968, Gwyneth had had enough. She left him and went back to live in Cwmbran. (Or *Old* Cwmbran as you now had to call it, ever since the New Town had usurped the name and begun to swallow up the valley's farms and villages.) Young Fred carried on almost undisturbed by the parting; cutting hair and shaving faces in the fashion he had learned out in India and perfected in Burma. As the Sixties grew, fewer and fewer people wanted that kind of haircut, but Fred was unwilling – or perhaps unable by now – to countenance extending his repertoire. So, his clientele became older and older, and their weekly visits to his shop became increasingly ritualised. As his wife had pointed out to him with more and more exasperation in her voice as the years passed, he was very cautious about raising his prices. When Harold Macmillan assured him that his customers had never had it so good, he took the bold step of raising the price of a haircut from two-and-six to three shillings. There it remained constant for over ten years, except for a conjuring trick which changed it magically overnight from three old shillings to fifteen new pence (although the coins still looked the same). Then the Seventies brought an oil crisis and ballooning inflation. Alarmed by the escalating costs of scissor-sharpening, electricity, shaving soap and Brylcreem, Fred gritted his teeth and pegged his prices to inflation, introducing annual incremental rises of two new pence. His loyal customers might have complained good-naturedly about the rises, but he and they knew that Fred's prices were less than half of what even the cheapest barber elsewhere in Newport was charging. When the Conservatives were elected in 1979, the price of Young Fred's haircuts stood at twenty-five pence. The Friday after the election, the regular customers came to the shop for their trims,

27

shaves and a post-mortem. They were all solid 1945 Labour men and, even though they had mistrusted Wilson and despised Callaghan, on that afternoon they shook their heads in sorrow, the fragmentary remnant clippings that had escaped the attention of Fred's brisk brush drifting down on to their hunched shoulders. Not just a Tory government, they barked in disbelief, but a Tory government led by a *woman*. Fred kept his thoughts to himself as he sheared and snipped at their rage-red necks. He remembered how efficiently Gwyneth had managed their household on her meagre budget. Perhaps that was what the country needed; a bit of no-nonsense feminine housekeeping. As a mark of faith, he had frozen his haircut price at twenty-five pence, and there it had stayed for seventeen years.

Nigel suspected that the packets of Durex racked in the cardboard display tray in the glass-fronted counter cabinet had also been loitering there, unsold and disregarded, for at least seventeen years. As far as he knew, he was the only one of Fred's customers under sixty, and they no longer had much use for such items. On the other hand, the same seemed to be true of the pyramid of Brylcreem tubs and the black plastic combs elastic-strapped to a rectangle of cardboard beside them. Since first coming in here six months ago, the number of combs on the card had remained at seven. He had also noticed, queuing in Boots one day, that their Brylcreem tubs had a completely different design on them than Fred's; redesigned years ago to compete with gel in a modern market.

Fred had finished shearing and snipping Nigel's hair, and was preparing to shave him. He selected a razor, flipped it open, and scrutinised its edge under the dingy yellow glow of an ancient light bulb before grasping the strop and swishing the blade back and forth along its polished surface.

Dai Davies cleared his throat noisily. His haircut done, he had sat down with the others to exchange gossip. 'I seen Dr Thomas got isself one a them shotguns,' he said loudly. 'I was down the surgery this mornin and seen it.'

Fred paused for a moment and glanced at Dai, then went back to his stropping. 'Fancy that,' he murmured.

The other men lowered their papers and stared at Dai with open incredulity. 'A shotgun?' repeated Bill Morgan. 'Dr Thomas?'

'Aye,' said Dai, his wizened little face beaming with pleasure at having got everyone's attention so quickly.

'What's e want with one a them?'

'Dunno,' said Dai. 'For pullin is caravan, I spect.'

The others looked at each other, then back at Dai. 'What the bloody ell are you on about, mun?'

It was Dai's turn to look puzzled. 'You know shotguns – them four-before things.'

Nigel grinned through the thick blanket of soap that Fred was daubing around his mouth. 'You mean *Sho*gun,' he said.

'Oohh,' they chorused, their faces falling in disappointment as the intriguing picture of the local GP arming himself for his daily surgery crumbled away.

'Shogun, you silly old bugger,' said Bill irritably. 'Not shotgun . . . Bloody twp,' he muttered.

'That's what I said,' Dai protested.

'Oh, shut up.' Bill shook his head and went back to his paper.

Nigel was still smiling when he felt Fred's ushering fingertips on his forehead and obediently dropped his head back on to the tilted rest. The smile vanished and his face tautened involuntarily as the blade sliced through the layer of lather and began to skate across his skin.

'Seen this?' said Bill.

From his reclined position, Nigel could see in the

mirror that Bill was holding up the front page of the *South Wales Argus*, but he couldn't read the headline.

Fred didn't look up from his work, but he nodded. 'Aye,' he murmured. 'Awful it is ... Keep still, Nige, there's a good boy.'

Nigel tensed up again; the razor had finished skimming his cheeks and chin, and Fred's bony fingers were guiding the edge down over his throat.

Bill and his friend muttered, 'Aye, awful,' in unison.

'What?' asked Dai.

'That,' said Bill.

There was a crackling of newspaper. 'Oh aye,' Dai agreed. 'Awful ... Pretty girl, wunt she? Always did ave a thing for nurses, me.'

Bill tutted disapprovingly. 'You shouldn't say things like that, mun. Terrible things e done to er. It says yere—'

He was interrupted by a loud gasp from the chair. The sheet billowed, and Nigel sat up suddenly, clutching at his neck. Blood was oozing over his fingers and mingling with the milky lather. 'Shit,' he gasped. 'Shit! You bloody clumsy old sod!'

Fred was aghast, holding the razor up in horror, a bulbous bobble of blood-tainted foam trembling on its tip. 'It wunt my fault! Wha'd you jump like that for?'

Nigel glared at him. 'Don't just stand there, you old fool – I'm bleeding to death here!'

'Now then,' said Bill calmly. He walked across and crouched over, peering at Nigel's neck. He prised the clutching fingers away and looked at the wound. 'You'll live, boyo ... Yere, give it a wipe with this.' He took a wad of tissues from a box on the shelf and handed them to Nigel. 'Careful, mind.'

Fred was still holding up the razor, petrified, his old eyes shocked and vacant. 'I never done that,' he whispered. 'Never in fifty years.'

'Never mind, Fred boy,' said Bill. 'He's all right. Ent you, butt?'

Nigel stood up, trailing the sheet behind him, and examined his neck in the mirror. He nodded reluctantly. The cut was about an inch long; the blade had peeled back a ragged flange of skin, and the blood was still weeping from under its soap-stung edge. 'Got any plasters?' he asked.

Fred didn't reply; he was almost catatonic with shock and shame. 'Never,' he kept muttering. 'Never done it before.'

'Come on,' said Bill. 'Got plasters upstairs, have you? Let's go and look.' As he led Fred away towards the door to the flat, he beckoned to Dai. 'Make yourself useful and do a pot of tea, butt.' He glanced at Nigel. 'Wait yere. Won't be a minute.'

Nigel sat down beside the counter, his heart pattering frantically. Trying to calm himself, he went through his routine of counting the unsold items in the dusty display. Durex: nine faded three-packs of Fetherlite, four of Gossamer. Brylcreem: a pyramid of six round tubs. Black plastic combs on their card: from the top, one, two, three, four, five, six ... He paused in his survey. That wasn't right; there should be seven combs. Surely Fred hadn't sold one at last? He peered closer; the seventh had been removed and replaced with something else. Crouching forward, his face close to the glass, he saw that it was a long, narrow slip of printed card. He glanced over his shoulder to check that Bill's silent friend was still engrossed behind his newspaper, then leaned around the end of the cabinet and took out the rack of combs. As he examined the intrusive slip of card, his heart, which had been beginning to calm down a little, started to thump more violently than ever.

'Yere we are,' said Bill, emerging from the door at the

back of the shop with a steaming mug of tea in one pudgy fist and a box of Elastoplast clutched in the other. 'Soon ave you sorted out.' He paused. 'Where's e gone?'

His friend shrugged. 'Dunno. Just took off, like.'

Bill put the mug and plasters down on the counter and stumped over to the door. He peered out, but there was no sign of Nigel from one end of Bacon Road to the other. 'There's strange,' he said, and headed back towards Fred's flat.

By the time Bill had finished making the tea and had located the plasters, Nigel had already reached the end of Bacon Road. The blood from his cut was congealing on his neck, and had seeped a deep russet stain into his shirt collar. He paid no attention to it, nor did he notice the stares of the people he passed as he hurried up the hill and turned right in Garw Row. At number 87, he stopped and fumbled in his pocket for his key. His fingers were shaking, and he had some difficulty getting the key into the lock. After several attempts, it rasped home and the lock sprang with a hollow *thunk*.

In the quiet semi-darkness of the hall, he leaned against the wall for a few moments to catch his breath, inhaling the familiar acerbic mixture of ammonia and cat hair which always hung in the air of the hall and stairs. From behind the door of Mrs Zymela's flat, he could hear the muted *thump-thump-thump* of the *Grandstand* theme music. Suddenly, there was a loud mewling behind him, and he flinched violently as a scrawny Siamese leapt over his shoulder from the top of the dresser and went skittering along the linoleum towards the kitchen at the back of the house. As he watched it go, the compressed energy of tension seemed to dissipate, leaving behind just an aching numbness tinged with apprehension. His shoulders slumped wearily, and he trudged up the staircase to his room.

Once he had shut himself inside and rattled the handle to check that it was locked, he went straight to the wardrobe. Standing on tiptoes, he reached up and felt around amongst the dry dust on its top until his hand fell upon the two objects which had lain up there, undisturbed, since he first moved into Garw Row six months ago; a dog-eared shoebox with its lid secured by a rubber band, and a battered green Golden Virginia tobacco tin. He carried them both over to the table and sat down. He gazed at them both for a while, then fished in his jacket pocket and drew out the slip of card he had removed from the comb rack in Fred's shop. *Brittany Ferries* was printed in a panel on the left, opposite a space for the passenger's name and address. It had been filled in, and although the handwriting (a hesitant, spidery scrawl) was unfamiliar and it had been years since he had seen or heard the words written there, he recognised the name and address as instantly as if they were his own.

Trembling again, he opened the shoebox, peeling back the rubber band and letting it ping away across the room. He set the box on the table and began to go through its contents: photographs in colour and monochrome, cuttings, clippings, notes, sheets of paper folded or rolled, one by one they piled up on the table beside the box. There were some letters and several small pieces of glossy coloured paper cut from a magazine, and a small poster rolled into a tight tube. Under this was a large sheet of thick cartridge paper which had been folded over several times. He paused and unfolded it. It was a drawing in pastels of two people standing in front of a wide doorway in a stone wall; a woman in a broad-brimmed straw hat and a long white dress, and a man in a blue shirt. The pastel was unfixed, and had blurred and eroded in patches along the folds. Nigel touched the woman's face with a fingertip; lightly, so as not to smudge it. He gazed at the picture for a long time, then put it aside and continued his search.

At last, under an empty, crushed Guinness can at the bottom of the box, where he knew it must be lurking, he found the other card. He laid it on the table beside the new one; they were identical except for the name and address and the handwriting (this one was composed of bold, rounded strokes). He put his head in his hands and closed his eyes.

He had been sitting there for some time, staring into interior darkness and trying to fight off the images crowding into his brain, when there was a soft rapping on the door. 'Mr Inkpen?' said a voice. 'Are you at home?'

Nigel considered ignoring the query, pretending to be out, but Mrs Zymela seemed to have a sixth sense that told her whether her tenants were in or not, despite the insistent racket of televised rugby at full volume. He stood up and unlocked the door.

'What is it?' he asked, opening the door a crack.

Mrs Zymela stood on the landing, a tiny woman wearing the pink gingham nylon overall which seemed to be an integral part of her spindly body. He had never seen her without it, even when she went out of the house. 'Good afternoon, Mr Inkpen,' she said, in a prim accent dusted with her native Polish. 'Did you have a good morning?'

'Not really. What is it?'

'Really, there's no need to be so abrupt.' She smiled. 'Can't a mother tend to her chicks without a good reason?'

'Sorry.'

'Well, never mind. Can you not open the door a little?

You wouldn't be trying to hide something from me, would you Nigel?'

'Hide?' Nigel looked suspiciously at her.

'Like a young lady, perhaps?' She inclined her head and gazed at him coyly from the corners of her eyes.

'No, there's nobody here.'

'Oh dear . . . Oh my dear lord, whatever has happened to your neck? Is that blood?'

Nigel fingered his throat. 'It's nothing,' he said. 'Just a shaving accident. Don't worry. Look, did you want anything in particular? I'm a bit busy.'

'Are you sure you wouldn't like a dressing? I'll go and get one . . .'

'No! Sorry, no, honestly, it's all right. Look, I've got to get back.'

He closed the door on her eager face. There was silence for a while, and he pictured her standing there on the landing, head cocked, listening for any interesting sounds from behind his door, then he heard her slippered footsteps padding across the landing and down the stairs.

He went back to the table and stared despondently at the two cards . . . It had begun again, and after such a short time. He prised open the tobacco tin, checked its contents and pressed the lid back on again.

Tap-tap. 'Nigel?'

He sighed and stood up. 'What is it now?' he demanded impatiently, opening the door again.

Mrs Zymela put a hand to her wrinkled rosebud mouth. 'I'm so sorry to disturb you again, Mr Inkpen. You will think me such a fool. I was so concerned about your poor neck, I quite forgot why I came up here. This came for you.' She took a small white envelope from her overall pocket and handed it to him through the gap.

'Thanks,' he said, pushing the door closed. 'Goodbye.'

'Nigel?' she called. 'Are you sure you do not wish a dressing for your cut?'

'No!' he shouted.

Before opening the envelope, he examined the outside. It was small and fat, its flap barely managing to enclose its contents. The address was written in tiny, neat capitals in blue biro:

NIGEL INKPEN ESQ.
87 GARW ROW
NEWPORT,
GWENT.

Orange first-class stamp, and a blurred Cardiff–Newport postmark. Not that he thought studying these details would tell him anything worthwhile; he already knew who had sent it. At last, he took a deep breath, slid his thumb under the flap and ripped it open. There were two items inside: a densely folded piece of newspaper and a sheet of bone-yellow writing paper. Putting his forefinger and thumb together, he tweezed out the yellow paper and unfolded it. This handwriting, unlike that on the boarding card, was depressingly familiar. As he stood and read the letter, his hands began to shake and his face turned ashen. The envelope slipped from his fingers and fell to the floor at his feet.

My dearest Nigel,
Forgive me for addressing you in such an affectionate manner, but I feel that over the years, our occasional correspondence (a little one-sided though it may have been) has led us to become firm friends. I venture to hope that you feel the same way, though my senses tell me otherwise. Why must you always run from me, Nigel? I always sniff you out sooner or later; at each turn it becomes easier, not harder. Don't let the sniffing turn to

36

snuffing, if you take my meaning.

I hope that by the time you read this, you will have received my little gift. Such small items can evoke such extraordinary memories, can they not? Memories that we thought were buried and forgotten. I hope (I do hope rather a lot of things, don't I? But what is a life without hope?) ... Let me at least phrase it differently ... J'espère (yes, that will do, so long as your French is as polished as it once was and you do not take me to task over my clumsy grammar) ... J'espère que tu as aimé mon petit cadeau et les souvenirs qu'il a relevé. How's that? Should there be a subjunctive in there somewhere?

But enough of the past. Let us speak of the present; your present circumstances, to be precise. Distressing intelligence has reached me concerning the manner in which you are now earning your living. You may conceal it from those around you (especially the charming Mrs Zymela, who would be quite <u>shocked</u>), but how could you think to try to keep it from my eyes? I had dared to hope that, after my last letter, you might have taken pause to reflect. But no – your moral standards, if anything, have declined. Shame on you, Nigel. If you continue in this manner, you may find yourself right back where you began, and I am sure that neither of us would wish that. Perhaps the item I have enclosed will emphasise my point.

Good health and the very best of good wishes,
The Strand Scourer

Nigel slumped down on the bed, staring into the growing gloom. Outside, slate-grey rainclouds were coalescing in the sky and drawing a premature dusk down over the streets. He gazed at the folded sheet of newspaper bulging from the envelope, still lying where he had dropped it in the middle of the floor. He knew what it would be without even unfolding it: only one

37

newsworthy event had occurred recently that would be of interest to the writer of the letter. He knew without looking at it that the cutting was from the front page of the previous day's *Argus*; the same story that Bill Morgan had pointed out just a few hours ago, making Nigel start so suddenly that the delicately poised razor had sliced into his skin.

He crumpled the letter in his fist and, clutching it to his chest, lay down on the bed and turned his face to the darkening wall.

3

When he woke for the final time, he was in bed. He had dreamt that she lay beside him; he could smell the scent of her body around him, pervading the pillow beneath his head. But when he woke and reached out, she was gone, the suspicion of her presence dissipating in the thick, warm air.

For so many years now, sleep – so long as it was untroubled – had been an escape for him, and waking a burden, a painful disappointment that ached in his bones like physical fatigue. Something was different now, though; for the first time in . . . he couldn't recall how many weeks, but for the first time in a long time, he was in a real bed. Rather a firm bed, he thought numbly, but nevertheless a bed; his head cradled by a single soft, fat pillow, his body cocooned under the limp weight of blankets.

And there was warmth; warm air and – strange, he thought – the residual smells of cooking. Curiosity dragged his fluttering eyelids fully open, but everything remained obstinately dark. Staring upwards, he could make out a pale ceiling and the black silhouettes of bulky furniture against the walls. Somehow, he sensed that this was evening darkness, not early morning, and a panic seizure gripped him; he had missed a whole day's travelling. He tried to roll over to his right, but his arm refused to lift him, so he rolled to the left, scrabbling and kicking the blankets away from his legs. Suddenly, his fumbling hand met empty space and he plunged forward, slithering down to the hard floor, his tangled legs dragging the blankets behind him. A blinding blast of pain shot up his immobile right arm from wrist to shoulder and exploded in his chest, making him gasp and gag.

When the pain had reduced to a throb, he eased himself cautiously to a sitting position, looking up accusingly at the bizarrely high bed. Only then did he realise that he had been sleeping on a table. His bewilderment increasing, he tried to reason with the situation; at least he knew now why the mattress had felt so hard. It also explained the cooking smells; in the relative clarity of full consciousness, he could make out the silhouettes of saucepans suspended from a rack on the wall, and the looming bulk of an Aga. However, he still had no means of explaining the biggest puzzle of all: how he had got here and why his arm was injured and bound.

'Hello?' he called. 'Anybody there?'

There was no reply, which did not surprise him; he knew the feel of an empty house when he sensed it. Gathering up and containing the panic which was beginning to ebb back into his mind, he started to work out a basic plan of action. First things first; find the light switch. He stood up, fighting against the haze of dizziness that was fogging his senses. After fumbling around the walls for a few moments, he found the switch and flicked it, then set about looking for his clothes. His jeans and socks were draped over a clothes horse near the range. The jeans were slightly damp around the ankles and the crotch, but he pulled them on anyway. His puzzlement deepened when he found his jacket and sweatshirt in a tangled heap beside the leg of the table. The sweatshirt had been slashed to ribbons, but the jacket was just about intact enough to wear, so he put it on, draping it loosely over his injured shoulder and zipping it at the bottom to keep it in place. Finally, he located his trainers. It took quite some time to find them, because someone had put them in the oven, presumably to dry them. They were baking hot, and he winced and huffed as he pushed his feet into them. At last, he was ready to investigate his situation properly. He shook his head and rubbed his eyes, trying to dispel the faintness and giddiness, then went cautiously in search of whoever had brought him here.

Carole dragged open the byre door and switched on the light. 'Well,' she said, 'I hope you're pleased with yourself. That poor guy – what if he'd been really badly hurt? What have you got to say for yourself, hmm?' She looked accusingly, but the red Morris just gazed benignly back at her, its headlamp lenses glittering in the harsh light. 'Let's have a look at you then, you old sod,' she murmured affectionately.

The key was still dangling from the ignition where she had left it, and she couldn't resist giving it another try. The battery had revived sufficiently to turn the starter motor, but the engine still churned uselessly and refused to fire. She couldn't understand it; only the day before, she had overhauled the whole ignition system, putting in new plugs, rotor arm, distributor cap, condenser and contact breaker. She had tuned the ignition timing and, while she was at it, even took the rocker cover off and adjusted the valve clearances.

She opened the bonnet and stared at the little engine nestling in its huge, oversized bay. In her mind, she went through all the mistakes she might have made, but the only ones which could have caused this total failure would have been forgetting to set the spark plug gaps or leaving off an HT lead. She checked that the thick blue cables were connected in the correct sequence around the distributor and that their rubber-capped sockets were pushed home firmly. No problem there. She was sure the plug gaps had been set, but she decided to double-check, removing each plug from the block and checking the clearance of its contacts with a feeler gauge. They were all correctly set, and all their insulators were in perfect condition. The only other possibility was a blockage in the fuel system. She didn't want to begin taking that apart right now; it would have to wait until the morning.

She was so engrossed in thinking through the possible blockage points that she didn't notice him pad softly through the doorway behind her. 'Hello?' he said.

She jumped, banging her head hard against the edge of the raised bonnet. 'Ow! Bastard!' she spat, clutching at her head.

He stepped forward and put a hand out towards her, but she stepped back, shrinking away from him. 'Are you all right?' he asked.

Trembling, Carole palpated the back of her head tenderly and nodded. 'Yeah, I think so, just a bump . . . So, you're awake at last. You scared the hell out of me, Steven.'

'I'm sorry.'

'That's twice in one day . . . How's your shoulder?'

Steven glanced down at the bandages under his tattered jacket. 'Don't know,' he said. 'Feels a bit numb. Aching a bit.'

She smiled grimly. 'I suppose it would,' she said. Yes, the accent was definitely London; the flattened vowels were lifted a little, suggesting a working-class background made good, perhaps with a bit of higher education. She found herself feeling slightly more relaxed; despite his dishevelment and his frightful beard (not to mention the acid *smell* of him), he had an inoffensively vulnerable meekness about him. 'Did you find anything to eat?' she asked. He shook his head. 'Come on, then. I'll make you some dinner . . . And, er, you'd better have a bath, okay? I'll dig out some clean clothes; you're not much bigger than me.' She moved around him and headed for the door, but he stayed where he was, gazing into the Morris's engine bay.

'What's up?' he asked, nodding at it.

She came back and stood beside him. 'I'm not sure. Could be a fuel blockage. I'll sort it out in the morning . . . Come on, let's go and get some food.'

'Won't it start?'

'No,' she sighed. 'I would have got you to hospital if it had.'

He peered at the engine, then his face brightened suddenly. 'Look,' he said, pointing at the ignition coil perched on top of the fat drum of the dynamo. 'The low-tension lead's come off.' He reached in and slotted the tiny wire's spade connector onto the tab on the coil. 'Try it now.'

Reluctantly, she climbed in and turned the key. The starter spun once and the engine clattered into life, roaring and settling down to a burbling rumble that echoed off the bare stone walls. She sat and stared at the dashboard, feeling humiliated; angry with herself for missing such a simple, obvious mistake, angry at him for pointing it out, and even more angry with herself for allowing him to.

'There you are,' he called from the far side of the raised bonnet. 'Listen to that; sweet as a nut. Someone's given this a good servicing, I reckon.'

It's not his fault, she told herself as she switched the engine off again and tried to adjust her expression to a grateful smile before getting out of the car. 'Where did you learn to do that?' she asked.

He seemed pleased with himself. The look of bewildered self-pity he had been wearing when he first wandered into the byre had been replaced by a wan but almost smug smile. However, as he considered her question – appearing to turn it round and about in his

43

mind like an indeterminate piece of jigsaw sky, trying to make it connect with something solid and recognisable – the confused expression returned. He frowned at the thin smear of grease on his fingertips, then looked at Carole's face. 'I don't know,' he said weakly.

She frowned back at him. 'Well, you must have worked on cars before,' she insisted.

He shook his head. 'I don't know,' he repeated miserably. 'I can't remember.'

4

Rosalind pushed her face-mask up over her head and turned off the welding torch. Its grumbling hiss died away and silence settled over the studio. 'He said *what*?' she demanded incredulously.

'He said he wanted to sleep in the barn.'

Carole smiled sheepishly. The waves of disapproval she sensed emanating from her friend made her feel as though *she* were the one who was acting strangely. She wasn't sure whether she was beginning to regret letting Steven stay (he had been with her now for nearly a week) or simply regretting having told Rosalind about him; either way, she had a manner of expressing opprobrium which never failed to make Carole feel foolish. She resented it, but it never stopped her from telling Rosalind everything, perhaps because of the glow of warmth she felt when her actions elicited approval.

Rosalind put the torch down on the bench next to the forest of blackened wire and steel plates which constituted her latest sculpture, and started peeling off her heavy protective gloves. 'Did he say why?' she asked.

Carole shrugged. 'Not really.'

She was especially disappointed by Rosalind's frowns and tuts and exasperated head-shaking because she felt that, on this occasion, she had been particularly resourceful. The problem of what to do about accommodating Steven had occurred to her while he still lay unconscious on her kitchen table. Her first thought was that she could perhaps persuade one of her male neighbours to take him in for the night. She rejected the idea at once; introducing him to a third party might lead to all sorts of awkward questions about how he had come by his injury. What if he wanted to press charges? She needed to have a chance to talk to him first, so there was no alternative but to let him stay with her. The idea of letting this strange man spend the night under her roof filled her with dread and even some revulsion, so she would have to arrange it so as to ensure her safety. She quickly formulated a plan. Her own bedroom had no lock on the door, but the larger of the two spare rooms did. After checking that the lock was sufficiently sturdy, she moved everything she would need for the night – bedding, nightshirt, fresh clothes for the morning – from one room to the other. She collected the shotgun and a box of cartridges from the living room and placed them beside her bed, then returned to the kitchen. He was still sleeping, so she quietly removed all the sharp knives from the drawers and took them upstairs, where she hid them in the wardrobe in her temporary new room. It occurred to her then that it was not only her person but also her possessions that could be vulnerable to this stranger. She had very little of value that would be portable, but what she had – her stereo, some CDs, a painting and a small silver cigarette case – she also carried upstairs and put in the wardrobe with the knives. Finally, she made up the bed in the smaller spare room and went back downstairs to resume her vigil.

Later that evening, after they had eaten and she was

feeling safer, she told him he could stay until the morning. Then, if he was feeling better, she would drive him in to Bradford or Keighley or wherever he wanted to go; preferably to a hospital.

He refused her offer. 'I ought to be going now,' he said.

'But it's the middle of the night!' she protested. She hated the idea of him wandering off on his own again. While he was shovelling down his helping of chicken pie and mashed potato as though he hadn't eaten for days, she had probed him quietly, trying to discern the depth of his amnesia. It was absolute; apart from a few fragmentary snatches from the last twenty-four hours, he could remember nothing about himself. She tested his general knowledge; did he know the name of the current Prime Minister? Or any Prime Ministers? He just stared blankly at her. Did he know who the Beatles were? Or Marilyn Monroe? *Star Wars*? Nothing elicited a response. All she had to go on was that he must have worked on cars. 'No way,' she said. 'Not until you're better. Look, I've already made up the spare room for you. You'll have to stay.'

His eyes widened slightly at that, a fearful expression creeping across his face as he glanced apprehensively at the curtainless kitchen windows. The way he looked at them reminded Carole of somebody; someone in a film or a book or something wearing exactly that kind of expression and saying, 'These are the sort of windows *faces* look in at'. The thought made her shiver.

'I can't,' he said, staring desperately at her. 'I can't stay.'

'Why?'

He shrugged. 'I don't know. I just can't.'

He was making her feel increasingly nervous, but she persisted. 'You'll have to stay,' she said, although her tone carried less conviction than before.

46

He chewed his underlip thoughtfully for a few moments, then appeared to come to a decision. 'I'll sleep in the barn,' he said.

'So, what did you say?' asked Rosalind.

'What *could* I say? I protested, obviously, but he was starting to give me the creeps a bit. I gave him some blankets and stuff and let him get on with it. What else could I do?'

Rosalind walked over to the corner of her studio and plugged in the small electric kettle which stood on the floor. 'You could have just booted him out,' she suggested.

'Christ, Ros, I'd *shot* him! I think I owed him a bit more than that! Anyway, you didn't see the state he was in. What if he'd wandered into a ditch or something?'

'All right, all right. Coffee?'

They sat down together on paint-splashed slatted wooden chairs and sipped from their mugs. Carole gazed vacantly around her at the congregated sculptures, and sighed. 'I mean, what could I do?' she asked again.

Rosalind pursed her lips severely. 'Don't keep asking me that if you don't want to hear an honest answer.'

'Sorry.'

'Look, Carole, how long have I known you? Four years? You're intelligent, practical, good-looking, but you let men trample on you. If it's not fathers or boyfriends, it's charity cases. You just can't resist them. I bet your best friend at school was the fat girl with the greasy hair and the lazy-eye patch that nobody else liked. And I bet you were the sort of little girl who was forever bringing home birds with broken wings that your father had to quietly kill while your back was turned.'

Carole smiled vaguely. 'Only once,' she said. 'And it was my mother. She told me it had got better and flown

47

away. I made a little splint out of a Zoom lolly stick. Michael told me years later he saw her kill it with a stone in the back garden.'

'Elaine did the same kind of things,' said Rosalind. Carole had heard stories of Ros's sister Elaine before; her name was often invoked because, in Ros's personal hierarchy of worldly competence and good sense, only Elaine ranked as more hopeless and sentimental than Carole. 'My father took us to the pet-shop once,' Rosalind recalled. 'We'd been on at him for months about rabbits, and he finally relented. We were allowed to choose one each. I picked a nice black and white lop-ears. Elaine, of course, had to go and choose the Rabbit Nobody Else Wanted – this big brown monster that looked like it was wild and had the beginnings of some sort of skin disease. It was all on its own in a cage at the back of the shop, and she couldn't bear to leave it there. The lop-ears was frightened of it. When we got them home, they established a sort of apartheid, which was just as well, because the monster died within a couple of months from whatever horrible disease it was carrying. Of course, Elaine was heartbroken. We had operatic wailing and teeth-gnashing for days until Dad brought home a replacement. Elaine wouldn't go near it – she was too bereft – so Muggins had to look after both of them while Elaine transferred her affections to some mangy stray cat that used to come into our back garden and spray on the clean washing.'

Carole looked resentfully at her. 'So you're saying I'm like that? That Steven's the equivalent of some diseased animal?'

Rosalind sighed. 'He's trouble, girl, a nightmare waiting to happen.' She leaned forward and looked earnestly at Carole. 'Christ, girl, you've had nothing but grief from men all your life, and now you're letting another one do it. What's the matter with you? For

48

God's sake, you don't even know who this guy is, where he comes from or anything. Fuck, *he* doesn't even know, or so he says. He could be a murderer for all you know.'

'Oh, come on . . .'

'No, I mean it. Okay, maybe not a murderer, but he certainly doesn't sound too well-balanced. What if he's mentally ill? You just said yourself he gave you the creeps.'

'Only for a moment. It was better the next day. He's not ill, Ros. At least not in the way you mean.'

'Really? How do you know? He sounds bloody strange to me. He's obviously paranoid for a start. What if he's schizophrenic?'

Carole shook her head. 'No. I've seen enough schizophrenics in my time. They were always in and out of Casualty, and he's not . . . well, he's not mentally ill. I think he's just frightened. Who wouldn't be if they'd lost their memory?'

Rosalind looked sceptically at her. 'If you say so,' she said grudgingly. She sipped her coffee. 'Where is he today?'

'Out, walking on the moors. He's been feeling a lot fitter over the past couple of days.'

'But he still lives in the barn?'

Carole nodded. 'He won't come into the house. I have to take his food out to him . . . Don't look at me like that! I can help him, I know I can.'

'Well, I'm sure you know what you're doing,' said Rosalind, in a tone which made it clear that she was sure of no such thing. She stood up and began cleaning the patina of carbon from the new sculpture with a wire brush. 'I think you should just bear in mind what happened with Ian and Beverley.'

Carole bristled. 'That's not fair. Don't bring Ian into this. You never knew him.'

'No, I didn't,' said Rosalind, pointing the brush at

49

Carole. 'All I know about him is what *you*'ve told me, so you can hardly accuse me of misjudging him.'

'It wasn't his fault.'

'No,' said Rosalind in a kinder tone. 'If you say so. But it wasn't yours, either; him leaving or . . . well, the other thing. I wish you'd accept that. What I mean is, you ought to have learned not to place men at the centre of your life. They're more trouble than they're worth, girl.'

'What about you and Richard?'

Rosalind turned studiously back to her work. 'Richard and I are different.'

'How?'

'We just are. I'm not some sort of man-hater, Carole; I just don't let them take centre-stage. Richard's considerate, for one thing. He knows he has to let me have my own life. That's what I like about him.'

'I suppose his owning the largest commercial gallery in Leeds has nothing to do with it?'

Rosalind was unfazed. 'It helps. I get a good reliable outlet for my work and he gets a good hard shagging on a regular basis. Fair exchange; no emotional robbery.'

'You don't think it sounds a teeny bit like prostitution?'

'Not at all. We both enjoy it, and we both understand the situation. He makes good money out of me; he'd still want my stuff even if I didn't sleep with him. I keep it up because I like it. The point is, we don't live together and we don't make unreasonable demands on each other.'

'Look,' said Carole wearily. 'You're talking as though I'm going to get involved with Steven. It's not like that; it's just a nurse–patient relationship.'

'There are more ways of letting them dominate your life than just giving them sex,' said Rosalind darkly.

'I'm *not* going to let him dominate my life. I just want to help him get his memory back.'

Rosalind finished brushing down the sculpture and stood back. 'You know,' she said thoughtfully. 'Something that's always puzzled me is why amnesiacs forget everything, but still know how to talk. How do they remember that?'

'Language is generated in a different part of the brain. It doesn't work in the same way as memory.'

'I see . . . You've been boning up on this, haven't you?'

Carole coloured slightly. 'Well, I've brushed up a bit; I need to know how it works if I'm going to help.'

'You don't think he'd be better off with a proper psychiatrist?'

'That's what I said, but he won't hear of it. He's scared stiff of seeing anybody.'

Rosalind gave her a knowing look. 'Why, I wonder?'

'Oh, for God's sake, Ros! Will you stop being so bloody suspicious. He's harmless. You don't know him like I do.'

Rosalind put up her hands as if in surrender. 'Okay, okay. Just answer me this, though: How come he knew how to fix your car? I mean, that's not like language. Or are you going to tell me the brain has a special area for knowledge of car engines?'

The same thing had troubled Carole at first: how could someone not know who they were or where they came from, but know that a loose low-tension lead could make an engine fail? He had to be faking it. It had bothered her all through that first evening until, by the time he went out to the barn, she was almost chewing her nails off with suppressed anxiety. As soon as he was out of the door, she had run to her bookshelves and searched out her one and only psychology textbook. Looking up Amnesia in the index, she learnt that some amnesiacs apparently lost what the book called autobiographical memory but still had access to other things, like technical knowledge and skills.

51

She explained this to Rosalind, but she still looked doubtful. 'What do you think caused it?' She asked. 'Like, has he had a bang on the head?'

'No,' said Carole. 'Not that I can tell.' Frustrated by her lack of knowledge and concerned that he might have some neurological problem, she had driven to Bradford at the earliest opportunity and equipped herself with a proper clinical textbook on neuropsychology and amnesia. Studying this revealed a bewildering variety of amnesias, of which Steven's was only one peculiar manifestation. There were retrograde and anterograde types, post-encephalitic, post-traumatic, organic, psychogenic, each with an array of subordinate forms. She was relieved to find that Steven's symptoms – complete retrograde memory loss but no deficit in short-term functions – resembled psychogenic amnesia and were therefore unlikely to be caused by brain disease or injury.

'You *have* boned up,' said Rosalind when Carole had recited this catalogue of disorders.

'I know I can help him, Ros.'

Rosalind came and sat down in front of her and touched her hand. 'You're really determined about this, aren't you?'

'Yes, I am.'

'Well, just you make sure you're careful, that's all.'

Carole withdrew her hand. 'Honestly, Ros, I'm not a child. I think it's about time you realised I can make my own judgements and look after myself.' She had had enough of this; she gathered up her bag and rose to her feet. 'I think I'd better be going now. Steven will wonder where I've got to.' This was partly true; she did need to depart, but the real reason was that she wanted to catch the shops in Keighley. Steven had been managing with T-shirts, a sweater and a jacket borrowed from her, but he was badly in need of a change of trousers and some underwear. She didn't dare tell Rosalind this, much less the fact that she was paying for the clothes herself. Steven had given her the last of his cash, but she had put it by in case he carried out his repeated threat of leaving.

At the front door, she turned back. 'Look, Ros,' she said. 'I'm smarter than you think. Just trust me, okay? I'll be fine.' Then, feeling a sudden surge of righteous happiness, she turned and tripped lightly down the steps to the pavement, smiling cheerfully to herself as she started the car and swung away down the hill.

Cold Harbour Pill

It was quite an ordinary housing estate, the Lodge. It clung to the skirts of the Iron Age hillfort from which it took its name, a quarter of a mile outside the mouldering Roman heart of Caerleon. Just an ordinary estate of four-square executive semis perched above the rich green flood plain of the brown, sinuous Usk. In one of the Lodge's artfully winding but nevertheless ordinary streets, stood an ordinary executive home; detached, four bedrooms, spacious garage with a Ford Scorpio parked behind a Rover Metro on the tarmac driveway. Just an ordinary house, but inside, something was happening which was quite extraordinary, at least in this part of the world, something which inquisitive neighbours suspected was a regular occurrence . . .

'What d'you think the problem is?' Cindy asked as the repairman emerged from behind her washing machine. She glanced at the plastic name-badge pinned to the chest of his blue overalls '. . . Peter? I've only had it two months.'

Peter shrugged. 'Don't know,' he said. 'The back side looks fine to me,' he added, winking suddenly at her.

Her eyes widened in obviously feigned shock, then she smiled coyly. 'What about the front?'

He watched appreciatively as she smoothed the clinging satin dressing gown over her breasts. 'I'll have a look.' He knelt down and opened the door, rolling up his sleeve and reaching in. 'Open it up and have a good grope around inside,' he grinned. 'Never know what you'll find.'

Cindy giggled and knelt down beside him, watching his thickly muscled arm as it fumbled around inside the drum. This close, inhaling the mixture of odours permeating the thin polyester of his overalls, she thought she detected the soft edges of something feminine; a soapy floral perfume which jarred with his heavily muscular body.

'Ah,' he murmured, 'what's this?' There was a short tearing sound, and his hand emerged draped in something red. The object had clearly once been lacy and diaphanous, but was now merely holed and flimsy. He held it up between them as they rose to their feet, dangling by its one remaining strap from his outstretched index finger.

Cindy giggled again. 'I wondered what'd happened to that!' she exclaimed. 'My favourite, too!'

'I'd like to see you in it,' he said, fingering its delicate fabric. Suddenly, he looked into her eyes. 'Put it on.'

She glanced anxiously at the window. 'What if my husband comes back?'

Peter grinned wolfishly. 'He can watch if he likes.' He parted the front of the dressing gown and cupped one of her large, broad-nippled breasts in one hand. As he massaged the dough-white flesh and thumbed its brown peak, her eyes closed and her lips parted. 'Go on,' he urged, offering her the tattered bra again.

'D'you like my tits?' she asked, taking it from his fingers and shrugging the dressing gown to the floor.

'Gorgeous,' he said thickly, gazing in rapture at her flame-red stockings and the neatly pruned triangle of blonde pubic hair.

'Well, what d'you think?'

The bra's right cup was intact, pushing its contents up to a high, bulging dome, while the other, torn and coming adrift from its strap, barely restrained her left breast from spilling out of its fragile hold. Without replying, Peter reached around her, grasped her by the buttocks and hoisted her up on to the washing machine. As he stumbled forward, his knee slammed the door shut, and the machine whirred and began to chug.

'Ooh,' Cindy murmured, 'that's nice.' Fumbling for support, her hand fell upon a large screwdriver. Eyes closed in ecstasy, she picked up the heavy implement and pushed its thick plastic handle between her parted thighs. There was a loud ratcheting noise as Peter twisted the programme knob, and the machine whined, screeched and juddered into its fast-spin cycle. 'Aah!' Cindy gasped, 'aaaahh!' She threw back her head and thrust her hips forward, grinding down on the screw-driver's fat plastic shaft. 'Oh, ah, *oooohh*!' Peter watched in delight as she shuddered, moaned and climaxed in a frothing swirl of tossed hair. With one last squeal, her body tensed, quivered and subsided as the machine reached the end of its cycle and, with a rapidly descend-ing whine, faded to silence.

Cindy wiped the wisps of hair from her face and looked hungrily at him. 'Right,' she panted, removing the screwdriver and tapping his chest with its tip, 'now I'm ready for some real cock.' In her haste, she failed to notice the look of alarm spreading across Peter's face as she seized the zip of his overall and swept it down to his crotch. She pushed her hand inside and fumbled around, then her eyes met his and her expectant expres-sion crumbled into exasperation. 'Oh, for fuck's sake!' she muttered. 'Mashed bananas.'

There was a bark of laughter from the other side of the kitchen as she shoved Peter aside and slid down from the washing machine. She pushed past the gig-gling cameraman and grabbed the long black coat which hung from the back of the door, putting it on and wrapping it tightly around herself.

'Cut!' yelled the director. 'What's the matter, love? It was going great.'

'Ask him,' she replied, lighting a cigarette and mumbling angrily around its filter. 'That's the third time this week, Derek.'

Derek sighed and put a hand on her shoulder. 'It happens to the best of us, love.'

'To some, maybe, but it's getting to be a permanent bloody state with Simon. Simon bloody Softy.'

Derek patted her arm and walked over to where Simon was trying to re-zip his overalls. The zip had stuck at waist-level, and he was tugging furiously at it.

'What's the problem, Si?'

Simon muttered something inaudible and carried on struggling with his zip.

'Come again?'

'I said it's this fuckin script,' Simon snapped. 'Why's there so many soddin lines? I ain't bloody Al Pacino.'

'You said it, mate,' someone murmured.

'Come on,' said Derek, 'there's not that many lines. Tessa's not having any trouble.'

Simon flushed. 'I dint say I was avin trouble, I just said there's too many lines. This is porno – you know, *action*. Not bloody yakkin.'

Tessa strode angrily across the kitchen, pushing the cameraman aside again. 'No trouble?' she said incredulously. 'You missed half your cues. When I put the bra on and say "What d'you think?", you're meant to say . . .' She grabbed the thin sheaf of paper from Derek's clipboard and read, ' "Lovely. Keeps them in place while I do this." Then we get going with the washing machine.' She shoved the script back at Derek. 'You don't just stand there looking like someone's rammed a poker up your arse.'

Simon turned puce and lifted a trembling finger to

57

her face, but Derek stepped smoothly between them, hands raised in a well-practised conciliatory gesture. 'All right, all right, let's calm down a bit,' he said. 'Now, you're both doing just fine. We'll just—'

'An that's another thing,' Simon interrupted, turning his anger on Derek. 'What's all this crap with the bra? I mean, she puts the bra on *after* we've seen her jugs? What the fuck's all *that* about?'

'It's different,' said Derek defensively. 'Makes it more interesting.'

'Interesting? Bloody stupid, I call it.' The zip finally gave up its grip on the fabric and rasped closed. With one last scowl at Tessa, Simon strode across the kitchen and out into the hall, slamming the door behind him.

Derek turned to his small crew. 'Okay,' he said, 'let's take a break.' With a martyred expression on his face, he followed Simon out of the room.

Nigel watched with some amusement, glad of the relief. He had been feeling uncomfortable during the filming; a little disturbed at how much the scene they had been acting out had aroused him. Tessa was a good-looking girl, with a great body; much too classy for this cheap set-up. He switched off his lights and approached her.

'Cadge a fag?' he asked.

Barely glancing at him, she handed him her packet and lighter.

'Hard work?'

She snorted. 'If only.'

Nigel laughed. 'I suppose he must be under a lot of pressure,' he suggested.

'Huh. Under a lot of smack, more like. Wait till you see him with his kit off; he's got more holes in him than a sieve. He's just lucky it doesn't show up on VHS or he'd be out of work.'

Nigel lit his cigarette and handed the packet to her.

She put it in her pocket and hugged the coat more tightly around herself.

'Bloody freezing in here,' she complained. 'I knew this would happen. I told Derek, "Do the fuck scenes while Ray's still around", but he didn't listen.'

'Who's Ray?'

She glanced at him. 'Go on, you must know Ray. No?' She smoothed the thick coat over her hips and sat down on a chair. 'He plays my husband – you know the sort of thing; comes home while me and Peter the Pecker are at it on the washing machine and tosses himself off watching through the keyhole. Like the sad wankers who buy the videos, I suppose. Anyway, he did his scenes yesterday and buggered off to London. Got a better offer.' She flicked her cigarette ash on the floor. 'Good stunt dick, Ray.'

'Good what?' said Nigel.

'Stunt dick,' she repeated.

'What's that?'

She raked him from head to foot with her eyes, and he felt himself blushing. 'Been in this business long?' she asked. Her tone was mocking, but her face looked friendly.

Nigel shook his head. 'First day,' he said.

Tessa nodded. 'Thought I hadn't seen you before.'

'How about you? Been doing it long?'

'Couple of years,' she said. 'And it's starting to show.'

'Nah,' Nigel smiled. 'You look great.'

She snorted derisively, but looked pleased. 'Well,' she said, 'you seen all I got. Turn you on, did it?'

'Course . . . So, what is a stunt dick?'

Tessa stubbed her cigarette out in a saucer. 'Well, what happens is, when the star can't get it up –' she sneered at the closed door behind her '– they bring in someone else who can to do the close-ups and the come-shot. Ray does that. Ugly as fuck – that's why he's usually the

59

dirty peeping-tom – but he's got a dick like a monster and permanent hard-on.'

'I see.' Nigel was beginning to feel flushed again in the presence of this woman, with her drowsily erotic eyes and pneumatic body, oppressively naked under the thick woollen coat, talking so languidly and unashamedly about dicks and come-shots. He cleared his throat. 'So, what d'you reckon they'll do now?'

She smiled up at him. Then, without warning, she reached out and cupped the front of his trousers, squeezing firmly. He flinched, but resisted the impulse to step back in embarrassment. 'Bloody hell,' she grinned, releasing him. 'You *were* turned on, weren't you?' She laughed and lit another cigarette, eyeing him speculatively. '*You* could do it.'

For a few moments, he just looked at her uncomprehendingly, then his eyes widened. 'No way!'

'Why not? They won't shoot your face, just your tackle.'

'Oh, and that makes it all right, does it? Why me?'

''Cause there's no one else. Terry's too old and Wayne's the wrong colour.' She indicated the cameraman and his assistant, who were opening their thick packets of sandwiches in the far corner of the room. 'Go on,' she said, her voice taking on a conspiratorial tone. 'If we don't get this done today, I'll have to come back tomorrow and maybe the day after, too. Ray says he can get me work in London. It's better money, but I'd have to be there by Friday to get a look-in.'

'Well . . .' he frowned.

'Oh, go on. Do it for me.' She smiled slyly and parted the front of her coat. 'Imagine it,' she whispered, 'getting paid. What most blokes wouldn't give . . .'

He hesitated. 'You're sure my face won't be in it?'

She stood up. 'Course not. That's what us stars get paid for, showing our bollocks *and* our faces.' She

60

opened the door and yelled, '*Derek*! Come in here – I've got a new stuntman for you!' She grinned at Nigel over her shoulder. 'Don't worry,' she assured him. 'It's easy.'

Nigel recalled that first day as he hugged the rubber-strapped shoebox tightly to his chest and clambered over the stile and up the high, steep grassy bank of the sea-wall.

It *had* been easy, he reflected; one minute a semi-skilled lighting technician, the next a professional penis stand-in, a jobbing erection. And the money had been useful; an extra ten pounds an hour, plus a fifty-pound bonus for a good ejaculation on camera. And, most importantly, they hadn't shot his face. Since that first day in Derek's kitchen, he had penetrated and been fingered, fondled and fellated by at least half a dozen different women, in different positions, locations and rudimentary costumes. The plots didn't vary much, and neither did the women. Most squeaked, humped and panted mechanically through the scenes. Off screen, they were dead-eyed and unfriendly, numb and cold from the repetitive pantomime enactments of animal lust, as though fake pleasure were the only pleasure left to them. That could explain why so many of them were up to their eyeballs on smack, although Nigel suspected it was more likely to be the other way around; they were in this business because it was a marginally better way than prostitution to stoke up their habit. Not Tessa, though. Tessa was different, as spirited and animated in life as she was on camera, and Nigel had grown quite fond of her. No chemical other than nicotine and adrenalin spiked her blood, and she seemed to delight in the obscenities of her play-acting. Nigel regretted that he only ever worked on two videos with her – and on the second he only got to stand by rather than stand in – before she received the overdue call from Ray and departed for London. He helped her carry her bags to the station and, swept along by an impulse, kissed her heavily and clumsily as the train pulled up to the platform. She hadn't minded, of course, and her tongue swept vicariously around his gums before she laughed and pushed him away. She promised to write, but she never did.

After Tessa's departure, his work had taken on an aroma of dullness, and – although it was never sufficient to put him off his stride when called upon to perform – the dullness had brought with it a vestigial tinge of shame at the work he had found himself doing. And now he had been found out. Standing on the concrete lip of the sea-wall, he took the crumpled letter from his pocket and read it again.

. . . Distressing intelligence has reached me concerning the manner in which you are now earning your living . . . Shame on you, Nigel . . .

How had he found out? A stupid question; the Invisible Man always found out everything (whatever strange names he might choose for himself, Nigel would always think of him as the Invisible Man). He had probably even seen some of the videos; probably – it wouldn't surprise him – even recognised Nigel's faceless, crudely edited-in body. He did feel shame, but having it brought upon him by this particular person along with other, older shames drew up anger within him.

He put the letter back in his pocket and looked around. Up here, his body was the highest point in the visible landscape. Behind him, the chessboard-flat fields of the Caldicot Level, incised with deep-cut reens, spread away in all directions. Before him, the vast, grey-brown mudflats of the Severn Estuary filled his field of vision, fading in the distance into a pearl-white mist which shrouded the pillars of the Severn bridges upstream and the chimneys of Portishead power station on the far shore.

He had been here many times before, drawn by the perfect bleakness of the place and its silent, subtle danger. It was Terry the cameraman who first brought him here to fish for salmon, and he had returned again and again. In the beginning, he always came with Terry, who taught him how to walk on the deep, soft, slippery mud without getting stuck, told him how to avoid the treacherous, dangerous places, and warned him of the tides; of how the rising water could race across the flats as fast as a man could walk. Eventually, he started to come alone. Catching the bus from Newport to Magor, he would walk down the rutted lanes to the sea-wall at Cold Harbour Pill and often spend whole days wandering the foreshore, exploring the little cliffs and coves cut into the beds of peat and blue clay by the endless erosion of the tides. Eventually, he came to know the place better than Terry himself, venturing further and further out each time, following the receding tide until he would find himself out at the distant sandbanks where the fishing boats sometimes beached and rested while their crews waited for the tide to turn. From there, the security of dry turf was miles away, and the colossal sea-wall was an almost invisible thread on the distant north horizon. Nigel had seen a lot of places in his life, but this place – for reasons he could not quite fathom – had more power than any other to draw him back. Here, he felt secure in an absolute solitude, a knowledge that he was miles from the nearest human being, that no intruder could hide their approach from him, and that here his enemies might be insidious and unforgiving, but at least they were natural and impersonal.

It seemed right that this should be the place where he

would bury his past once and for all.

He took the letter out of his pocket again and slipped it in under the lid of the shoebox, where it joined the cutting from the *Argus* and all the other accumulated artefacts. He checked that the rubber band was secure, then put the box under his jacket and zipped it up tightly. Squatting down on his haunches, he swung his legs out over the lip and dropped down on to the huge granite boulders that were banked high against the wall's concrete core. He picked his way carefully down the steep, jagged slope, hopping from rock to rock until he stood on the narrow strip of sand at the foot of the wall. Cold Harbour was one of the most desolate parts of the foreshore; not even the tough, ragged saltmarsh had been able to colonise this stretch.

He paused for a moment, then launched himself forward. Most people coming out here for the first time tried to walk normally on the mud, and found themselves bogged down to the ankles at every step by its thick, sticky grasp which pulled and sucked at your boots and tried to tear them from your feet. The technique Nigel had learned from Terry was to take advantage of the slippery surface and skate across it, feet splayed outwards to push with the insteps. Once mastered, Nigel had found it almost effortless, propelling himself across the flats like a waterboatman behind twin bow-waves of spraying mud, perfecting his style until he was able to cover ground faster than he could run on dry land. The liquid surface spattered and swooshed under his feet, and he smiled into the slipstream as the endless empty space opened up around him.

A quarter of a mile out, he reached the first break, where the strata of peat and clay shelved down. The insistent lapping waters perpetually undercut the layers, forming a miniature cliff-face six feet high, its lower edge littered with the chunks that had teetered from the brink under their own unsupported weight. Nigel paused to check his bearings, finding himself beside the familiar deep trench, about the size of a large grave, which had been dug through the peat near the edge of the shelf. During one of their fishing trips the previous spring, he and Terry had come across the people who had dug it; a small team of four people crawling about in the slop in smeared yellow waterproofs under the direction of their leader, an archaeologist from Cardiff University. He had been friendly, seeming grateful for the unaccustomed attention, and gave the visitors a lengthy tour of his tiny excavation. His workers had cleared the mud from an area five feet square, dragging it with their hands until they had exposed the underlying solid surface of blue clay. Underlying this in turn was peat, which showed through in patches where the clay was thin. The clay, the man told them, was the same material as the brown mud, having been deposited and turned blue by compression. The peat, he said, was the ground surface as it had been in the Bronze Age, when the foreshore had been heavily overgrown marshland, thick and heavy with tangled vegetation. The site they were digging was a trackway that had been laid across the marshes more than three thousand years ago. People had laid hazel hurdles and bundles of brushwood on the boggy ground and pinned them in place with long stakes. Nigel was fascinated by the way the constant waterlogging had preserved the wood; the sticks, twigs and stake-tops – some with carapaces of bark still adhering – emerging from the clay as the workers peeled and picked it away with agonising slowness looked as though they had been put down less than a month ago. The archaeologist demonstrated how deceptive their appearance was by taking one of the sturdier looking stakes and crushing it in his fist like a peeled banana. The diggers had cut a slit-trench beside the trackway to

65

investigate the depth of the stakes, and one had been exposed in the trench's side, crimped and buckled as the contracting peat had slowly squeezed and pulled at it through the centuries. At the bottom of the trench, the archaeologist told them, they were standing on the dying stages of the Palaeolithic, before the rising sea had flooded the land, when the ten-millennia marsh had been dense forest whose stumps – their cut wood still fresh and white – pocked and hummocked the bottom of the trench.

Now, the excavations seem to have been abandoned, and the trench had half-filled with mud. Nigel stepped around it and found a place in the cliff where the eroded layers shelved more gently, and slid down the slope from the Bronze Age to the last Interglacial, below the level of the marshland, below the forest that had grown when the infant Severn was little more than a rushing stream, past tens of millennia of clay which had accreted when no humans existed in this region of the world, and landed at the bottom with a heavy splash, his boots sinking deep into the mud. This was where he felt most at home; here, there was no human presence outside the African cradle. Here his own past could lie, insignificant and forgotten, forever.

He twisted his feet from side to side to break the suction. The mud gave up its hold with a reluctant, gurgling gasp, and he set out again, skimming and skating further and further out across the brown flats. His quick, practised eye scanned the subtle, almost invisible nuances of glossy tone that indicated the thickness of the mud, and he skirted adeptly around the places which hinted at dangerous depths.

It was near noon, and he was more than two miles from dry land, when his zigzag course brought him to the first sandbank of the Welsh Grounds. He had caught up with the tide, which was still running downstream a hundred yards ahead of him. Breathing deeply, he stopped on the firm sand and looked around. The mist had risen and thickened, hemming him into a bright bubble a mile in diameter. Neither shore nor any landmark were visible, and the only noise was the faint lap of the outgoing water.

'Here,' he murmured. 'This is the place.'

He unzipped his jacket and took out the shoebox, then dropped to his mud-soaked knees. The grey-black sand was hard and waterlogged, but he dug furiously at it with his fingers until they were sore and grazed. He excavated a hole two feet deep, splashing about as it half-filled with frothy water. He opened the box and gazed one last time at the things inside: *In nomine Paul, Michael, et Alan sancti*. He filled the box to its brim with the loose sand, resecured the lid and lowered it into its watery grave, where it lay submerged while the remaining sand splashed and plopped over it.

He stood beside the grave for a few minutes, gazing inwardly at an interior landscape which now seemed as barren and featureless as the mudflats and sandbanks before him; razed and wiped clean. Satisfied, he turned for the shore.

The mist had thickened and closed in even more now, and he had to rely on his own tracks to take him back. He skated along, following the tacking seam of splayed, staggered skids, losing them in patches of still, standing water, picking them up again and continuing onwards. The third patch of water he came to was much wider than the others; he paused at the edge, scanning the mud on the far side in vain for skate-marks. He thought he remembered crossing it at an angle, but he couldn't remember what angle. He skated up and down the edge, feeling increasingly nervous, but there was still no sign of any tracks beyond the water. Eventually, he decided to cross it anyway, and try to pick up the trail on the other side. When he had splashed across, he stood still and studied the diminishing area of mud remaining visible within the encircling mist. Still no success. He was starting to feel the pang of nausea which presaged panic, and he concentrated on regulating his breathing, calming the fear . . .

Something had changed. Somewhere in the vast weight of dead air, something had altered, a sound had disappeared . . . It was the water; the subtle sound of the river lapping as it flowed down the estuary had gone. It had reached its standstill and the tide was turning. It had probably already covered the grave in the sand, and would be seeping on to the mud at any moment. He concentrated his ears, scrutinising the spectrum of sound . . . and there it was; faint, almost inaudible, the trickling, rippling whisper of water on the wet mud.

He gave up on the lost trail and, turning his back to the channel, leapt forward, skating for all he was worth, searing through the mud, splattering great dark fountains of glutinous spray that coated him from face to feet.

He had gone no more than a quarter of a mile when, suddenly, an inexplicable post loomed out of the mist in front of him; as thick as a telegraph pole, five feet high and canted to the right. Nigel, registering only the briefest surprise, skirted deftly around it. In all his explorations, he had never come across such a post before, and he wondered how far he must have wandered from his outward course. He was about to dismiss the thought when something made him slither to a dead stop. He looked around him in surprise. He was surrounded by wood – two wide, neat arcs of short, jagged stumps protruding from the mud, all leaning like the post he had just passed – and now he knew what that post was. He was standing in the midst of a hulk, a ship sunk in the estuary and forgotten, settling slowly into the soft surface as the decades passed and the water-borne silt piled up, filling its cavernous hull with mud. Nigel looked down at his feet; they had sunk less than an inch into the mud, and he could feel something solid beneath. Scraping with the toe of his boot, he uncovered a blackened timber. Its bulk sloped down steeply, and he was standing on its precarious tip. The nausea returned again, and he looked around desperately, but the mud's glistening surface was inscrutable, giving no indication of its depth. The only way out would be to turn around and retrace his steps until he was well clear of the wreck, then continue on his way, giving the sunken hulk a wide berth.

Now that he was conscious of the delicacy of his position, his effortless balance slipped away, and he was shaking as he turned carefully around, daintily poised on tiptoes, feeling the ancient, fragile timber creak beneath him. It was only a short leap to the nearest of his incoming skid-scoops. There must be more solid wood under that place. He tensed his body and, as he raised one leg to spring, the timber under his foot sagged. He felt rather than heard it crack, and he was pitched sideways. His raised foot – deprived of coord-inated guidance – slapped down awkwardly and sank to the knee, while the other, its support gone, buried itself all the way to the thigh.

Panic finally swamped rational thought, and he fought against the mud, twisting and flexing his legs, trying to break its cold, sucking clutches. But every movement pushed him deeper, until the thick brown glop gripped him from feet to groin. He was trapped; any effort to move was futile, only serving to drag him deeper still. Somehow, a shaft of reason pierced the turbulent panic in his mind: this mud was not like quicksand; so long as he didn't struggle, he would not sink any further. But being sucked into the mud was not the problem; he was stuck fast and somewhere out there, beyond the mist, the rising tide was quietly, relentlessly skimming across the flats towards him.

He closed his eyes and waited for inspiration, but none came. He would die here. He had come to bury his past, and now he would be drowned and buried along with it. He felt curiously calm about it. Perhaps this was what he had really, secretly desired; the little box in its little grave in the sandbank merely a symbol of the oblivion and eternal forgetting he really longed for. He laid his arms limply on the wet surface, closed his eyes again and waited for the waters to engulf him.

When they came, they came quickly; a thin rippling film at first, spreading quickly, advancing, washing and frothing around the hulk's broken timbers. It swirled about his hips, soaking through his jeans and chilling his skin, rising to his waist as it raced onwards and past him, swallowing the mudflat until all that could be seen was swelling water. He felt it lap at his lower ribs and begin creeping up his chest, and wondered how long it would take to reach his chin, his mouth, his nostrils. He anticipated the rush of cold liquid into his throat and lungs, and terror returned.

'No!' he bellowed. 'NO!'

He made one last despairing effort to free himself, twisting his body with all his strength, arms flailing and splashing in the water, but the mud still held him tenaciously. Then, as he relaxed and prepared to try again, he felt a cold trickle on the tops of his thighs. He twisted again and the trickle spread. The water was seeping between his body and the mud, beginning to break its suction. The desperate numbness of defeat melted away, and he was back in the game. He twisted again and again as the brackish water enveloped his chin and licked at his lips and at each twist, the water – his saviour and his executioner – seeped deeper until with one last wrenching, writhing effort, the mud gasped and belched up a cloud of brown silt and bubbles. His feet slipped from his boots and he slithered free just as the water was running up his huffing, panting nostrils.

When he had finished retching and coughing the silt-laden water from his gullet and sinuses, he lay back and floated motionless and exhausted on the lapping surface, his face turned to the pearl sky. Then, when his heart had stopped pounding and his breathing had settled down, he rolled over onto his chest and began to swim for the shore.

He stood on the sea-wall and looked out over the estuary. The mist was dissipating, the vast sky was filling with heavy black clouds, and the rain was beginning to fall, spattering on the surface of the choppy water which ebbed against the wall of boulders. He remained standing, buffeted by the rising wind, until he could feel the raindrops coursing in his face, then he turned and slithered down the grassy bank. He walked along the pot-holed, puddled track until he came to the culvert where the swollen Cold Harbour Pill ran under the sea-wall and emptied onto the foreshore. Pushed in amongst some reeds and brushwood on the bank was a bulging plastic carrier bag. He opened it and took out a pair of jeans, a top, a jacket and some shoes. Quickly stripping off his wet clothes, he pulled on the dry ones and sheltered in the lee of the culvert's concrete wall until the shower abated. At the bottom of the bag was a roll of ten- and twenty-pound notes as thick as his wrist, secured by an elastic band. He unrolled them, split them into three smaller rolls and distributed them amongst his trouser and jacket pockets.

71

When the last drops of rain had fallen and the clouds had retreated from the sky, he set out along the lane which led back towards Magor. At Magor, he caught a bus to Chepstow, then another to Bristol. At Temple Meads station, he bought a one-way ticket for the first train going north.

5

Breathing heavily, Steven strode up the last few yards of the hillside, the front of his borrowed jacket flapping and billowing in the wind that rode roaring from beyond the north moors. The hill was capped by a cairn of stones on which a triangulation pillar had been set. He climbed to the top of the cairn and, resting his elbows on the flat top of the concrete pillar, gazed back the way he had come.

During the past three hours of restless walking, he had described an irregular quadrangle over Rombalds Moor, trekking from peak to peak. Now he stood on the highest point and surveyed the landscape from west to east before settling his gaze to the south. Away in that direction, the moor rolled downwards, bisected by the broad gouge of Airedale. Sprawled in the bottom of the scoop, in the middle of the vista, he could see Keighley. At this distance, the town's buildings had the appearance of a grey-brown rash choking the throat of the Worth Valley where it opened into the wide dale.

That was where Carole would be now – not in Keighley itself, but further along the valley at Haworth. She had gone to visit some friend of hers, she said – Rosalind or something. She had asked Steven if he would like to come with her, but her tone of voice was not enthusiastic and, when he declined, she made no attempt to persuade him. He told her he would rather go for a walk. Before she left, she gave him an Ordnance Survey map, a pocket compass and a warning not to stray too far or stay out too long. 'The weather doesn't look too promising for hill-walking,' she had said, glancing up at the gusty, cloud-scudding sky. 'I'll be all right,' he assured her.

Apart from the wind, the bad weather she had warned of had so far failed to materialise. But what a wind it was; for hours he had battled against it or been borne along in its grasp as he tacked and turned across the face of the moor. Now he understood what *wuthering* meant; the word's blunt Norse syllables perfectly evoked the effect of the battering north wind on the body and the mind. He supposed the locals grew accustomed to it eventually. He had watched as Carole went about her work in the farmyard and her few small fields. She barely seemed to notice it, except to remark on its absence when it dropped.

Carole ... The thought of her made him feel depressed. For a whole week he had been firmly predicting his imminent departure, but each time he raised the subject, she protested. No, she said, she wouldn't hear of it until he was completely better. Really, his shoulder wasn't an issue; he should stay until he could piece together his memory. She dreaded to think what might happen to him, wandering the roads alone with no knowledge of who he was or where he was going. He could sense that she wanted to probe him with questions, and each time, she shied away from the brink of her curiosity. Only once had she suggested outright that if he could work out what it was that made him want to leave, he might get some clue as to what trauma had caused his brain to erase his memory. There was a degree of anxiety in her suggestion. He had seen her little book on amnesia; there was a subheading in it on Psychogenic Amnesia and Crime, and, although neither of them had mentioned it, he worried that she might have read this chapter and been frightened by it.

The situation was altogether too complicated and delicate for him. One of Carole's motives for keeping

74

him here was obviously inquisitiveness – and after all, she was entitled to some sort of explanation of how and why he had blundered into her life – but he also believed she really wanted to help him. It was this that made him feel depressed; teased out the first trace of guilt. He had cloaked himself in so many lies before now, and had drawn them so tightly about him, that each old one shed and each new one donned seemed as real as any subjectively remembered truth. But now, for the first time, he felt a hot breath of shame on his face each time this new lie was aired. He had not lost his memory, much as he might wish he had. He would have been only too pleased to see it sink irretrievably into the blackness of dead, forgotten past time, but it was still there in all its stark, sharply drawn ugliness. It was not the pull of the road ahead that disquieted him; rather, it was what was behind him, always present at the back of his mind, that was pushing him forward.

There and then, he resolved to leave the next morning; steal away before dawn if necessary. *And where will you run to then?* an interior voice asked him. Standing on top of the cairn, he slowly turned full circle, considering all the directions of the compass: South, perhaps; a diversionary doubling-back? Hmm, maybe; lose himself again in the press of civilisation until he could regain the initiative and take control of his life again . . . East was quickly dismissed; he dared not risk crossing the sea again, at least not in that direction . . . North was an attractive possibility, striking onwards towards Scotland . . . Or there was the west and Ireland. As he gazed into the nexus of all his possible futures, the sharp wind drew tears from his eyes. They trickled over his cheeks and gathered in droplets at his chin, and he wiped them away impatiently. Why postpone the decision, or even the departure? Why not leave now and just go where chance took him? If he was quick, he could get back to the farm, collect his few belongings and be gone before Carole returned.

He descended to the foot of the cairn and, taking a bearing from the map and compass, began to make his way back across the moor.

The first fat raindrops began to splat on the windscreen as Carole steered off the main road into Riddlesden. By the time she had left the village behind and the Morris was whining in lower gear up the steep road towards Holden Gate, the black clouds rolling over the moortops were darkening the last dregs of daylight and pouring down a torrent. She flicked the headlamps on and peered through the ambiguous arc left behind by the wipers as they clunked and swished unhurriedly back and forth. At last, she crested the rise and the Morris's little engine roared and sped, tyres splashing through the puddles gathering at the road's edge. She grimaced at the drystone walls and banks of dripping heather rushing by on either side, and hoped that Steven was not still out on the moor. Dusk would be closing in soon, and he might wander for hours without hope of shelter. In his present condition, the last thing he needed was another frigid nocturnal soaking.

Carole was still smarting from Rosalind's harsh comments, and her resentment only served to redouble her concern for Steven's welfare. Ros had made no effort to disguise her scepticism about his amnesia or – by implication – her supercilious contempt for Carole's alleged naïve belief in it. But Carole had seen rather more of the world outside the green folds and honeyed brownstone houses of the Dales than Rosalind had; she knew something about how quixotic the human brain could be, and she knew when to trust or be suspicious. Growing up in London and spending five years working in a busy inner-city hospital had taught her a thing or two. She was still a little nervous of Steven – after all, she was alone, and his behaviour *was* odd and disconcerting – but she no longer felt fearful of him (she had read 'Psychogenic Amnesia and Crime' and dismissed it; her judgement of his symptoms and personality suggested that some emotional trauma, a personal tragedy, lay at the root of his problem). Indeed, now that she had overcome the shock of his sudden, alarming arrival, she welcomed his presence; it was as if he had been sent by fate as a medium for atonement. Through helping him regain his memory – and therefore his identity and his life – she might be able to darn up the gaping, thread-bare patch in her conscience and make good the guilt that lurked there.

As the car rolled and rocked slowly down the pot-holed, muddy lane towards the farmyard, she resolved to make a renewed effort to entice Steven into the house that evening, at least to eat. His apparent fear of the house had begun to affect her slightly, and for the first time, she was conscious that her solitude within its walls and spaces was vulnerable as well as emancipat-ing. She would be glad to warm away its chill with the presence of another person.

Her train of thought was simultaneously interrupted and given resonance by the sight she saw as she swung the wheel and set the car splashing across the yard, the headlamp beams sweeping across the stone faces of the barn and the house. She stamped on the brake and brought the car to a slithering stop in the middle of the yard, her heart accelerating and pounding. The front door was open; not merely ajar, but gaping on its hinges, swinging and banging in the howling wind. Trembling, she switched off the lights and the engine and sat for a few moments, staring in disbelief. Then, deciding that she had no choice but to investigate, she reached under the passenger seat and drew out the car's starting handle. She climbed out into the maelstrom of rain and, holding the heavy, cranked steel bar aslant at her shoulder like a club, walked slowly and deliberately towards the open door.

Steven was closer to the farm than he had reckoned, and by the time he had hiked back across the moor, there was still at least an hour of daylight left. There was no sign of the Morris in the yard, and the byre door was shut and padlocked. He went straight to the barn and swung open the door.

Inside, at the far end, he had built himself a makeshift cot from straw bales. Three bales made up the base, with several more stacked up at one end and along both sides to form a draughtproof cabinet. The base was covered with bedding borrowed from Carole; a layer of blankets, a sleeping bag and another layer of blankets. At the foot of the bed, a wooden packing case served as a table from which he could eat the meals she brought out to him. A Calor Gas storm lantern was perched on one corner of the table, alongside the woollen gloves she had given him and which he had forgotten to take with him that morning. He put them on now, then rolled back the bedding from his cot. In the centre of the base was a patch of loose straw into which he pushed his hand, groping about in the prickling stalks until he found the only possession he had brought with him to the farm; a scratched and dented Golden Virginia tobacco tin.

All the while, he kept his ears alert for the sound of the car approaching from the lane. He would have to strike out across the field and straight on to the moor to avoid meeting her on the road. He slipped the tin into his inside jacket pocket and stood up. Pushing the barn door closed behind him, he set out across the yard towards the kitchen garden and the field beyond. Then

78

he stopped. The front door of the house was ajar. He glanced at the byre again, but it was still shut and locked. Strange; she usually only locked it at night or when she left the farm ... He was about to carry on walking, when he heard the telephone ringing inside the house. If she was in and answered the phone, she would be able to see him from the window if he went any further, so he froze in his tracks and waited, listening intently. The ringing went on and on, then stopped. He walked quietly up to the front door and cocked an ear to the crack, but there was only silence. The first possibility to cross his mind was burglary, but there was no sign of damage to either the door or the jamb. Of course, they could have come in through a window at the back and left through the front door. Fighting down the alternative and much more frightening explanation which was whispering inside his head, he nudged the door with a forefinger, letting it swing open onto the dingy hallway. He stepped over the threshold and padded softly along the hall. He kept his ears open, scanning the pregnant silence, but the only discernible sound was the deep tocking of the mantel clock in the parlour. He felt an overwhelming urge to arm himself. The shotgun cabinet was securely padlocked, so he went to the kitchen instead. After quietly opening and closing several drawers, he found the cutlery; tableware, an assortment of utensils, but no sharp knives. There were none on the draining board or in the sink, either. He frowned; this was getting more peculiar by the second. As a last resort, he looked in the small utility room which adjoined the kitchen. There, amongst the dust and cobwebs under the work bench, he found an ancient cricket bat, its padded handle fraying and the blade blackened and pitted.

Holding the bat out in front of him like a clumsy broadsword, he went cautiously from room to room, treading tentatively on the uneven floorboards. The light outside was fading by the time he had checked the upstairs rooms and finished the circuit back in the darkening parlour. There was nobody there. He had only been inside the house twice before, and on both occasions he had not had all his wits about him, so he could not tell whether anything had been taken or moved, but there were certainly no signs of disarray or damage. Then he noticed the shelf unit beside the huge stone fireplace: there was a stack of cassettes at one end and some LPs on a lower shelf, but only a large empty space and a glossy square of bare wood in the matt patina of dust where a stereo should stand. He leaned on the cricket bat and sighed with relief; it was just a burglary after all. He had found no sign of a break-in so it must have been an opportunist; Carole must have left the door open, the dozy cow.

Still, he had no time to stand around feeling satisfied; the darkness was closing in fast and the rain which had just been starting when he began his search was getting heavier all the time. He wondered whether he should leave her a note; it had occurred to him that she might think he had stolen her stereo, and the last thing he needed was to have his description handed to the police. But he decided to risk it anyway; she had good enough reasons of her own not to bring the police in, due to the small matter of an unreported firearms acci-dent (or assault, depending on whether they believed his version or hers). Laying the cricket bat across the arms of a deep leather armchair, he quickly checked his pockets and headed for the front door.

The wind had risen, and the door was swinging back and forth, a frigid torrent of rain-misted air blasting into the hall. As he approached the doorway, the telephone suddenly jangled to life again in the parlour behind him. Startled, he flinched and swivelled. At that moment, something hard and heavy slammed against the back of his head. Feeling as though his skull was crumbling into his brain, he stumbled forward and, as he fell, his temple collided with the corner of the hall table. His body slumped to the floor and everything turned black.

Shades of Grey

*W*omen, Paul muttered into the breeze, staring out across the pin-cushion bobbing masts in the Ocean Village marina. His lip curled over into a snarl. *Fucking tarts,* he said out loud. He had half a mind to go up there and give her a . . . what? The thought took him by surprise and deflected him from his rage. If he only had half a mind to start with and then he gave her a piece of it, he wouldn't have much left. He smiled suddenly, then frowned again as the wheels rattled out of this brief siding and slotted back on to the rails; he couldn't have had much of a mind in the first place to let her take advantage of him like that, a bloody woman. Oh, they were clever all right, he'd give them that; the ways they had of turning men's brains into jelly and taking advantage of their resulting weaknesses. Not that he would be able to go and see her anyway, he concluded, not now he didn't have a car any more.

Two adolescent girls with precocious black tights and powdered candlewax skin below long gloss hair walked along the quayside behind him. As they entered the periphery of his vision, he saw them whisper to each other and bubble with stifled giggling. Paul turned round suddenly. 'What's so bloody funny?' he demanded angrily. Their heads turned simultaneously, startled, and he glimpsed soft reddened lips and pencilled eyes before they walked on, hurrying their pace and glancing back nervously until they had turned the corner and walked in through the sliding doors of the shopping arcade.

Paul looked down at himself; he was still wearing the dark blue overalls he had put on that morning. They were what he thought of as his clean overalls, which meant that they had been washed and only bore the spatters of dried paint and island patches of deep grey ground-in workshop grime, rather than the dampness of fresh oil with floor grit and silvery speckles of swarf adhering. He hadn't had a chance to get them dirty; almost as soon as he had walked in to work that morning, it had been, *Old Bailey wants to see you* and before he knew where he was, *Here are your wages to the end of the week, it's more than you deserve but I'm a generous man now get out of my sight*. He hadn't even been home yet, and it would be tea-time soon.

He found his reflection in the smoked glass window of the cafeteria. No wonder he was the source of giggling; standing there with his baggy, shapeless jumpsuit, big boots ballooning ludicrously from the trouser-ends, his uncombed hair all scrunched up on one side. There had been a time when he had taken care of his appearance, but he had recreated himself since then, and this slovenly mess was the outward, world-turned façade of the remodelling. In fact, the burying of the old foundations and overbuilding had been so thorough that he sometimes found his thoughts running in strange chimeric patterns, so that he no longer knew which were his own.

He turned away from the glass and walked quickly along the quayside. He would have to go home and work out what to do next.

The car he had come to see was standing on the gently sloping driveway beside the shrub-cluttered front garden; a Morris Minor convertible in creamy white – Old

English White, the BMC catalogue called it – with a cherry-red hood and matching upholstery. The bulging body panels gleamed and the hood was bright and taut, without the dulling and slackening of age. Paul parked the truck by the kerb and consulted the slip of paper he had been given: *1965 CONV. WHITE. MRS AGNEW, 12 NEWBURY GARDENS, WINCHESTER.* There was a phone number, and that was all. In the breast pocket of his overalls was a pre-signed blank cheque; he was authorised to go up to a thousand pounds, not a penny more.

The front door was answered by a tall, middle-aged woman. Like her car, she wore her age well, accepting its mellowing effects but evading deterioration. The strongly structured face under the dome of fading coppery curls was only lightly lined around the mouth and eyes. 'Mrs Agnew?' he inquired. She peered perplexedly at him. 'Paul Chapel,' he explained. 'Morris Minor Restorations.'

'Yes, of course,' she said. 'I don't know what I was thinking of. Wait here – I'll be with you in just a moment.' The door closed a polite distance; angled far enough to discreetly block the view into the hall. Paul pressed a hand against it, near the hinges, letting it swing wider slowly, as though caught by the breeze. She was slipping her feet into a pair of loafers and speaking to someone through an open door on the left of the hall. 'Righty-ho,' she said brightly, stepping outside to join him on the driveway. 'This is the car, as I supposed you've guessed. It's in such beautiful condition, isn't it,' she said, a comment rather than an invitation to concur. 'My son took awfully good care of it. Actually, he had it completely restored, more or less, not long before . . . well, not long ago.'

'Who did the work?'

'A friend of my husband. Very good. Owns a garage,

you know. It does look good, doesn't it?'

This time it was a question. Paul nodded; it did look good, with no rust bubbles on the brightly polished paintwork of the body panels. It even had a pair of stainless steel sill finishers. He took a long, narrow-shafted ball-pein hammer out of his overall pocket.

'My husband and I,' she was saying, '– oh, that does sound dreadful, doesn't it. Like the Queen. We bought the car for Simon after he'd finished his A-Levels – four grade As. He loved it, drove all over the New Forest, down to Dorset, Brighton, all over . . . Good Lord, what on earth is that for?' She was staring wide-eyed at the hammer.

'Checking underneath,' he explained, kneeling down and crouching, craning his neck to look up under the boot apron. He shifted his grip on the hammer in the confined space under the car and swung it upwards, banging repeatedly along the apron, the noise resonating throughout the hollow metal spaces. He felt rather than saw Mrs Agnew flinch at each blow.

'What are you *doing*?' she demanded. 'You'll damage it.'

He ignored her and went on hammering. As the rapid blows juddered off the apron and went further along past the leaf springs, the tone became deeper, duller, booming. There was a sudden crunch and a shower of rust flakes scattered on the ground.

'*Now* look what you've done. I *told* you you'd damage it.'

Paul wriggled out from under the car. 'You've got a hole near the right front spring hanger,' he said.

'Which *you* made,' she glowered. 'I shall want—'

He interrupted, shaking his head. 'If there's rot like that, you might as well have a hole. Then you know what you're dealing with.'

'I told you, Simon had it all restored.'

'They must've missed that bit.' He moved around to

the side of the car and knelt down again, resuming the hammer blows along the underside of the sill and the cross-member.

Mrs Agnew followed and stood over him, wringing her hands. 'Do you *have* to hit it so hard?' she pleaded.

He stood up again and moved on to the front. 'What decided him to sell it?'

'What?'

'Your son. Why is he selling it? If you don't mind me asking.' He knelt down and started examining the front chassis.

'He died.'

'Pardon?'

'Simon is dead. He had leukaemia. He died last November.'

Paul sat up. 'I'm sorry,' he said, feeling his cheeks reddening. 'I didn't—'

'He would never have sold it. It was his pride and joy.'

'I didn't know. I'm sorry.'

'It's been six months now, and we've no use for it. Too many painful memories.' She walked slowly around the car and laid a hand on its fat haunch, smiling sadly. 'He used to be out here every Saturday morning, polishing and polishing. Even after his illness was starting to take hold. Sometimes he'd get started, but be too tired to finish it off. That was what really upset him, not being able to look after his car properly. He wasn't afraid of dying, but his weakness infuriated him . . .' She stood up straight and looked Paul in the eye. 'Well, what's it worth?'

Paul stared at her over the hills and valleys of the bonnet, disoriented by the sudden change of tack. 'What?'

'Mr Bailey said two thousand pounds, perhaps more.'

'Mr Bailey—?'

'I spoke to him on the phone.'

'Has he seen it?'

She hesitated. 'Well, no, not actually in person, but I did describe it to him. He said it would be worth that.'

'He told you that? Two thousand?'

'Perhaps more. Simon maintained that the car was worth over two thousand pounds after the restoration. I told Mr Bailey and he agreed. I can't bear seeing it parked out here any longer. I want it to go soon. Will you take it?'

'Are you sure Mr Bailey said two thousand? I mean, he wouldn't normally quote a price over the phone, not without giving the car a good check over.'

Mrs Agnew blanched slightly. 'Well, you have checked it. Is it or is it not worth two thousand pounds?'

Paul stood up and rubbed his jaw. 'I haven't finished yet, but what I've seen, I'd er, I'd have to say no.'

'*No?*'

'Well, it needs some work underneath – that spring hanger. Even if the car was worth two thousand in theory, then that's what we'd be selling it on for, you see. Now, some of that is going to be VAT, some is going to be the cost of work to bring it up to value, and then we've got to make a profit. So we can't *buy* it for two thousand.'

As he talked, Mrs Agnew's mouth turned down more and more steeply as she gazed at the car's vinyl hood. 'How much *would* you give?'

He sighed. 'Let me finish checking, and I'll tell you. I'll need to take it for a test drive. Is it MOT'd?' She shook her head. 'Doesn't matter,' he said. 'I won't go far.'

After he had warmed up the engine, he backed smartly out of the driveway and puttered off along the crescent. He drove for a couple of miles around the streets of Winchester. The brakes were sharp, with no binding or fading, and the engine ran well, whining and roaring happily through the gears. He found a steep hill and ran up it fast, tilting his head and listening for the resonant thrum of worn main bearings, but the bottom end was sweet and silent. When he returned and parked in the drive, he finished his checks by looking for rust under the carpets and bouncing the shock absorbers.

'Well?' said Mrs Agnew, who had watched him anxiously, hands clasped in front of her. 'How much will you give me?'

Paul stared at the car, avoiding her eyes. 'I'm only allowed to go up to a thousand,' he said. 'I *could* ask for a bit more . . .'

She didn't hear. 'A *thousand pounds*?' she repeated incredulously.

'If you let me phone, I'll ask for twelve hundred.'

'That's still not two thousand, is it.'

'You could always sell privately,' Paul suggested.

She sucked in her lower lip and sighed, gazing at the car for a long time. 'Oh, very well,' she conceded in a tone of extreme exasperation. 'I can't bear seeing it standing there any longer. One thousand two hundred pounds.'

'I'll have to get permission.'

'You can use the phone in the hall. Wipe your feet first.'

He got through to Dave Ingrams, the company's deputy director, who authorised the deal on Old Bailey's behalf. After they had exchanged documents and the cheque, Paul drove the Morris up on the truck's trailer, lashed it in place and set off for Southampton. It was his afternoon off, so he deposited the car in the yard, handed the documents in to the office and went home.

The next morning, Paul arrived early for work. He put on his overalls and went straight to the paint shop to continue the work that had been interrupted by his visit to Winchester. A customer had brought in a Series II saloon the previous week for a complete, ground-up restoration, and Paul had been given the job of preparing the bodywork. Over the past few days, he had hauled out the engine and gearbox, dismantled the brakes, suspension and steering gear, taken off the rear axle and springs, stripped out the electrical system and the glass, removed all the seats and trim, and stored all the parts in the room next door. He had also taken off the bonnet, boot-lid, doors and wings, propping the panels against the walls of the paint shop until the hollow shell of the body was bare on four pyramid axle-stands in the middle of the room. The whole car had been steam-cleaned and was now ready for sand-blasting in preparation for the welders, who would cut out the ragged rotten metal and suture in bright new pieces.

He pulled on a mask and goggles and propped the boot-lid in the blasting booth. Then he switched on the compressor, and the morning silence was flooded with its thrumming, juddering racket, a high-pitched hissing cutting in over the top as pressurised air escaped from the safety valve. He dragged and whipped the stiff rubber hose across the floor until he had enough slack to work with, then aimed the nozzle at the top corner of the lid and squeezed the trigger. The noise of the compressor was sheared out by the plangent, hissing rasp of the jetting grit careening off the steel panel and showering around the perspex walls of the booth. The pale green paint began to erode quickly to white primer and grey metal in slow-moving waves across and down the gently curving surface.

Paul enjoyed sandblasting; the visual and sonic stimuli were powerful enough to make the task aesthetically satisfying, but it was also sufficiently mindless for his thoughts to be able to wander. He tracked the nozzle slowly and smoothly back and forth, watching the glossy green melt to matt white then shining grey, and thought about colours.

He had never taken much of an interest in colours until he met Cressida Allan, who had taught him to take notice of the chromatic world. She told him that the retina was made up of two different kinds of cell: long, rod-shaped cells which responded to the frequency of light and told the brain about light and shade, and stubby cones which contained a selection of photosensitive pigments that reacted to different photic wavelengths and allowed you to see colour. There were only a few of these pigments, she said, but together they could give the brain enough information to reproduce in the mind all the infinite variety of tone and shade that were present in the world. He had liked Cressida, despite her wretched Twins, and he enjoyed their conversations. Now, he missed her whenever he found himself looking at the coloured world. He remembered her saying that dividing the spectrum of colours into categories was entirely artificial, and that other cultures had different groupings. This had come as a surprise to him; he had always thought that red was red and blue was blue. She said that in some cultures, blue and green were categorised as variant shades of the same colour. Thus, the sky, the grass, the leaves on the trees and the sea were all of one hue; variations of the one true colour of nature. He wondered whether, if you grew up thinking blue and green were the same colour, you actually *saw* them differently from someone who thought of them as blue and green.

Cressida's eyes had always been turned towards nature; towards the trees and the grasses and the wild flowers under woods and the borders of worked fields. As Paul blasted the paint from the panel, he reflected that he would have liked to have shown her the colours of machinery. He felt sure he could have proved to her that there was as much richness and variety in the works of metal and materials as there was in nature. Grey, for instance. He had never realised that there could be so many shades of grey. The grey he was looking at now as the paint was whipped back – the sheeny dove-grey of clean, fresh sheet steel – was his favourite. And within that one tone were a hundred graded variations in the reaction of light and surface curvature and the swirls of a million microscopic dust scratches. There were also the greys of dust on metal, toned and blended by the qualities of the metal and the composition of the dust. A deep, bone-yellowed ash-grey on the cast steel of the steering swivel pins and trunnions; slightly different, slightly less yellow than the same road dust dulling the copper brake pipes snaking out of the chassis and across the backs of the wheel hubs. The same grey dust gathered in spray-rushed ripples inside the wheel arches, and there it was browner than in the thin patinations on the moving parts. There were other greys also: the charcoal-grey of ageing rubber bushes, striated with black cracks where it had perished; and the glossy, mottled greenish grey of old grease when it oozed in thick ribbons out of the suspension joints as new yellow grease was pumped into the nipples. Then there were the other colours: the browns of corrosion were the commonest. Rust in the sheet metal structure was a deep russet, its surface knobbled, bubbled, and gradated in tone, sometimes dust-dulled, sometimes stained darker by smears and dribbles of grease, oil, petrol or brake fluid, each adding a different tint to the ruddy brown base. Rust on the strapped steel leaves of the rear suspension was a completely different kind of brown from the rust on sheet panels: when they were dry, the thick strips turned a rich, bright terracotta that gave the spring steel a brittle, frangible appearance. These were the car's natural colours. There were also the primers and paints, with their fanciful catalogue names: Almond Green, Smoke Grey (which looked to Paul like pale blue), Old English White, Trafalgar Blue, Rose Taupe. Each of these in turn had its own variations according to weathering and oxidation and different paint batches.

Paul had finished stripping both sides of the boot-lid, and was about to start on the doors, when someone tapped him on the shoulder. Submerged in the noise of the compressor and lost in thought, he had not heard anyone come in, and he jumped, almost dropping the hose. It was Dorothy from the front office. Seeing the shock in his face, she smiled apologetically, then pointed to her ear and at the compressor. Paul switched it off, experiencing the momentary feeling in the sudden silence that his eardrums were being sucked out of his head by a vacuum.

'Mr Bailey wants a word,' said Dorothy.

'What about?' he asked, conscious that he was shouting over the imaginary noise still echoing in his head.

'He's in the office,' she said, turning to leave. 'I think it's about the car you brought in yesterday.'

He put the hose down and followed her out of the paint shop, across the yard and along the narrow, dingy corridor to the front of the building.

Morris Minor Restorations was housed in a crumbling Victorian villa at the lower end of Portswood Road. The house itself contained the front office and Old Bailey's office, with the remaining rooms given over to storing spare parts. In front of the house, the large garden had been paved over and served as a forecourt for displaying the selection of saloons, convertibles, vans and Travellers that were for sale. The vast back garden – consisting of the house's garden and a quarter-acre of waste ground next door – had mostly been built over with workshops, stores and the paint shop where Paul had been working. What remained of the weed-grown, gravel-sown ground was cluttered with body shells representing a spectrum of stages of dilapidation and corrosion, from mostly intact Minors awaiting restoration, to hollow, holed husks from which all the usable parts had been stripped, waiting for rust to complete its infestation and cause the remaining structure to crumble to nothing.

The front office was the public face of the business, and was a little less dusty and grimy than the rest of the house. Dorothy's huge desk, with her plastic trays, pots of pens and bulky electric typewriter, took up one end of the room, beside the ornate, blocked-off fireplace. In front of the desk was the waiting area; like a barbershop, with half a dozen moulded plastic chairs set against the walls surrounding a long, low coffee table on which sat a heaped scatter of classic car magazines, parts price lists, insurance brochures and leaflets detailing the company's modification and restoration programmes. The walls, below the yellowed plaster cornices, were covered with pictures. The wall behind the desk was devoted to a vast mosaic of photographs: Morrises undergoing restoration in the workshops; unusual finds like the 1953 Series II Traveller discovered in a barn near Wareham, shrouded in tarpaulins and with only ninety-six authentic miles on the clock; oddities such as the Morris Minor fire engine and the custom-built dormobile constructed on a pick-up chassis; and, most frequently, shots of customers' cars after restoration, gleaming and flawless on the company forecourt. The other three walls bore a mixed papering of faded newspaper cuttings about the company – mostly taken from the *Southern Evening Echo* – and facsimiles of advertising posters; from the late 1940s with the blocky primary colours of lingering art deco (MORRIS MINOR: BRITAIN'S TOP CAR), through to the washy, sub-realist watercolours of the 1960s.

By the time Paul reached the office, Dorothy had resumed her post behind the desk and was clattering the typewriter's keys. Bailey was sitting on one of the plastic chairs, talking to someone on the phone. 'You need to do something about the tie-rod brackets,' he was saying. 'The last batch were wrongly angled . . . Yes, we welded one of the buggers on and couldn't fit the bar without distorting the rubbers . . .' He glanced up at Paul as he walked in, gazed impassively at his face for a moment, then swivelled in his seat, turning to face the corner. The plastic helix of the cord stretched out tightly over his shoulder as he turned, dragging the phone across the desk. Dorothy tutted silently and moved it nearer to him, rearranging her stationery around it.

Paul tried to gauge the tone of Old Bailey's glance, but it had been unreadable. Bailey was really a lot less frightening than he looked, Paul had found. His pugnacious, almost brutal face – narrow, heavily browed dark eyes closely flanking a fleshy, upturned nose with deep furrows sweeping down and bracketing a truculent, slackly lipped mouth full of large, slabby teeth – was belied by his voice; instead of the guttural aggression people always expected from him, he spoke with soft gentleness. He could, however, be abrupt and even frankly insulting when he chose to be.

Paul stood idly at the end of the desk and waited for him to finish the call. His eyes drifted over the posters and clippings on the wall. There was a new cutting inserted in one of the few remaining patches where the faded floral wallpaper had shown through; fresh, supple cream amongst the curled, almost friable bone-yellow. It was a half-page piece, apparently cut from the *Sunday Times*, with a large photograph of Bailey smiling forbiddingly over the divided windscreen of a black convertible the company had rebuilt for a peripheral member of the Royal Family (' "Minor" Royalty', said the headline). Next to this cutting was a poster from the mid-1960s advertising the new Minor 1000. The car shown – a cream saloon packed with a grinningly idealised nuclear family – was speeding joyfully away from an open-mouthed car ferry which loomed white in the right-hand background against a cobalt sky. At the bottom of the picture was the caption *'Now better than ever!'* in bold, optimistic brush-strokes. With a lurch of horror, he noticed that the poster had been adulterated: someone had drawn, with grooves of hard-pressed black biro, a stick-figure with a round head falling towards the water, trailing motion lines which led back up to the ferry's top deck, where a second stick-figure stood at the rail, arms raised as if in alarm.

Paul stepped back involuntarily from the poster, his lips parted, eyes wide, mouth going dry . . . No, he told himself, it was just coincidence, but his mind filled with the rushing water webbed with foam and the splash engulfed by the churning wake and waves. *Just a coincidence*. It had to be. One of the apprentices, probably, bored and doing a little dull mischief . . .

'When can you get them here?' Old Bailey was saying. Paul's ears picked up the tone of a winding-down conversation, and he waited tensely. 'Okay. Cheers, then.' The receiver rattled in its cradle, and Bailey stood up. He leaned over the desk and shuffled some papers in one of the trays, consulting Dorothy briefly about some of them, then turned to face Paul. Another long, expressionless gaze. Paul was about to speak when Old Bailey crooked a finger. 'Come with me,' he said softly.

Paul followed him out of the door and along the passage to the back yard. They crossed the corner of the yard, past a stack of newly delivered, cellophane-wrapped radiators, heater units and rubber hoses, to the wide-open doors of the main workshop. Old Bailey strode up the shallow concrete ramp, then stopped suddenly on the threshold and turned. '1965 convertible,' he said. 'White.'

Paul nodded. 'What about it?'

'You brought it in, didn't you? I was out. I spoke to Dave.'

Paul nodded again. 'Mmm.'

'How much did you pay? How much company money?'

'Didn't Dave Ingrams tell you? He okayed it.'

'Yes, he told me. Now I want you to tell me.'

'Twelve hundred. It was a good deal.'

'A good deal of money. Yes, it was.'

'No, I mean—'

Bailey interrupted: 'Let's go and examine your purchase, shall we?' He turned and went into the workshop.

There was space inside for three cars to be worked on. The first work space, immediately inside the doorway, was equipped with a hydraulic lift. A van with dustily oxidised maroon paintwork sat on the raised platform, and one of the mechanics was welding the underside. The MIG trolley with its towering blue gas cylinder clicked and hummed intermittently as the man worked, the lumpy grey shadows under the chassis sporadically illuminated electric blue, the sizzling metal spraying showers of yellow-white sparks past his masked face to the oily floor, where they ran and bounced and danced for a few brief moments before dying. In the next space, a Trafalgar Blue Traveller mounted on axle stands had been stripped of its woodwork and been left to await rebuilding. At the far end, in the last space, was the car-roller; a car had been bolted by its offside wheel hubs to the deceptively delicate-looking steel frame and tipped over on its side, exposing the black and russet maze of its belly. Simon Agnew's convertible.

'I got back yesterday evening,' Bailey was saying. 'I spotted the car in the yard, so I had a look at it. Robbie was still here, so I got him to help me put it up on the roller, because I *couldn't bloody believe* what I saw.'

As they came closer, Paul could see that the nearside chassis leg, which should have been a smooth, box-section member, looked lumpy and uneven. Bailey took a heavy screwdriver from his pocket and began prodding and scraping at the thick black underseal. In places, this revealed patches of shiny steel, but as he worked forward towards the vital union with the front suspension, chips and flakes of rust emerged under the screwdriver's chiselling tip, as well as gritty lumps of white powder and bits of shiny aluminium foil. When he had reached the end, he stopped and looked at Paul. The chassis member was a holed, ragged, rusting mess.

'You didn't even *look* at it, did you,' he said. 'Look! The whole bloody thing's packed up with filler, patches. God knows what. Fucking Chinese takeaway tins! I've never seen anything like it.'

'But I—'

'The sills are the same, and so are the spring hangers, the cross-member and half the floor.'

Paul stared at it in a daze. 'She told me it'd been restored!'

'Restored? *Restored?* Well, yeah: new set of carpets, bit of filler and whack on a good thick layer of underseal. That's about all the restoration this fucking thing's had.'

'I'm sorry.'

'Sorry?' Bailey paused and smiled ominously. 'Let's do our sums, shall we. Even a moron like you should be able to work it out. You paid twelve hundred for it. We

97

do about fifteen hundred's worth of work on it and we can maybe sell it for two thousand including VAT. What does that add up to?'

'Well—'

'I'll tell you: it adds up to you being fucking fired, mate.'

6

He had been floating through a tunnel; its walls were formed of pinpricks of phosphorescent green, spiralling around him, darts of multicoloured pain shooting out of the dark, distant epicentre towards his face. Then a voice started speaking to him in a foreign language dotted with words he recognised but which carried no sense or compulsion to understand . . .

Mwah murble but fwah bibbih hear me?

. . . He concentrated on the voice. It was pleasant, soothing, familiar . . .

Breeble . . .

. . . As he strained to catch the words, the tunnel stopped revolving and advancing, and the lights began to fade . . .

Arrgh fooble awake?

. . . He opened his eyes into a yellow haze lurking with indeterminate shapes . . .

Verbal oowah . . .

Carole smiled; a wan, patient smile which tried to be reassuring but couldn't quite achieve the necessary degree of relaxed confidence. 'At least the sick-bed's a bit more comfortable this time,' she said as his blank eyes gazed woozily up at her.

She had laid him on the sofa with a pillow propping up his injured head. He had two wounds; the worst was on the back of his skull behind the left ear. The scalp was grazed and bruised and dark blood had matted his hair. She had cleaned it up and bandaged it, finishing off the last of the strip she had used only a week ago to bind his shoulder. The second was smaller; just a bump on the forehead near the temple, a slightly raised lump which was now flowering subtly in an array of sombre bruise purples tinged with yellow.

She knelt down by the sofa and stroked his hand, which was lying limply across his chest. His skin was hot to the touch, and his fingers stretched and flexed under hers like a small animal waking. He shifted on the sofa. 'No, don't try to get up,' she said, laying a hand lightly on his shoulder to restrain him.

Showing no sign that he had heard her or even felt her touch, he levered himself awkwardly by degrees into a sitting position, wincing and making little gasping sounds through clenched teeth. When he had completed the slow, painful manoeuvre, he gazed dully around the room.

'Do you know where you are?' she asked tentatively.

He continued surveying his surroundings, then looked at her face. His eyes were bloodshot and slightly yellowed, the pupils shrunk to barely visible black pinpoints. He gazed at her unsteadily, blinking slowly, for several moments. Finally, it seemed to register in his brain that she had spoken. 'Hnn?' he grunted.

'Do you know where you are?' she repeated.

Again, the question seemed to take a painfully long time to reach his brain. It was like watching thick oil sink into soft sand. Eventually, he nodded; a tiny, almost imperceptible tilting of the head. 'Yes,' he said, his voice barely more than a gruff whisper. 'I think so,' he added cautiously.

She held up a finger in front of his face. 'How many fingers can you see?' she asked.

He frowned, puzzled. 'One,' he said.

She relaxed. There didn't seem to be any signs of concussion. 'And what's your name?'

Another long wait while the question penetrated the

fog that she herself could almost see cloaking his senses. 'Steven,' he mumbled. 'Steven Goldcliff.'

She leaned closer. 'Where were you born?' she asked, a note of eagerness in her voice.

Pause. Deep frown. 'Don't know,' he said.

She slumped back on her heels in disappointment. She had hoped (rather foolishly, she realised) that the blows might have jolted his dormant memory back to life, but it evidently hadn't. Still, at least he didn't seem to have lost what little he had.

He resumed his scanning of the room. Suddenly, his eyes widened. She followed his gaze; he was staring at the starter handle, which she had left lying on the rug in front of the grate. She guessed immediately what he was thinking, and she laughed. 'No, it wasn't me this time,' she said. 'Mind you, I can't guarantee I *wouldn't* have clouted you if you hadn't already been flat out on the hall floor. I'm telling you, it scared the hell out of me.'

'Then who . . .?'

'Nobody,' she grinned, enjoying the puzzle and pleased that he was showing signs of returning to a normal level of alertness. 'I found a mark on the edge of the door; a little smear of blood. The wind must've caught it when you were looking.' She pointed at his forehead. 'Then you hit the table on your way down. You're lucky; you must have a skull like armour plate.' She paused, and the smile faded. 'What exactly were you doing? I mean, how did you get in?' He looked into her eyes, and she felt suddenly flustered. 'I'm not accusing you of anything,' she blurted hastily. 'I mean, I would've let you have a key if you'd—'

'Burglars,' he said, interrupting her. He pinched the bridge of his nose between his forefinger and thumb, and closed his eyes as if concentrating hard. 'The door was open,' he said. 'I remember the door being open. I

101

thought it might be burglars . . .' He looked up suddenly. 'There *were* burglars.'

She stared at him in alarm. 'Did you see them?'

'No, I didn't . . . They took your stereo.' He pointed to the empty space on the shelf. 'Funny,' he added. 'They took your knives, too.'

'Oh,' she murmured, looking down at the carpet. 'Yes . . .' She cleared her throat. 'Look, Steven, this is going to sound a bit silly, but I don't think there were any burglars.' Her cheeks glowing red, she explained the precautions she had taken on the afternoon of his arrival. 'I don't know why I haven't put them back,' she added. 'Just haven't got round to it, I suppose.'

He nodded, not seeming at all fazed by her distrust of him. 'Are you sure there's nothing else gone?'

She got up off her knees and sat on the sofa beside him. 'No. I mean, I haven't really looked, but no, nothing I've noticed.' She glanced at his profile, ragged with beard and bandages, against the firelight in the hearth. 'How're you feeling?' she asked. 'Any better?'

'Bit better,' he said. 'My head aches like buggery. Have you got any aspirin?'

She looked doubtful. 'I'm not sure you ought to take anything at the moment. Will you be able to wait for a bit?' He grimaced, but then nodded reluctantly. 'God,' she sighed, 'you've really been through the wars since you got here, haven't you . . .'

He turned to face her then, wincing as he moved his head. Suddenly, he smiled. It was the first time she had seen a smile on his face since she met him; it was a broad smile that suffused his face, his eyes shining and radiating warmth. She smiled back and, seeing his grin broaden and the skin about his eyes crinkle with mirth, she laughed, a sudden bubble of joy expanding within her.

'It looks like I'm never going to escape from here,' he

said, his voice pleasantly warm under the veneer of mock bitterness.

Caught off guard by this unexpected breach in the implacably blank wall he had so far presented to her, her words were out before she could check them: 'I hope not,' she said.

His smile wavered and faded slightly. 'I'll have to leave eventually,' he said quietly.

'I know,' she said, reddening. 'Not yet, though . . .' He murmured in acquiescence. 'Now, how about a drink? Hot chocolate do you?'

'Perfect,' he said.

She patted him on the knee and rose to her feet. She paused in the doorway and looked back at him. 'Steven,' she said. 'You're not in any state to go back out to that horrible dirty barn. There's still a bed made up for you in the spare room. Tell me you'll use it.' He looked back at her doubtfully. 'Just for my sake?' she added.

'Okay,' he conceded. 'Just for you.'

While she pottered about in the kitchen, setting the saucepan of milk on the hob and lining up the mugs, she hummed happily to herself. She had no idea what had made him laugh so suddenly, and she had no inclination to examine their conversation in order to seek out an explanation. All she cared about was that, at last, he felt happy and comfortable in her company. And so did she with him. The last vestige of doubt and insecurity had melted in the warmth of his smile. She had never really noticed until that moment that, underneath that wild hair, unkempt beard and haunted face, there was a disturbingly attractive man pleading to be let out . . . She curtailed this line of thought as soon as she realised that she was gazing dreamily at the row of saucepans hanging from the rack on the wall and shivering as she imagined the sensation of his arms around her. *Stop it*, she told herself, even though she didn't want to. *You're not that desperate*, she added, even though she knew she was: four years along had to have cost her something.

The milk was boiling over, hissing and skitching on the hob. She snatched up the pan and wiped the top of the Aga with a damp cloth, cursing herself good-naturedly.

When she returned to the parlour with a steaming, sugar-smelling mug in each hand, she found Steven standing by the fireplace. His face was a ghastly, ghostly white, and he was holding on to the edge of the mantelpiece for support. She put the mugs down hastily in the grate and took him by the shoulders. 'Are you all right?' she asked anxiously.

'Just went a bit dizzy,' he said, smiling wanly as she guided him back to the sofa. He sat down heavily and blinked a few times, opening his eyes wide as though trying to focus. 'It's okay,' he said eventually. 'It's gone now.'

'Are you sure?'

'Mmm . . . I think I'd like to get to bed now.'

She sighed as the cosy atmosphere dribbled dismally down the plughole. 'Okay. I'll help you up.'

Lightly gripping his elbow, she steadied him as he rose to his feet. He stood still for a few moments, concentrating and waiting for the onset of dizziness. He smiled. 'I'm okay now,' he said.

'Probably low blood sugar. You'll be fine as long as you don't stand up too suddenly.'

He looked down at her. 'I'm sorry to be such a pain.'

'You're not,' she said firmly.

'No, I mean it. You've been brilliant. Thanks.'

She laughed awkwardly, rubbing his arm in a brusque, matey fashion. 'Don't be daft. It's been a pleasure. And it's not over yet – you've still got a long way to go, you know . . . Now, let's get you up those stairs.'

He made no attempt to move. He was still looking into her eyes. She returned his gaze and, without any conscious control, found herself reaching up and, with the tips of her fingers, gently touching his hairline just above the darkening bruise. With the lightest touch, she pushed the hair back from his forehead, then let her fingers trail down over his temple, his sideburn and his cheek. He closed his eyes, and let out a long, low sigh which trailed off into a luxuriant purr. Suddenly, he grasped her wrist, and she felt a wild rush of excitement. His grip was strong, immovable; stopping just short of the threshold of pain.

'No,' he said, his eyes still closed.

'No?' she repeated, confused.

'Don't.'

The excitement that had leapt up in her suddenly tripped over its own feet and fell on its face in the dust. His grip tightened, and she gasped. 'You're hurting me,' she yelped.

He opened his eyes, looked at his hand around her wrist, and released her as suddenly as he had grasped her. 'Sorry,' he said, avoiding her eyes. 'I'm really sorry. I, I think I'd better go.'

She rubbed at her wrist, trying to ease away the livid weals that had risen around it, and stepped back from him, looking down at the floor. 'Yes, I think you'd better.'

With a last apologetic glance at her, he headed towards the front door.

'Where are you going?' she asked, following him out to the hall.

He paused, but then just shook his head and walked on.

'Oh, no,' she said. 'No, you can't go back out there! You're not well. Your bed's all made!'

He didn't reply. There was a brief gust of wind as the

door opened, then he was gone. Carole slumped down on the foot of the stairs, her head in her hands, and swore a stream of muttered curses at herself.

Steven lay shivering in his straw-bale cot, feeling damp and cold despite the tightly wrapped cocoon of sleeping bag and blankets. His eyes were open, staring into the pitch darkness, and he listened miserably to the rain susurrating on the barn roof, the wind humming around the eaves, and the occasional grate and thump of tiles as they lifted briefly and fell back into place.

That knock on the head must have been worse than he thought, one part of his mind suggested. For the past week, he had been more or less indifferent to this woman; apart from the trace of unaccustomed guilt at the lies he had told her, he had given her little thought. He had been more concerned with getting away from this place. There had been her voice, of course; that richly toned, lightly carried voice had seeped mellifluously into his mind and soothed him while he still lay unconscious after his first encounter with her. But he hadn't really noticed before how pretty she was; long past the bloom of youth, but even in those ill-fitting jeans, shapeless, chunky jumpers and not a single smear of make-up on her face, she was uncomfortably attractive. He had felt the draw of strong physical attraction plenty of times and – much more rarely, for only a tiny number of women – he had harboured a fondness, a sentimental affection, but he had never before felt both simultaneously and so strongly about one woman. And it had all come upon him in that brief, sudden instant, with her cool fingers on his aching face, the smell of her close to him and her eyes warm with reflected firelight.

He rolled onto his side and fidgeted restlessly, closing his eyes tightly against the pain from his battered head. What was it with women? Just when she had been coming on all mumsy, she had to go and spring a massive pass on him. More to the point, what was it with *him*? There had been a time – not even that long ago – when he would have greedily grabbed such an opportunity, neatly side-stepping any consequences that might shower down in his vicinity afterwards. *Guilt.* Christ, he had never felt guilty about anything before . . . He backtracked and corrected himself; he had never felt *this* guilty about anything *so trivial* before.

He rolled over onto his other side and tried to unpick himself from his thoughts and drift off to sleep, but it was futile; like extricating himself from a vat of glue. The sooner he got away from here and away from her, the better.

Paper Mirror

Fired. Bloody fired! That had been it; no protest, no apologies accepted, just get out and don't come back. He had never been fired from anything in his life before, and the feeling of abject, impotent humiliation was new to him. He had gone down to Ocean Village to clear his head, in the hope that watching the boats on the water might calm his mind and allow him to work out what to do about the situation, but his brain had just kept churning round and round, grinding out a sickening mixture of despair, hatred, humiliation, bile, self-pity, fear and rage.

As he trudged back through the town towards St Mary's, he decided that the only solution to his sacking would be to go back to see Bailey in the morning and, grovelling if necessary, offer to do the work on the convertible himself for no money. The very idea of it revolted him; not so much the thought of begging Bailey for his job back; worse than that was that the sight of the big yachts in the marina had kept reminding him of the adulterated ferry poster in the front office. The more he dwelt on it, the more convinced he became that it couldn't be coincidence; it was clearly aimed directly at him, a sick reminder which only he would understand.

His eyes cast down at the pavement and vacant with interior regard, hands deep in his overall pockets, he turned the corner into St Mary Street and crossed the road, ignoring the cars that squealed to a halt and blasted their horns at him. A few seconds later, though, he was abruptly jerked out of his inner world as he was passing the entrance to Cook Street. Three boys on mountain bikes shot out of the side-road and whisked past him so close that the handlebar of the second bike caught him a glancing blow in the stomach, knocking him off balance and winding him. They didn't even pause; by the time he had straightened up, they had already crossed the street and were pedalling furiously down Chapel Road. Not bothering to waste breath by hurling abuse at them, he turned and looked back the way they had come. A little way down Cook Street, a blue Peugeot was parked, its alarm keening its shrill, futile wail to the indifferent street. The only other person present was a man in black jeans and a white bobble-hat, who was pasting a poster to the wall opposite, and he was paying no attention to the alarm.

Paul walked up to the car and examined it: the nearside window had been smashed, and a large lump of yellow brick lay on the front seat amongst a snowdrift of glittering glass particles. For the first time that day, Paul smiled with genuine pleasure, schadenfreude momentarily undercutting his own misery. He was about to make some remark to the man fly-posting, but when he looked up, the man was gone.

This wall was a favourite location for fly-posters, and had accreted a dense, colourful palimpsest, rich with the torn and ragged remains of layer upon layer of paper in a variety of fluorescent shades. The latest addition, however, was smaller and plainer than the rest; just an A4-sized sheet of white paper standing alone in the centre of the wall. Drawn by nothing more than idle curiosity, Paul crossed the street to look at it. When he saw it close-to, he almost vomited. In the centre of the poster, below the bold type of its legend, staring back at him in crude greyscale, sternly impassive, almost smug in its bland formality, was his own face. Or rather, a version of his face; a version he had not seen in years.

He stared dumbly at it for several moments, then looked frantically up and down the street, searching for the man who had put it there. At the far end, between a parked van and the street corner, he caught a glimpse of a white bobble-hat. He ran towards it, but his progress was impeded by his heavy, clumping boots and the drag of his baggy, oversize overalls, and by the time he reached the end of the street, the man was gone. He leaned on the rail which separated the pavement from the racing lanes of traffic and scanned the scene in front of him: the broad sweep of St Mary Place, the buildings on the far side, the tree-lined expanse of Hoglands Park . . . Then he saw him; a distant figure walking up towards the Hanover Buildings. Paul scrambled over the rail and ran across the road, dodging the traffic, climbed the rail on the far side, and set off again in pursuit.

Now he was getting closer to the city's shopping centre, the crowds were becoming denser, and he had to keep pausing at every junction to stand on tiptoe and scour the undulating, mottled sea of heads. Each time, he managed to spot the distinctive white hat, and each time he set off again in pursuit, breathless, heart thumping, until he came to the next corner. Then, suddenly, much closer than he anticipated, he saw the hat turn left near HMV and head down the alley which led to the indoor Bargate Centre. With a surge of renewed energy, Paul elbowed and shoved through the press of shoppers, oblivious to their squawks of protest, and charged in through the swing doors, skidding to an uncertain stop on the polished floor of the arcade.

He gazed around him: shoppers – escalators – shops – shoppers – more doors – the street beyond – shoppers – lifts – brightly-lit display windows – escalators up, escalators down – more shoppers milling all around him. He searched desperately in every direction – shop doorways, escalators, around and around the central rotunda with its open well giving onto the café terraces on the level below – but there was no sign of the white hat. He had lost him; he had almost had him, and then he was gone.

Panting, his chest throbbing with pain, he leaned back against the plate glass of a bookshop window and closed his eyes. All signs of life and will drained out of him, and he slid slowly down the glass until he was crouched, abject and moaning, on the dusty floor.

Later, when he returned to Cook Street, the poster was still there. He had forlornly hoped that he might have imagined it, but there it was, still damp with paste. Glancing around to check that nobody was watching, he carefully peeled it off the wall and rolled it into a tube. Then, at last, he continued on his way home.

Setting down one of her bulging shopping bags on the step and holding her open purse between her teeth, Christine just about managed to insert her key in the lock. The door clunked open and the familiar musty humidity of the hallway welled out into her face. With the purse still clamped in her mouth and leaking its sour plastic flavour onto her tongue, she picked up the bag and staggered in through the doorway, bumping the door closed with her bottom.

She had put away the purse and was halfway to the foot of the stairs when the door of the ground-floor flat opened and Arfur ve Landlord's large, shiny face appeared. Pretending not to notice him, Christine carried on walking. 'Art'noon, Zeta,' he said, making a show of looking at his watch. 'Free o'clock an up an about! Crack a dawn fer you, innit, Zeta?'

She paused and looked at him, from his pink, domed head with its sideways scrape of wiry, greying hair, to his distended belly straining the buttons of a stained nylon shirt and the short, spindly legs terminating in holed maroon slippers.

'It's Christine to you,' she said with dignity. 'Or Miss Harris, if you prefer.'

He nodded sardonically and leaned against the door jamb. 'Oh, right, I forgot. It's only yer punters calls you Zeta, int it.' His face darkened to a glower. 'No need ter put on yer ladylike airs wiv me, missie. I know what sort of filfy fings you get up to. Disgustin, it is. Dint oughta allow sluts like you in my ouse.'

She sighed. 'Did you want something, or is this just you having a go?'

'Avin a go? I got better fings to do van stand round avin a go at scrubbers, darlin.' He paused for effect. 'Na, vis come fer im upstairs. Be a good gel an take it up for us, will yer.'

He produced a letter and held it out to her.

'All right. Put it in there.' She held up one of her shopping bags, and he slipped the envelope inside. This close, the acid, ammonious odour of his body made her nostrils twitch and the corners of her mouth turn down. 'I'll see he gets it.'

Arfur stayed where he was, uncomfortably close to her. 'I bet you will,' he leered. 'Night off tonight, is it?' He nodded at her bags. 'Entertainin?'

'What's it to you?' She was edging away from him, but he kept following her, his watery eyes glittering.

'Just wond'rin, you know, if you ain't busy, you might wanna come downstairs and see what a *real* man can do for yer . . .'

A movement caught her eye, and she glanced down involuntarily. There was a dark, shiny patch on the fabric around the crotch of his grey trousers, and his stubby, nicotine-brown fingers were idly stroking and fiddling at it. 'What d'yer say?' he whispered. 'Fancy a good big moufful a pork, do yer?'

In spite of herself, Christine laughed.

Encouraged, Arfur glanced furtively over his shoulder. 'I know what a gel like you wants,' he said eagerly, fumbling with his trousers. There was a sudden, plastic rasp of a zip, and Christine found herself looking down at something resembling a half-cooked sausage, greasy and partially engorged, stained fingers twitching its wrinkled stub-end urgently in her direction. 'Come on,' he whispered excitedly. 'I know you wannit. Get yer teef round it – Right here, right now!'

Smiling sweetly at him, she put down her shopping bags and laid a hand lightly on his chest. She leaned close and whispered softly, seductively in his ear. 'Are you sure? Do you really want to feel these luscious lips around your cock?'

He flushed bright red to the tips of his ears. 'Yes,' he squeaked.

'Really? And you'd like me to lick you with my tongue?'

He nodded dumbly, his eyes wide as billiard balls.

She leaned even closer, her whisper as rich and thick as honey: 'I'd sooner go and suck the dogs on the common, you filthy old pervert.'

He was so absorbed by the sensual hypnotism of her voice that she had picked up her bags and got halfway up the stairs before the words registered. Fumbling himself back into his trousers, he stamped furiously to the banister. '*Slut!*' he yelled. 'You'll come beggin fer it one a vese days, yer poxy prick-teasin little *whore!*'

Christine turned at the top of the stairs. 'Have you always been a greasy old wanker, or do you have to work at it?' She paused and, gazing down at him with drowsy eyes, she parted her lips and licked slowly, lasciviously around them, then giggled and was gone.

'*Bitch*!' he screamed as her flat door snapped shut. 'Fuckin *slag*!'

Binnie was in the living room, perched on the arm of the sofa and making up her face in a mirror propped on the windowsill. 'I heard that,' she said as Christine walked through to the kitchen. 'Old Arfur try it on with you, did he?'

Christine reappeared in the doorway. 'Oh God,' she moaned, taking off her coat and slumping down on the sofa. 'It nearly made me puke. I mean, I've been with some pretty disgusting blokes, but Christ . . .'

Binnie pulled down her lower lid and began pencilling black eyeliner along its rim. 'How much'd'e offer you?'

'Nothing.'

'Nothing? Shit . . .'

'Must think I go crazy for fat old geezers who stink of piss.'

Binnie tutted. 'He's getting worse. At least he used to offer to pay. Once told me he'd deduct it from my rent if I'd suck his dick.' She finished lining one eye and started on the other. 'Story is – Linda told me this, right – there was this old girl who lived upstairs who weren't too choosy. You know, the old sort, a bit past it. Right old slapper. Used to work the pubs down by the docks on Friday nights. Anyway, she used to give old Arfie hand-jobs at two quid a throw. Special rate for the landlord, see. Now he thinks any of us'll yank his grotty old chopper just for the privilege of living in this shite-hole.'

Christine grunted. 'Well, next time he tries it, I'm gonna be ready with a pair of scissors.' She paused and gazed at Binnie. 'What are you up to, by the way? Isn't it a bit early to be getting the slap on?'

'Appointment,' said Binnie, putting her eyeliner away

and rummaging through her bag for a suitable lipstick.

Christine sat up. 'Yeah? Is this a freelance, or does Gary know?'

'He arranged it. All-nighter over at the Mayflower. Some business friend of his.'

Christine sighed. 'Wish he'd fix me up with something like that. How much?'

'Two hundred after he's had his cut.'

'Lucky bitch.'

Binnie laughed and stood up, sweeping a little red cocktail dress off the ironing board. 'What d'you think?' she asked, smoothing the silken fabric over her front. 'The old flame-thrower. Worth an extra fifty quid tip?'

'Lovely. Won't work with that lipstick, though. Go for something brighter. Look, I'm going for a nap. Wake us up on your way out, will you?'

Binnie nodded absently, and Christine left her concentrating on alternately pouting at the mirror and frowning at her dress.

She was woken by the sound of the front door slamming. Its report resonated throughout the house's flimsy fabric and up the legs of her bed, jarring her from sleep. The slam was followed by heavy footsteps on the stairs and another, quieter slam of the door across the landing.

That would be Paul, she thought, then remembered the letter.

She wandered into the living room. Binnie had gone, and there was a heavy, cloying aroma of Opium in the air. Silly tart; she had been so keyed up for her big appointment she'd forgotten to wake her up. Oh well, she had plenty of time. She retrieved the letter from the Safeway bag and took it across the landing. She rapped on the door and called his name, but there was no answer, so she jammed the envelope in the crack of the

115

door and went back to the flat.

Two hours later, bathed, dressed and made-up, she was on her way out to work. As she closed the door, she noticed the letter, still stuck in the jamb where she had left it. There were people living here who would steal anything, so she went across the landing and knocked again. There was a long pause, then she heard a chain rattle, the door opened a crack and a fearful, suspicious pair of eyes peered out. 'Hi, Paul,' she said, grinning at the anxious look on his face.

'Oh,' he said, relaxing. 'It's you.'

'Aren't you gonna open this door?'

'What? Oh, right. Sorry.' The chain rattled again and the door opened wide.

'You okay, pet?' she asked, walking past him into the tiny bedsit. 'I knocked earlier and there was no answer.'

'Must've been out.'

'No, you were in. I heard you come up the stairs.'

'Oh ... Er, d'you want a cup of tea?'

Christine was gazing around the room. Under the window was a rickety table with a faded orange formica top. On it was a shoebox which was overflowing with bits and pieces of paper, as though he had been rummaging through it when she knocked. Beside it was a tube of rolled-up paper. Paul noticed her looking at the box, and slipped the lid back on.

'Sorry,' she said. 'Didn't mean to be nosy. I dunno if I'm coming or going today. What was it you said?'

'D'you want a cup of tea?'

'No, ta – just on my way to work ... Are you sure you're all right? You look a bit pale.'

He sighed and sat down on the bed. 'Oh, it's nothing much. I only lost my sodding job today.'

'No.'

'Yeah. I reckon I'll have to move on, Chrissie.'

She sat on the chair by the table and lit a cigarette.

'Christ, Paul. That's really shitty.'

He gazed silently at her for a few moments, a strange, absent look in his eyes. 'Yes,' he said, keeping her held in his gaze.

She wavered, and made a show of looking around for an ashtray. There wasn't one, so she tapped her ash onto the lid of a tobacco tin which stood next to the shoebox on the table. 'Didn't know you smoked rollies,' she said.

'I don't.'

'Oh.'

'You said you were on your way to work.'

'Yeah, yeah, I was.' She leaned forward and touched his knee. 'Paul, you know you can always talk to me.'

'So?'

'Well, you know, if there's something on your mind . . .?'

'Right, yeah.'

'Okay,' she sighed. 'I know when I'm not wanted.' She stood up, and he followed her to the door. Before opening it, she turned to him. 'I'll see you later, I suppose.'

'Eh?'

She nudged his arm and smiled. 'It's Friday. You do still want me to come, don't you?'

He sighed. 'I told you, I lost my job. I can't afford it.'

'Oh. You're the best of all my regulars, too.' She looked coyly at him. 'You know, I could still come . . .'

'I haven't got any mo—'

She put a manicured finger to his lips. 'I said,' she repeated slowly, 'I could still come.'

At last, his eyes came to life and he grinned. 'Yeah? What would Gary say if he knew you were giving away freebies?'

'He doesn't need to know. Anyway, he doesn't know you're on my client list at all, payment or no payment.

117

He doesn't like his girls playing at home . . . So, do you want me to come or not?'

He nodded. 'Okay.'

She tweaked his collar. 'Only, tidy yourself up a bit first, eh?' She opened the door and was about to walk out when she remembered the letter. 'Oh shit. I told you I wasn't with it today. I was meant to give you this. Ta-ra, then. See you about half-twelve.'

And she was gone, trip-trapping lightly down the stairs and leaving him with a waft of perfume in his nostrils and the envelope in his hand.

When Christine returned home at midnight, she went to the bathroom and freshened up. After an evening spent cramped in the darkness of strangers' cars, she was no longer in any mood for her liaison with Paul, and she regretted having arranged it. She could not imagine what it was that had made her offer herself like that. Okay, he was broke, and he wasn't bad looking under that beard, and he was less rough in bed than most of her customers, and she was fond of him in a funny way, but none of those things were good enough reason to hand over her goods gratis. Still, she wasn't the kind of girl to break her promises lightly. She would just have to make it clear that this was a one-off, a consolation, never to be repeated without full and proper payment.

She finished abluting and touching up her make-up, and went across the landing to Paul's bedsit. Once again, there was no answer to her knock, so she tried the handle. The door opened into darkness. She switched on the light and stepped inside. He wasn't there, so she sat down on the bed to wait. Twenty minutes passed, and still he didn't come. After half an hour, her patience utterly exhausted, she took a pen and an old receipt from her clutch bag and wrote an angry note. Leaving it on the table, she went out and slammed the door behind her.

The note was still there a week later, gathering dust, when Arfur came up to demand Paul's overdue rent. He noticed it and picked it up.

You fucker – Next time you fucking well pay.

He read it several times, his moist lips forming the words, his eyes alight with interest, then he folded it and slipped it into his trouser pocket. Grinning to himself, he went across the landing and tapped at Zeta's door.

Paul crouched over the hand basin and sluiced water over his face. The blood had congealed, and he had to scrub with his fingers to remove it, wincing in agony as he scraped around his nose. When he had finished, he looked at himself in the cracked, dirty mirror. Yes, still just about recognisable; he would be back to normal, whatever that was, when the swelling went down. 'You fucker,' he said to his reflection. 'You stupid cunt. You nearly paid for that one big-time.'

It had begun about two hours earlier. He had been sitting at the bar of the Firkin in the centre of Newbury, a double whisky half-drunk between his palms, staring at the row of optics, the glasses, the bottles and the little chopping board with its row of lemon segments. On an impulse, he drained the whisky in one go and slammed the glass down on the bar. The barman, who was pulling a pint of bitter, glanced up at him. 'Another one of those, mate,' said Paul, tilting the empty glass at him.

'In a moment, sir,' said the barman with professional patience.

Paul nodded laconically and turned to two who were standing a little further along the bar. They were both heavily built and wearing matching denim jackets and red baseball caps. He leaned over and tugged on the nearest one's sleeve. 'Oi,' he said. 'Whaddya think of the service in here?'

The men stopped talking and stared at him. 'What?' said the nearest one.

'The service,' Paul repeated, nodding at the barman.

'It's all right.' The men turned away from him and resumed their conversation.

'Oi, Tweedlefuckindum twinnies, I'm talking to you.' He looked at the barman. 'Tell me, mate, is there two of em or have I had more'n I thought? Oi, you pair! Listen, I was asking—' He leaned across to nudge the nearest of the pair again, but lost his grip on the bar and lurched forward, swiping the man's pint glass onto the floor.

'Jesus! You stupid cunt!' the man shouted, grabbing Paul's jacket.

His friend stepped quickly between them. 'Okay, okay, cool it, Dave,' he said. He looked at Paul. 'I think you oughta buy my mate another drink and say sorry.'

Paul nodded enthusiastically and looked at Dave. 'Okay,' he said. 'Very well. Let's see, what'll it be?'

Dave looked mollified. 'Budweiser,' he said. 'Pint.'

'Budweiser,' Paul repeated. He leaned towards the man and laid a finger on his chest. 'Only queers,' he told him authoritatively, 'drink Budweiser. *You* must be a fucking qu—'

He didn't even see the fist that swooped out of nowhere and slammed into the middle of his face. The room blurred and tilted, and he was on the floor before he even felt any pain.

'Why did you do it?' he asked his reflection. 'What did you think it was going to achieve, *hn*?'

His face was looking just about passable now; his nose was a little swollen and there was some slight purpling under his eyes, but he had never been prone to severe bruising, so he was fairly sure the effects would progress no further. Hoisting his rucksack onto his shoulder, he left the public toilet and walked out into the street. There was a fine drizzle blurring the street-lights and glossing the pavements. He turned up his collar and started walking towards the edge of town, pausing and holding out his thumb to each thundering lorry that swooshed past in a cloud of gutter-spray. He didn't bother with cars. After about half an hour and four attempted hitches, an articulated lorry swept by him. There was a squealing hiss of air-brakes, and the lorry pulled over, its brake-lights lit up like a fairground ride. As he hurried along, he glanced up at the name on the side of the container. It was a general freight firm, and appeared to offer three home destinations, all in South Wales: Cwmbran, Newport and Bridgend. The cab door opened, and he climbed up onto the step.

'Where to?' asked the driver, a short, wiry man with a deeply lined face that looked eerily green in the dash-board lights.

'Newport?' Paul suggested.

'I'm going to Bridgend, butt. I can drop you at the Malpas roundabout if you like.'

'Okay.' He had no idea where the Malpas roundabout might be, but he could work that out when he got there.

'Get in, then.'

'Cheers, mate.' He climbed on to the seat and slammed the door. The engine roared and grumbled beneath him and they pulled slowly away into the night.

The driver, whose name was apparently Les, if the sunstrip on the windscreen was to be believed, was thankfully uncommunicative, and they rolled along in a mutual silence accompanied by Les's collection of Dire Straits and Celine Dion tapes. The only time Les spoke

121

during the journey was as they set out: 'You got a name, butt?' he asked.

'Nigel.'

Les nodded, apparently satisfied that his duty to sociability had been fulfilled.

Nigel. He had no idea why; the name had just popped into his mouth. There was something he liked about its flavour, though, so he decided to stick with it. All he needed now was a surname, and he decided to take one from the next road sign they passed. When it came, it offered three options: Avington, Kintbury and Inkpen. He liked the sound of Inkpen best; Nigel Inkpen sounded like someone he wouldn't mind having a go at being. He hadn't much liked being Paul Chapel. In a sense, he felt that Paul rather deserved to be punched in the face, even if it did mean that Nigel had to go on enduring the residual throbbing pain. To be fair to himself, he had to admit that Paul had been quickly and expediently constructed from the resources which had been lying about at the time; Nigel, he decided, would be more carefully built.

It was not until half an hour later, as the lorry was carving its way on to the M4, that he remembered the letter. He hadn't even opened it; as soon as he saw the writing on the envelope, he had instantly decided to move on. He was packed and gone within forty minutes of Christine giving the letter to him. Now, with nothing to occupy him and feeling more cheerful, he dug the envelope out of his rucksack and opened it. Angling it to the glass, he read it by the intermittent orange lights sweeping overhead.

Dear Paul,

Ha, he thought. You're already out of date, friend. I've outrun you.

Well, well, well. That was a rather rapid departure. It took me quite by surprise. It seems that I chose my own particular appellation most appropriately, now that you have shown yourself such an accomplished strandloper. Still, I confess to a degree of bewilderment as to exactly what it is you are loping from. I thought you seemed to be leading such a contented life. Surely the cause of your departure cannot have been me? . . . It was? But Paul, you should know, even after such a brief courtship, that faithlessness and desertion simply will not do. You should have taken my measure better than that. I wish you would trust me, but then I do admit that, in these circumstances, this may be asking too much. Put faith, then, in your ignorance: ignorance is, after all, second best to trust. Ask any politician.

It gladdens me to learn that you have found honest employment. However, my cheeks burn with sympathetic shame at the mere thought of the company you keep: the society of harlots, Paul, is not for the likes of you and I. She is not good for you, my friend: forsake her, or I shall find myself compelled to tease her away from you in my own gentle way.

Isn't it quite astonishing about the poster? (I am sure you will have seen it by now: I shall take care to place it where you will find it.) Of course, they never used them, did they? By the time the wretched things had been printed, they were quite redundant. Little point in pursuing a dead man, is there? Unless, of course, one happens to be me. This brings me back to the matter I wrote of in my last letter; their eyes, unlike mine, are turned upwards rather than downwards. They may consider themselves men of wisdom who know the shadowy corners of the human heart, but they have not my willingness to put their hands into the darkest slime. Only when one takes full and untempered pleasure in those places can one truly have absolute knowledge; and knowledge, as we both know, is power. There lies my genius and their foolishness.

I hope, Paul, that you will not make any more attempts to elude me. You will have noted that I have not taken so long to find you this time. Next time – if you are so foolish as to allow there to be a next time – I shall smell you out even more quickly. Eventually, I shall be at your back every step of the way. It is your choice: flee and be scoured or stay and be comforted by my little trinkets. A man should never forget his past, Paul. I am here to ensure that you do not.

With fondest and sincerest good wishes
I am still here,
The Strand Scourer.

Not this time, Nigel thought, folding the letter and putting it away. You can't track me this time. He leaned against the window and gazed out past the beading rainwater at the pale ochre of the carriageways and the deep darkness beyond, letting the vibrations of the truck soothe the tiredness from his bones.

Part II

Mutandum

7

'How's the bacon?' asked Carole, sipping her coffee and watching as Steven forked and sliced off a crescent of the thick, pink meat, wiped on a smear of egg yolk and pushed it greedily into his mouth.

'Mm-Hmm,' he said, chewing vigorously. 'Mmmmm.' He swallowed and licked his lips. 'Superb. Where d'you *get* it?'

'Old Mrs Willis. Her husband farms the pigs and she slaughters them. They're just about the last people around here who still do the whole bit, from breeding to butchering. The meat's organic, too. But then I suppose the Willises never went *in*organic in the first place.'

Steven looked up from his plate and smiled, his jaw working around another forkful of bacon, egg and mushroom.

Three weeks had passed since the burglary that never was. Neither of them had referred to it since, and they had settled down to an improvised routine. Steven continued living in the barn, but ventured into the house for meals, rarely going further in than the kitchen. He contributed what little help was needed around the farm, but spent most of his days either walking on the moors or sitting on his cot in the barn, reading books that he borrowed from Carole. The intention he had avowed to himself of leaving at the earliest opportunity seemed to have slipped away. Each time it raised its hand and asked for attention, he waved it aside, giving himself a stream of excuses (he wasn't well enough yet; he needed a proper plan; he should break it to Carole but hadn't got round to it yet) which he knew were feeble or even blatantly untrue. The simple truth was that the things which made him want to go – indeed meant that he *must* go – had been outweighed by his desire to stay. So, he just tried not to think about it, and Carole helped by not mentioning it either.

He swallowed the last mouthful and pushed his plate away.

'More coffee?' she asked, taking the jug from the stove and bringing it back to the table.

Running his tongue around his teeth, he raised a palm and shook his head.

She sat down and poured herself a second cup. 'I don't know how you can eat first thing in the morning,' she said, taking a cigarette from her packet and lighting it. 'Anything more solid than coffee this early makes me retch.'

'That's women for you,' he said, leaning back in his chair and smiling contentedly.

She snorted. 'That's greedy bastards for you. I hope you're going to rinse that plate.'

He nodded. 'I'll wash up if you like.'

'Okay,' she said. 'You thought I was going to say "No, leave it, I'll do it", didn't you?' she grinned, glancing at the mound of dirty crockery which had been lurking in and around the sink since the evening before.

He raised his hands in a surrendering gesture and shook his head. 'No, honest. I'll do it.'

They sat quietly for a few minutes, content in the light fuzz of post-breakfast early morning. Carole smoked her cigarette slowly. In between puffs, she prodded at the pellets of ash in the ashtray with the tip, breaking them down into powder. Suddenly, without looking up, she broke the silence. 'Have you remembered anything else?' she asked. 'Any little memories knocking on the door you want to tell me about?'

He raised his eyes from his plate and gazed at the

ceiling. His face was a study in calm inscrutability, but inside, his mind was working feverishly.

This had all begun with a mistake last week. He liked to imagine that it had happened because he still wasn't quite thinking straight after the blows to the head, but he knew perfectly well that he had just been sloppy and careless, letting his emotions interfere with the cold calculation needed to establish a believable character with a believable ailment. Carole had devoted a lot of time to devising unsuccessful therapies for him: plying him with general knowledge questions, making him listen to tapes of old songs, and so on. They spent several evenings overhauling the Morris; lifting out the engine and gearbox, stripping them down and rebuilding them with new bearings, gaskets, oil seals and valves. His oily hands scampered and twiddled expertly among the tools and components, but no personal memories were disinterred. Carole would have begun to lose heart had it not been for one unexpected glimmer of progress: It was a Sunday, and there was little work to do on the farm, so she had accompanied him on his walk. Together, they hiked for miles, searching little hollows, splashing across streams, examining the ancient, lichened stones. All the while, she told him stories about the moors: local histories and legends, mingled with anecdotes about her childhood.

'You grew up here, then?' Steven had asked as they strode across a stretch of open grass studded with patches of heather.

'Good God, no,' she laughed. 'London born and bred, I'm afraid.'

'I thought you didn't talk like a local. So how . . .?'

'Oh, it's a long story.'

'Tell me anyway.'

'Well,' she began. As she spoke, she slipped her arm through his; the gesture seemed so natural that it was

129

only much later that he wondered how she had got so close so quickly. 'The farm originally belonged to some distant relative of my father; the Fitchett branch of the family. The Percevals hadn't had anything to do with them for – oh, generations, I suppose. Then, the last of the Fitchetts – an old guy called George – died unmarried and childless. He was a bit of an eccentric, apparently; lived alone on the farm well into his nineties. Anyway, it turned out that my father was the closest living relative, so he ended up inheriting everything. Dad was a solicitor – he's retired now – and *he* had no intention of taking up farming.' She laughed, glancing up at Steven. 'I suppose you'd have to meet him to get the joke . . . So, he sold off most of the land to the neighbours and did it up as a holiday home. My little brother Michael and I used to come up here with my mother every summer holiday. Dad hardly ever came. Too busy, I suppose.'

'Didn't he worry about your mum?' Steven asked. 'Up here on her own with two kids?'

'Not that I was aware of. Anyway, we weren't always alone. Dad's brother used to bring his family sometimes. Uncle Tony and Aunt Gemma. They had a son my age – Kieran. We used to play together, go on long exploring trips across the moors . . . God, we walked miles and miles, the two of us. One favourite game was this thing we called Wuthering Heights. It was so silly. What we did was, if we came across a high bit of moor like this where we are now, the kind that seems to go on forever, one of us would whisper *Wuthering Heights*. That was all – just "Wuthering Heights" – and we both knew what to do. I'd walk off in one direction and Steven . . . I mean, Kieran; Kieran would walk off the other way, like in a duel. Then, when we were about a hundred yards apart – somehow, we always knew the right moment – we'd both turn round at the same time and start running like mad towards each other, arms out, crying out "Cathy!", "Heathcliff!", "Cathy!" ' Carole paused, breathless with laughter, ' "Cathy!", "Heathcliff!" ' she continued, wailing the names with melodramatic passion. 'God knows where we got that from. Off the television, I suppose. Anyway, by the time we reached each other, we'd be totally breathless with running and shouting, and we'd just fall into each other's arms and topple over into the grass, laughing like madmen. You know the sort of laughter you get when you're a child, when you can't breathe and your chest hurts . . . I wonder where that goes when you grow up . . .'

'What happened then?'

'Nothing really. We just rolled around for a bit until we'd got our breath back. I mean, we were only about ten years old. There wasn't much else that could have happened . . . Kieran. God, I had *such* a crush on him. I wonder if he ever knew.'

Steven looked at her, eyebrows raised. 'So, all that . . .?'

'Hmm? Well, yes, of course. What else? Children have funny ways of expressing it. I remember always feeling a bit strange afterwards; a bit excited, a bit frightened, a bit wicked, even a bit unsatisfied, as though I knew there should be more to the game than that. Like I was missing out on some essential, arcane element, but at the same time feeling frightened of finding out what it was . . . God, who'd be a child? Anyway, after we'd got our breath back, we'd get up and head for home, suddenly all embarrassed and shy and not talking to each other. Unless, of course, we found another suitable hilltop. Then it would be "Wuthering Heights?" and off we'd go again.' She laughed.

Suddenly, Steven stopped walking. 'What's that place?' he asked, pointing. They had come to a point where the moortop peaked and swept down into a valley whose distant floor was choked with houses looking like crumbs and grit gathered in a blanket fold.

'That's Ilkley,' she said. 'This is Ilkley Moor, famous in song. You know the one.'

He looked blank, so she hummed the tune. After a few bars, his lips started moving, mouthing the words. 'I know that!' he laughed. 'My granddad used to sing me that song when I was a kid. I hated it, it was crap!'

'Was he from Yorkshire?' Carole asked, a note of surprise in her voice.

'Yorkshire? No, he was East Anglian. I remember him singing it in this thick Norfolk accent. Tickled me pink, that did . . .' He paused. 'What?' Carole, still clinging to his arm, was looking up at him with a look of wonder and triumph in her eyes. 'What?' he repeated, smiling nervously. 'What are you looking at?'

'You,' she said, squeezing his arm excitedly. 'You remembered something!'

He stared at her. *Shit, shit, fuck and buggeration!* What was he thinking of? He had allowed himself to become preoccupied, gathered up in Carole's reminiscences; one momentary loss of concentration, and look what had happened! He concentrated now on keeping the self-disgust and fear out of his face, carefully constructing instead an expression of bewilderment. 'What?' he said again.

'Your memory's coming back!'

'Is it?' *Tch, clumsy; concentrate.*

She threw her other arm around him, turning him to face her, squealing with delight. 'Yes, yes, yes!' she shouted. 'I knew it would come back, I *knew* it!' She kissed him on his bearded cheek and hugged him.

And that had been it; the skilfully woven fabric was torn, and no amount of thread could stitch it up again.

During the days that followed, all he could do was embroider around the sudden rent as Carole – her carefully husbanded patience bubbling over with good intentions – poked and peeled at its edges, trying to widen the hole. In the end, it had worked out all right. Improvising carefully, he had even managed to turn the situation to his advantage; finally convinced that she could help him recover his memory, Carole's kindness to him and tolerance of his eccentricities became greater and more confident. At the same time, he found that he was feeling increasingly comfortable with her, no longer having to be quite so alert to every word he uttered in case it revealed a trace of memory. Every so often, he would deliberately deliver a fresh morsel – invariably chosen from the safe larder of his childhood – to feed her appetite for improvement. The snippets were always true, because it was easier to be consistent with the truth. Any accidental slips could quite easily be play-acted away.

This morning, as they sat lingering over the remains of their breakfast, was typical. She always wanted to know if anything new had surfaced during the night; she had some pet theory that dreams could be the route back to his memory banks. While she waited, he continued gazing thoughtfully up at the ceiling. Outwardly, he appeared to be probing his mind. Inwardly, he was deliberately slicing and trimming the choice cut he had prepared for her.

Carole sucked on her cigarette, watching him apprehensively. 'Anything at all?' she prompted, sounding slightly disappointed.

'Yes, there was something,' he murmured. 'Do-it-yourself price reductions,' he said, looking at her and laughing.

'Do-it-yourself what?'

'Price reductions,' he repeated. 'Don't ask me how I

came up with it. It just popped into my head when I woke up.'

'What does it mean?'

'I'm not absolutely sure, but I think I've managed to work it out. It started making me think about huge rows with my parents ... I'll tell you what I've pieced together. For some reason I still can't get hold of, it feels really important – you know, more significant than it sounds.' The fragmented story he told was, like all his recollections, a genuine memory, and he knew its significance perfectly well; how his actions had come back to haunt him later, but he wasn't ready to think about that himself right now, let alone tell Carole about it. 'I'm a kid, right,' he said. 'About thirteen. Fourteen, maybe, and I used to shoplift with my mates. The usual sort of stuff: sweets and crisps from the Spar at dinnertime. Anyway, we were nicking other stuff as well. I must've been into making models – you know, plastic kits – because I remember we were nicking stuff like that. Pocketing little things like pots of paint and tubes of glue, but sometimes the actual kits if they were small enough ... I think this was mostly in Woolworth's ...' He paused and grinned. 'I remember something else now. I remember having this snorkel parka – d'you remember snorkels? Fucking horrible they were, and this one was blue and it had all these burn holes inside the cuffs from hiding our fags in the playground if a teacher was looking ... Anyway, I remember I had all these pockets cut out in the lining; you know, for pinching things.'

Carole smiled. 'Where do the price reductions come in?'

'Ah, that was the clever bit,' he grinned, leaning forward and resting his forearms on the table. 'I had this mate, my best friend, I suppose. I can see him now, as clear as I'm looking at you. Buggered if I can put a name to him, though. Funny, isn't it; I've got all this stuff about him, but not a ghost of a name. Anyway, he was a shoplifting genius, a master. He had a parka like mine, and you wouldn't believe how much gear he could get in it in one go. I think he must have been into models too, but he got ambitious. Some of those kits came in bloody big boxes, much bigger than even he could sneak out unnoticed. So, he invented do-it-yourself price reductions, and pretty soon I was doing it too. What you did was pretend you were looking at something – something you had enough money for – and meanwhile you'd be peeling the price label off it. Really carefully, so you didn't scag the edges. Then you'd use it to replace the label on the big expensive thing you really wanted. Obviously, you could only do it in the big shops where the old dears on the checkouts hardly knew what day of the week it was, let alone what the real price of an Airfix Panzerkampfwagen should be.'

'Before the days of bar-codes, then,' said Carole.

'What? Oh, yes. Still, I reckon this guy – I wish I could put a name to him – I reckon he would've found a way round those eventually.'

'So, how long did this go on? Can you remember?'

He shook his head. 'I don't know. It all seems rolled up with this picture I've got of an awful screaming match at home. My old man going *purple*. Maybe we got caught, or *I* got caught, or maybe someone split on us. I don't know . . . I do remember something else, though; this friend shoplifting a stereo.'

'A *stereo*?' Carole repeated, her mouth dropping open.

Steven laughed and slapped the table with the palm of his hand. 'A real genius. I mean that's what genius is, isn't it – going for it; doing the things that nobody else can conceive of as possible. Sheer audacity . . .

Now, here's the problem: how do you get a stereo – this bloody big ghetto-blaster, or the nearest they had to ghetto-blasters in those days – how do you get something that size, in its box, out of Woolworth's without getting caught?'

Carole shrugged. 'I give in.'

'Well, he goes in with a big carrier bag in his pocket and sidles up to the hi-fi section, nice and casual, and when nobody's looking, he slips the stereo off the shelf and into the bag. Now he's got to get out of the shop. A schoolkid walking out past the checkouts with a big bag like that? Forget it; suspicious as hell; they'll be on him straight away. This is the clever bit, the work of genius. In this Woolies, they had this counter near the exit where you could leave stuff – heavy bags and things – while you went and did your shopping. So, bold as brass, he walks straight up to the counter, hands over his bag, gets his little ticket or whatever and just strolls out. This is lunchtime. He goes back to school for the afternoon, then at hometime he returns to Woolies, hands in his ticket and Bingo! He's out of there with a new stereo.'

'I don't believe it,' said Carole. 'Surely they'd check it?'

'Why? They're probably rushed off their feet at this counter, looking for old ladies' bags and brollies. And what is there to be suspicious of? A kid just walking out with a stereo in a bag is one thing, and they're always on the lookout. But a kid collecting his bag – who knows, probably his mum's shopping – what's suspicious about that? So, he's not only shoplifted from Woolies, he's actually got the *staff* to collude with him.'

'I read a story once,' Carole said. 'True story, about a woman who was a secret agent in France during the War. She used to forestall suspicion by flirting with German soldiers if they spoke to her. Sometimes, she'd even get them to carry her bags for her, even if they had stuff in them – I don't know, radios or whatever – that would have got her tortured and shot if they were found.'

Steven nodded. 'It's the same thing. Okay, it's in a different league, but it's the same principle.'

Carole sat forward and smiled. 'This is wonderful, Steven. I've been thinking; maybe it would be a good idea to start writing all this stuff down. If we put it all in chronological order, then you might start seeing connections that'll help you remember more.'

He shrugged. 'I don't know. Maybe . . .' He paused, listening to the sound of a car pulling into the yard. 'Who's that?'

Carole's eyes widened in alarm and she jumped up from her chair. 'Oh shit!' she said, looking at her watch. 'It's Ros. I'm supposed to be giving her lunch. I totally forgot she was coming . . . Where are you going?'

Steven had retreated from the table and was hovering near the back door, looking anxious. 'Well, you know. Got things to do.'

'No, don't. Stay and meet her . . . Please. Have lunch. You'll like Ros, honestly.' There was a loud hammering on the front door. 'Please?' she persisted.

He looked gravely doubtful, but came back to the table and sat down. Carole smiled gratefully and went to answer the door.

8

Steven browsed idly along Carole's bookshelves. The shelf at eye-level was jammed solid with novels, and he read their titles, beginning from the left. It was an eclectic mixture, ranging from the glitzy spines of science fiction to the orange and white of Penguin Modern Classics: *Use Of Weapons, Complicity, The Castle, Behind The Scenes At The Museum, Portrait Of The Artist As A Young Dog, The Lord Of The Rings, The Liar, Darkness at Noon* ... He had read a few of them during his long nights in the barn, but there were several here that he had never heard of. He prised *The Castle* out and riffled through the yellowing pages, but the dense, solid look of the text was offputting, so he put it back again. He felt uncomfortable; bored and anxious at the same time. He could hear Ros's voice barking loudly in the kitchen, harsh alongside Carole's quieter, melodic tone. He continued methodically grazing the titles, praying for the afternoon to be over.

Rosalind stood in the kitchen doorway, sipping from a glass of white wine and watching Carole slicing vegetables at the table. 'I wish you'd let me help,' she said insistently.

Carole swept a mound of sliced carrots into the basket of the steamer and shook her head. 'Not a chance. I feel bad enough as it is, without you having to help cook your own lunch.'

Rosalind laughed. 'You need treatment, my girl. You've got an overactive guilt gland. Check into a clinic and get yourself a guiltectomy.'

She turned and wandered through to the parlour. Steven was in there, standing about like a spare part. He reminded Rosalind of a man waiting in the lingerie section of a clothes shop while his girlfriend lingers out of sight in the changing room: all awkward restlessness, trying to be casual and at the same time desperate for something neutral to look at, trying not to appear too interested in the merchandise on display or the other female shoppers fondling it. He had finished examining the spines of the books on the shelves, and was now studying a framed picture which hung on the wall beside the window.

'Alfred Wallis,' she said, coming up behind him.

'What?' He glanced at her in surprise.

'The painting; it's an Alfred Wallis original.'

'Is it? Oh.' The name meant nothing to him, but the painting was interesting. It showed a two-masted boat of some kind – a trawler, perhaps – against a background of harbour-side streets. The picture was completely uncontrolled by perspective or depth; the boat seemed to hover slightly above the surface of the greyish water and, although its profile suggested a sideways-on angle, the oval deck was in view. The houses in the background were drawn in crooked lines, with little hot-cross-bun windows in each corner, and the streets beyond could be seen, like a medieval map that shows the façades of buildings.

Rosalind smiled. 'I see you've not been introduced to Wallis's work.'

Steven shook his head. 'I thought it was a kid's drawing.'

'Ah-ah,' said Rosalind. 'If you want to get by in artistic circles, you should say "naïve" or "primitive". Don't you find it has a certain charm?'

Steven contemplated the picture. 'Well, sort of. Did he have something wrong with his eyesight, or was it a gimmick?'

'Neither. That was his natural style.' She lowered her voice slightly. 'Don't repeat this to Carole, but I wouldn't really describe Wallis as a true artist.'

'Why not?'

She sipped her wine and gestured at the painting with her glass. 'Wallis was a Cornish fisherman, born in the 1850s. He lived in St Ives. Gave up going to sea and took up the rag-and-bone trade. He even sold ice cream for a while. He married a woman called Susan who was more than twenty years older than him. After she died, he took up painting to keep his mind off his grief. No training or anything; he just painted with and on anything that was available; boatbuilders' paint, bits of wood and cardboard. In the Twenties, he was discovered by this clique of intellectuals and artists from London. They went wild for his work, because of its naïveté and its simplicity.'

'So, he got rich?'

'No, he didn't. He died very unpicturesquely in a workhouse in 1942, without a penny. His paintings go for thousands now. Most of them had been bought up in the Thirties by the artist Ben Nicholson on behalf of his intellectual friends for a few shillings a go.'

'And they didn't help him out of the workhouse?'

'Nope.'

'What a bunch of bastards.'

She sipped her wine and shrugged. 'Still, at least they sorted out his funeral for him, so they can't have been all bad, eh?'

'Why wasn't he a proper artist, though?'

'Because of the very naïveté that made his work so beguiling to Nicholson. In my opinion, the term "naïve art" is an oxymoron.' She glanced at Steven. 'That's a contradiction in terms,' she added.

'I know what an oxymoron is.'

'Sorry. I'm being patronising, aren't I?'

'Never mind. I'd still like to know what a real artist is.'

'Well, how can something be naïve *and* be art? I mean, we use *art* to mean all sorts of things; anything from cooking to football or conversation are referred to as "an art", by which we mean that in some people they're finely-honed skills. So, that strikes Wallis out on one count, because he was basically crap at drawing.

140

But we're talking fine art here, so the more important factors are depth of signification and originality. Now, Wallis's painting didn't signify anything except that he liked boats and the Cornish coast. His reason for painting was to keep himself occupied. As for originality, you said yourself you thought it was a child's drawing. And it's true; kids do paint more or less like that. Now, if Wallis had painted in that style as an experiment, as a conscious effort to see the world in a particular way, like Nicholson did when he aped Wallis's style, then you could call it art. Otherwise, it's just drawing.'

'So crap drawings can be real art if they're crap on purpose?'

Rosalind smiled. 'Got it in one. We'll make a critic of you yet.'

'Poor old Alfred,' Steven sighed, looking at the painting again. 'Sorry, mate, you're not an artist.'

'Have you ever known any artists?' Rosalind asked.

'Yes,' he said absently.

She looked sharply at him. 'Really? How do you know?'

He coloured slightly, but didn't seem unduly flustered. 'You're an artist,' he said. 'I know you.'

'Ah, I see . . . By the way, Carole tells me Mnemosyne has been whispering in your ear recently.'

'Pardon?'

'Your memory's coming back.'

'Bits and pieces. It's like little scenes cut out of a film that don't join up. And it's mostly really old stuff from when I was a kid.' He paused and listened to the sounds of rattling crockery and cutlery coming from the kitchen. 'Sounds like it's going to be ready soon. Had we better . . .?'

He was turning to go, but Rosalind took hold of his arm and looked at him with intense, appraising eyes.

'You know,' she said, 'when Carole first told me about you, do you know what my first reaction was?'

'No . . .'

'I thought you sounded like a creep and a fraud. She couldn't see it, of course; she never can, or perhaps she just refuses to. You'll be happy to know I've changed my mind now, though. I don't think you're a creep at all; I think you're a nice, intelligent guy.'

'Well, I—'

'But I still think you're a fake.'

He stared blankly, uncomprehendingly at her. 'A *fake*?'

She smiled. 'That's very good, Steven. Bashful innocence; I like that, it's almost convincing, that wide-eyed *what, me?* look. What's the next stage? Carefully crafted indignation followed by bewildered anger? I'm on to you, mister. Now, I don't know what's going on, but for some reason, you've found it convenient to lose your memory. Maybe you've done something or you're running away from something – whatever it is, I don't believe in you, Steven.' She paused to assess the effect of her charges, but he just continued looking blankly at her. 'That's all by the by, really. I'm reasonably satisfied now that you're not some psycho, and at least having you here seems to make Carole happy for some reason.' She lowered her voice to a threatening growl. 'But I'm telling you, if she comes to so much as the slightest harm as a consequence of whatever it is you're mixed up in . . . well, you won't know what's hit you. She's been through some seriously bad shit in her time, and I'm not going to stand by and see her go through any more. Is that clear?'

Steven shrugged and looked confused. 'I don't know what you're talking about.'

She smiled at him with sarcastic sweetness. 'Well, that's all right then, isn't it?'

142

'It's on the table,' said Carole, appearing in the doorway.

Rosalind turned and smiled warmly at her. 'Steven and I were just admiring your Alfred Wallis.'

Carole smiled and joined them in front of the painting. 'It's lovely, isn't it. My grandfather was a friend of Christopher Wood. He left it to me when he died, because I always loved it so much. Sometimes, I sit in that chair there and just gaze at it for ages. It's like hypnotherapy.' She leaned towards Steven. 'Ros doesn't like it, you know,' she said in a conspiratorial tone. 'She doesn't think it's real art.'

'That's not fair!' Ros protested. 'I've never said I didn't *like* it. I think it's sweet. I just don't think it's, well . . .'

'Real art,' said Carole. 'It's all right, I'm not offended; I mean, *I* didn't paint it, I just look at it . . . Anyway, let's go and eat.'

Steven remained mostly silent throughout lunch, only speaking when called upon to offer an opinion on whatever subject was being discussed. He listened carefully, however. He was interested in the way Rosalind and Carole negotiated their conversation; although they were both relaxed and informal and spiced their talk with the kind of gossipy innuendoes and mild insults only exchanged between close friends, there was a faintly-drawn but still detectable frontier between them. He was struck by the way Carole deferentially disclaimed any right to an opinion of her own on any subject except those which bordered on medical or psychological matters. On every other subject, ranging from local news to art, literature and international politics, she seemed to fight a delicate rearguard action which involved being heard without being argumentative. She set out nebulous, vestigial defensive positions which were quickly adapted or surrendered as Rosalind

143

marched confidently forward deploying and detonating high-explosive opinions like a conversational panzer division.

After lunch, she stayed for coffee, then afternoon tea, and it was not until after six that she climbed into her little blue Renault and slithered up the track to the main road. Carole stood in the yard and waved her off, watching until the car was out of sight. 'Well, that wasn't so bad, was it?' she said when she and Steven had sat down again in the kitchen, amidst the day's culinary detritus.

He nodded slightly, noncommittally, looking around at the stacks of dirty dishes. 'Hmm. Lunch was nice.'

'I don't mean the cooking, I mean Ros. I'm glad she got to meet you at last.'

'She doesn't like me.'

Carole looked at him in surprise. 'Doesn't *like* you? What on earth makes you say that?'

'She thinks I'm a fake.'

'A fake?' Carole repeated, looking puzzled.

'That I'm faking amnesia, to take advantage of you in some way . . . You don't think that, do you?'

She reached across the table and held his hand. 'Of course I don't. You know I don't. What makes you think Ros thinks that? No, I'm sure she doesn't really, not now she's met you. You seemed to be getting along so well – you were thick as thieves in the parlour earlier . . .' She frowned. 'Hang on a minute, did she say something to you?'

'No . . . It wasn't anything like that. It was the *way* she said things. It was just a feeling I got.'

'Are you sure? I know Ros. If she's said something to upset you . . .'

He smiled and squeezed her hand. 'She didn't, honestly. I just got a feeling she didn't believe in me somehow. Let's just forget it, eh? Shall we finish up this wine?'

Carole picked up the bottle and tilted it. 'Not much left. There's another bottle in the fridge. D'you fancy making an evening of it?'

He smiled. 'Why not?'

9

Humming to herself, Carole nudged her clock's alarm pointer forward to seven-thirty and checked that the button was out. Then she peeled off her thick woollen socks and eased herself gratefully into bed. Her head was pleasantly drowsy from the wine, but not fogged or giddy, and her body relished the soft embrace of the duvet. It felt so good that, after switching off the bedside lamp, she held back sleep for a few minutes just so she could savour it. Little by little, consciousness seeped out between her interlaced fingers and the vacuum of sleep rushed in to replace it . . .

Bang!

—Her head leapt from the pillow, gasping, staring wildly into the darkness. The noise was like a gunshot going off right behind her left ear, and its echoes were still battering around inside her skull as she reached out and flipped the light back on. She sat up and waited for her breathing to level out and her heart's insistent thumping to die down. She cursed herself for drinking the wine. Hypnagogic hallucinations, they were called – sensory blips experienced on the brink of sleep – and she had been prone to them since childhood. It was always auditory, always sudden, short and sharp, and always loud; like a drumbeat or a door slamming or a gunshot, and they almost always occurred when she had been drinking in the evening.

145

When she had calmed down, she switched off the light and lay down again, pulling the duvet tightly around her chin for comfort, and waited for sleep to return. And waited. It was no use; the few moments' half-sleep and the shock of the bang had weakened and scattered the advancing drowsiness, leaving her wide awake. Each time she rolled over and tried to concentrate on oblivion, thoughts leapt out of the shadows like goblins and stamped around inside her head, shouting and chanting at her. She thought about Steven, she thought about Ros, about Ros and Steven, about herself and Steven. What if Ros *had* said something to him? What if it unbalanced him, impeded his recovery. What if Ros was right and Steven *was* faking it, but what about the little snatches of memory, how could those be faked, why couldn't Ros just mind her own business, should she let the two of them meet again, what if Ros antagonised him, or he antagonised her, but how could she cut Ros out of her life, and what about the farm, should she be devoting so much time to Steven – was the farm likely to suffer, how did Steven feel about her, how did he feel about being here, he seemed to be happy with her, sort of, but it was so difficult to be sure, and why was she so concerned, were her feelings about him entirely innocent or did she feel something deeper, the way he looked at her sometimes, walking across the moor with arms linked, holding hands across the table, touching his knee, his eyes closed, gripping her wrist, how might it feel to have his arms around—

She sat up and opened her eyes, and the thoughts receded and muted to a muffled murmur. She was hot; there was a thin film of perspiration on her face, and the bedclothes which had been so comforting now felt viscous and cloying, like hot mud. She flung back the duvet and sat on the edge of the bed, wide awake. On an impulse, she got up and walked to the window, parting the curtains and peering out into the night. The moon and stars were shut out by a thick blanket of cloud, and the yard was utterly dark, except for a thread of pale light trickling out across the ground from between the doors of the barn. So he wasn't sleeping either; perhaps he was having the same thoughts as her . . . No, surely not.

He might be.

I doubt it.

Well, you could find out . . .

I can't.

Why not?

I just can't go intruding on him.

He might want you to.

No.

What if something's wrong?

. . . Like what?

He could be ill or something.

Well . . .

You ought to check . . .

. . . I don't know . . . No, I can't . . . I'll just get back into bed and try again.

With a heavy greatcoat pulled on over her nightdress and the rubber rims of her wellington boots slapping loosely around her bare legs, Carole stepped lightly and quickly across the dark farmyard, heading towards the faint crack of light between the barn doors. The ground was sloppy and slippery from a light fall of rain earlier in the evening, and she almost lost her footing twice.

The doors were unbolted and slightly ajar. She peeped in through the gap. Steven was sitting on the end of his straw-bale bed, bent over his crate table, writing in the small blue notebook she had given him for recording his recovered memories. He seemed

147

utterly absorbed, his pencil flowing back and forth across the page without a pause. Standing on the table next to the storm lantern was the bottle of wine they had been halfway through when Carole had decided to call it a night. As she watched, he put the pencil down and took a deep swig from the bottle.

After a momentary hesitation, she pulled the door open and stepped on to the threshold. Steven looked up in alarm at the sound of squealing hinges, then relaxed. She was pleased to see a warm, welcoming smile suffuse his face, but could not help noticing the furtive way he closed the notebook and pushed it away behind the wine bottle and the lantern.

'Couldn't sleep,' she said, hovering uncertainly in the doorway.

'Me neither.'

'I saw your light on. I thought I'd come and see if you were all right.'

'Yeah, I'm fine. Just an attack of the wide-awakes.'

'Me too.'

He nodded sympathetically. She nodded sympathetically.

'Oh well,' she said brightly. 'I suppose I'd better go and leave you in peace.'

'No, don't . . . Look, why don't you come and help me finish this bottle?'

'No, no thanks. I don't think I'd better have any more.'

'Well, come in anyway. Pull up a bale and sit down.'

She closed the door and walked slowly towards him. He stood up and pulled a bale from the stack, dragging it into place beside the table. Carole glanced at it, but didn't sit down; instead, she ambled around the end of the barn, examining the walls and the roof and the milk-churns with absent-minded curiosity, like a visitor in a museum. 'It's not too bad, is it,' she said. 'You've done a good job with it. It actually feels quite homely in this light.'

'Well, I like it,' he said, sitting down again on the end of his bed.

'You could put a screen across there, if you liked. You could use some of that tarpaulin from over there.' She nodded towards the other end of the barn. 'Make it more like a proper room, keep the draughts out.'

He shook his head and patted the straw wall of his bed. 'This works well enough. Besides, I like the open space around me.'

She looked at the straw-bale structure and smiled. 'It must be like sleeping in a four-poster.'

He laughed. 'Yeah, I suppose.'

'When I was a little girl, I used to dream of having a four-poster. When I grew up, I was going to have one of my very own and I'd be able to get in it at night and draw the curtains and be all snug and secure inside.' She laughed. 'When I was about eight, Dad took us on holiday to this big old hotel in Scotland – this was before we had the farm. Huge old gothic place it was, with all this dark wood panelling everywhere. It was on a loch, with forest all round it. We'd gone out of season and it was practically empty, so Michael and I had our own rooms. Mine was huge, with all this gigantic knobbly furniture in, and paintings on the walls and a view over the loch, and – guess what – this *enormous* four-poster! I can see it now: it had big fat posts and dark red curtains and a mountain of big white pillows, just like the beds you see in stately homes. The first night, I felt like a princess. I got my little Andy Pandy pyjamas on and climbed in and drew the curtains. And then – guess what again – I couldn't sleep a wink. The hotel was full of draughts, and the curtains around the bed kept twitching every so often. I just lay in bed, staring at them, waiting for them to move. I was convinced there

149

were ghosts in the room, prowling around outside the curtains, and any moment they were going to come through and get me. I suppose I must've fallen asleep eventually, but the next night, I wouldn't even set foot in the room. I wanted to swap with Michael, but *he* wouldn't go in there either after I'd stupidly told him the reason. I ended up having his room and he went in with Mum and Dad.'

She went on to describe the rest of the holiday; walks in the woods, fishing on the loch with her father. Steven listened intently as she stood by the wall in the pale, thin light of the lantern, fiddling with a loose piece of stone while she talked. She seemed uncomfortable, avoiding his eyes, telling stories to mask her embarrassment. At last, the flow of her monologue trickled and halted, and she looked at him. 'I'm boring you, aren't I,' she said.

'Of course not.'

'Yes I am. I can see it in your face. I'd better go and let you get some sleep.'

'Carole,' he said, 'I love hearing all this stuff. I want to hear more about you; all about how you grew up and where you came from and how you got here. Everything.'

'Honestly?'

'Honestly.'

She smiled uncertainly. 'Why would you want to know about me?'

He shrugged. 'I just do. I'm interested. Besides, it helps me remember.'

She brightened. 'Really? Have you remembered anything new?'

'A few things.'

Hesitantly, she approached the table and, at last, sat down on the bale. 'Tell me,' she said excitedly.

'You don't want to hear it now.'

'Yes I do. You listened to mine, so let me hear yours.'

'I don't want to say it. I'll tell you another time.'

She glanced at the wine bottle. 'Have you written it down?' He looked up at her, and she explained: 'I noticed you were writing when I came in . . . Can I see?'

He gazed at her for a few moments, then reluctantly took out the notebook. 'It's all a bit disjointed,' he warned as he fanned through the pages and held it out to her. 'And the handwriting's awful.'

She took the notebook and opened it at the first page, which was headed 'SHOPLIFTING', and began leafing through, skim-reading a few lines from each page. The writing filled about a quarter of the book, consisting of passages which varied in length from several pages to a single paragraph or even a solitary phrase, mostly under headings such as 'RIDING A BIKE', 'CAMPING', 'SMOKING', 'FIRST(?) DAY AT SCHOOL'. As Carole turned the pages, she came at last to the final entry; the piece he had been finishing when she came in. It ran to five pages and was headed 'LOSING VIRGINITY'.

In spite of herself, she looked up from the book and grinned. 'When did you remember this?'

He blushed slightly – just a little, vulnerable pink shading above the line of his stubble beard – and squirmed in his seat. 'Few days ago,' he mumbled.

'You didn't tell me.'

His blush deepened. 'No, I er . . . you know, it was a bit . . . personal.'

She smiled and closed the book. 'I won't read it if you don't want me to,' she said quietly.

'You can if you like, if you think it'll help. I don't mind, I'm not shy.' He looked relieved, though, when she laid the book down on the table.

'Maybe another time,' she said.

'Okay.'

She wondered what had prompted such a memory to

surface; whether it was just part of a pattern of significant events which one would expect to be prominent, or whether something specific had teased out the recollection. Unable to help herself, she felt her eyes drawn back to the little blue notebook.

He followed her glance. Sighing, he picked up the book and held it out to her again. 'Go on,' he insisted. 'Read it.' She reached out to take it, but he suddenly snatched it back. 'Hang on,' he said, and riffled through to the last written page. To Carole's surprise, he tore it out and crumpled it into a ball. 'There,' he said, finally letting her take the book.

'What did you do that for?'

'I wasn't happy about that bit. I started thinking about ... well, that is, I started getting a bit carried away.'

'Steven, it's all important.'

He looked at the ball of paper in his hand and shook his head. 'Not this. It wasn't right ... Well, are you going to read it or not?'

She hesitated, gazing at her hands as they nervously fingered the edges of the book. They were nice hands, Steven thought; long and slender and pale, well cared-for, the scarred nails and the small pads of callus on her palms the only traces of her heavy work around the farm. As he looked at them, and at the white bulbs of her knees protruding from the skirt of the greatcoat, and her calves curving into the wide throats of her black wellingtons, he felt a tightness in his chest and stomach.

'Can I take it away with me?' she asked. 'Or will you need it?'

'No,' he said. 'No, feel free. Take as long as you like. It's all in there; everything I've remembered so far.

Clutching the book to her chest, she stood up and kissed him on the forehead. 'Goodnight,' she whispered.

'Try and get some sleep.' Then she ruffled his hair and left.

'Goodnight,' he whispered as the door closed behind her.

She told herself it was excitement at the accelerating pace of his recovery rather than any prurient curiosity that made her so eager to read what Steven had written in those last five pages. Whatever the cause, she knew she would not sleep until she had read it. Back in her room, she lay down on the edge of the bed and opened the book.

Forcing herself to be systematic, she turned to the first page and began from the beginning. As he had warned, the handwriting was dreadful, and she had to keep repeating whole sentences, teetering uncertainly on some especially illegible words, trying to calculate their meaning from their syntactical context. Slowly, carefully, she worked her way through the episodic passages. They were all written more or less exactly as he had told them to her verbally; some flowing and full of detail, others fragmentary and incoherent. All, that was, except the last. With growing excitement, she turned over the last page of 'SMOKING' and came to 'LOSING VIRGINITY'. Unlike the other pieces, it was written urgently, as though he were writing the memory down as it came to him, which was strange if it had really come a few days ago.

Excited Running up the stairs No not excited – more like I'm sort of imm no not like that. Where am I? Running, yes running up the stairs "excited" More excitement than And she's there shes waiting for me sitting on the edge of the bed, a little bed in my bedroom. I run up the stairs and run into the room and see her Have they gone? Its funy I can't see a face this time but

theres a name KERRY   It makes me think of him maybe
shes his sister   Shes older than me shes done it before
she's not frightened like me   Then shes gone and Im
lying on the bed and staring at the skirting board which
is whit going yellow and a blue furry carpet and Im
~~burstin~~ full up like being filled with hot honey with
happiness and excited   The toilet flushes and she comes
back   Are you ready? She lies on the bed and I can see
the sticker from the Dark side of the moon stuck on the
headboard above her head   And and and this is the
best bit she pulls up her skirt and shes got no knickers
just white thighs and curly black pubes with the skin
showing through   Then she takes off her top and her
~~bra~~ white bra with little purple flowers on it the first Ive
ever seen for real they're small like ~~se~~   ~~apple~~ like little
marshmallows with jelly tots   Darren says he likes red
jelly tots best because theyre like womens nipples   She
wants me to kiss her but I want to look at her first My
arms around her thighs pushing my face in her stomach
in her pussy she says   stop it but I want to lick every
bit of her tasting fresh and soft She makes me kiss her
properly before we do it then she undoes my flies
Strange how it feels someone else's fingers And then it
happens   I'm looking at her face but I cant see her my
eyes are closed and her fingers are pulling my cock about
slippery then its done she makes a squeaking noise and I
feel like my cocks being squeezed in a vice a soft vice all
round it   I love you I love you I love you Shut up
and do it quick The beds bouncing and squeaking and we
are too I think Ive hurt her but she tells me not to stop
red cheeks eyes closed and then Im blind and there are
~~ligh~~ coloured lights in my eyes and my stomach turns
over It feels like its never going to stop pouring out and
my teeth are grinding and creaking   Then she's
pushing me off her and lying there   Holding my
hand and putting it between her legs its all wet and

154

dribbling on the bedspread That all comes from you and I go ugh but really I think its brilliant   She goes to the toilet then puts her clothes back on I don't want you to go can we do it again? Maybe I'm seeing Gary Does Gary know about me?   No and youd better not tell him or noone else But can we do it again? I love you No you dont She's broken something in me taken something away and put back something else more precious and she doesn't even know it   She's still

The writing stopped abruptly at the end of the fourth page. Carole stared desperately at the ragged fringe where Steven had torn out the last page, reeling as the frantic pace of his words catapulted her off the edge of a cliff and left her floundering in empty air.

Trying to gather up her confused feelings, she started reading the passage again; more slowly this time, poring over particular sentences, mentally punctuating the eager, uninterrupted flow. As she worked through it, the scene grew in depth of detail in her mind, becoming clearer, the ambiguously attributed snatches of speech making more sense. No wonder he was shy about this piece; it was more than the sexual content that made it personal; he had clearly fallen desperately in love with this girl Kerry, and she had just used him. Poor guy, how old must he have been? There were no clues, but Kerry was apparently older, more worldly and already going out with somebody else. And now it was as if he had to relive the whole painful experience over again.

It was then that the alarm went off. While she had read and puzzled out the words, the night had been passing its last hours, and the light was growing outside the window. She stood up, her head aching and dizzy, and switched off the buzzer. Opening the curtains, she looked down at the barn, wondering if he had managed

155

to get any sleep. The day was bright, with only a few patches of cloud drifting across the lightening sky, and she had a lot of work to do. It would just have to wait for once. Winding the clock's pointer on to ten-thirty – she hesitated guiltily and advanced it to eleven – she climbed into bed and was sound asleep within five minutes.

Waking up at eleven, she felt no better than she had before. Her head still felt muzzy, and there was a dull pain behind her eyes and a weary, aching weakness throughout her whole body.

As she ambled around the kitchen making breakfast – one extra-large pot of ultra-strong coffee – taking three times as long as usual to do everything, she resisted the urge to go and call Steven. He seemed to have an unerring instinct for knowing when breakfast was being made, and if he hadn't shown up by now, he must still be asleep. If he felt half as tired as her, he wouldn't welcome being woken.

She sat down at the table with her coffee and sipped it. She had brought the notebook downstairs with her, and could not resist having another look at that last passage. Feeling the way she did at that moment, it did not have the same power to arouse her. Instead, she found herself homing in on quite different words and phrases, smiling at the reference to nipples like jelly tots (*how* old must he have been?) and the sense of proud seminal achievement in *I go ugh but really I think its brilliant*.

Gazing at the space where the last page should have been, she noticed that the blank page below it bore the indentations of the writing. She hadn't noticed it by the light of the bedside lamp, but by daylight the marks were quite clear; a spidery scrawl of undulations and curls. Tilting the book back and forth to catch the light, she scrutinised the marks, trying to make out the words. Most of them were too faint, but she managed to identify some letters and – more tentatively – whole words. Suddenly intrigued, she hurried to the parlour and came back with a pen and a piece of paper. While the remains of her coffee turned cold in front of her, she began to copy the marks, pausing every so often to review her progress. After half an hour, her piece of paper was covered with markings, letters, crossings-out and hesitant words. The only part which seemed to make any sense was near the bottom of the page, where the marks were deeper, perhaps because they had been written more slowly than the rest.

I had for(?gotten) what it . . . . to . . . .
(?way). I had it . . . . (?Now) (s)he . . .
(?bought) it . . . . again. I can't . . . . . myself
to . . . . . I love her (?voice) and her . . . ., I . . . . love her
st . . . . sto . . . I . . . . ly keep . . . . ing her . . . .
. . . .'s . . . . me. (?This) . . . . be hap(?pening) to me. I love
her.

As she had suspected, this page seemed to expand on his feelings about the first girl he had made love to; how much in love he had been and how hurt when she treated the incident as no more than a bit of fun. Of course, Carole knew from her own experience how besotted some people could become with their first sexual partner, however casual the circumstances. For Steven it must be like experiencing that hurt all over again the way the narrative was written suggested that this ancient, long-healed wound had suddenly opened up his mind, as raw and livid as when it was first made.

As she read the transcribed fragments again, she

experienced a surge of sympathetic love for him. Helping him to burrow inside and unblock his collapsed memory was going to be harder and more painful than she had ever expected, but she vowed to redouble her efforts to make him a whole, healed person again.

Commune

*O*ne man went to mow, went to mow a meadow . . .

Cressida hummed the tune to herself as she walked across the small courtyard, enjoying the knobbly sensation of the worn cobbles through the thin rope soles of her espadrilles. Everything here – even just the sensation of walking – was an aesthetic thrill to her. She couldn't understand why they hadn't made the move years ago. As she swung the high wrought-iron gates open, she glanced back at the farmhouse. The Twins' shutters were still firmly closed against the hot morning sun. She smiled, indolent slobs though they may be sometimes, she loved them both to death. She continued humming as she ambled down the lane.

Hm-hm-hmm-h-hmmm, da-da-daaa-dadum-dumm . . .

'Good morning,' she said, addressing two horses who were standing close together in the sparse shade of a hawthorn tree in the paddock beside the lane. One of them, an elderly chestnut mare, glanced at her and snorted, then went back to staring dolorously at the pale grass around its partner's hooves. Cressida made a few *kitch*ing noises at the back of her tongue and held a hand out over the wire fence, but both horses ignored her. 'Poor things,' she said. 'I know how you feel. Mornings get to me like that sometimes.'

At the end of the lane, the stone-studded baked earth gave onto the tarmac of the single-track road which led from the town of Camus down in the distant valley bottom and wound its way up through the woods and the fields to the village of Chevalette. At the entrance to the farm lane, a brand-new sign had been nailed to an ancient wooden post. The small board was painted white, with 'le Temple' in carefully drawn, quasi-runic red lettering. Cressida paused to admire it before heading up the road towards the village.

After about a kilometre, the hill crested and the road widened slightly as it assumed the role of meandering village street. Chevalette was a large agricultural hamlet, the nexus, in effect, of several large farms and numerous smallholdings, so most of its houses and farmyard outbuildings were widely spaced, sprawling over the whole of the broad plateau. This morning, the place seemed dead and deserted: as Cressida walked along, her espadrilles scuffing lightly in the soft dust at the roadside, the only signs of life were a tractor rumbling slowly across a distant field and a small brown dachsund trotting along the other side of the road towards her. She stopped and smiled as it approached, stooping down and holding out a hand. Without breaking step, the little dog met her eyes and, laying back its ears, increased its pace, stubby legs pumping, darting nervous glances back at her until it had disappeared beyond a bend in the road.

'Seems like no one wants to know me today,' she muttered.

She took off her broad-brimmed straw hat and wiped away the film of sweat from her hairline with a tissue, blinking as the white sunlight hit her full in the eyes. A few metres further on, she came to the village well – long abandoned, its stone wall crumbling and its crank, chain and bucket deep brown and wafer-brittle with decades of rust – and, beside it, a small stone house which was in only marginally better condition. It was clearly an old outbuilding – probably once belonging to the large, modern farm complex which lay beyond – and had been roughly converted to habitable condition by the reduction of its doorway to human size and the addition of some small windows. Its wooden eaves and lintels were dry, pale grey and deeply fissured with age, and the terracotta tiles on its roof were sun-bleached and discoloured by patches of lichen.

This was the place she had been told about. 'Charming,' she whispered delightedly to herself. 'Absolutely charming.' She stepped up to the door and rapped briskly on it with her knuckles, grimacing as several flakes of the peeling blue-grey paint fluttered to the ground. She waited for a while. No response. When she felt that politeness and patience allowed another try, she knocked again. Another little shower of curled flakes and another long silence. She was about to give up when there was a grating clatter as the bolt was drawn back, and the door creaked open. She quickly laid a polite smile across her face and peered into the dust-moted gloom.

The man who had opened the door stood framed in the rectangle of darkness, blinking and staring at her in silence and with unconcealed hostility. He was tall and lean, with tanned, weathered skin and wearing a stained white vest. His face was long, with stern eyes and a thick black moustache which drooped around the corners of his mouth.

'Bonjour monsieur,' said Cressida brightly. 'Vous êtes Monsieur Viveau?' He just glowered back at her, so she went on hastily: 'Je suis votre voisin depuis quelque jours. J'habite le Temple.' His frown deepened. She wished he would respond, at least indicate that he understood what she was saying. She had always thought herself good at French, but that had been written School French; this was something altogether more challenging. 'Je m'appelle Mademoiselle Allan,' she continued, struggling hard. 'On m'a dit que vous êtes, er ... oh, er bricoleur, oui, vous êtes bricoleur. N'est-ce pas?' He nodded, a small movement barely discernible in the gloom. *'Ah, bon . . . er,'* She hesitated. *'Aussi, on m'a dit que vous parlez anglais. C'est vrai?'*

His frown deepened from hostility to suspicious hostility. 'Hnh?' he grunted.

'Pardon, monsieur. Moi, je parle français comme une vache allemande. On ma'dit que vous parlez anglais.'

He nodded slowly. 'Yes,' he muttered. 'Yes, I do.'

'Oh, thank goodness,' she said. She went on, speaking slowly and loudly: 'My name is Cressida; Cressida Allan. I've just moved in to le Temple, down the hill –' she pointed '– and I need some jobs done. I was told you are a, er, a *bricoleur*. Is that correct?'

'What?'

'I said,' she repeated, increasing the volume. 'I need a han—'

He shook his head impatiently and interrupted her. 'What jobs?' he demanded.

'Oh, er, I would like you to look at the roof of the barn and, well, one or two other little things.'

He was silent for a while, then said, 'Busy,' and, without another word, the door closed in her face.

She stared at it in stunned silence for a few moments, then knocked again. *'Monsieur!'* she called. *'It's only*, oh, bugger it . . . *je ne veux que deux ou trois petits*, er petits, er, *a couple of little jobs!'* . . . Silence . . . 'I'll pay you well!' she added. There was still no response, so she knocked again, muttering under her breath. *'Monsieur?'* she called again.

There was another long pause, then a muffled voice: 'Tomorrow. Now go away.'

She smiled in satisfaction. *'Merci, monsieur!'* she shouted, then turned and walked back down the road.

Monsieur Viveau did not come the next day, nor the day after that. By the end of the third day, the Twins had to

162

restrain her from storming up the hill to pay another, slightly less polite call on him. Then, late in the afternoon of the fourth day, as Cressida was standing in the lane trying to coax the horses to take a clump of grass from her palm, he appeared, walking down the road with a lumpy canvas bag slung over his shoulder and a faded blue cambric shirt, open to the waist, pulled on over what looked like the same vest as before.

She ran to the end of the lane to meet him. 'Bonjour, monsieur,' she said. 'Were you coming to me?'

He nodded. 'I was coming to you.' He pointed at the board nailed to the post. 'Nice sign,' he said, seeming in somewhat better humour than he had been at their last meeting. 'Did you make it?' He spoke with the slightly halting manner of someone whose command of a language has had its edges slightly blunted by lack of use, but his pronunciation was almost flawless, with barely a trace of an accent.

'No,' she said loudly. 'My Twins made it, bless them. When we bought the place, the—'

'Excuse me,' he interrupted, his face colouring. 'You don't need to talk in that tourist way to me. I am not a, er, a retard.'

She put a hand over her mouth. 'Oh, goodness, I'm so sorry. One gets so used to . . . you know . . .'

'You were telling me about the sign,' he prompted.

'Yes. The agent who handled the sale told us the farm originally *was* a temple belonging to the Knights Templar.'

'That sounds reasonable,' he said.

'You've heard the story?'

'No. This village has a lot of storytellers in it. A lot of history has happened here.'

'I'm sure it has . . . Er, would you like to come this way? I'll show you what needs doing.'

She led him around the outside of the house, the barn

163

and the courtyard, pointing out the work she wanted him to do. By the time they had completed the tour, he had a long list of jobs, ranging from a broken hinge on one side of the courtyard gates to mending the tiles on the barn roof and restoring the floor in the hayloft.

'These jobs will take a lot of time,' he said, standing in the cool shade of the barn and examining the rotting, broken floorboards above his head. 'Very expensive,' he added.

'You'll do the work, though?' she asked.

He paused. 'I may,' he said cautiously. 'Okay, I'll do the work.'

She smiled broadly. 'Excellent. Now you must come and have an aperitif.'

'No thank you. I have other jobs to do. Please excuse me . . .'

'Oh, come on. Just a little glass of pineau? Come on, come and meet my Twins. They're dying to meet you.'

'Okay,' he mumbled reluctantly.

'I hope you don't mind my saying,' she ventured as they walked across the courtyard towards the house, 'but you speak English awfully well for a . . . um, well, a, er . . .'

He raised his eyebrows. 'For a *paysan*, you mean?'

'Well, yes.'

'It's not such a mystery. I grew up in England. I was born there.'

Cressida stopped in her tracks. 'Really? How extraordinary! What part?'

'Croydon,' he said gravely.

She smirked in spite of herself. '*Croydon?*' she echoed incredulously.

'What's so funny? Do you know it?'

She shook her head and patted his arm, still grinning. 'I'm sorry,' she said. 'I'm so sorry . . . er, goodness, I don't even know your first name.'

'Michel,' he said stiffly.

'Look, Michel, I'm so sorry, but it's just . . . oh, I don't know, it's this place. We came over here for the authentic French Experience; you know, the gallic rustic idyll. And this place is *it*, all the way from the eaves to the cobbles, as French as . . . well, as French as French, and then the local handyman – who incidentally happens to look like he's stepped right off the pages of a Marcel Pagnol novel – turns out to be from Croydon. It's priceless, just utterly priceless.'

She laughed, and Michel smiled; a small, slightly bewildered smile. 'We go and meet your cheeldren now?' he said, affecting a thick gallic accent. 'Ow eez zat? You like better?'

'There you are,' she grinned. 'Lighten up, Monsieur Michel le Bricoleur . . . Yes, now we go meet my boys.'

She opened the kitchen door and led them inside. '*Timothy!*' she shouted. '*Jeremy! We have a visitor!* Put your tools down there and take a seat. *Boys! Come on down!*' There were sounds of movement from upstairs, followed by a cacophony of heavy feet on the bare-boarded stairs, then the Twins appeared in the doorway. 'Michel Viveau,' said Cressida. 'Meet my boys, Jeremy and Timothy.'

Michel stared at them; her 'boys' were no younger than Cressida herself. Possibly even a little older; about mid-thirties, he would guess. Nor did they look like twins. True, they were about the same height, and wore identical clothes – highly polished two-tone shoes, artfully crumpled linen trousers, crisp white collarless shirts, buttoned-up waistcoats of identical cut (green peacock pattern on Jeremy's, red paisley for Timothy), and identical crew-cuts – but there the resemblance stopped. Jeremy's hair was dark and his features were heavy and swarthy, whereas Timothy had pale blond hair and a pinkish complexion with fine-boned aristocratic features.

'Good morning,' said Jeremy, smiling vacantly at Michel.

'Good morning,' Timothy echoed, grinning gauchely from Michel to Cressida and back again.

'Boys,' said Cressida. 'This is Monsieur Viveau. He's going to be doing our little jobs for us. Don't slouch, Jeremy.'

Jeremy flinched and stood to attention with his hands behind his back. '*Enchanté de faire votre connaissance,*' he said fluently in unison with Timothy.

Michel, disorientated, just nodded back at them.

'Monsieur Viveau speaks English, boys, what do you think of that? Their French is so much better than mine,' she whispered aside to Michel.

Timothy cleared his throat and nudged Jeremy. 'Oh, yes,' Jeremy said, bringing a large sheet of paper out from behind his back. 'We've got something to show you.'

'Another picture?' said Cressida delightedly. 'For me? Oh, that's so sweet!' She took it from Jeremy's hands and held it up for Michel to see. 'Isn't it sweet? Oh, my boys are so talented!'

They were indeed. Michel gazed in wonder at the picture. It was large – about one metre square – and done in pastels. It showed a corner of the courtyard outside the house. The colours were bright; shot through with such an intensity of golden light that the whole scene looked slightly hazy, exactly the effect of the late afternoon sun on a day like this. Standing half-in, half-outside a triangle of shadow in the entrance to the barn was a figure he recognised instantly as Cressida; not just by her huge, ridiculous straw hat, but also by the perfect way the drawing captured her bird-like posture, heels together, head cocked slightly to one side as she listened to the man standing in front of her.

With a shock, he recognised the man as himself.

He pointed at it. 'This . . .' he said incredulously – 'This was less than twenty minutes ago!'

Timothy stepped forward and, grinning slyly, took the picture back. 'Yes,' he said. 'We hope you don't mind us putting you in.'

'That was my idea,' said Jeremy.

'That was Jeremy's idea,' said Timothy. 'I drew you, though.'

'And I drew Mother,' Jeremy added.

'Very good,' said Cressida fondly. 'It's beautiful. Now, would you boys like to go and play outside while Monsieur Viveau and I talk business?'

'Shall we go to the bakery?' Jeremy suggested, looking at Timothy.

Timothy nodded and nudged Jeremy in the ribs. *'Pain au chocolat!'* he said excitedly. As they turned to go, Timothy tossed the picture carelessly onto the table. 'You can have it if you like,' he said to Michel. *'Au revoir.'*

'Au revoir,' Michel replied mechanically. 'Thank you,' he added, glancing again at the incredible picture.

Cressida opened a cupboard and took out a bottle of pineau and two glasses, pouring out a large measure for each of them. 'Well, they're my boys,' she said proudly as they sat down at the table. 'They must have taken a liking to you to have put you in one of their pictures like that.'

'Where did they learn to do this?'

'They're both eidetic.'

'Identic?'

'Eidetic. They have eidetic vision; what some people call photographic memory. Eidetics have the ability to just look once at a person or a scene or an object or whatever and then produce a perfect mental image of it. Let's see, what would be a good example . . . I know; the

167

Eiffel Tower. You've probably seen it countless times, as it were, *but* could you tell me, just from visualising it in your mind, how many criss-crossy girder things there are on each leg? Or in the whole structure? Or, say, how many windows there are on the front of Buckingham Palace? No, of course not. You can close your eyes and produce a pretty good general mental image of the building, because you've seen it so many times, but an eidetic person – even if they've only seen it once – can produce an image which is so accurate that it's like having a photograph. *They* could tell you how many windows or girders there are.'

She pointed at the picture. 'Of course, nobody could do all that in twenty minutes; they were probably making a picture of the courtyard before we arrived and they just added us to it. The thing is, most artists couldn't have drawn us so quickly because they would have to keep looking up; Jeremy and Timothy only had to look once and then draw what they could see in their heads. And it's perfect; truly perfect.'

Michel nodded. 'I never heard of this – what is it? – eidetic thing before.'

Cressida sipped her pineau. 'It's very rare. Actually, it quite often occurs with autism. When it happens in children, you sometimes get an element of sideshow freakery associated with it, you know, which I hate: *Roll up and see the incredible five-year-old autistic boy. He can draw St Paul's Cathedral in minutes!* Parading them on television. It makes you sick.'

'So they are autistic?'

'Who, the Twins? Goodness, no. The kind of people who gape at little autistic prodigies just don't understand eidetics or the difference between it and artistic talent. If you look at their drawings, the overall proportions and many of the lines tend to be a bit wonky, like you would get if someone with normal vision were to trace a photograph which gets moved a fraction every so often. That's exactly what the common eidetic person is doing; just tracing a slightly unsteady photograph. The only difference is, the photograph is in his head. He images it and *projects* the image onto the paper to trace it.' She paused and took another sip of pineau. 'No, Jeremy and Timothy are different, much more sophisticated than that. They have a gift; they are *artists*. What is more, they are *trained* artists.' She looked defiantly at him, as though expecting him to deny it.

'I can see that,' he said.

'Can you?' Cressida challenged him, rising in her chair. 'Are you really sure?'

'Yes, of course.'

'Plenty of people think they can see these things, Monsieur Viveau; they think they can recognise talent, but they cannot, they *will not* see . . . Let me show you something.'

She stood up and led him from the kitchen into the adjoining room. It was a large, bare room with a tiled floor and two high, narrow windows looking out onto the courtyard. Apart from a squat stove in the heavy ashlar fireplace and three large cane armchairs ranged around it, there was no furniture. The rough, unplastered stone walls, however, were covered with pictures. In the centre of each wall hung a large canvas, and each canvas was surrounded by smaller paintings and drawings, all framed and spaced with a perfect asymmetry which resonated harmoniously with the proportions of the room and its fittings. Still more pictures, trailing streamers of shredded newspaper, protruded from a tea-chest which stood in the middle of the floor.

Many of the hung pictures were portraits, and of these, most were of Cressida and the Twins. One painting in particular caught Michel's attention; a large canvas about three metres by one and a half, which dominated the broadest wall and therefore the whole room. In it, the three of them were sitting side by side on an ornate wrought-iron garden seat; Cressida in the middle and the Twins either side of her. They were dressed almost exactly as they were today: Cressida in a long, diaphanous summer dress and the two men in matching shoes, trousers and waistcoats. The only differences were that Cressida's hat was absent and the Twins wore cravats under their shirt-necks. All three were sitting primly, with feet and knees neatly together, backs upright, palms resting on their laps, but there was no suggestion of stiffness; one could easily sense the presence of living, moving human flesh under the painted clothes. Although they were facing the viewer, none of them were looking directly out of the painting. Timothy, sitting on Cressida's right, was leaning towards her and whispering something in her ear; clearly something amusing, because a smile was emerging on her face. Michel looked at the face for a long while, trying to work out how this arrangement of paint seemed so real and convincing, then he hit upon it suddenly: the artist (or artists, he supposed, since all the works seemed to be signed by both of them) had not made the mistake of painting the smile fully formed. A lesser painter might easily have done that; depicting the effect of the joke before its telling had been finished. Instead, Cressida's face wore the incipient hints of a smile – something in the eyes cast down at her lap and a tension in the muscles of her cheeks – which anticipated the joke and foreshadowed amusement. Jeremy, sitting on her left, was grinning broadly, but not apparently at Timothy's joke. His eyes were looking away to his left, beyond the frame, and seemed filled with a gleeful wickedness rather than amusement.

'Can I ask you a question, Monsieur Viveau?' Cressida demanded suddenly.

'Hnh?'

'What is art?' she asked, a hint of aggression in her voice.

'What is art?' he repeated. 'I don't know ... Drawing things, I suppose.'

'No, Monsieur Viveau, it is not drawing things.'

He frowned. The didactic tone that had been growing in her voice during their conversation, and which was now taking on a hectoring edge, was beginning to grate on him. 'Well, making things as well.'

She smiled ruefully. 'No. Ask most people that question and they say something similar. The truth is, they simply do not know. Even critics do not know: they'll regurgitate a stream of unspeakable drivel for you, but they're just as ignorant as anybody; worse, if anything, because they *ought* to know. Here, look at this—' She reached up to the high mantelpiece and took down a yellowing newspaper cutting. 'I saved this because it encapsulates the whole wretched shower of them ... Listen to this. This is from a *national* newspaper: "Turning to the works by the so-called 'Twins', we see a further deterioration in the standard of this exhibition. Unlike Gilbert and George, upon whom Jeremy and Timothy clearly model their public image, the Twins are not a gay couple; also unlike Gilbert and George, their work has no viscera, no energy and no originality of thought. Their paintings have a certain naïve charm, certainly, but also a lightweight sentimentality not seen in any major body of work in this country since the dissolution of the Pre-Raphaelite Brotherhood. Like the Pre-Raphaelites, the Twins pursue a form of photorealism, but this style (although undoubtedly pleasing to the uncritical eye), when it is devoid of the PRB's density of symbolism and socioreligious commentary, is of questionable artistic value ..."' Cressida stopped reading and snorted. 'See? Trivia, sexual gossip and carping about who did what first! And what the hell is "viscera"? . . . I ask you again, what is art?'

Michel shrugged helplessly and shook his head.

'Art, Monsieur Viveau, is *representation*. It's as simple as that; *re*-presentation. To take the world inside you and re-present it back in the exterior. Once the world has been through the mill of your soul and you have poured it out onto the canvas, then it becomes *art*. What is originality or precedent or – what does this mongoloid say? Energy? – What is "energy"? Or *viscera*? *Love* is the thing. How can one hope to process and alter the world and re-present it if one does not love it, if one is preoccupied with what the critics will approve of or what nobody else has thought of doing before? Great painting can only be born out of *love*. And that is what my twins have; passionate, loving hearts.' She thumped her chest with her clenched fist. 'Who cares if somebody did the same kind of style before? It's *irrelevant*.'

Cressida's indignant ire had reached a peak. Her cheeks were flushed and her forehead was perspiring. Suddenly, as she looked up at her visitor's bewildered frown, she laughed. 'I'm sorry, Michel,' she said, breathing hard. 'I didn't mean to gallop off on a tirade like that. It's an unfortunate habit.'

'Don't worry,' he said stiffly. 'It's very interesting for me.'

'That's very kind of you . . .' She gazed into his eyes for a few moments, then her voice dropped to a conspiratorial pitch: 'Let me tell you my plan, Michel. *Our* plan, I should say.' She paused for effect. 'A *commune*, Michel, a commune for artists. What d'you think of that? A sanctuary where all the great painters who have been scorned and spat upon like my Twins by those *hacks* in their nasty little coterie can come and practise their art where their gifts are appreciated. This is where

172

you come in; I want more than a few little jobs, Michel; I want you to help me make this a place where *great art* can be created. What do you say?'

He hesitated. She put a finger to his lips. 'No, don't say anything yet; come and have another drink.'

Michel woke up sweating and groaning, a sharp pain stabbing at the backs of his eyeballs. He had forgotten to draw the curtain the night before, and now the morning sun was glaring ferociously through the window, full across his face. He rolled over in bed and dropped his bare feet onto the rough stone tiles, letting their coolness suck some of the excess heat out of his body while he nursed his head in his hands.

'Merde,' he moaned. '*Merde.*'

He stood up painfully and wandered across to the sink, filled the kettle and set it on the gas ring. He put a fresh paper core in the filter and began spooning coffee into it: one, two . . . he hesitated, then added two extra spoonfuls. While he waited for the kettle to boil, he gazed lethargically around the room. Something seemed odd, but he couldn't work out what it was. He had been staring straight at it for several seconds before noticing it; it was the picture.

He clearly remembered bringing the pastel drawing home with him late last night, rolled up under his arm as he ambled drunkenly up the hill from le Temple. He also remembered dropping it on to the floor just before collapsing into bed. He certainly had no recollection of hanging it up, but there it was now; suspended from a nail beside the front door, the upper corners of the limp paper drooping down under their own weight.

He shrugged and finished making his coffee. He had

no time for mysteries. He had promised the English-woman he would begin work on her barn roof this morning, and it was already after ten.

Cressida slid a baking tray laden with croissants into the oven and slammed the door, making as much noise as she could. She filled the kettle and crashed it onto the gas hob, then went searching through cupboards, banging the doors and rattling about amongst the cups and plates.

'*Boys!*' she shouted, kneeling down and hunting through bags and boxes under the table. '*Come ON! How many times do I have to call? It's BREAKFAST!*'

'There's no need to shout,' said Jeremy quietly at her shoulder.

'Oh God!' she gasped, clutching at her chest. 'You startled me, you naughty boy. Where did you spring from?'

'Ah,' he said, glancing mysteriously over his shoulder at Timothy, who was standing just behind him. 'Where indeed?'

'From our beds, of course,' said Timothy. 'As soon as your sweet voice drew us gently from our dreams.'

They were both dressed, their faces scrubbed pink and shaved, and their hair neatly brushed.

Cressida rose to her feet, a jar of *Bonne Maman* blueberry jam in one hand and a packet of *Maison du Café* in the other. 'Good,' she smiled. 'Now be good boys and sit up to the table. Your breakfast's just coming.'

They sat down, sniffing the air. 'Do we smell croissants?' asked Timothy.

'Yes, you do. Is blueberry all right?' she asked, putting the pot of jam on the table and swivelling it for their inspection.

They nodded in unison. 'Confiture Good Mummy,' said Timothy. He looked Jeremy in the eyes, and they recited together: 'Yummy, yummy, Mummy's jam in our Tummy!' They clutched at their sides, helpless with stifled giggles.

Cressida smiled and went about making the coffee and taking the croissants out of the oven. The Twins watched her, turning up their faces and inhaling deeply as the rich buttery smell pervaded the room.

'Can we have the big cups?' Jeremy asked. 'We want to dunk.'

'Already taken care of,' said Cressida, laying their cups, plates and the jug of coffee on the table.

They clapped excitedly. 'I think our Mummy is psychic,' said Timothy.

Cressida smiled again, staying for a few moments to gaze rapturously at them both as they began their breakfast. Then she turned away and began clearing up the worktop.

Jeremy leaned forward, his lips dotted with flakes of pastry, and addressed Timothy in a loud whisper: 'She's happy this morning, isn't she?'

'Oh yes, very happy,' Timothy replied. 'Quite pleased with herself, in fact.'

'Now, what do you suppose she's so smug about?' Jeremy turned to Cressida. 'What is it, Mother? What's tickled you so much?'

'What do you think?' she replied teasingly.

Jeremy glanced at Timothy, then back at Cressida. 'It's your Frenchman, isn't it? Did he agree to our plan?'

Timothy put his piece of croissant down. 'He did, didn't he?' he said. 'You were up with him *all night*. What on earth did you talk about?'

'It was *not* all night,' Cressida insisted.

'Well, you were still at it when we laid down our heads,' said Jeremy, making a *yakkety-yak* gesture at Timothy with his fingers. 'We didn't even get our goodnight kisses. So, did he agree or not?'

'Yes,' said Cressida, running hot water into the sink for the washing-up. 'He agreed.'

The Twins whooped and applauded. 'How did you do it?' asked Jeremy. 'He seemed so stiff and starchy.'

'And hairy,' added Timothy, mimicking Michel's moustache with a downturned croissant under his nose.

Jeremy guffawed and gave him a knowing look. 'Mother likes them hairy,' he said. He wiped his lips and fingers on his napkin and stood up, carrying his empty plate over to the sink, where Cressida was washing the baking tray. 'Did Mother use her feminine wiles to snare her Frenchman?' he asked, lifting her pony-tail aside and kissing the nape of her neck.

She shivered. 'Of course not,' she giggled. 'Don't be silly. Anyway, he's not *my* Frenchman.'

'I bet she did,' said Timothy, still sitting at the table and watching as Jeremy delicately fondled her neck and shoulders. 'Don't you?'

Jeremy nodded. 'He didn't stand a chance once Mother came out to play.' Suddenly, he slipped both hands around her body and cupped her breasts. As he stood there fondling them, he sang softly in her ear: 'Boys and girls come out to play, and Mother's rolling in the hay.'

'Stop it,' she scolded, slapping gently at his hands with foamy fingers. 'I don't want to play. I've got washing-up to do, not to mention other things.'

Jeremy ignored her and began unbuttoning the front of her dress. 'But Mummy always wants to play with her Boys,' he insisted, sliding a hand inside and stroking her skin.

'Not now!' she said with sudden sharpness, slapping his hand hard.

Jeremy jumping away from her as though stung, an expression of startled horror on his face as he stared at

176

Cressida and at the pink mark emerging on the back of his hand.

'Oh dear,' said Timothy. 'That's torn it.'

Jeremy's cheeks were flushing red. 'It's her fucking Frenchman!' he spat petulantly. 'Him and his nasty hairy moustache!'

'Don't be ridiculous,' she said crossly, turning away from the sink and scowling at him as she buttoned up her dress. 'How could you say such a thing, Jeremy?'

'How could *you*, you mean,' he sneered. 'I hate you! You let him put his filthy garlic hands all over you!'

'*Jeremy!* That's outr—'

'*Whore!*' Jeremy screamed, almost apoplectic. 'I hope he gives you the pox and your fanny blows up like a balloon!' With one last furious glare, he stormed out into the courtyard and slammed the door behind him.

'Oh dear,' said Timothy again. He stood up slowly and followed Jeremy out, glancing nervously back at Cressida as he closed the door.

She heard them talking outside, their voices receding as they walked away. When they had faded away to silence, she sank down heavily in a chair and sighed the long, deep sigh of the eternal martyr.

10

Steven did not wake until the middle of the afternoon. When he went across the yard to the house, he found the back door unlocked. On the kitchen table was his notebook together with a piece of paper.

Steven,
I'm up in the top field. Back by seven, I hope. There's coffee and stuff – well, you know where it all is by now, I should think. Got to dash, already missed a whole morning.
Love,
C
P.S. Thank you so much for letting me read this.

He folded the note and placed it between the pages of the little book, put the book in his hip pocket, then went back outside. The top field was about twenty minutes' walk from the house, separated from the farm by some of the fields which had been sold off to neighbouring farms by Carole's father. Steven set out past the kitchen garden and across the wide, sloping fields.

The dream was becoming real. Fantasy, façade, charade: whatever you chose to call it, the membrane was closing over him and solidifying. He hadn't quite realised it until the night before, when he started writing down these episodic memories. The effort of will he had summoned up in order to invoke genuine memories, dust them down and present them as startling revelations had thrown every dull, half-remembered detail into glaring, fire-drawn clarity; so

178

bright against his more recent memories that they really did feel as though they were all he had to cling to; even he almost believed in his amnesia now. Rosalind claimed to have seen through it, but he was convinced that this had more to do with an innate cynicism and a particularly livid shade of jealousy about his relationship with Carole than any true perspicacity; more lucky guess than judgement, he thought. No, the real threat of exposure came from a far more sinister direction.

He spotted Carole straight away; as he climbed over the gate which led into the top field, he could see her acid-green Suzuki parked at the far end, where a section of the drystone wall had collapsed and spilt its stones out onto the grass. As he watched, her head bobbed up behind the wall as she hefted a large, angular stone into place. He waved. There was a pause, then she waved back; a tiny, yellow-gloved hand swaying briefly against the grey sky.

'Hi,' she said as he approached. 'How're you feeling?'

'Knackered.' He sat down on the mound of rubble, breathing heavily. 'Didn't sleep much.'

'Have you had breakfast?'

'No, not yet.'

'Oh. You could have; I left the door open.'

'I know. I got your note.'

'Steven, you really shouldn't come out without a proper breakfast.'

He smiled sardonically at her. 'And what did you have?'

'Touché,' she smiled. 'Just some coffee. Some very, *very* strong coffee.'

He leaned back against the upstanding part of the wall and watched as she went back to work, her fingers dancing and darting in and out amongst the heaped stones, selecting one, flipping it over and placing it precisely in the wall, then stooping and selecting another. 'You've had a lot of practice at this,' he commented.

'Mmm,' she said, turning over a heavy slab. 'I learned how to do it when I was on this outward-bound thing from college. Never dreamt it'd come in useful.'

'What did you study at college?'

'Medicine.'

'Ah,' he said. 'That figures. So, how did a doctor end up as a farmer?'

She glanced at him. 'I never became a doctor. I dropped out.'

'Oh. How come?'

She lifted the heavy, triangular slab into place and paused, leaning on the wall and wiping her brow on the back of her thick glove. 'It's a long story. I'll tell you about it another time . . . Did you pick up your book? I left it on the table.'

He patted his pocket. 'Safe and sound. Er, what did you think?'

'Of the book? I thought it was really good.'

He thought he detected uncertainty in her voice. 'I'd rather you were honest,' he said. 'You didn't like it, did you? You didn't like that last bit.'

'It's not a question of liking, Steven. It's meant to be therapy; a way of helping you remember more.'

He looked downcast, gazing at his fingers. 'I know, but . . . I don't know, I just sort of want you to like it as well.'

She sat down on the stones at his feet. 'You mean you want me to like the person who's revealed, don't you? I do understand. That's part of what makes us who we are, isn't it; where we've been, what we've done, who we've known. I understand; I can imagine what it must be like to have to start from the beginning, to feel like you're a stranger to yourself.'

He nodded. 'So, did you like the me you found in there?'

'I like you as you are, Steven.' She hesitated, seeing a painful anxiety in his eyes. She took off her gloves and laid her hands on his. 'Yes,' she said quietly. 'I really liked it.'

'Even the last bit?'

'Especially the last bit. It was really touching . . . Look, I've been thinking. You know you said telling you my memories helped? I thought we could have a proper day out, let me show you a bit more of the area, the places I used to go.'

'Okay. Where, exactly?'

'I thought we could start with Haworth.'

His face fell. 'Haworth?'

'Don't worry, we needn't visit Ros. It was your note-book that gave me the idea. You see, when they were children, the Brontë sisters used to write stories in little notebooks. You've never seen such tiny, perfect writing. There's a museum there in the Parsonage where they lived. You can see one of Charlotte's dresses – it's so *little* – and the sofa Emily died on, and we could walk up to Top Withins, where *Wuth*—'

'Wait,' he interrupted, holding up a hand.

'What?'

'Will there be a lot of people there?'

'Well, it's not holiday season yet, but I suppose there'll be some there.'

'I don't want to go.'

'Oh,' she murmured, crestfallen. 'Oh . . . Okay.'

'Sorry.'

'It doesn't matter.'

'I just don't want to be anywhere where there are lots of people. They make me feel nervous.'

'It's okay, Steven, I understand. Honestly, I do.'

He stood up and looked out across the moor. 'That's

181

why I like it up here. I love it: the emptiness, no people. It's the sort of landscape that just says Fuck You to everything human. I mean, well, it's just sort of *there* . . . I don't know, I can't explain it . . .' He sat down again and shrugged helplessly. 'I *like* being alone,' he added weakly.

She stared intently at him. 'I think I understand you perfectly. You don't need to explain.' Suddenly, her eyes brightened and she slapped his leg, making him jump. 'I've *got* it!' she cried. 'Oh boy, have I got a place for you! It should be virtually deserted at this time of year.'

'Where?'

'I don't know why I didn't think of it before. Brimham Rocks!'

He smiled. 'Sounds like a volcano.'

'Not quite. We can go there tomorrow.'

He frowned at her. 'Carole, it's the middle of the week. What about work?'

'Oh, sod that. There's nothing to do that can't wait.'

'What about this?' he insisted, indicating the broken wall.

'Well,' she said, standing up. 'If you pitch in, we could have it done by dinnertime. Have you got any walling experience?'

'Not that I know of.'

'Well, we'll soon find out. You stand there and hand me the stones. See if you can find me a biggish, flattish one for this gap . . .'

Carole finished assembling the sandwiches, stacked them up into a tower and sliced through them with a long knife. Then she divided them between two polythene bags and set about filling the Thermos with coffee. When the picnic had all been packed into a holdall, she glanced out of the window. There was still no sign of Steven. It was still early, though, so she decided to let him lie in a while longer before fetching him for breakfast. Besides, she had to get changed yet.

She trotted up the stairs, almost skipping from tread to tread. In her bedroom, she opened the wardrobe and frowned at the row of neglected garments. Not much to choose from; she didn't have a great deal of time for accumulating or wearing a large collection of clothes these days. Nevertheless, she considered each item carefully; she was determined to have a change from her eternal uniform of jeans and jumper.

Why are you doing this?

She pushed her hands between the folds of fabric and spread them apart; jacket, skirt, trousers, skirt, woollen waistcoat . . .

You're not usually this choosy.

Too short . . . too thin . . . I'd freeze in that . . . no, that'll get dirty . . . too *frumpy* . . . too baggy . . . not sure about that colour any more . . . definitely not appropriate . . .

Excuse me, it's only Brimham Rocks . . .

Too thick . . . wait a minute . . . no, maybe not . . . good God, how did I think I was ever going to dare to wear that? Don't know, though, maybe one day . . . not sure . . . no, I want a change from trousers . . . ah, got it!

She pulled out a long denim button-through skirt and turned to the mirror, holding it up against herself.

Isn't it a bit chilly for that?

She pulled open a drawer and rummaged around inside until she found a pair of thick, black woollen tights. She held them up to the light, stretching the legs and checking for holes. Taking off her jeans, she sat on the stool by the dressing table and drew on the tights, then stood up, wrapped the skirt around her waist and buttoned it down the front, rejoicing in the sensation of airy freedom around her legs.

183

By the way, what was all that about having nothing urgent to do? Have you forgotten what came in the post yesterday: you know, the electricity bill, the feed supplier's bill, that nasty letter from the bank . . .?

Leave me alone. She hesitated for a moment, then sat down again on the stool and gazed at her face in the mirror, tracing the fine lines and crinkles of fat around her eyes with her fingertips, and touching the weather-roughened skin of her cheeks.

Hang on . . .

She opened another drawer and stirred a hand through its contents. Underneath a nest of belts, hairbands, scarves and bits of old costume jewellery was a small black bag which had not been opened in more time than she cared to recall. She unzipped it and took out the bits and pieces one by one, arranging them in an arc on the dressing table: three half-used lipsticks (one with cracked case); one eyebrow pencil; one eyeliner; one tube of mascara (leaking and sticky); three dusty plastic cases (one cracked, one with lid coming adrift) each containing three small tablets of eyeshadow; two applicators; one small can of foundation mousse; and one compact.

Make-up? This wouldn't by any chance be what I think it is, would it?

Not too much; nothing obvious. He probably wouldn't even notice – men never did unless it was slapped on with a trowel – but it would make her feel better. She had grown so accustomed to wearing workaday clothes and doing nothing to her face other than wash away the day's grime, that she felt a wicked exhilaration as she contemplated the possibilities offered by her small and ageing collection of cosmetics. In the end, she settled for eyeliner, some subtle eyeshadow and a lipstick only half a shade darker than the natural colour of her lips.

Well, that's not too bad. I hope you know what you're doing . . .

Despite her body's protests at the intrusion of the unfamiliar chemicals (the eyeliner stung and the lipstick tasted bitter), she was excited by the startling transformation such a modest application of make-up had wrought on her features . . . Then there was her hair. She had always been proud of her hair; it was rich and dark and heavy, and age had not yet marred it with anything worse than an occasional grey strand. However, the short, straight bob which was so fuss-free and sensible for farm work was just . . . well, *dull*. She ran her fingers through it, sweeping it this way and that, seizing it and pulling it up, down, sideways, but nothing seemed to quite work. She gave up, and simply brushed it straight. Anyway, it would have been a wasted effort: the wind on the moors would have just pulled it to pieces within ten seconds.

I was just wondering, by the way: what happened to the nurse–patient relationship?

It still is a nurse–patient relationship. Except now he's got a slightly prettier nurse.

So this is for his benefit?

Don't be ridiculous. Shut up.

She took one last look in the dress mirror, smoothed the wrinkles out of her tights and twitched her skirt straight, then went downstairs to start Steven's breakfast.

As she had predicted, the place was deserted. There was only one other car in the car park, and that was only the orange and black burnt-out husk of a Nissan Sunny. The red Morris pick-up rolled slowly over the gravel and parked at the edge of the grass.

'What do you think?' asked Carole, pulling up the handbrake and switching off the engine.

'I think you chose well,' said Steven. 'I like it.' He unbuckled his seatbelt and leaned forward, gazing out at the landscape. It had an undertow that connected it to the moorland he was familiar with – desolate and hostile, clothed in harsh, rough grass studded with thickets of heather and the occasional stunted, twisted tree – but it was formed differently: in place of the smooth slopes and sudden scarps, the land here was puckered and ridged with hollows and hills and miniature valleys. Scattered about the landscape were eerily globular formations of brown gritstone: some massive, towering and deeply fissured, others smaller and smoother.

Carole looked at his face as he stared in rapture at the view. 'Come on,' she said. 'Let's get out and have a proper look.'

They walked slowly down the grassy slope from the car park. At the bottom, the way was cut off by a rearing ridge like a breaking wave of earth and rock, with two small valleys leading off to either side. Steven chose the right-hand way, which sloped gradually upwards and curved around to the left.

'We used to bring the dogs here,' said Carole. 'There always seemed to be a thunderstorm. It probably only happened once or twice, but it seems like always. Everyone would run back to the cars to watch. It terrified me, the lightning flashing over the hills, hitting the rocks – and the *noise*! It was like sledgehammers on the roof of the car, and I'd be sitting there waiting for a bolt to hit us. Dad told us we were safe because of the rubber tyres, but it didn't help much.'

Steven stepped up onto an outcrop of rock and looked back the way they had come. 'What sort of dogs did you have?' he asked.

'They weren't ours, they were Uncle Tony's. Golden retrievers.'

'What were their names?'

She smiled. 'Eric and Ernie. Which tells you all you need to know about my Uncle Tony.'

'Pardon?'

'Never mind.'

'How old were you the last time you came?'

'Pfff! God, let's see ... *It would've beeeen ... 1973*, so I'd be twelve. There, now you know how old I am now.'

'It's 1997 now, right? So that makes a grand total of ...'

'Never mind! And less of the *grand*, please.'

He jumped down off the rock, landing with a muffled thump on the soft turf. 'Twelve,' he said thoughtfully. 'Tell me what you used to do here.'

'Well, we used to walk, mainly. Or at least, the grown-ups walked. We mostly ran around like crazies. These rocks are great for hide-and-seek.'

He shook his head. 'Tell me something specific. I want a detail, a little picture of you here.'

'Umm ... Yes, I know one. It happened on the last visit. I think it may be the reason why I'd never come back. It makes me blush even now.'

'Tell me about it,' he said eagerly.

'Well, there was this huge rock formation with a big crack down the middle. I was hiding behind it, waiting for Michael and Kieran to walk past on the other side. I was going to stick my head through suddenly and make them jump.'

'And did they?'

'I don't remember. I put my head through the gap and couldn't bloody get it out again. The boys just rolled about, crying with laughter, and I was stuck there, going redder and redder and my ears getting sore from chafing on the rock. I honestly don't remember how I got out, but I remember this bloody *audience* gathering.

187

Jesus, the *shame*! Imagine it: I was twelve; just at that age when your self-consciousness needle is well into the red and starting to shoot right off the scale. It took me *months* to get over it.' She looked at Steven: his lips were pinched tightly together and trembling. 'It's all right, there's no need to burst a blood vessel. Feel free to laugh. I'm over it now.'

The laughter burst out of him like a dam breaking. 'I'm sorry,' he gasped when he had got his breath back. 'It was just the look on your face, like you were still *angry* about it.'

She smiled and took him by the arm. 'Come on, let's walk. There's lots to see yet.'

'Show me,' he said suddenly.

'What?'

'Show me where it happened. I want to see it. Can you remember where it was?'

'God knows. It could be anywhere.' She looked around. 'I suppose it might be . . . umm . . . that way.'

'Okay, let's go. It's a quest; a quest for Carole's most embarrassing moment.'

They walked for more than an hour, trekking along gullies and through hollows, scrambling up hillocks and scanning the horizon. At each likely-looking rock, Carole would walk around, lips pursed, scrutinising the fissures, then shake her head. 'I told you it'd be difficult,' she said after the fifth attempt. 'It was twenty-odd years ago. The rock might not even look the same now, what with erosion.'

'Nonsense. We just need to find one with ear-prints on. It shouldn't be hard to spot.'

'Cheeky sod, are you saying I've got big ears?'

He didn't answer; he was looking towards the horizon, where there was a pinpoint of red in the centre of a deep fold. 'I can see the car from here,' he said. 'We've come miles.'

'Shit!' she exclaimed. 'The car! I left the sodding picnic under the seat.'

'Uh-oh,' he murmured. 'D'you think we ought to head back?'

She looked up at the sky and nodded. 'I think so. Anyway, it looks like the weather's closing in.' While they had been engrossed in scouring the hills and stones, charcoal clouds had been surreptitiously colonising the sky until, as they turned and began retracing their steps, there was not a patch of blue to be seen. They had covered less than a hundred yards when the rain began; a smattering of heavy droplets at first, rapidly proliferating into a drenching downpour. 'Shit!' shouted Carole, breaking into a run. '*Shiiiiit!*'

Steven was running just ahead of her. Suddenly he stopped and she rammed into his back, almost knocking him over. 'Down there!' he shouted. 'Come on!' Before she even had a chance to gather her senses, much less reply, he seized her wrist and she found herself stumbling frantically behind him down a steep slope and being hauled across the bottom of a deep gully. 'In here,' he said, pushing her forward.

On one face of the gully was a massive rock formation as tall as a house. It had been undermined by the erosion of a smaller tributary gully and some of its lower strata had partially subsided, forming a small shelter about five feet wide by four feet high. Carole crouched down and scuttled inside, closely followed by Steven.

'Here,' he said, taking off his jacket and spreading it on the dusty floor. 'We can sit on this. Budge up a bit.'

The hollow went back several feet, and there was room for both of them to sit comfortably in its mouth, huddled together on the jacket and gazing out at the falling rain.

'Bugger,' Carole muttered, taking out her cigarettes

and lighting one. She inhaled deeply and blew a long billow of smoke into the rain. 'I'm soaked. Look at this.' She held up her cigarette, which was blotched and soggy from her wet fingers.

'It could have been worse,' said Steven. 'It hasn't gone through your clothes. Take your jacket off and drape it over you so the wet doesn't soak through.'

She did as he said, using the jacket as a blanket, then she settled down against him, shivering and absorbing his warmth. 'And we didn't even get our picnic,' she sighed, exhaling another long streamer of smoke.

'Are you hungry?' he asked, gently stripping the beads of water from the ends of her hair and flicking them away.

'Not really.'

'D'you think it'll last long?'

'Ten minutes,' she said. 'Maybe an hour; maybe all day. Who knows?'

They fell silent, watching the shivering haze of rain, listening to it splattering and trickling on the rock above their heads. The diminishing cigarette rose and fell regularly, each movement punctuated by a crackle of burning tobacco and a jet of smoke. Carole tossed the stub out onto the wet grass and settled down. 'Steven,' she murmured.

'Hm?'

She raised her head suddenly. 'Oh, am I getting you wet?'

'No,' he lied, ignoring the damp patch where her hair rested on his jumper. 'I'm fine. What were you going to say?'

She nestled against his chest again. 'It's funny. I was about to ask you whether you believe in God.'

'Why?'

'Do you?'

He shook his head. 'No, not really . . . Not at all, actually.'

She giggled. 'I'll laugh if we find out you're a priest in real life. I could blackmail you.'

'Why do you want to know?'

'I don't know. I was just wondering.'

'Do *you* believe in God?'

'I don't know . . . No, I don't really, not in God as such. But I think there's *something* out there, some force that makes things happen, guides things. You know, creates a *pattern* in everything.'

'Like astrology, you mean?'

'Not specifically, but I suppose it could be that. More like fate or karma or something. I think everything happens for a reason – every decision we make, every person we meet; everything that happens to us. It all has to have a meaning.'

'Why? I mean, why *must* it?'

She paused. 'Because everything in nature is patterned, orderly: it all follows an ideal logic; everything from genes to stars and planets. So, why shouldn't spiritual things be like that too?' She hesitated. 'I'm talking rubbish, aren't I?'

He kissed the top of her head. 'No. I like hearing you talk.'

'You're a good listener. I'm sure Ros thinks I'm just an airhead sometimes.'

'Huh. Ros is a *fat*head, if you want my opinion. I don't know why you put up with her.'

'Don't say that. She's been a good friend to me.'

'She's a control freak. I've seen the way she speaks to you. She should show you more respect.'

'Maybe . . .'

'Anyway, what were you saying about patterns?'

'What? Oh, yes. I think everything has a purpose. When we encounter people, it's for a reason . . .' She

191

paused and rummaged for another cigarette. 'Like you and me,' she added, trying to make it sound casual, like an afterthought rather than the whole point of her long preamble.

'You and me?'

She lit her cigarette. 'Well, you lost your memory, right? And there I was, with more memories than I could cope with . . . You know, I came here to escape from things, retreating into the past, running away, but of course I brought it all with me.'

'You can run but you can't hide?'

'Exactly. And the more I tried to burrow my old memories, the more purposeless I felt and the more unhappy I became. I tell you, when you showed up, I'd been seriously considering giving up the farm – just packing it in and moving on. But there you were: someone who needed me. I saw it straight away. And it fits, do you see? There was me with too many memories, a glut of memories, and there was you with no memory. You see, it worked on two levels: you needing me, me needing you to need me on one level, and the *way* we needed each other, which is sort of poetic. That's what I mean by a pattern. Do you understand now?'

'Yes,' he said, sounding surprised. 'Yes, I do.'

She sighed, deeply and contentedly. 'It's all too perfect. You know, you're the first man I've been able to talk to like this in four years . . . Actually, you're the first man I've *ever* been able to talk to quite like this – you know, this close, without any embarrassment. It's been four years since I've really talked to a man at all.' She took a last puff of her cigarette, and sent it spinning out to join the first. 'I wish I could keep you here forever,' she murmured.

Without saying anything, and feeling that he might be about to make a big mistake, Steven reached into the pocket of his jeans and took out a crushed ball of paper.

He unpicked it and rubbed it flat on his thigh.

'What's that?' she asked.

He offered it to her. 'Go on, read it.'

With a jolt of surprise, she recognised it as the page torn from the notebook. She took it from him and sat up, staring at the uneven pencil strokes. The first lines were clearly a continuation of the passage she had read. The last paragraph, however – the one she had tried to transcribe from its indented impression – seemed different now that she could read it in full. Unlike the preceding lines, it was clear and coherent. She stared at it in disbelief for a moment, then read it again.

I had forgotten what it was like to feel that way. I had it under control. Now she has brought it all back again. I can't bring myself to leave. I love her voice and her face, I even love her stupid stories. I can hardly keep from touching her when she's near me. This can't be happening to me. I love her.

He squirmed as he watched her eyes tracking intently back and forth. 'Sorry about the reference to your stories,' he said as she raised her head and turned her wide eyes on him. 'I didn't mean that – I was just angry with myself.'

'Did you mean the rest of it?' she asked, her voice toneless.

'Well, yes. Of course I did. I didn't write it for fun.' She was still staring at him. 'Look, please don't be offended. I only—'

He thought she was going to attack him, and he raised his arms in self-defence. She seized him by the hair, and the back of his head thumped against the stone wall of the shelter. He opened his mouth to plead with her, but all that came out was a muffled, truncated gasp as her mouth closed over his.

193

Every moment of loneliness and regret, layer upon layer, piled up over four years of solitude, was channelled into her kiss; every feeling of longing and despair contributed to its ferocity. She plied and twisted his hair around her fingers and straddled him, squeezing his body between her thighs until the muscles burned. When she broke free, panting and gasping, her lips were sore and smeared with saliva and smudged lipstick, and her cheeks were red and wet with tears. She stared wildly into his startled eyes for a brief moment, then kissed him again. This time, she grasped the shoulders of his jumper and hauled him forward, lowering herself until she lay on her back in the dust, his body arched above her. She fumbled clumsily with the front of his jeans, making little squeals and gasps of frustration and desire, and at last they came loose and she pushed them down, his cock springing out and hovering, quivering above her. She unbuttoned her skirt and clawed at the crotch of her tights with her fingernails until the seam gave way and ripped, then, pulling aside her knickers with one hand, she guided him inside with the other. Ecstatic clouds spangled with lightning-flickers of pain billowed and burst inside her head and groin, and she squealed as the charge flooded through her limbs and sparkled at her toes and fingertips. She wound her legs around his, but still it wasn't enough; she hauled up the fronts of both their sweaters and pulled him down, desperate to feel his weight on top of her and the heat of his bare skin on hers. Still not enough. Her lips slithered away from his and nuzzled his neck. 'Fuck me,' she gasped. 'Go on, just do it, *please* just do it.' She didn't care about coming; she just wanted the lustful violence she felt suffusing her whole body to be echoed in him, for him to reinforce it and then batter it down. 'Faster!' she urged, cupping his buttocks and hauling with all her strength. 'Faster, faster, harder ... yes ... yes,

194

fuck . . . fu—aahhH!' When he came and she felt the spurt
of his fluid within her, she opened her eyes and stared
with wild, crazed joy into his face; eyes clenched closed,
skin stretched tight over straining, ridged muscles,
sheening with sweat and blotched with red. When he
had twitched and shuddered and grunted to a standstill,
he hung over her for a few moments, supporting himself on shaking, splayed arms, then his weight collapsed
onto her again. She coiled her arms and legs around
him, closed her eyes and sighed deeply.

11

He opened his eyes.
   The throbbing, pulsing, ululating buzz snapped
down to a quiet, barely audible hum. The hazy wash of
phosphorescent colour stilled and cleared, shapes drifting together slowly, imperfectly. He pinched the bridge
of his nose and gouged his sticky eyes with his finger
and thumb.
   —He opened his eyes again. That was better . . .
slightly. He relaxed, concentrating on the hum. When
the beams and rafters in the roof had coalesced into
recognisable geometric forms, he sighed and smiled,
then turned onto his side and raised himself on one
elbow. Carole was lying beside him, her back to him,
one hand curled loosely in the crook of her shoulder. He
blew gently on her fingers; they twitched briefly and
settled. Some strands of straw had fallen from above
and were clinging to her dark hair. He carefully picked
them out and tossed them away; one snagged and
pulled, but she didn't wake.
   This was one of the many surprising things he had

learned about her recently, during the weeks that had passed since that wet afternoon at Brimham Rocks; that for such an habitual early-riser, she was an incredibly heavy sleeper. So deeply did she sink that he had been able to rise, kiss her face and put on his clothes without waking her, leaving the house and making his way across the midnight-black yard back to his cot in the barn. She would only notice his absence when her alarm woke her the next morning. At first she had been hurt; she tried again to persuade him to move once and for all into the house, but he still could not bring himself to do it; he felt insecure there, he told her. Not half as insecure, she said, as she felt when she woke up to a cold, empty space in the bed where his warm body should be. Then had come the occasion when, for the second time, she visited him in the barn in the middle of the night, to talk. She had ended up staying until the morning, sharing his makeshift bed. As the weeks passed and the weather grew warmer, she visited him more and more, and now slept with him in the barn more often than in her own comfortable bed. She didn't like the chill or the discomfort, but she was happy to endure them so long as it was the only way to wake up with him still beside her.

Also, as the weeks passed, the little blue notebook filled up. The deepest seams of his memory were probed and mined and the rich yield was set between its pages. Eventually, virtually all the significant events and images of his childhood were contained there, and he gradually came to feel that he only existed in two places: the distant written past and the immediate sensate present. In effect, he had become the man he had set out to be.

Carole grunted softly in her sleep and pulled at her earlobe. Steven smiled; gently, he lifted the edge of the blankets and drew them back, taking a long, lingering look at her body; the folds of heavy hair across her neck (she had been letting it grow recently), the long, curved sweep of her back rising suddenly and swooping over her hip and swelling out to the orbs of her pale—

'*Hey!* I'm freezing!' She raised her head from the pillow and twisted round to look at him.

'Sorry, I thought you were asleep.'

'I was until I got an Arctic gale down my back.'

He smiled at her. 'I wanted to look at you. It doesn't usually bother you.'

She turned over to face him. 'D'you mean you make a habit of ogling my body when I'm asleep?'

'I can't help it,' he said, kissing her on the lips. 'You're so beautiful.'

She pulled the blankets up over her nose. 'No I'm not,' she said. 'I'm getting old.'

'*You,*' he said insistently, '*Are. Beautiful.*'

Her large, round eyes peeked over the blanket at him. 'Am I really?'

'You'd better believe it,' he said, burrowing a hand through the rumpled bedclothes and stroking his palm lightly over her breasts.

She wriggled closer to him and snaked an arm around his waist, resting her head on his chest. 'I love you,' she whispered.

'I know.'

She kissed his chest and sat up reluctantly, rubbing her eyes. 'Suppose I'd better get up and have my bath. Loads to do today.'

He lay and watched her dressing, pulling on the cold clothes from the night before, shivering in the damp, chill air.

'It's icy in here,' she complained, not for the first time. 'You know, if you're really going to insist on being so stubborn, I think we ought to see about getting a space-heater in here.' When she had buttoned her shirt, she crawled back onto the bed and knelt beside him. 'I wish you'd sleep in the house,' she murmured.

He sighed. 'I've explained all that.'

'I know. I just wish, that's all.'

He slipped a hand under her shirt. 'I think we generate enough heat by ourselves.'

'Stop it!' she laughed. She retrieved his hand and held it between hers, spreading his fingers and looking closely at them, one by one.

'Found something interesting?' he asked.

She smiled absently and kissed his palm. 'This,' she said, holding up his ring-finger.

'What about it?'

'I don't know. Just being silly.'

'Tell me.'

She hesitated, her eyes cast down at her lap. The question she was about to raise had been on her mind for some time, ever since their relationship had burst so suddenly into flower. She had always shrunk from raising it, because she was frightened of the consequences; frightened that his reaction might lay a blemish on their relationship, or even tear it apart by triggering the one memory which, as far as she was concerned, was unwanted.

'What is it?' he persisted, sitting up and brushing the hair away from her face.

'I was just wondering. What if you're married?' She looked into his eyes with sudden candour: now that the problem had been whipped out, she wanted to see every nuance of his reaction.

'What?' he said dully.

'We don't know, do we? You might have a wife somewhere, Steven.'

'A *wife*?'

'It's possible, isn't it; you might even have children for all we know.'

He stared blankly into space. 'A wife?' he repeated. '*Children?*'

'Think about it. You must be ... what, about late thirties? What are the chances that you'd be single and childless by that age?'

'I don't know ... I *might* be single.'

'You *might* be, but we don't know for sure.' She looked down at her hands again, and her voice shrank to a hoarse whisper. 'I can't get it out of my mind. Every time ... every time, after we've made love, or when we're lying in bed together, I keep thinking about her lying in her own bed, all alone, not knowing where you are or what's happened to you or if you're even al—'

'She probably doesn't even exist, Carole.'

'She probably *does*.'

He shook his head. 'No, it doesn't feel right.'

'How would you know?' she insisted. 'I've been so selfish; I wanted to keep you here for my own sake, and there she is, frightened half to death for you, and you're here and I'm just hanging on to you for my own selfish reasons. Why did I ever—'

'Hush,' he said, putting his hand over her mouth. 'You're getting hysterical. Calm down.'

'How *can* I? Steven, we should have done something about this *ages* ago. God, I've been so *stupid*! We should have taken you to the police. They could get your picture on the telev—'

'*No!*' he shouted. 'No, Carole, we can't.'

'Why *not*?' she wailed.

'Because ... because I don't *want* to! I'm not going to do it. Don't push me like this, Carole.'

There were tears welling in her eyes. 'I'm sorry,' she said, and the tears brimmed over.

'Come here,' he said softly, wrapping her up in his arms. 'Ssh ... It's all going to be all right. There isn't anyone else, I just know it. Just trust me.'

'I do trust you,' she sobbed. 'I just feel so *guilty*.'

'Well, don't. I'm sure there's no one else. Even if there was, how could I go back now? I'm with *you*; I could never leave you now.'

'Never?'

'Never. You're stuck with me.'

She looked up at him, her eyes pink and wet and swollen, then threw her arms around his neck. 'I love you so much,' she whispered.

'Come back to bed,' he said. 'Lie down.'

They lay together, clasped tight, and Carole gradually grew quiet and calm. Steven could feel her heart settling down to a steady pulse, bumping gently under his hand.

'What if you remember her?' she couldn't help asking. 'You might want to go back to her.'

'I won't remember her, because there's no one to remember. And I could never love anyone like I love you. Now be quiet.'

She fell silent, concentrating her mind on feeling his warmth against her body. She hadn't meant to become so upset, but the thought of another woman standing in the shadows like a ghost, bereft of the man both of them loved, made her bones ache. His recall had been developing so well that it seemed inevitable that more recent, adult memories would begin to emerge before long. But he was right; all she could do was trust him to still love her even if a wife or a lover did walk forward and identify herself to him. And she did trust him, she did believe in him.

Carole was still and quiet for so long that Steven thought she had gone back to sleep. He relaxed and listened to the distant humming, which had grown slightly during the past few minutes.

'Carole,' he said.

'Hn?' Her voice was drowsy. 'I was just dropping off . . . Better get moving.'

She was about to lift herself up again when Steven stopped her. 'What's that noise?' he asked.

She frowned blearily. 'What noise?'

'That one. Listen.'

'I can't hear anything . . . What sort of noise?'

'Humming.'

She listened intently for a moment, then a broad smile dawned across her face. 'Oh, *that*. Has it been bothering you?'

'No. Well, yes it has, actually. Ever since I got here, I've been trying to work out what it is.'

'Why didn't you just ask?'

He shrugged. 'I don't know. Never remembered to.'

'Come on,' she said, sitting up. 'Get dressed and I'll show you.'

Carole inserted the key and snicked the padlock open. Steven stood behind her in the yard as she opened the door to the annexe. The humming deepened and increased in volume, and a billow of hot air rolled out through the doorway, but he could see nothing.

'Bugger,' said Carole, looking at her watch. 'It should've come on by now.' She stepped inside and fiddled with something on the wall. There was a rasping sound like a ratcheted dial being twisted, and fluorescent lights flickered on, intensely bright. 'I think the timer's getting a bit dicky. Come on in, then. Meet my livestock.'

Steven followed her in and found himself standing inside a small, glass-walled cubicle which enclosed an area about three feet square just inside the door. Beyond the glass was a room which filled the whole of the large annexe. He could see vegetation in there – several small structures made from branches – and some metal framing around the walls. But what made him stare, aghast, was the stuff covering the walls and the floor; a thick, greenish-brown carpet, a thick carpet that *moved*. It

201

writhed and shivered and undulated and, as the lights kicked in, began to evaporate into a dense, swirling cloud, the humming swelling to a loud, deep rumble tinged with a thin, hissing rattle.

'Oh my God,' he choked, his throat tightening.

'Impressed?' said Carole, smiling wickedly at his discomfiture.

'What the *fuck* . . .?'

'They're locusts,' she grinned.

'*Locusts?*' He gaped in disbelief at the heaving, shimmering mass, his face turning ashen.

'Mm-hmm. *Locusta migratoria*. You're just in time for feeding.'

'*What?*'

There was a bucket just inside the door, filled with a sort of powdery mash. She unhooked a plastic scoop from the wall and began shovelling the mash into a transparent chute which was set into the glass and sealed off by hinged flaps at either end. The food scattered on the floor of the cage, and the rumbling swirl coalesced into a hurricane as thousands of insects homed in on it.

'Oh Christ,' said Steven. His face had turned white. Suddenly, he turned and rushed out of the building.

'Steven?' she called. 'Are you okay?' Puzzled, she put down the scoop and followed him out. She found him standing in the yard, leaning against the wall of the barn and gasping for breath. 'What's the matter?' she asked. 'Are you ill?'

Some colour was coming back into his face, but he could still scarcely breathe. 'Insects,' he gasped, 'I – can't – stand – *insects*.'

Carole put a hand to her mouth. 'Oh no. No! Oh God, I'm so sorry; I should have warned you. I just didn't think.'

He scowled at her. 'It's not funny,' he said.

'Sorry,' she repeated, suppressing her smirk.

'Why didn't you *tell* me I was living next-door to a fucking *locust*-house?'

She shrugged. 'You didn't ask.'

'Didn't *ask*? Well, it's not the sort of thing you think of, is it? "By the way, there aren't any plagues of fucking great insects next-door, are there?" I mean . . . shit!'

'Well, how did you think I managed to make a living from such a small farm?'

'Well, you could . . . I don't know. I've never really thought about it.'

'Surely you must have seen me going in and out?'

He was nonplussed. 'Well, yes, sometimes. I thought you had a generator or something in there.'

She laughed. 'Well, now you know.'

He stared at her. 'But *why*?' he asked, shaking his head.

'Why what?'

'Why locusts? What the fuck do you *do* with them?'

'Sell them. I've got a distributor in Bradford. They go to zoos, pet shops and so on. Reptile food. Some of them go to schools, for biology – you know, dissection and—'

'Stop it,' he said. 'I don't want to hear the details. I'll be sick.'

She put her arms around him. 'I'm so sorry,' she giggled. 'And I thought you were so butch.'

'Carole . . .' He hesitated, chewing his lip.

'Mm?'

'Can I move into the house now?'

12

Steven walked out of the Parsonage and headed towards the street. He had paid his entrance money, but had only managed to look at two rooms before the press of people had become too much for him and he had to hurry to the exit and out into the fresh air.

The main street was also busy, families and parties of tourists ambling up and down the steep cobbled hill or loitering in front of shop windows. Steven stopped, looking nervously to left and right, then turned back and entered the churchyard. In here, he could still hear the bustle and chatter of the street, but felt more at peace amongst the tightly packed rows of green-grey stone slabs and monuments. Apart from an elderly couple who were stooping to examine a gravestone in the near corner, he seemed to be the only person present. He walked slowly along until he was in the centre of the burial ground, then sat down on the edge of one of the raised grave slabs, letting the tension that had built up amidst the swarming maelstrom of people in the Parsonage ebb away.

That was when he noticed the man sitting in the far corner of the graveyard; like Steven, he had chosen a raised slab for a seat, and was sitting with his ankles crossed and his hands resting in his lap amongst the folds of his beige raincoat. He was gazing intently up at the tall Georgian windows of the Parsonage, his face obscured by a shadow falling from the brim of his hat. There was something familiar about him . . .

'You should have seen his face,' said Carole. 'I really thought he was going to throw up.'

Rosalind came through from the kitchen with two mugs of coffee and a packet of chocolate digestives on a tray. She put the tray down on a table and sat in the armchair opposite Carole. 'Then it's just as well you didn't tell him how you harvest the wretched things,' she said. 'That gives *me* the willies.' She sipped her coffee. 'I mean, locusts are bad enough dead. I remember dissecting them in Biology at school – they were all brown and wet and squishy. They stank as well. I can still smell it – like coffee made with rancid milk and gone cold.' She glanced at her mug and pulled a face.

'It was unbelievable,' said Carole, still smiling at Steven's comical discomfiture. 'I mean, it's not exactly unknown for there to be the odd rat scurrying around in that barn, but that didn't seem to bother him at all. And yet locusts next-door, with a thick, sealed stone wall between him and them, that scared the hell out of him.'

'Phobias are strange,' said Rosalind, opening the biscuits and offering them to Carole. 'Elaine once went out with a guy who was a lion-keeper at Knaresborough. Quite happy to get in with these huge brutes, but if he found a spider in his bath, it was like mad half-hour in Bedlam.' She sat back and crossed her legs. 'Did you say he's moved into the house, then?'

'Yes. He was still reluctant, but the locusts must have worried him more than whatever it was he didn't like about the house.'

'And you're happy to have him there?'

'Of course. It makes life a lot easier.'

Rosalind nodded. 'So, it wasn't a wasted effort after all.'

'What wasn't?'

'Setting up the spare room.'

'Oh, I see,' said Carole, colouring a little. 'No. I hadn't thought of it like that.'

'Lucky it's such a big place. Plenty of rooms.'

'Hmm.'

Rosalind leaned forward. 'You're completely transparent, Carole. You're sleeping with him, aren't you?'

Carole blushed scarlet. 'No! . . . Well, yes. Yes, I am.'

Rosalind sighed. 'Oh, for God's sake. How long has this been going on?'

'A month or so . . .'

'And how many times?'

Carole shrank into her chair and looked into her mug. 'Pretty much constantly, really,' she mumbled.

'I wondered how long it would take before you were well and truly suckered.'

'Ros!' Carole cried. 'That's a horrible thing to say!'

'Well, it's true, isn't it? How did he persuade you? No, don't tell me – he claimed he loved you and he was so gra—'

'He *does* love me! Anyway, it wasn't like that. I made the first move.'

Rosalind's eyes widened. '*You* did?'

'Yes.'

'*You* seduced *him*? Meek little Carole?'

'Don't tease me, Ros. You make me sound like an imbecile. Anyway, I wouldn't quite call it a seduction, either.' She paused and leaned forward, smiling wickedly. 'Ros, it was incredible: I practically *raped* him.'

'What?'

'Well, almost.'

Suddenly, unexpectedly, Rosalind laughed. 'Way to go, girl,' she said.

Carole looked up, surprised. 'It's wonderful, Ros,' she said, emboldened. 'God, I can't tell you how good it is. I've never known anything like it. We've done it everywhere: in the barn, in the house, in the kitchen, outdoors . . .'

'Where outdoors?'

'Brimham Rocks. That was the first time. We were sheltering out of the rain in this little cave.'

Rosalind listened to the story, a light of wonder – almost admiration – growing in her face. 'Well well well,' she said when Carole had finished. 'Brimham Rocks . . . You know, I've always thought there was something a bit primal about that place. Good God.'

'I feel so wicked and naughty and fulfilled and full up with everything. For the first time in years, I feel really *human*, Ros. I love him so much. I'm sure I'm doing the right thing; even you must see that.'

'In a way. It's occurred to me more than a few times that what you needed was to get really well and truly laid.' She paused. 'It's just a shame that it had to be him.'

Carole's face fell. 'Why?'

'You know perfectly well why.'

'Ros, I swear you've got him all wrong.'

'Have I? Then why do you feel so guilty about it?'

'I don't!'

'Yes you do. You're a walking guilt factory, girl; you always have been. I can read it all over you; it's in everything you say. It's not just being *wicked* or *naughty* or anything twee like that. There's good old-fashioned honest-to-goodness guilt going on in there somewhere. Tell me what it is.'

The man hadn't moved; for several minutes he had remained entirely motionless, gazing up at the Parsonage. There was something vaguely familiar about his posture. Steven puzzled over it for a while, then realised that it was the exact mirror-image of how he himself tended to sit. Looking down at himself, he found that he was doing it now: ankles crossed, hands resting on his lap. Steven still couldn't see his face, and felt impelled to look closer. He stood up and started walking. To reach the far corner, he had to walk along the grave-lined pathway to the end and skirt around a cluster of tall monuments. He kept one eye fixed firmly on the man as he walked, but there was still no sign of him moving. Visual contact was only broken once for a few short moments as Steven rounded the monuments at the end of the graveyard, but when he emerged on the other side, the man had gone. Not just moved, but vanished.

Lying on the slab were two small flowers. They had

small, densely clustered petals of deep, silky black, and their stalks were freshly cut. Steven held the dark blooms to his nose and inhaled. Black flowers? It was not what he had expected to find: black flowers meant nothing to him. Perhaps his notion that the man seemed familiar had been mistaken.

With a shrug, he placed the flowers back on the slab and walked away.

'No, Ros, he is *not* married,' Carole insisted. She was regretting having confessed to the turn her relationship with Steven had taken, and was feeling every conceivable species of fool for having admitted to her fears about it.

Rosalind looked sceptically at her. 'And how exactly do you know that?'

'For a start, he hasn't got a ring, and there's no sign of a mark or anything on his finger.'

Rosalind snorted. 'That doesn't mean a thing.'

'Look, he swears he's certain there's no one else.'

'I see. And you believe him?'

'Of course.'

'Well, I suppose he'd know, wouldn't he?'

Carole frowned. 'What's that supposed to mean? Oh, I get it; he's a fake, of course. Is that what you're saying?'

'Carole, he walks, looks and quacks like a fake, so I call him a fake. What he's got to hide is all I wonder about.'

'Oh, for Christ's sake! Will you stop being so bloody suspicious. You said something to him, didn't you, that day you came to lunch . . . Yes, I thought so. I asked him and he denied it, but I could tell he'd been upset.'

'All I did was—'

Carole jumped up from her chair. 'All you did was interfere! Jesus, Ros, I'm sick of this. Why do you have to be so ... so fucking *cynical* about everyone? Nobody does anything without some self-serving motive in your book, do they? Well, you're wrong: not everyone has your standards.'

'What d'you mean, my standards?' Rosalind was disorientated; simultaneously affronted and impressed by Carole's uncharacteristic onslaught.

'I mean you and Richard. Just because *you* exploit people, doesn't mean *every*one's at it. You screw this guy in order to sell your sculptures, and – *shit!* – then you have the bloody nerve to lecture *me* about relationships. And don't tell me it's about "having your life under control", cause it's not. I'll tell you what your problem is: you're scared stiff of committing to someone. I bet you've never really loved a man in your whole life. And you tell me ... and, and I'm *stupid* enough to listen to it all!'

'Have you finished?' asked Rosalind quietly.

'I've barely even started. Remember Peter from Harrogate? I really fancied him, but oh no, *you* didn't like the look of him and I let you persuade me not to go out with him.'

'He was *married*, Carole!'

'He wasn't! He was separated!'

'*Bull*shit! He was after a quick leg-over, and you would have let him if I hadn't said anything. Anyway, that was years ago.'

'Exactly; look how long I've been putting up with it!'

'Well, *I've* never asked you to come round here whining about your bloody problems.'

'No, but you got a great power-kick out of all that condescending advice. Steven's right; you're a control freak. You treat your friends like shit!'

Rosalind stood up, her face suffused with rage. 'Oh, do I? Well, at least I haven't *killed* any of them! Does *he* know about that? I mean, does he, hn?'

The rising, swelling tumult froze abruptly and tee-tered precariously on the brink of an abyss. They stared at each other. Carole's eyes were wide with horrified shock, as though she had been physically struck, while Rosalind's expression of righteous, triumphant fury crumbled slowly into abject remorse. It took several moments before Carole could even activate her voice so far as to choke incoherently, by which time Rosalind had rushed forward and seized her by the arms.

'Oh Jesus, I'm sorry,' she whispered. 'I didn't mean that, I swear.'

Carole gazed impassively back at her. 'So that's what you think,' she said calmly. 'As least I know now.'

'No!' Rosalind cried desperately. 'I didn't mean it; I didn't know what I was saying.'

Carole continued to gaze coolly at her. 'I think I'd better go.'

There was a loud knock at the front door, but neither of them moved. A few moments passed, then the knock came again, slightly louder.

'Hadn't you better answer that,' said Carole.

Rosalind nodded dumbly and went out to the hall. There was a sound of the door opening, followed by muffled voices, then she reappeared with Steven behind her. 'It's Steven,' she mumbled. Carole smiled warmly and went to him, taking his head between her palms and kissing his face.

'Come on,' she said. 'Let's go home.'

'Carole, please,' said Rosalind.

Carole ignored her. Without looking back, she took Steven by the hand and led him to the door.

'What was all that about?' he asked as they drove away.

'Nothing,' said Carole. 'I've just had enough of having my mind controlled.'

'Did you have a row with her?'

She glanced at him. 'Of course I had a row . . . Steven, what would you say to a nice night in with a bottle of wine and some proper conversation? You remember you said you wanted to know everything about me and how I came to be in Yorkshire; well, I think it's time I told you.'

In the graveyard, the black marigolds were already wilting, their tiny petals curling and falling. A gentle breeze tugged at them and scattered them across the surface of the grave slab, some of them catching in the shallow grooves of the worn inscription. The slab had been eroded by centuries of rain and wind-blown dust and was spotted and patched with yellow and green lichen, obscuring all but a few of the carved words. All that remained legible was a pair of christian names, one male, one female. The man who had sat here had noticed them and felt their significance, even if Steven had not, and he had left the flowers to mark their forgotten deaths.

The Beech Tree

A t the bottom of the hill, where the steep slopes levelled out into a broad, shallow dish, there was a small spread of woodland, and near the centre of the wood was a small grassy glade through which a narrow, slow-flowing stream meandered before leaving the wood, passing under the bridge which carried the main Sainte Claudine–Camus road, and spilling into the Savonne. Squatting on their haunches beneath the fronds of a tall weeping willow at the edge of the stream were two neatly dressed young men, talking to each other in low voices, occasionally reaching up and breaking off willow twigs which they tossed idly into the water.

'It's all very well for you to say that,' Jeremy was saying gloomily. 'You didn't smell her.'

'No,' Timothy conceded. 'No, I didn't . . . Er, what did she smell of, exactly?'

Jeremy had broken off a thick twig and was peeling off the yellow bark with his long fingernails. 'Him,' he said darkly. 'I could smell his breath on her skin. I could even smell his spunk in her belly.'

Timothy raised his eyebrows and shifted uncomfortably. 'In her belly? Are you sure?'

'Yes, I'm sure. His spunk smells of garlic and snails.'

'Really? How could you sm—'

'I thought I'd find you here!' said Cressida brightly, stepping out into the glade.

Timothy jumped guiltily to his feet, startled, but Jeremy remained where he was, excoriating the twig with concentrated, methodical viciousness.

'Are we playing pooh-sticks?' she asked.

'Don't be silly,' said Timothy. 'You need a bridge for that. We were talking.'

'Talking? What about?' She glanced inquiringly from one to the other of them.

Jeremy kept silent, his back remaining resolutely turned against her. Timothy hesitated and cleared his throat. 'Just things,' he said defensively, then with more confidence: 'Men's things.'

Cressida's face looked ironically impressed. 'Men's things? Are you sure one of you wasn't just being a silly spoilt little boy?' There was a painful silence. Timothy looked down at his shoes in embarrassment. Cressida went and squatted down beside Jeremy, carefully gathering up the long white skirt of her dress and tucking it behind her knees so that it wouldn't trail in the black mud at the water's edge. She gazed at the steady, hypnotic motion of the stream. 'It's beautiful here, isn't it,' she said quietly. 'I think you should make a picture of it one day soon.'

Out of the corner of her eye, she saw Jeremy's fingers stop picking the twig. When she turned to look at his face, his eyes were brimming over with anger and pain and resentment. 'What do you care?' he spat contemptuously. 'Why don't you get *him* to make you a picture?' He snorted. 'Ha! I'd like to see *him* paint like we do.'

Cressida put an arm around his shoulders. He shrugged; just enough to register distaste, but not enough to dislodge her touch. He was silent for a while, then he whispered: 'Get rid of him.'

She frowned. 'Who? Monsieur Viveau? I can't, Jeremy ... Listen, darling, you're being a very silly boy. Silly and spiteful.'

'Then *we* shall leave.'

Cressida glanced up at Timothy, who nodded defiantly in agreement. 'Jeremy, listen,' she said patiently. 'There is nothing between myself and Monsieur Viveau. How could you even think such a thing? How could you think I would *ever* be unfaithful to my Boys? You're my darlings, nobody else.'

Jeremy raised his head and looked her in the eyes, searching and probing them for signs of a lie. He glanced over his shoulder at Timothy, then leaned closer to her, shutting his eyes and sniffing daintily at her skin; along her outstretched arm, over her shoulder and under her armpit, across her chest and neck and around her ears. His nostrils dilated to capture every nuance of smell, and his breath huffed in and out in little staccato bursts. When he had finished, he opened his eyes and looked at her again.

'What do you think?' asked Timothy.

'I'm not so sure now.'

'She might have bathed.'

Jeremy shook his head. 'No, she hasn't bathed.' He was still gazing into her eyes, and she gazed steadily back. There was silence for several minutes as they searched each other's faces. Suddenly, Jeremy whispered: 'Prove yourself, Mother.'

'What?' she said, then: 'Oh . . .' She paused, then stood up and went to Timothy. 'Would you be a good boy and leave Mummy alone with Jeremy for a little while? He's very upset.'

Timothy nodded doubtfully, glancing at Jeremy. 'Will you comfort him?'

She nodded. 'Yes, I'll comfort him.'

Timothy's pale complexion coloured slightly. 'I'm upset too. Will Mother comfort me as well?'

She smiled and touched his hand. 'Later, my darling, later. I know it doesn't seem fair, but leave us alone just this once, yes?'

'Very well.' Timothy turned to go, then hesitated. 'You won't leave us, will you? Not for your Frenchman?'

She sighed. 'How many times, you silly chump? He's *not* my Frenchman. Now run along.'

She watched him walk away through the trees, then turned back to Jeremy. He had stood up and was smiling slyly at her. She smiled back and walked towards him, unbuttoning her dress.

Michel wrenched free the last piece of broken tile from its neighbour and tossed it off the roof. It landed and smashed amongst the pile of pieces that had accumulated in the corner of the courtyard, raising a little cloud of orange dust. He stood up and stretched his body, rubbing the small of his back and groaning. The sun was past its zenith now, and the air was furnace-hot. He wiped the runnels of sweat out of his eyes and sat down on the tiles to rest.

'Hello?' called a voice from down below. The top of the ladder shuddered and rocked, then a small dome of white-gold hair appeared between its tips, followed by Cressida's face. 'There you are,' she said, peering at him from under the shade of her hand and holding up a straw basket. '*Déjeuner*. Sorry it's so late.'

'Thank you,' he said as she picked her way carefully up the shallow slope of the roof, stepping around the gaps. 'There was no need to come up. It's dangerous. You should have called me down.'

'Nonsense. I wanted to see the view.' She sat down beside him on the ridge and opened the basket. 'There's a baguette for you. Cheese and ham. And some fruit and half a bottle of Bordeaux. It's not much, but I haven't had a chance to go down to the shop this morning.' She gazed out over the valley while he took a swig of wine from the bottle and began chewing on the stuffed baguette. 'It's beautiful,' she sighed. 'I could stay here

215

and look at this view for a hundred years and never tire of it. Couldn't you?'

He glanced up and swept his eyes across the sun-warmed treetops and bright yellow fields of sunflowers on the far side of the valley, the silver-blue ribbon of the Savonne glittering in patches between the woods and farms, the pale orange roofs of Camus away in the distance. 'Hnh,' he grunted. 'It's nice. Where are your men friends this afternoon?'

She paused. 'Painting, the last I saw of them. Down there.' She pointed towards the woods in the valley bottom.

He took another bite. 'I think they do not like me very much,' he said, mumbling around the mouthful of bread and ham.

'My Twins? Whatever makes you think that?'

He swallowed. 'I passed by them when I came this morning, and the dark one – what is his name?'

'Jeremy.'

'Jeremy, yes. He looked at me like he could spit in my face.'

She nodded. She could picture that look. 'You shouldn't pay too much attention to it, Michel.'

He took another bite of baguette. 'I don't.'

'My boys are a little temperamental. That's the way artists can be sometimes. Ordinary people, like you and I, well, we just have to tolerate these little foibles if we are to enjoy the fruits of their genius. Don't you agree?'

'An artist lived in my little house once.'

'Really? That's fascinating. What sort of artist was he?'

'She. I don't know, but she was temperamental, they say. She hanged herself from the beam which is now above my bed.'

Cressida blanched and put a hand to her mouth. 'How horrible! Doesn't it give you nightmares?'

He shrugged. 'It was a long time ago. Before the War. She's gone; it's just a story now. It frightens the villagers, I think. Aside from the German soldiers, I am the first person to live there since her.'

'There were *German soldiers* here?'

'Of course. For a time, the border between Vichy France and occupied France was just down there, where those trees are. This farm was the last building before the frontier. There was a – what is the word? – a checkpoint on the road over there with guards and wire fences and soldiers patrolling in the woods. Many people in the village had relatives in Camus, and if they wanted to visit each other, they had to present their papers and be searched by the guards. There were hundreds of soldiers. My house was one of the buildings they seized for their billets.'

Cressida looked around at the idyllic vista, trying to picture it crawling with soldiers and bristling with hatred and fear. 'It must have been awful,' she said weakly.

He glanced at her and took a swig of wine. 'You should talk to old Monsieur Lacroix,' he said. 'He could tell you some stories. He was a young man when the Germans came. He made some trouble for them, I think, he and his friends. In the end, they imprisoned him and took him away to a slave factory in Germany. When he came back after the War, his own mother barely recognised him.'

Cressida sighed. 'How could such terrible things happen in such a beautiful place?'

He shrugged. 'People are cruel. All of them, in their hearts. Cruel and selfish. Why think about it? Life is good now, so just forget about it: it's all just stories.' He drained the last of the wine and stood up. 'I must get back to work now. I was late this morning. Thank you for the food.'

217

She just looked down at her feet, showing no sign of moving. 'Michel, I hope you won't think me dreadfully rude. It's about your work here.'

'What about it?'

'Would you be offended if I were to ask you not to come tomorrow?'

He stared at her. 'You don't like my work? I've hardly started it yet!'

'No, no, it's not that! Goodness, no. I'd just like you to stay away for a couple of days. Don't worry, I'll still pay you for your time.'

He glowered. 'The money is not important. I shall have nothing to do. I have said no to other work to come here.'

'Please, Michel. I just need to sort a few things out.'

He nodded. 'This is about your "boys", isn't it? I was right; they do not like me.'

'It's not their fault,' she pleaded. 'Over the years, you see, they've become so accustomed to having my undivided attention. Just give me a little time to persuade them you're no threat to them . . . Please?'

'Okay,' he sighed. 'Call on me when you are ready for me to continue. If you don't mind, I will finish these tiles before I go.'

The sun was arcing over and lowering in the sky as Michel walked up the road at six o'clock. Its light was still fierce, but the intense heat was fading to a warm, humid glow. His muscles were aching comfortably from the day's work, but the relaxed cheerfulness he usually felt in this state had been dampened; even the thousand-franc advance that Cressida had pressed on him and which was now forming a reassuringly solid bulge in the hip pocket of his trousers, even that could not raise his spirits. Here he was, getting his life organised – nearly a year it had taken him to become completely absorbed as an integral part of the village – and along had come this eccentric Englishwoman with her strange ideas and her loathsome protégés to remind him of why he would never be truly at home here. Still, he consoled himself, the money was good, and there were months of steady work ahead of him.

Walking up to his front door, he dropped his heavy toolbag on the ground and hunted through his pockets for his key. He found it at last under the roll of notes in his back pocket. But he had no need of it; as soon as he pushed it into the lock, the door clicked off its latch and swung open. Leaving his toolbag where it lay, he stepped cautiously across the threshold. After the bright sunlight outside, it seemed darker than dusk inside the house, and he stood still, just inside the door, waiting for his eyes to adjust, peering around at the deeper shadows of the cooker, the armchair, the table, his bed . . .

He gasped; sitting silently on the edge of the bed was the figure of a man, his face in shadow. 'Bonsoir, Michel,' said the man, then laughed: a harsh, scornful laugh that made the back of Michel's neck prickle. 'Nothing to say for yourself, Monsieur Viveau?' The man pronounced the name with distaste. 'You weren't expecting to see *me* here, were you?'

Cressida slid the large casserole dish out of the oven and carried it over to the table, inhaling the rich aroma of meat, vegetables and herbs. This was to be a special dinner; she was giving them their favourite, boeuf bour-guignon with pommes de terre dauphinoise, julienne vegetables and fresh wild mushrooms. She had laid out a crisp white linen tablecloth and her best silverware, and a freshly opened bottle of Chateau Latour was breathing its aroma into the air of the kitchen.

She adjusted the layout of the cutlery and looked at

her watch. It was past seven. She had told the Twins to be home and freshened up by quarter-to. She walked to the foot of the stairs and called their names, but there was no response; apart from the ticking of the oven as it began to cool, the house was as silent and dead as a tomb. Where could they have got to? Tutting to herself (without rancour; she was well accustomed to their habit of becoming so absorbed in the detail of a painting that they often lost track of time), she put the casserole back in the oven and went outside to search for them.

'How the hell did you get in here?' Michel demanded angrily.

'Now, now,' said Jeremy calmly. 'There's no need to be aggressive.'

'How did you get in?' Michel repeated.

'The door was open already,' said Timothy, who was standing behind him.

Michel spun round. 'You too!' he shouted. 'I might have guessed! What do you mean, trespassing in my house?'

'He told you, the door was open.' Jeremy looked around with distaste at the shabby fittings and the rumpled, discoloured blanket on which he was sitting. 'We wouldn't be here from choice, I can assure you.'

'No,' said Timothy. 'We like things to be clean.'

'Clean and wholesome,' Jeremy added.

'What do you want?'

'To keep things clean and wholesome,' said Jeremy simply. 'Especially our Mother.'

Michel snapped: 'What the hell is this stupid "Mother" business about? She's not your mother.'

'She is!' Timothy shouted. 'And don't you dare say otherwise! She's ours, and you can't have her!'

'What?'

Jeremy stood up. 'She's *our* Mother, and we're going to keep her.'

'Yes,' Timothy said. 'So keep your dirty Froggy hands off her nice clean skin, okay?'

Michel stared at him, then laughed suddenly. 'Is that what you think?' He jabbed a finger at his temples. 'T'es fou! Both of you, madmen!'

'Then explain this,' said Jeremy, holding up a large sheet of paper.

It was the picture of Michel and Cressida, its top edge torn where it had been pulled down from the nail on the wall. Michel frowned at it, puzzled. Looking closer, he saw that it had been altered; someone had added, in pen, a crudely drawn pair of pointed horns to his head.

'How dare you do this to our beautiful picture,' Jeremy fumed.

'Betraying his devilish intentions,' said Timothy.

'I didn't do this!' Michel insisted, but they weren't listening.

'Devil!' Jeremy shouted. 'Pimp!'

Michel held up his hands. 'I assure you, I have *no* intentions towards your mo—, towards Madame Allan.'

Jeremy sneered. 'It's *Mademoiselle*, you great hairy ignoramus!'

That was it: Michel had taken enough. He drew himself up and looked defiantly at Jeremy. 'So what?' he said quietly. 'So what if I wish to fuck your precious Mother? What will you do about it, hnh?'

Jeremy's face turned white. 'You filthy *pimp*!' he screeched. He leapt forward faster than Michel had anticipated, but his small, wildly flailing fists failed to connect. Michel ducked the left one and snatched the right by the wrist, swivelling Jeremy around and flinging him face-first against the wall, where he held him pinned securely, his arm crooked halfway up his back. Jeremy swore a stream of barely intelligible obscenities at him through clenched teeth, tears of frustrated fury welling from his eyes.

'Let go of him!' said Timothy. 'Let go – you're hurting him!'

'Good,' said Michel calmly. He bent Jeremy's arm further, until the swearing stopped and he squealed in agony. 'Now listen to me, you mad bastard,' he snarled, leaning close until his face was inches from Jeremy's. 'Your so-called Mother thinks you are both little geniuses. Myself, I think you are little shits, but then I am an ignorant peasant. But if you ever want to paint with this arm again, you will listen to me good and careful. I have no *intentions* to her at all, other than to earn my bread by helping her make your little commune. Your stupid behaviour is not helping. I don't want to have to warn you any more forcefully than this, so pay attention: I am no threat to you unless you choose to see me as one. You understand?'

'I understand,' Jeremy gasped, his eyes shut tight against the pain.

'Now, here is what you will do. You will go back down the hill to your Mother like good little boys, and you will tell her you are happy for Monsieur Viveau to continue with his work. After that, you will start to show her the respect she deserves. Believe me, I will know if you do not.' He released Jeremy's arm and stepped back. 'And tidy yourself up before you see her. Now go.'

Timothy went to Jeremy and put an arm around his shoulders, glancing at Michel with a mixture of fear and resentment, then led him out through the door. Michel slammed it behind them, then went and lay down on his bed, breathing hard and trembling with subsiding rage.

'I'm amazed,' said Cressida, stepping over a fallen branch. 'Quite amazed. The Twins have really quite taken to you now.'

She looked up at Michel and smiled. In this light, under the intermittent canopy of leaves, the filtered sun turned her burnished hair from white-gold to a softer shade of green-gold, echoing the colour of her eyes, which were glittering with happiness.

Michel shrugged. 'They think I am okay, maybe.'

In fact, over the past few weeks, Jeremy and Timothy – especially timid Timothy – had gone to almost embarrassing lengths to make a show of accepting his presence at le Temple, even attempting – in a rather ineffectual, mincing sort of way – to help him with his work when they were not busy with their art. Michel suspected that this latter action had more to do with keeping a close watch on him than with showing themselves to be friendly.

Today was marked by a superlative effort on their part. It was a Sunday and, rising unusually early, they had badgered Cressida to invite Michel to accompany them on their customary walk. They hustled her about the kitchen, giving her instructions for the collation of a picnic, then sent her up the road to call on him. He had been surprised by the invitation, but glad to escape the boredom of his day of rest. He offered to show them his favourite walk. This was a long, winding path leading through the woods which covered the hillside to the north of Chevalette, descending in long zig-zag sweeps to a place where the Savonne fed into a broad, still pond lined with rushes.

They were halfway down the hill now, and the Twins had trotted on ahead. Before long, they had disappeared from view beyond the trees, and Cressida and Michel were left alone to amble in peace.

'No,' she said. 'They really do like you. I can tell.'

Michel doubted it; from time to time when he had looked without warning at Jeremy, he had found in his eyes a look of loathing so profoundly bitter that it made his skin prickle. He kept his thoughts to himself, though. Instead, he posed a question which had puzzled him for some time: 'How did you meet them?' he asked.

'The Twins? Oh, that's a long story. In short, I had just come down from Oxford, and I was working for my Uncle Toby, who used to have a gallery in Cork Street. I met the Twins at their graduation show at Goldsmith's. Of course, I fell in love with their work right away and I offered to sell some of their paintings for them through the gallery. We've been together ever since.'

'And this was how long ago?'

'Um, let me see . . .' She muttered to herself, counting on her fingers. 'Good Lord, it's been fifteen years! It feels more like five.'

'They are not really twins, are they?'

'They might as well be. Aside from their colouring, you couldn't find a pair of true identical twins more alike than my two. And yet they had never met each other before arriving at art college. Imagine the odds against it.' She paused. 'So, you've heard our little story; now tell me how Monsieur Viveau le Bricoleur came to be born in Croydon.'

'That's easily told. My father volunteered as a soldier in 1939. He was little more than a boy. When the Germans came, his regiment was fighting alongside the British. He was evacuated from Dunkirk with them and he ended up in the Free French Army under de Gaulle. One day, he met a pretty young girl in London and they fell in love. After the War was over, he came back to England for her and they settled down and were married.' He counted off on his fingers: 'First they had my brother Jean-Marie, then my sisters Yvette and Arlette, then there was a long, long time when they thought they could have no more children, but suddenly there I was.'

'What made you come back to France?'

'My father died when I was eight years old. When I was twelve, my mother remarried another man. An Englishman. I hated him; he used to beat her, and me. When I was eighteen, I left and came to France to find my father's family. I did my military service and got my passport.'

'And this was how long ago?' She smiled as she repeated his phrasing.

'Sixteen years. I came to live in this village, though, only a year ago.'

'Why?'

'Oh, to be alone. I got tired of the city.'

Cressida was about to ask which city, when they were interrupted by a shout from further down the track. She heard the Twins calling her name, then Timothy came trotting around a bend towards them, his pale cheeks flushed with excitement. 'Come and see what we've found!' he said breathlessly, taking Cressida by the hand.

'What is it, Timothy dear?' she asked.

He tugged at her hand. 'Come and see!'

'Timothy, don't. It's too hot for running. You'll make your poor Mother faint away.'

Still holding her hand, Timothy fell into step with her, occasionally tugging gently at her fingers to urge her on.

'What is it you've found?' she asked. 'Where's Jeremy?'

'You'll see,' said Timothy slyly. Then, unable to contain his excitement, he blurted: 'It's a *sculpture*!'

'A sculpture?' Cressida glanced at Michel, but he just shrugged. 'What sort of sculpture, Timothy?'

'You'll see,' he repeated.

After about another fifty metres, the narrow forest track widened suddenly and opened out to a small clearing about ten metres across. In the centre stood a large beech tree whose heavy lower boughs stooped almost to the bare earth of the forest floor, forming a shady dome above their heads. From many of the outer branches, small, shiny black objects had been suspended with lengths of thread like baubles on a Christmas tree. Jeremy was standing under the tree on the far side of the trunk, peering at one of the objects. He prodded it, and it swung gently back and forth on its thread. He looked up at the sound of their approach.

'They're *Guinness* cans!' he said incredulously.

'See?' said Timothy, squeezing Cressida's hand. 'I told you; it's a sculpture.'

'The Guinness Tree!' said Jeremy.

Timothy ran to him, and they both began swaying the branches, making the hanging cans swing and rattle against the leaves and twigs.

Cressida looked at Michel. 'Is this some strange local custom?' she asked. 'Or has there been a party al fresco, do you think?'

He shook his head. 'I don't know.'

'How extraordinary . . . Oh, *Jeremy*, be careful; you've broken it!' One of the swaying, bouncing cans had broken loose from its branch and fallen to the ground with a hollow, tinny clatter.

'A windfall!' cried Jeremy, and he rushed to pick it up.

Michel watched intently as Jeremy examined the can, turning it over and over in his hands and picking at the remains of the thread noose around its rim. He was so absorbed in watching that he barely noticed Cressida speaking to him.

'Hnh?' he grunted.

'I said I had no idea they even drank stout in France.'

'No,' he said absently. 'No, it is not a popular drink.'

'*Somebody* obviously likes it,' she said.

He wasn't listening. Jeremy had stopped picking at

the thread and was now shaking the can, every so often turning it upside down and peering into the opening in the top. 'There's something in here,' he said. 'A piece of paper.'

Timothy stepped up and looked over his shoulder. 'Perhaps it's a message,' he said.

'Telling us where to find the treasure!' Jeremy cried, trying to insert a finger in the hole.

'Let me do that, my darling,' said Cressida, taking it from him. 'We don't want you cutting your fingers, do we.' She turned it up and looked inside, then reached in and tweezed out the object between two fingers. It was a strip of thin card which had been folded in half lengthways.

'Mine!' shouted Jeremy, snatching it from her fingers and unfolding it.

'It's not a treasure map,' said Timothy, peering at it.

'What is it?' asked Cressida.

Jeremy looked at her with a puzzled expression. 'A boarding card,' he said.

'A what?'

'A boarding card from a ferry. Look: it says "Brittany Ferries".'

'Oh,' said Cressida. 'I rather think some British tourists have passed through here, don't you?'

'Why would they have one of these, though?' Timothy said. 'We had to hand ours in, don't you remember?'

'There's a name on it,' said Jeremy. 'Michael Spring, I think. The handwriting's awful – all big and blobby, like a girl's.'

'Curiouser and curiouser,' said Cressida. 'Who, I wonder, could Michael Spring be?'

Jeremy gazed at the card for a few moments, then slapped it triumphantly with his fingers. 'Michael Spring!' he said. 'Michel Viveau! It's the same name!'

'Good Lord,' said Cressida, turning to look at Michel.

227

'Oh . . . Darlings, did you see—'

'No it isn't,' said Timothy. 'Spring in French is *la source*, not *viveau*. There's no such word.'

'But there could be,' Jeremy insisted. '*Vive eau*: lively water, spring; it's more poetic than *la source*.'

'Hush a moment, children,' said Cressida. 'Did either of you see where Michel went?'

They looked up and shook their heads. Suddenly, Timothy pointed. '*There* he is! Michel! Look at this!'

He had wandered off to look at the hanging cans on the far side of the tree, and was half hidden by the trunk. He looked up at Timothy's call and walked back to them. 'What?' he inquired.

Only Cressida noticed the expression on Michel's face when he looked at the card. The Twins were too excited by their find. Under the sun-browned surface, the colour drained from his cheeks, his eyes widened fractionally and his jaw slackened. He recovered quickly, though, coughing and waving the card nonchalantly. 'I understand now,' he said. 'I think I know who has done this. Some of my friends in the village find my English ancestry amusing to joke about. They sometimes call me *l'Immigrant*. This is one of their jokes, I think. They know I often walk this way on a Sunday.'

Cressida relaxed. 'Oh, I see. These rustic types can be rather odd, don't you think?'

'Yes . . . I wonder if you would excuse me. I'm very sorry, but I think I should go home now. I'm sure you can find your way from here.'

Cressida's face fell. 'But what about our picnic?'

'I'm sorry. Please don't be offended. I have to go see someone. Good day.' Without another word, he turned and walked away.

'Michel!' she called after him. '*Michel!*'

It was no use; he was out of sight amongst the

trees. The Twins came and stood either side of her.

'What a strange man,' said Timothy.

'Come along, Mother,' said Jeremy, linking arms with her. 'Just think: all the more sandwiches and drinkies for us!'

Reluctantly, stealing anxious glances over her shoulder, she allowed them to lead her on down the track towards the reed pond.

He strode frantically through the forest, panting up the steep hill, a hazy curtain of blinding confusion rising around him. He stumbled over roots and clumps of undergrowth, overhanging branches flapping and slapping in his face. At every turn, he almost veered from the beaten track, his panic flight exactly matching his state of mind as his reason staggered helplessly through a tangled forest of inexplicable contradiction and half-buried, weed-grown memories.

Several times, he tripped and almost fell; at least twice, he dropped the empty can and the slip of card and had to rummage for them amongst the mossy litter of the forest floor. It was on the second occasion, when he was straightening up after retrieving the card from inside a cluster of exceptionally vicious stinging nettles, sucking his stung fingers and cursing, that his mind received its second jarring blow.

Just a few metres in front of him, something small was fluttering in the light breeze against the bark of a tree. Treading down the nettles, he walked closer. The object was a small strip of glossy paper which had been attached to the bark with a dressmaking pin. It had clearly been cut from a magazine, by the look and feel of the paper; not clipped, however, but carefully removed with a single razor cut which followed the sinuous contours of the photograph's subject. Or a part of it. It was a leg; a woman's leg sheathed in a white stocking and wearing a high-heeled white shoe. Above the stocking was a brief expanse of bare flesh which ended in a scalloped edge as though the cut was following the hemline of a very short skirt.

Michel unhooked the paper from its pin and stared at it, his panic sliding into simple bewilderment.

A few paces further along the track, he found another carefully cut piece of paper pinned to another tree: this time a slender arm, cut off just above the elbow, which was bent, fingers splayed as though resting on a hip. A little further on again, and his next find was the other white-stockinged leg, then the second arm. The fifth piece was the largest, including the clothed torso and shoulders in one piece. It was wearing a very short, tight white dress with short sleeves. A small, dark triangle of pubic hair peeped from below the hem, and the front of the dress was unbuttoned from the neck to the broad belt at the waist and drawn back to expose a pair of large, pink-nippled breasts.

It was while he was standing there examining the jigsaw pieces, turning them around in his fingers and matching them together, trying to make sense of them, that the thought struck him: he turned around and looked back down the track, sighting on the trees which had yielded this strange fruit. There was no doubt about it: had they been there earlier, he would have seen them. That meant they had been put there within the last thirty minutes.

His panic redoubled, and he hurried on. As he ran, he glanced at the tree trunks, but there was no sign of the figure's missing head. He had no desire to hunt for it; not when the person who was responsible for this could still be out there; watching him, waiting to seize him and do to him what he had done to this photograph.

At last, the track came to an end. He burst out of the

forest and hit the road running. He didn't stop or look back until he arrived, panting and shaking, at his front door.

Mon cher Michel,

Oh, how are the mighty fallen! I am told that you are earning your living as a <u>bricoleur</u>. How quaint. And such a picturesque setting. Indeed, when I saw your pretty little cottage (so delightfully <u>Charentais</u>) I almost turned away and left you to your new life. Imagine it! But no, I was compelled to harden my heart and don the full weight of my responsibility, burdensome though it may be.

Who am I? I am sure you are wondering. (At least, I assume you must be wondering, since you must by now have received my little <u>cadeaux</u>. I hope you like them and that they bring with them happy recollections of times past.) I suppose I really ought to have a name, oughtn't I? You already know me by one name, but such a pathetically unimaginative one that I cannot force my pen to inscribe its forlorn shape upon the page. So, taking my cue from your own libertine relationship with names (really: treating them like whores to be cast aside when they no longer satisfy; how many have you raped and abused in this manner, Michel? Three? Names deserve a little more respect, my friend) . . . Where was I? Oh, yes; taking my cue from you, I shall invent a name; something appropriate fashioned from my own pure brain. Let me think . . .

A memory is surfacing . . .

When I was but a snot-nosed urchin, I developed an unhealthy, Sméagol-like passion for gutters, alleyways and other dingy, unpleasant places. I became adept at rooting out all the dark little secrets that accumulate in such places, unseen by the rest of humanity as they walk by with their eyes raised towards a brighter heaven. Indeed, I think in another life I may have earned my bread working the shores in the deep sewers of Victorian London. I am digressing again . . . The nub is that my dear old Granny (as embittered an old Aberdonian as ever croaked a curse at an innocent child, may the Devil scorch her shrivelled soul) sometimes caught me with my guilty fingers coated in black gutter-slime, and shrilled at me: 'Ye filthy wee strand scourer!' Like the gutter-slime, it stuck, and became her name for me.

In a sense, I have never lost my fascination with the grubby, discarded secrets of the world; I am still a Strand Scourer at heart, and so that is what you may call me.

Think of me as your Conscience, Michel. I am not sure whether you already have one of your own. (I mean, that unfortunate business aboard the _Esprit de Cotentin_; how could you, Michel? And _Guinness cans_? They're not that heavy, are they; the Channel is sure to give up its dark secret eventually.) But never fear: I am here to remedy your deficient sense of shame. You can rely on me not to shirk: I shall always be there in the shadows, never sleeping, helping you to remember. I am with you; within you, part of you. _We are One Soul_.

So please be assured, Michel, that I remain
Your Faithful and Conscientious
Strand Scourer.

Michel laid down the letter on the table beside the Guinness can, the boarding card and the completed jigsaw cut-out. He had found it waiting for him inside his locked house. Enclosed with it was the woman's missing head; a bob of dark hair surrounding a drowsy-eyed, pouting face under a small white bonnet. That explained it; what he had taken to be a dress was in fact a stylised, fetishised uniform.

He put his hands over his face and dug his fingers into his eyes. He hadn't expected it to end this way. This little community was so obscure; deeply buried in the heart of a foreign country, and he had camouflaged himself so thoroughly within its fabric that even he had to look hard to see the join. Of course, there had always been that uncomfortable little part of his mind which harboured doubts, making him glance over his shoulder for fear of discovery, but he had never imagined it like this. In his mind, it had always been the unexpected knock on the door; the gendarmes with their handguns at the ready, perhaps accompanied by one or two familiar faces; the long ride home in handcuffs and the endless questions. Not this cryptic, faceless taunting.

He was left with no option. He stood up decisively and went around the room, gathering all his belongings into a pile on the table. It didn't take long: apart from his tools, all he owned barely added up to a bucketful. He had no bags, so he packed the things he wanted in the old, sturdy shoebox his *bricoleur* boots had come in. When he had finished, the box was less than three-quarters full. He hesitated, then added the Guinness can, the cut-up photograph, the card and the letter. He also folded up the Twins' picture and added that. (Now he knew where those devil's horns had come from.) The last item to go in was a tobacco tin which he had kept hidden between the layers of his palliasse.

When he had finished and had checked his savings (nine thousand five hundred and twenty francs, plus fifty pounds Sterling), he sat down on his bed and waited.

'I think we've waited long enough, don't you?' said Cressida plaintively.

The Twins glanced at each other over the tops of their

newspapers, but said nothing. 'I mean,' she continued, 'I've tried to keep a polite distance, but don't you agree, four days is rather a long time for someone to remain incommunicado like this?'

Jeremy put down his copy of *le Monde*. 'Leave him, Mother. You've knocked at his door. What more can we do. If he chooses to be a silly old sulky-pants, it's his funeral.'

'But what if he's ill?' Cressida asked anxiously.

'Then he should see a doctor,' said Timothy. 'It isn't our problem.'

Cressida shook her head and stood up. 'No,' she said, looking sternly at them. 'I rather think you boys are more than a little pleased about this. I'm going to call on him. If he were ill or in trouble and I had done nothing, I should never get over it.' She noticed them both staring at her and flushed slightly, adding: 'I mean, I am technically his employer, so I have a certain responsibility.'

Cressida stood at the door of the shabby little house by the broken-down well and knocked. And knocked again. And again. She called his name, but there was no reply. The shutters were open, and she tried to peer in, but it was dark inside and the glass was hazed with grime.

She tried again several times over the following days, then reluctantly gave up. None of the villagers she asked had seen him; indeed, they seemed rather vague about him and did not seem unduly surprised by his absence, but she put this impression down to the limitations of her command of the rustic dialect.

Although Cressida continued to wait, Monsieur Viveau never did return to le Temple, and his work on her commune for great artists remained unfinished.

★ ★ ★

At the very moment when Cressida was knocking uselessly on the door of the empty house, the *Duc de Normandie* was carving its way past the tip of the Isle of Wight and aiming its bulk towards the mouth of Portsmouth Harbour. Perched on a stool at the bar, Douglas Bailey was ordering a drink for his new friend.

'Same again, Paul?' he asked. 'Right – Another couple of halves over here, if you please.'

They had struck up a conversation while they were standing at the stern rail, watching the beach of Ouistreham recede towards the horizon. Returning from a holiday with his family, Bailey was in a relaxed, contemplative mood. He had turned to the stranger with the heavy moustache that was becoming lost within an advance of new beard growth, and remarked: 'See that? Sword Beach, that was.' He pointed towards the distant sands. 'Thats where my old Dad went ashore on D-Day.'

The stranger had responded with recollections of his own father's wartime service; something hush-hush in bombers, apparently. Their conversation ambled along with ease, turning before long to classic cars, for which they discovered a common passion. By the time the ferry was halfway across the Channel, Bailey had heard most of Paul's life story.

'So,' he said, swigging his beer. 'Got any work lined up in Blighty?'

Paul shook his head. 'Not a hope, mate.'

'And I don't suppose you'll get the dole, being out of the country so long.'

'No, I suppose not.'

Bailey took another long sip and turned to face him. 'Look, I hate to see an expat come back to his home country and get the cold shoulder. Why don't you come and work for me?'

'For you?'

'Yeah, why not? I can always use a bright bloke with a

feeling for old cars. Besides, I like your face. Always could spot a good honest bloke. Got a genius for it, I reckon: good judge of character, me.'

'Well, it's really kind of you . . .'

'Kind bollocks. You'd be doing me a favour.' He drained his glass. 'Now, how about another before we bump dock?'

13

'Say when . . .' Carole tilted the bottle, and the red wine glugged into Steven's glass. He held up a hand to stop her when it was two-thirds full. She filled her own glass to the brim, took a large mouthful, then topped it up again. She set the bottle down in the grate and sat in the armchair, lighting a cigarette.

'Won't you sit here?' he asked, indicating the space next to him on the sofa.

She shook her head and took another long sip of wine. She doubted that she would sleep much that night anyway, so it would make little difference how much she drank or what hallucinatory noises she heard.

Steven gazed at her. She had been very quiet ever since they had got back from Haworth, hardly speaking at all during dinner, refusing to reveal why she had argued with Ros. And now she was slinging back the wine like there was no tomorrow. Something significant had clearly happened between her and Ros: more than just a squabble; something that had provoked this desire to unburden herself at last of whatever brooding secret she had been carrying around deep inside her. He was well aware, from a variety of hints, allusions and half-told tales, that there was a deep shadow cast across the years before she had become a reclusive locust-farmer; something she had done or that had been done to her which she considered terrible and shameful. Her big secret. He wondered how it would compare with his.

'Confession time, eh?' he said, trying to get the conversation moving.

'You could say that . . . Steven, do you love me?'

'You know I do. Look, I wish you'd sit over here.'

'No . . . I want to be able to look at you. I hope you'll still love me after I've told you what I'm going to tell you.'

'Try me. I'm sure I will. I can't see what you could've done that's so awful.'

'Well, you can judge for yourself.' She topped up her glass again. 'I wonder if I ought to bring another bottle in. I think this might be a two-bottle story.'

She was having trouble getting started. 'Let me help,' he said. 'Why don't you start with the reason you didn't become a doctor. I presume that's connected?'

'Sort of. I didn't become a doctor because I didn't want to enough. Or wasn't good enough. Or both. It was my father who wanted me to study medicine. I wanted to be an actress or a singer. I used to be in all the school plays and concerts and things.'

He smiled. 'I bet you were good. You've got a lovely voice.' It was true; he had heard her sing snatches from time to time, and she was no run-of-the-mill singer, either: her singing voice, like her speaking voice, had a gorgeously rich sweetness to it. Indeed, he remembered how it had been her disembodied voice seeping into his uncertain consciousness that he had first started falling in love with.

She smiled. 'Maybe. But it wasn't a proper career as far as darling Dad was concerned. Plan A was for me to be a lawyer like him. Then he realised I was better at the sciences, so Plan B came into force – medicine. He had me earmarked for a London consultancy when I was still doing my O-Levels. Anyway, I got into Nottingham to study medicine. I didn't exactly hate it, but my heart wasn't in it. By the end of the third year, my marks were so crap that the Medical School and I agreed it would be better for both of us if we parted company. After that, I faffed around doing nothing in particular for a few years. That was when Dad stepped in with Plan C – use the training I'd managed to get and become a nurse instead. By this time, Dad had lowered his sights as far as I was concerned. Michael was at university doing engineering, and he'd taken over the role of big achiever, so I was off the hook.

'I tried hard at nursing. I was surprised to find I really did enjoy it: it felt like I'd really found my niche. I never gave up on my ambitions, though. I applied to RADA, and they actually offered me a place, but my father put his foot down; I wasn't entitled to a grant because I'd already had my shot at university, and he refused point-blank to sub me.'

'Couldn't you have supported yourself?' asked Steven. 'You seem pretty resourceful to me.'

'Maybe, but there was more to it than that. Looking back on it, I think his approval was as important to me as his money. Always has been, I suppose. And he didn't approve of acting as a career. "Do you know how many actors there are in the world?" he used to say. "Do you realise that more than ninety per cent of them are unemployed? No daughter of mine is going through that . . ." and so on. So I stuck with nursing . . . ' She fell silent, sipping at her wine.

'And what went wrong?' Steven prompted.

She shook her head. 'Nothing. After I qualified, I worked in Casualty for a couple of years. I found that too stressful, so I did some retraining and went into paediatrics. Everything worked out fine from that point on. I moved out of my parents' house and rented a flat with Beverley.'

'Beverley?'

'Sorry, I'm getting ahead of myself. I met Beverley when I was working in Casualty. I told you how it was too stressful for me; I mean, Casualty takes its toll on all the staff after a while, but Beverley was incredible. It never got to her. And I don't mean she was cold or insensitive, because she wasn't; she was kind and patient, and she never got stressed-out or tired or confused like the rest of us did. She just coasted along, always there when you needed her. She was like the original angel of mercy.

'There was one time on the night-shift. It was one of the worst nights I ever knew. There'd been this riot between football supporters. They were all over the place. Some of them with horrific injuries. Right in the middle of all this, they started bringing in an overflow of casualties from a massive road accident somewhere near Dartford. A juggernaut had jack-knifed across two lanes of traffic, I think, and there were burns, neck injuries, contusions, broken bones, dozens of them all coming in on stretchers. We were going frantic trying to deal with it all, and we were running low on anaesthetics and blood. Then, one of the football men started going crazy. He burst into one of the cubicles where they were trying to give a transfusion to someone who'd had his neck slashed with a knife. I think he must've been an opposing supporter or something, because this nutcase started screaming abuse at him and at the staff, then he grabbed hold of the drip and tried to pull it out. There was a young junior doctor there who'd been called back after a twenty-six hour shift. He was exhausted, almost going out of his mind, and he just lost it. He was all set to punch this man out, but Beverley stepped in and stopped him. I'll never forget it: the drunk started screaming at her, saying all sorts of obscene things – threatening her. And she didn't even blink. She just talked really gently to him and ushered him out to the waiting room like a lamb, and sat him down, and . . . well, it was just unbelievable. Then she went back to dealing with the casualties.

'It wasn't just things like that, either. I remember

another time when they brought in a guy who had a . . . well, you know, this . . . vibrator thing, lodged in his rectum. He was brought in on a trolley, face down with a sheet draped over him, and this –' Carole smirked and made a little tent shape with her hands '– this *thing* sticking up.'

'I don't believe it,' said Steven, grinning.

'It's true. It wasn't a little one, either, it was this great big . . . God, it must've been the size of a cucumber. Christ knows how he'd got it in. It really is true. If you want to see the sort of thing perverts'll do for a thrill, just go and hang around your local casualty department. We had men in with bondage injuries, mangled penises from trying to masturbate with vacuum cleaners and food-mixers and God knows what, stuff you wouldn't believe that they'd tried to do with electricity. Some of them were just mysteries. One time, we admitted this couple. The man had horrible lacerations to the penis, and the woman who brought him in had bruises all over her face. We thought it was a domestic at first. It turned out, though, they'd been, er, well, she'd been doing him an oral favour. The thing is, she was epileptic, apparently, and—'

'Don't,' Steven interrupted. 'I can guess.'

'Well, exactly. The bruising was caused by him trying to beat her off . . .' Carole paused, staring blankly into space, her smile fading. 'I've got off the point, haven't I? Where was I? Oh yes, the man with the vibrator. Beverley dealt with him. He was absolutely *beetroot* with humiliation and agony, but Beverley just took the whole thing in her stride; not so much as a blink or a twitch of a smile. Treated it as though it was no more embarrassing than a splinter in the finger. You see, what I'm saying is, it didn't matter how strange or perverted you were, or how angry and violent, Beverley treated everyone exactly the same; kindness and patience and respect.

'Anyway, as I was saying, we ended up renting a flat together. She was the best friend I'd ever had. She was the only person I've ever been close to who hasn't tried to influence me or tell me what I should do with my life. She just listened whenever I told her my problems, and gave me love and support; no disapproval, no judgement, no advice I didn't want . . .

'I transferred to paediatrics about six months after moving in with her. We didn't see so much of each other after that; we weren't working together any more and we were on opposite shifts a lot of the time. We had some great times together, though. I was a lot happier in paediatrics, and things were going really well. Then, after about a year or so, it all started going wrong. I can even put an exact date on it: April the seventeenth. I remember it because that was the day our new paediatrician arrived. His name was Ian Laithwaite, and all the nurses swooned over him. He looked a bit like Ralph Fiennes, with a bit of Alan Rickman on the side, all brooding and handsome. I mean, the only other man in the department under forty was a junior consultant called Sturdy who looked like Marty Feldman and used to frighten the children.

'I'm afraid I went totally stupid over Ian. I got this enormous crush on him. I used to try to rig my shifts so that I'd be there when he was. I used to think he didn't notice me, didn't even know I existed. There were at least a couple of paediatric nurses who were far prettier than me, so I just couldn't believe it when he asked me out. I was standing in the corridor, and he sidled up to me like a schoolboy, all red around the ears, as though I'd be the one making *his* dreams come true. It was so sweet, I just crumpled up inside . . .'

'You probably were making his dreams come true,' Steven said.

Carole drained her glass and refilled it. 'Don't be

'ridiculous,' she said, without humour.

He watched her down half the glass at one go. 'Shouldn't you slow down?' he suggested. The bottle was already two-thirds empty, and he had only drunk one glass.

'No,' she said. 'I'm determined to tell you this story, and I don't think I could do it cold sober.'

He sank back on the sofa and sighed. 'Okay, so what happened with the wonderful Dr Ian?'

'It was fantastic,' she said dreamily. 'At least, it was at first. We went out that weekend, then again the next. After that, it . . . well, it just exploded. We were seeing each other almost every night we were both off-duty. I was so much in love with him, I . . .' She hesitated, and lit another cigarette, inhaling deeply and blowing out a huge cloud of smoke. Then she pressed her fingers into her eyes, the tip of the cigarette twitching dangerously close to her hair. 'I was obsessed,' she said at last, removing her fingers from her eyes, which were now red and sore. 'I went crazy; in the end, Ian started backing off. I just wouldn't leave him alone – ringing him all the time, turning up at his house in the middle of the night, screaming at him. He wanted to finish it. Christ, I made such a fool of myself. You can hardly blame him, can you? We couldn't work together any more. Then, one weekend, I came down with flu, really horrible gastric flu. I was off work for two weeks, and when I came back, Ian had gone. The senior consultant had seen what was going on and used his contacts to fix Ian up with a position somewhere in the West Country. I never saw him again.

'About a week after that, I found out I was pregnant.' She looked up at Steven, tears tipping from the corners of her eyes. 'Our last fling, trying to rescue our relationship. We'd only slept together that one time in the whole previous month. Once! Every other time,

and no mess-ups, but once when things weren't working, and Bingo!' She laughed: a bitter, hollow bark.

'What happened?'

'What d'you think? I had an abortion. After that, I
finally gave up work. I couldn't cope any more. I went
back to live with my parents, but that didn't work out.
In the end, it was Michael who suggested I should move
up here. He'd started work with a firm in Sheffield. He
said he'd keep an eye on me. Dad finally coughed up
some money to help set me up, and Michael used to
come over at weekends to check I was all right.'

Steven sighed. 'Poor Carole. I wish you'd told me all
this before. You shouldn't have to carry all that by
yourself.' He leaned forward and stretched out a hand
towards her. 'How could you think I'd think any less of
you because of it?'

Carole smiled and wiped her eyes. 'You really do love
me, don't you?' she said, touching his outstretched
fingers with hers.

'Of course I do.'

Her smile faded. 'Good, because I haven't told you
the rest of the story yet.'

'What? I thought . . .'

'It's my fault,' she said, withdrawing her hand and
pouring more wine into her glass. 'Bugger. This bottle's
empty. I'll go and get the other one . . .' She stood up,
slightly unsteadily, and went to fetch the second bottle
of wine from the kitchen. When she had pulled the cork,
she sat down again, dropping heavily into the chair and
sighing wearily. 'Where was I?'

'You were saying it was your fault.'

'True,' she said resignedly. 'It's always my fault.
Everything . . . Yes, that was it. I'm not telling this story
very well. I've got it all back-to-front. I haven't told you
why it all went wrong. My brain wants to forget that bit.
I want to forget that bit,' she added, as though she and

her brain were opposing, antagonistic forces who for once happened to be in agreement.

'What bit?'

'Beverley . . .' She paused. 'What d'you think of betrayal, Steven?'

He shrugged. 'I don't know what you mean.'

'Betrayal. Betraying someone's trust, betraying their love . . .' As she spoke, her face crumpled and she began to cry. Steven went to her, but she pushed him away. 'Don't,' she sobbed. 'Please.' She blew her nose and sniffed. 'I'll be all right in a minute.' When she had drunk some more wine and lit another cigarette, she settled down and continued talking: 'After I started seeing Ian, my friendship with Beverley began suffering. I kept cancelling dates I'd arranged with her and . . . and I even started feeling jealous. You see, Ian was a dreadful flirt, and Beverley was very attractive. I told her to keep her hands off him. I said some terrible things to her. I always felt awful about it afterwards, because she was so bloody patient and understanding all the time, but then I'd be at it again. One afternoon, I came home from work early and found Ian at the flat. I went ballistic. I screamed at them. I remember slapping Beverley across the face and calling her a bitch and a slut and God knows what else. Ian pulled me off her and slapped *me*. He said I was hysterical. I told them they could get on and fuck each other senseless for all I cared, then I stormed out. When they finally caught up with me, they both swore that nothing was going on. I must've been insane; I mean, they hadn't even been *doing* anything when I walked in. As far as I can remember, Beverley was making tea in the kitchen and Ian was in the living room reading a newspaper. He'd only come round to be sure of catching me when I got home. He'd got tickets for a concert that evening and wanted to surprise me. A nice, kind surprise. He was so thoughtful, and look how I repaid him.

'I tried to make it up to Beverley. We arranged a girls' night out. We were going to see a film – I think it was *Ghost* or something. I didn't fancy it much, but Beverley was crazy for Swayze, as she used to put it. Then, after that, the plan was to go on to a club to dance. She loved dancing. I was supposed to meet her in the foyer of the cinema at eight, because she was going straight from work. About seven o'clock that evening, I got a phone call from Ian. He'd got tickets from some friend of his for a weekend in Vienna. The problem was, we had to be at Gatwick by eight-thirty. I phoned the hospital, but Beverley wasn't available, and there was no one who could give her a message. Then I phoned the cinema and tried to get them to give her a message not to bother waiting, and they said they'd see what they could do . . .

'I don't remember anything about Vienna. The next thing I remember is getting home late on the Sunday night. Beverley wasn't there. I didn't give it much thought at the time; I assumed she must be on her shift.'

Carole was completely calm now, although her voice was slightly unsteady from the wine. She had stopped drinking, and her half-empty glass was resting on her thigh, forgotten as she gazed at the ceiling, looking beyond her physical surroundings into a past that she could see as clearly as the present. Steven, rigid with tension, never took his eyes off her face, not even to blink.

'I didn't find out what had happened until the next day,' she continued. 'It seems she went to the cinema as arranged. The woman in the ticket kiosk remembered seeing her, and one of the usherettes remembered seeing her leaving alone after the film. There was an unconfirmed sighting of her on a bus in Oxford

Street at ten-thirty, and that was the last anybody saw of her ... Her body was found on the Saturday morning, on some waste ground in Limehouse. They identified her by the contents of her purse. She'd been asphyxiated, but there were no signs of a struggle. Her body—' There was a catch in her voice, but she pressed on doggedly, picking the details out of her brain and enunciating them sharply, as though their cruel, unsheathed edges could replicate on her own soul the horrors she had caused to happen to Beverley. 'The body was naked, and all her hair had been cut off. All of it: her head, her arms, her pubic hair, all shaved as neatly as though she'd been hot-waxed. Her clothes and the cut hair had all been removed. They were never found, as far as I know. Only the purse was left there. There was a piece of paper in it that her killer must have put there. I can still remember the exact words that were written on it. It said "My name is Beverley. Soon my face will be famous" ... That was all: "Soon my face will be famous." Her face had been ...' Carole stumbled again, but this time couldn't recover herself. 'Her face ...' she repeated thickly. The wine glass slipped from her fingers and toppled off the arm of the chair, smashing on the stone grate, but she gave no sign of noticing. 'It was found ...' She choked on the words, and gave up trying to describe what had been done with Beverley's face. 'The note was right,' she went on. 'Her face did become famous. The victim without a face whose face became famous for not having a face. Christ. The photograph they used for all the television news reports was one I'd taken. Her parents didn't have any recent ones. I took it one night when we'd been drinking. I was even drunker than I am now. It was all fuzzy, and she hated it because she thought it made her look fat. They chose it because she looked happy in it. They said the happier she looked,

247

the more public sympathy there'd be, and the better chance there'd be of catching someone.

'I've no idea if they ever did catch anyone. They told me later he disappeared, whoever it was who did it. Died. Something like that. I heard there were more murders, but I stopped watching the news and reading the papers, and I wouldn't let anyone talk to me about it. I was going out of my mind. Everything fell apart with Ian after that . . .'

Carole turned her gaze on Steven, searching for a reaction, searching for the inevitable transformation of love into disgust, loathing and condemnation. He was staring at the floor between his feet, his face taut and pale. 'So, there you are,' she sighed. 'Now you know. The best friend I've ever had was killed because of me, because I betrayed her, because I was selfish. *I* might as well have killed her myself.'

Steven was silent for a long while, then he stood up. Carole watched him nervously. 'I, er,' he said hoarsely. 'Look, I think I'll . . .' He gestured helplessly, then, avoiding her eyes, he turned and left the room.

Carole watched him go, her face slowly creasing and crumpling. When she heard the back door closing, the tears finally welled up and spilled out.

14

Carole woke just as the alarm was about to go off. Opening her eyes and noticing the time, she felt she could almost hear its startling shriek; a curious effect, like hearing the echo of a sound before the sound itself. She rolled quickly out of bed and slapped down the button to forestall its noise.

Sitting on the edge of the bed, she rubbed her eyes and yawned, then slid back under the duvet. It was Sunday: the world could wait another half an hour. After the past couple of days, she felt that the world could go to hell for all she cared. She pulled the heavy duvet tightly around her body and allowed herself to slip back into the fuzzy haze of hovering half-sleep.

She had woken with Beverley's gentle voice floating in her head. She had dreamed that she was back in the hospital, trying desperately to remember how to administer an intravenous drip. She ought to know how to do it, but it all seemed so long ago, and her expertise had deserted her. Whichever way she tried it, she could not make the needle fit onto the end of the plastic tube. The patient in the bed was Steven; his body was torn and bloody with shotgun wounds – wounds that she herself had inflicted – and she knew he would die unless she could get the drip into his arm. His eyes were open and full of baleful reproach as he watched her fumbling clumsily with the needle. 'Let me,' said a familiar, quiet voice beside her, and the needle and tube were taken from her by gentle hands. The nurse slotted them together easily and slipped the needle into Steven's arm. His eyes closed and his body seemed to glow from within as the miraculous fluid dripped into his veins. Carole had known that voice, those gentle, patient fingers. The nurse turned to face her. 'I knew you'd come back,' said Beverley. She evaded Carole's eager questions, but not her hug. 'I haven't been anywhere,' Beverley insisted, laughing as Carole embraced her again. 'I've always been here. Waiting for you.'

She had woken up then, tears forming in her eyes and her chest aching with longing.

She replayed the dream now, hearing the voice again, scrutinising the sharply focused features. It had been so long now since she had seen her alive that Carole usually found it impossible to recall an accurate image of Beverley's face; all she was left with in her conscious mind was a vague, unfocused impression of burnished corngold hair so rich that it seemed to give out its own internal light, haloing a soft, melting kaleidoscope of features. Only on the rare occasions when Beverley came out of her inviolable sanctuary in deep memory and walked into Carole's dreams did her features snap into focus. Every few months or so, the dream would return, taking place in different settings and with different casts of supporting characters, but always the same emotions: relief, desperate yearning simultaneously fulfilled and doomed, but curiously little surprise. It was as though there were a small part of her mind which still didn't quite believe that Beverley was dead, saying to her, *There, I told you so. Now everything will be all right.*

That part of her mind was diminishing all the time, until it had become a tiny lacuna in a smooth, seamless weave of dull acceptance. On the day of the funeral, the doubt had been at its strongest: as Carole stared at the polished coffin with its bright, brassy handles, perched on velvet-covered trestles at the front of the church, she found herself utterly unable to believe that Beverley's body was inside it. (*Denial*, her therapist called it, and she accepted the verdict, even though it distressed her so much that she never went back to see him again.) She had been quite heavily sedated that day, and her conscious memory of it was irrevocably hazed, blurred and fragmentary, even more than her memory of Beverley's face. Now, though, as she lay in bed with the dream fresh in her head and the route between the busy reading room of her conscious mind and the vast, darkened library of her visual memory still wide open, she found whole chunks of the ceremony and all its inconsequential details unfolding before her; even things she couldn't remember remembering: Beverley's brother in the pew in front, the gold braid around the cuff of his naval uniform catching the light from the window as he fingered the pages of his hymn book, open at Psalm 23; watching nervously as the professional pall-bearers provided by the undertaker hefted the coffin off the trestles on to their shoulders, wondering abstractedly whether they had ever fumbled and dropped one of these heavy wooden boxes so that it clattered and crashed onto the flagstone floor; leaning on Ian's arm as they walked in procession up the aisle behind the family; the look of scornful resentment she thought she could read in the mother's face as she caught her eye in the crowd outside the church; the blank incomprehension transfixing the father's face as he stood there in his cock-eyed, ill-fitting suit; and, last of all, the gathering at the graveside. She had never attended a burial before (all her dead relatives had been cremated), and she had expected to be repelled by the visceral immediacy of the open grave. Instead, it had been almost comical, in a grim sort of way: the vivid green fake grass covering the sides of the pit and the adjacent spoil heap like an empty grocer's window; the frail, elderly vicar squirting holy water into the grave from a small plastic bottle rummaged from a pocket under his vestments; several of the mourners stumbling and almost falling over the surrounding monuments in the congested graveyard. She looked around the congregation, her gaze jumping from face to face, barely registering their identities, flitting from the faces at the graveside to some men in suits standing under a yew tree some distance away, then back to the grave, then back to the strangers again. She peered at them, trying to penetrate the Valium fuzz. They were wearing rumpled suits – work suits, not best – and token black ties. The two on either side were watching the ceremony, but the one in the middle was staring steadily at her; directly into her eyes. He held her gaze for a few moments, then turned and walked away. She had been holding the image of his face freeze-framed in her mind for several moments before she realised that she knew that face as well as she knew her own . . .

—She gasped. Her eyes flicked wide open, staring up at the grey, dimly-lit bedroom ceiling, her heart racing and her breathing laboured, the image of Steven standing under the tree in the graveyard strobing behind her eyes.

The telephone seemed to go on ringing for a long time, *prrp*ing relentlessly in her ear. Carole sighed and drummed her fingertips nervously on the desktop. On the fifteenth ring, it clicked. 'Hello?' said an agitated, irritable voice.

'Oh, hi, Ros,' said Carole, trying to honey her voice placatingly, feeling intrusive and guilty before she had even said anything. 'It's me.'

'Carole! I was worried I'd never hear from you again.'

'Yes. Look, I'm really sorry about yesterday, Ros.'

'No, it was my fault. I really didn't mean anything I said. Especially . . . Can you ever forgive me, darling?'

'Don't be silly. Of course I can. I do. Listen, I . . .' Carole paused. She could hear noises in the background. 'Are you busy?'

'I am a bit, yes,' said Rosalind, quickly becoming brisker now that forgiveness was vouchsafed. 'I've got to get the *E-Motion* pieces to Oakworth by the end of the afternoon, and the movers they've sent over are bloody . . .' Her voice suddenly muted to a hoarse half-whisper – 'bloody hopeless. Bloody awful. Cups of tea, I

252

don't know what ... They've already broken one of the stems off *Breath IV* and I've been trying to weld the bugger back on *and* keep watching them in case they smash anything else. I don't know *where* they find these people.'

The tirade went on for several more minutes. When Rosalind eventually paused for a moment, Carole broke in tentatively: 'Would you prefer it if I called you back later?'

'Oh, I don't know, Carole. I'll be in Oakie till late. Tell you what, I'll call you.'

'Oh,' A note of despondency crept into her voice. Waiting for Ros to call back usually meant a miniature eternity.

'Are you all right, darling?'

'Yes, I'm fine. I just, you know ...'

A deep sigh rasped in the earpiece. 'Come on. Talk to me.'

'I told Steven about Beverley.'

There was a long pause. 'What, everything?'

'Yes,' said Carole quietly.

There was another pause – even longer this time – and Carole could feel the familiar waves of exasperated disapproval and impatience pulsing down the line from Haworth. 'And?' said Rosalind eventually, in a tone which implied that she could probably provide the answer herself.

'He went out to the barn. I haven't seen him since ... Then, this morning I had this dream – or at least I think it was a dream, but I don't know now if it was or if it was something I really remember. I'm so confused, Ros. I don't know what to do ...'

'You sound pretty messed-up, girl.'

'Oh God, Ros—'

'Look, I'm really sorry. I'd love to stay and listen, but – *Don't hold it like that*! – God, cretin. I'd really love to,

253

but I can't. Why don't you meet me in Oakworth for lunch tomorrow.'

'Well, I suppose . . .'

'About half-twelve? Come to the station and we'll drive out somewhere.'

'Okay.'

'Get away from the hustle and bustle, eh?'

'Mm . . .'

'Look, I've got to go. Bye.'

The line clicked, and Carole was left alone with the dialling tone buzzing in her ear.

Carole sat alone in the compartment, leaning back, eyes half-closed, letting the motion of the train roll her head gently from side to side, and the rumbling of the wheels and the chuffing and hissing of the steam engine soothe her. Taking the train had been an impulse; driving through Keighley, she had been passing the railway museum when, on a whim, she pulled suddenly into the car park and left the Morris there. Luckily, a train had been just about to depart when she arrived on the platform.

She had not ridden on the Worth Valley railway since the childhood holidays that seemed as unreal to her now as a dream. *As unreal as a dream*: the phrase struck resonantly inside her. All her memories before Beverley had that same fogged quality of remembered dreams; conscious and subconscious mingled and their boundaries blurred. Only now did she realise what must have been obvious to her friends and family all along. Resigning from her job and moving to York-shire, which she had insistently rationalised to herself and anyone who queried her actions as a desire to escape from the stress of the city and do something to fulfil herself, as well as – when they pressed her on the subject – to escape from her guilt: all this cloaked (from her own eyes at least) a very simple core; her desire to retreat into her childhood. Not the generality of her pre-adolescent years, but the honeyed times where there was no school, no homework, no pressure, no restrictions; an archipelago of islands in the past where there were only leisurely rural breakfasts, outings with gifts at the end, long treks over the moors and games of Wuthering Heights. Those games were the focus of it all, in a strange way: the pleasant itch of sexuality without consummation or even the desire for consummation; without even the knowledge that consummation was supposed to be the point, and without the bitterness, the awkwardness, the disappointment and the recriminations of its aftermath. Reckoning, responsibility and culpability receded into an endlessly telescoping tomorrow.

She smiled wanly to herself as she recalled the intoxicating intensity of these feelings. Not only had they been marred by the inevitability of adulthood, but they were also contaminated by a cancer that grew silently inside them, embodied in her and Kieran's very choice of game. A couple of years ago, Carole had attended a one-day seminar in Bradford on semiotics and eroticism in the Brontë novels. One of the speakers – a female professor from Durham – pointed out that Heathcliff, the foundling, was clearly the bastard son of Earnshaw, and therefore Catherine's half-brother. Carole's skin had prickled uncomfortably up and down her back at this as she thought about her childhood play with Kieran, her first-cousin. The professor had gone on to itemise all the veiled erotic references in the novel, her dénouement, her *coup de grâce* being the ultimate act: marshalling her evidence, she outlined her case for Heathcliff having committed an act of necrophilia with Catherine's body. It was at that point in the lecture that Carole had run from the room in distress, provoking a half-heard comment from the professor about people of a sensitive disposition as the door swung closed behind her.

A squeal of brakes and a gush of steam: Carole glanced out of the window to see the buildings of Oakworth Station looming beyond a bend in the track. For several moments, as the train slowed and drew up beside the platform, she had to struggle to remember what she had come here for. It was only when she saw the small blue poster pinned to the station notice-board that she remembered Ros.

SLEEPERS

An Exhibition of Paintings and Sculptures by Local Artists

Works by

SU ANNA

ROSALIND BARTON

JIM FRIED

NOEL KOVACIK

GLORIA SCOTT

The Station, Oakworth

26 MAY–8 JUNE 1997

Carole wandered from the platform into the small booking hall. Most of the other passengers had already passed through; apart from a middle-aged couple who had paused to glance around at the display of art works, the place was deserted. She tried the waiting room, but there was no sign of Ros in there either. She walked slowly around, looking at the exhibits. The sculptures ranged from pastoral to pseudo-industrial in appearance, and in size from a small, polished piece like a distorted egg on a white board pedestal, to an object which stretched to the ceiling and looked like a space rocket built from rusty corrugated iron by someone on drugs. She recognised the sculpture; she had gazed at it countless times in the studio. A small white card stuck to the wall beside it read: 'PENETRATE VI. ROSALIND BARTON. SHEET STEEL AND BRASS WIRE. 1993'. Further along the wall was a large canvas, about five feet by four, the whole of its white surface crowded with small, coloured ellipses, closely spaced in neat, regular rows. Each perfectly formed ellipse was a different pastel shade and had its long axis orientated slightly differently from its neighbours, so that the whole canvas seemed simultaneously calm and alive with restless motion. The printed card beside this one read: 'HOPE. JIM FRIED. ACRYLIC. 1996'.

'Talk about a triumph of style over content,' said a loud voice right behind her shoulder.

Carole flinched and spun around. 'For God's sake, Ros. You scared the life out of me.'

Rosalind grinned. 'Sorry. I've been out in the car park waiting for you.'

'Oh. I took the train.'

'Thought you might have.' She stepped up beside Carole and nodded at the canvas. 'Awful, isn't it,' she said in a stage whisper.

Carole looked at it again. 'I thought it was nice,' she said.

Rosalind glanced at her sidelong and smirked. 'Nice. Hmm, yes it's nice. Probably the fact that it's so nice explains why it's been done to death. God, even Damien Hirst has done stuff like this, and Bridget Riley was churning them out decades ago. *And* hers were better. I mean, it's all very well, but what does it *signify*?'

Carole shrugged, as though abdicating responsibility for her own opinion. 'Well, I suppose I don't know much about art,' she said.

257

'But you know what you like. Oh well, you're entitled, I suppose . . . Anyway, let me give you a guided
tour of the show, for what it's worth.'

Carole only half-listened to the stream of commentary
as they ambled together from piece to piece, around the
room, into the booking hall and out onto the platform,
where some sculptures too large to be housed indoors
were displayed. Rosalind's flow of information was
liberally studded with barbed criticism and breathless
praise – significantly more of the former than of the
latter – and by the time they emerged from the station
into the car park, Carole felt disorientated, over-
whelmed, no longer sure what to think; whether to trust
her own gut reactions or contemplate the layers of
significance, precedent and implied moral value
ascribed by Rosalind to each work. She had noticed, not
for the first time in the course of their friendship, that
her own aesthetic tastes were grossly at odds with the
things that Ros seemed to imply she had an imperative
moral duty to admire.

Rosalind was so full of the exhibition that they were
almost out of Oakworth, cramped close in the narrow
space of her Renault 4, before Carole had a chance to
redirect the conversation.

'It was nice of you to make time for me,' she ventured.
'You're so busy at the moment, I feel awful dragging
you down with my problems.'

'Nonsense, girl. Just tell me what's happened. You
weren't terribly coherent on the phone.'

'Are you sure you want to hear all this?'

'I've swept all artistic thoughts out of my brain. I'm a
willing receptacle. Just talk to me, woman.'

Carole drew in a deep breath. 'Well, it all started on
Saturday night . . .'

'Are you sure you won't have anything?' asked Rosalind

as the barman placed a mountainous ploughman's lunch on the table in front of her.

Carole looked away from the food and shook her head emphatically. 'I couldn't,' she said.

'You'll waste away,' said Rosalind sternly. 'You're already looking a bit pasty.' She rotated the gigantic plate. 'Here, eat the salad. You know I can't stand green salad. Go on, eat it up for me.'

Carole picked out a disc of cucumber and a roundel of red pepper, both going dry and slightly wrinkled on one side, and nibbled them reluctantly. 'Why did I have to go and tell him, Ros?' she moaned.

Ros shrugged. 'I don't know. Why did you?'

'It was like a sort of test, I suppose. I thought: If he still loves me when he knows this, then . . . I don't know, I'd be saved or something. Cleansed, forgiven.' She picked up a wedge of tomato trailing strands of cress. 'Afterwards, he didn't say anything. He couldn't even bring himself to look at me. He just stood up and walked out of the door.'

Rosalind tore open a hot bread roll and began buttering it. 'Well, to be fair on him, it was a hell of a heavy thing to lay on someone in one go like that. I remember when you told me the story. Took me a few days to get my head round it.'

'This was different, Ros. He thinks I'm evil, I can tell. And who can blame him? It *was* all my fault.'

'Start talking like that and you and I might have to have another argument.'

'Well, it was. I mean, *you* blame me, don't you.'

'No I bloody don't. Listen, Carole, what I said on Saturday was . . . well, you know how it is in an argument; you reach a point where you're so angry, you just want to kick the other person right where you know it'll hurt the most. I don't think you deserve any blame at all.'

'Well, Steven does . . . You know what it reminded me of? Ian. The way he got up and walked out, that was exactly how it was the last time I ever saw Ian. He stood up and left without saying anything, not looking at me. *He* blamed me, and he was right. They both are.'

Rosalind sighed. 'Have you seen Steven since? Spoken to him?'

'No. He hasn't come out of the barn. I left him some food outside the door yesterday, but when I took some breakfast out for him this morning, he hadn't touched it. I know he's in there, because I saw the light on last night. I can't bring myself to go and talk to him.'

'Give him a few days. If he really cares about you, he'll come round.'

'If, Ros, *if*. I'm not so sure. I wish I'd never told him.'

'Carole, it was bound to come out sooner or later. If he really thinks any the less of you afterwards, it's no fault of yours. It only reflects on him.'

'No it *doesn't*!' Carole shouted. The people at the next table looked up from their meal and stared at her. She reddened and continued in a hoarse whisper: 'It doesn't, because I *am* to blame. If I'd been a true friend to Beverley, I'd have met her at the cinema that night, and she'd still be alive.'

'But how were you to know? Something might still have happened to her.' Rosalind glanced at Carole, then went back to piling slivers of Stilton on her bread roll. 'Anyway, I've got my doubts about this *true friend* stuff. You've told me about Beverley, and I don't want to seem nasty, but the way you tell it, she does sound a bit too good to be true.'

'What d'you mean?'

'Well, I'm always suspicious of these people who are nicely-nice. People who come across so saintly they sound as though they piss rosewater. I mean, I'm not doubting your ability to judge character, but . . . well, yes, I suppose I am doubting it . . .'

Carole frowned at her. 'What are you suggesting? That it was *her* fault she got killed?'

'Of course not. Don't be ridiculous. What I'm saying—' Rosalind put down her knife and pushed her plate to one side, as though she needed physical space to expand her argument into. 'What I'm saying is this: Think about things logically for a moment. There's no way on earth you could have known what would happen to Beverley that night, is there?'

'But—'

'Just answer yes or no.'

'Well, no . . .'

'Good. That's a start. Given that you couldn't have known, you can't be held responsible for her death. *You* didn't kill her, and you didn't know she was *going* to be killed. Yes?'

'Right.'

'So, that eliminates her death or any *rational* notion of your responsibility for it from the picture. Right?'

'If you say so.'

'I do say so, cause it's true. So, now we've eliminated that, what we're left with is the idea that you betrayed her friendship by choosing to go to Vienna with Ian when you'd already arranged to meet her at the cinema. Her death is something you've used to punish yourself for *that*. Now, can you remember *why* you arranged to go out with her that evening?'

'Of course. You know the story well enough by now. It was to make up for the way I'd behaved over her and Ian. I was horrible to her.'

'You were horrible to her. You know, I've always felt uncomfortable with your description of that incident. There's something about it that doesn't ring true.'

'What d'you mean?'

261

Rosalind paused and put her fingers together, resting her chin on them. 'You arrived home early, didn't you?'

'Yes.'

'Tell me, how long did you spend in nursing altogether?'

Carole shrugged. 'About five years if you include being a student.'

'And in those five years, how often did you finish your shift *late*?'

'Late? I don't know. Maybe a couple of days a week. Maybe three or four days if you include being a few minutes late. Sometimes it could be up to an hour or more if it was a really heavy day. Why?'

'And how often did you finish early?'

'You're starting to sound like a barrister,' said Carole, smiling nervously. 'Okay ... well, there was that time ... and, er, another time when I was coming down with something, and, er, yes, once when I was moving into the flat.'

Rosalind nodded. 'Three times in five years. And yet Ian was there, supposedly waiting for you, even though he would have been sure you wouldn't be home for at least another half-hour. Quite likely longer.'

Carole shook her head uncomprehendingly. 'He had concert tickets for that night. He wanted to be sure of catching me.'

'He wanted to be sure of catching you. Were you in the habit of dashing straight out after you got home?'

'Not really.'

'Not really?'

'Well, no. I usually went and laid down for half an hour, then had a shower.'

Rosalind nodded. 'Hmm ... Did you ever *see* these concert tickets?'

'No. Well, I wouldn't, would I – I stormed out.'

Rosalind patted the table with her hand to emphasise

her point: 'Exactly. You thought there was something going on.'

'Ros, I wasn't thinking straight. I was crazy with jealousy. Emotions like that aren't rational.'

'No,' Rosalind conceded. 'But your reaction might have been triggered by something subliminal in the atmosphere.'

'Something *subliminal*? Christ, Ros, it'd have to be subliminal – it's not as if I caught them in bed together! Ian was reading the paper and Beverley was in the kitchen. It was all totally innocent.'

'At that moment, perhaps, but let's put the facts together. You come home early to find Ian already there, even though he knows you shouldn't be home for at least half an hour. It also happens to be a day when Beverley is at home because she's on nights. Then let's add the final fact: It all looked perfectly innocent when you walked in, but *how long had Ian already been there*? You don't know, do you? There's no way you could know. Maybe it didn't even occur to you. When you calmed down, you just assumed that he'd only arrived shortly before you.'

Carole was staring at her, her mouth opening and closing but no sound coming out. After several attempts, she managed to splutter, 'But . . . but—'

'Let me ask you one last thing,' Rosalind interrupted. 'Beverley was on the night-shift. At that time of day, what would she normally have been doing?'

'I don't know. Just getting up, I suppose. Having breakfast.'

'Okay, correct me if I'm wrong, but on this occasion she was up and fully dressed. Did she *look* as though she'd only just got up?'

'I can't remember . . . No, I suppose not.'

Rosalind sat back in her seat. 'She'd been up for hours, hadn't she. So, tell me: What would a busy casualty nurse with one hard night behind her and another one ahead of her be doing up and about when she could be getting valuable sleep?'

Carole shook her head. 'I don't know, it doesn't make any sense! You're just confusing me. They *can't* have been doing anything. I'd have known.'

'You *did* know, or you suspected. Carole, you're always putting people on pedestals and yourself in a pit. Face it: Beverley *wasn't* an angel; she was just a human like the rest of us. You didn't betray her any more than she betrayed you.'

Carole drove home in a daze. Her thoughts were tumbling like animals fighting in a sack; she could sense the turmoil, but she felt divorced from it, unguided, unable to know how to reach a conclusion, much less know what conclusion to reach. By the time she alighted from the train at Keighley and got into her car, her mind was so numb and fogged that she couldn't think about what Ros had said to her. It didn't make sense: she *had* to be guilty, otherwise what had she been doing for the past four years? Nothing made sense; there were no certainties to grasp hold of any more. However painful it was, her knowledge of her responsibility for Beverley's murder had at least been a grim lodestar pointing pitilessly at her weakness, her selfishness and her treachery. It at least let her know how things stood in the ineluctable pattern of betrayal, culpability and remorse. And Steven had been meant to be part of that pattern; the mechanism by which she would achieve absolution. But the mechanism had simply and inexplicably fallen to pieces in front of her eyes. He had been meant to forgive her: she would tell him her terrible secret, and he would lift the mantle of guilt from her shoulders and it would crumble to dust in his fingers. He would enfold her in his arms, and . . .

and she had to wipe away the blue of tears which were obscuring her view of the road . . . Perhaps she had tried too soon; should she have waited until he was fully cured? . . . Had she not earned her redemption yet?

She was so confused and bewildered that she had arrived home and parked the car in the byre before realising that she had forgotten to tell Ros about her dream. Now, that was something she *was* certain about, she thought as she pushed the byre doors closed. Clear though the vision of Steven's face had been, she was convinced now that it had been a trick of the imagination. It was all perfectly rational (she hadn't studied dream analysis for nothing), who should she see in a dreamlike evocation of Beverley's funeral but Steven – the person who had become more important than anyone else in her life, the person who now knew her deepest secret before he was ready, and judged her evil for it.

The barn door was closed tight. Carole walked across the yard and knocked hesitantly on the wood. 'Steven?' she called nervously. There was no response, so she opened the door a few inches and peeped inside. It was dark, and there was no sign of him. She opened the door wide and walked in. His bed had been neatly remade, and the storm lantern was back on the crate at its foot. This was how he measured her: she had sunk lower than the locusts in his world-view. He would rather endure the creeping horror he felt near them than be under the same roof as her.

There was a squeal of hinges behind her, and she flinched and spun round. Steven was standing in the doorway.

'I . . .' she stammered. 'I was just . . . Have you been out?'

'Just over there,' he said. 'In the field. I heard the car.'

'Oh . . . I've been . . .'

He walked in, stepping past her and avoiding her eyes. He took an Ordnance Survey map out of his pocket and dropped it onto the table, then sat down on the edge of his bed.

'Carole, I've—'

'Steven—'

They both halted awkwardly. Carole indicated that he should speak first.

'I've been thinking,' he said, still not looking at her. 'I think it's time I moved on.'

She was aghast. *'Move on?'*

'It's for the best. Things aren't working out.'

This remark revealed a capacity for understatement that was quite giddying. *'Not working out?'* she repeated in disbelief. 'Why don't you just come out and say it? You—'

'Carole, listen. Ever since I got here, all I've done is cause trouble. Look at what I've done to you and Ros. You're at each other's throats.'

'No,' she said. 'You don't understand. It's all okay with Ros now. We're friends again.'

'And why?' he insisted. 'Because you were upset by me. As long as I stay here, I'll just cause—'

'You bastard,' she breathed, her bewilderment and anxiety finally turning to anger. 'You lousy, cowardly *bastard*!' She lashed out and struck him across the face.

'Ca—!'

'You coward!' she shouted, lashing wildly at him while he tried feebly to resist. 'Bastard – bloody – coward! You can't even tell me the truth – Go on, tell me – tell me the real reason! At least allow me that. You just can't stand the sight of me!' Steven grasped her wrists, but she continued struggling and swearing at him through furious tears. Suddenly, she broke free and lunged at him. He was too slow to avoid her, and he

braced himself for the attack, but instead of the anticipated blow, she hurled her arms around his neck.
'*Please*,' she sobbed, clinging desperately to him. 'Please
– don't – go . . .'

'Carole, I have to.'

'*Please!* I can't stand you hating me.'

'I don't hate you.'

'You think I killed her. You think I'm evil!'

'Carole . . .' He disentangled himself from her arms
and held her away from him. 'I don't think you . . . I
don't think you've done anything wrong.'

She stared at him with red, puffy eyes. 'Then *why*?'
she pleaded.

He let go of her arms and stared silently at his hands,
at the floor, at his feet. Carole waited for a reply, but
none came. At last, when she could stand the tension no
longer, she turned and fled, slamming the heavy door
behind her with such violence that he could feel it
resonate through the floor beneath his feet. A few seconds later, the house door slammed too, then there was
silence.

Yet another sleepless night, yet another tense, sweating
dance with the duvet, over and over, back and forth
across the hot pillows. Several times, she got out of bed
and went to the window. He hadn't left yet; all that
night, the chink of light leaked from the barn doors.
What was he waiting for? Why couldn't he just leave, if
he hated her so much?

The truth took some time to come to her . . . At
around five o'clock in the morning, in a delirium, her
body weak for want of sleep and her head aching, she
was visited by a revelation. Perhaps not quite a revelation, but certainly a sudden, bright spear of insight. It
had just been a throwaway remark, something Ros had
said when they were driving back to Oakworth that

afternoon. In a tone of mock despair, she had said: 'How on death did two such messed-up people manage to get together?' Carole had barely registered the remark at the time, but now it leapt back into her brain with all the plangent clarity of a cymbal crash. She repeated it to herself under her breath, staring sightlessly with sore eyes at the lightening curtains, her heart suddenly thumping, her skin going cold.

Exchange

Michael walked out of the men's toilet and shower room on C-deck and stood at the foot of the stairs for a few moments, holding on to the banister rail and bracing his legs against the ship's yawing roll and pitch. He was still having a little difficulty seeing through his new glasses, and his moustache had been tickling his nostrils infuriatingly for the past eight hours. When he had got his bearings, he climbed up the stairs to B-deck. As he climbed, the two bulging plastic carrier bags swung like pendulums with the ship's motion, bumping heavily against his leg and clunking on the metal railing.

He had picked the ideal night for his crossing: high winds lashed and furrowed the sea, flinging curling, spraying waves against the ferry's diving, rising prow as it surged on across the Channel. He liked this sort of sea, and he inhaled deeply as he opened the glazed door on to the darkened deck and stepped out into the wind-rushed flying spray. He walked unsteadily along the deck, heading aft, past the dimmed, fogged oblong windows of the bar, weaving as the shifting deck tried to pitch him against the rust-bubbling painted steel of the lifeboat davits.

At last, as he passed the third lifeboat, he saw Alan (Michael found it helpful to think of him as Alan) waiting for him as appointed, standing huddled in the corner between the side rail and the steps leading up to the sun deck. Michael hesitated for a moment, then stepped forward into the well of spray-sparkled floodlight.

'Cheer up, son,' said Michael. 'It might never happen.'

The boy looked up at him, his expression of despondency slowly metamorphosing into irritation. Michael had spotted him from the far side of the booking hall; a spindly youth – probably about sixteen or seventeen by the look of him – sitting on the floor in the corner by the Europcar desk, a scruffy yellow canvas kit-bag under his knees. He was gazing miserably through owlish glasses at a family buying paper cups of Coke from a kiosk opposite. Now, as he looked up, Michael could see that his narrow, pale face was blotched and streaked and his eyes were puffed, as though he had been crying. 'It already fuckin as appened,' he said sullenly.

Michael smiled in sympathy. *Worth a try*, he thought, crouching down on his haunches. 'What has?' he asked.

The boy looked down at the floor. 'Lost my fuckin wallet, ant I,' he muttered. He raked his bony fingers through his spiked, rain-matted blond hair. 'Dunno what I'm gonna do now. Can't go nor get ome nor nuffin.'

'Where are you going?'

'France.'

Michael smiled. 'Yes, I guessed that,' he said. 'But which port?'

The boy frowned. 'Cairn or Corn or somefin, they said.'

'You mean Caen,' said Michael. 'Who said?'

'Me mates. I was meant ter meet em in . . . Caen, d'yer say? Yeah, Caen.'

'What happened to your wallet?'

'Dunno.' His eyes narrowed, and he said, 'I reckon it was that bastard trucker nicked it . . . Fuckin arseole . . . Ticket, dosh, everyfin's gone.'

'So you're all on your own, then?'

The boy nodded, then looked suspiciously at Michael. 'What's it ter you, anyway?' he demanded. 'Oo are you?'

Michael beamed at him and patted him on the shoulder. 'Just call me Santa Claus, son,' he said. 'I think this could be your lucky night.' He rooted around in his trouser pocket and pulled out a handful of loose change. 'Go and get us a couple of coffees,' he said, holding out two pound coins and nodding towards the kiosk. 'And we'll talk about it.'

The boy glanced at the money, but didn't take it. 'You an arse-bandit or somefin?' he asked, glaring at Michael. 'I ain't fer sale, mate, so fuck off.'

He started to get up, but Michael restrained him with a firm hand on his arm. 'No, I'm not after your arse, son, I'm—'

'An don't call me son, I ain't yer fuckin son,' the boy snarled, wrenching his arm free.

'Look,' Michael hissed, trying to regain control of the situation, 'I'm not a queer, and I'm not after anything. I just thought I could help you out of your problem, and you'd be doing me a favour as well . . . What d'you say?' The boy just glowered silently at him. 'Just go and get those coffees, okay? I take it white, one sugar.'

The boy hesitated, then took the coins grudgingly. He hitched his kit-bag over one shoulder and walked over to the kiosk. He returned a few minutes later with two polystyrene cups.

'There y'are,' he said, handing one to Michael and quietly pocketing the change.

Michael blew gently on the steaming, muddy liquid and sipped it while the boy sat down again on the floor, keeping as far away from Michael as he could without actually breaking the thread they had established between them by the transaction. 'So, what d'yer want?'

he asked, with affected indifference.

Michael peered at him for a few moments, weighing up the situation and scrutinising it for any flaws which might be revealed as plan unfolded into practice. Satisfied, he reached into the pocket of his rucksack and drew out two glossy paper envelopes. 'This is my ticket for the eleven thirty sailing,' he said, peeling back the flap of one envelope and glancing at the name: M. SPRING. 'And this,' he added, holding up the other, 'is yours, if you want it.'

Looking Michael steadily in the eyes, the boy leaned forward and took the ticket. 'Who's A. Gorvin?' he asked, reading the name inside.

Michael sighed. 'My mate Alan,' he said. 'He didn't show up. We were supposed to be doing this building job – holiday home renovation in Normandy – but his missus has come down hard on him. You know what women can be like. I was meant to meet him here, and I'd bought him a ticket and everything . . . I was just on my way to get my money back when I clocked you. Hello, I thought, there's always someone who's got worse problems than your own.'

The boy fingered the shiny ticket noncommittally. Michael could see that he was strongly tempted to accept it, but a residual suspicion still coloured his expression. 'But why d'yer wanna give it me?' he asked. 'What's in it fer you?'

Michael shrugged. 'The pleasure of doing a good turn?' he suggested. The boy looked even more suspicious, so he went on: 'Look, if I go and cancel it now, they'll take off a ten-quid administration fee, but if you use the ticket and give back the docket later, like when we're on board, I can claim it back from my gaffer later. I'll say Alan did a runner when we got to France. Then everyone's happy.'

'Except your gaffer,' said the boy, looking more

relaxed and even smiling slightly. 'What if he don't pay yer?'

'Oh, he will.'

The boy grinned. 'What a sucker. All right then, mate, I'll take it.'

'Right,' said Michael. 'I'm off. Meet me . . . er, let's see . . . I've got to change some money first, then get my duty-frees before the queues start. Then I might as well get some kip. Let's say we meet up just before Caen . . . say five a.m. on the port side near the stern. Got that?'

The boy frowned, and repeated, 'Five a.m., port side, er . . .'

'Near the stern.'

'Got it. That's the back end, innit?'

'That's right.'

'An the port side's the left, yeah?'

'Yes. See you later.' He stood up, then hesitated. 'Oh yes, I nearly forgot. When they give you your boarding card, put Alan's name and this address on it, okay?' He fished out a slip of paper and handed it to him.

After they had parted, Michael trailed the boy discreetly to ensure that he boarded. He followed him from the booking hall to the toilets, then to a café where he bought a Mars bar with the change from their coffee, then to the queue for boarding. Michael joined the queue about twenty or thirty places back from him, and collected a boarding card from the uniformed attendant as he entered the covered gangway. He held the narrow slip of thin card daintily by the edges as though it were a strip of photographic negatives, peering at it with a puzzled expression.

'Scuse me,' he said, leaning forward and addressing a couple of young female backpackers who were standing just in front of him. He showed them the card. 'What's this for?'

273

They glanced at each other. 'It's a boarding pass,' said the one standing nearest to him. She had dark hair which was cut short like a boy – fuzzy on top – and a stud in her nose. (*Dyke*, he thought.) He frowned uncomprehendingly at her, so she added, 'It's so they know who's on board if we sink – you know, after Zeebrugge.'

'Oh, I see,' he said dully, frowning at the card with deepening perplexity.

The two women looked at each other, then the second one explained, 'You write your name and address on it . . . There –' she pointed '– where it says "Name and Address".'

'Oh,' he murmured. Out of the corner of his eye, he saw them whisper to each other. 'Er,' he began, 'er, I couldn't trouble you to do it for me . . .'

The lesbian looked at him doubtfully, but the other, who was blonde and attractive, took it from him with an understanding smile. 'What's your name?' she asked.

'Michael Spring,' he said. 'I never had much of an education, you see,' he said sheepishly to the lesbian while the blonde wrote his name on the card. She nodded sympathetically, her gold nose stud glinting in the overhead strip light.

'Address?' asked the blonde.

Michael shifted uncomfortably and looked down at the floor of the tunnel. 'Er, no fixed abode, really,' he said. She looked sadly at him. 'Er, you could put the Sally Army Hostel, Battersea. That was sort of my last residence.' She finished filling in the card and handed it back to him. 'Thanks,' he said, taking it by the edges again without looking at it.

The women smiled and turned away, falling into muted conversation with each other. *What a palaver*, he thought. Still, it was worth it for its own sake; the blonde one was pretty nice-looking and had a good meaty arse – he gazed appreciatively beneath the over-hanging shelf of her rucksack at the twin swells of her buttocks within their tight denim carapace, and fol-lowed the bisecting crease down to where it curved suddenly under between her solid-looking thighs. The dyke might be quite a peach as well, he judged, if she grew her hair properly and got rid of that stud ... He deliberately suspended this train of thought. Should Michael really think like this? Maybe it would be best not to start developing character traits – especially ones like this – without seriously weighing them up first. On the other hand, a shade of lascivious misogyny seemed appropriate somehow.

At the top of the tunnel, he handed his filled-in card to a second attendant, and stepped through the door into the body of the ferry. His first stop was at the bureau de change, where he exchanged two hundred pounds for francs. Then he headed for the duty-free shop, where the chromed racks of bottles were already rattling as the deep harbour swell bobbed the ship up and down. The shop was crowded with a milling mass of early customers. He spent the last of his sterling on a slab of Guinness and a half-bottle of Bells, then, with the heavy slab balanced on his shoulder, he went off in search of a quiet corner.

Kevin stood by the rail smoking a cigarette he had scavenged from a drunk in the bar and watching the black water sweep by far below. He was wondering what he would do for cash when he got to the other side. Even if he met up with Dave and Wayne – and he was starting to have anxious doubts about this – it might take him a while to get there. They had given him an address in Caen where they said he could find them, but he had got talking to a couple of bikers in the bar who said the ferry actually docked at a place called

Weestham or something, which was miles from Caen. He asked if he could hitch with them, but they said they were overloaded already with all their camping gear.

He was starving, too: the last thing he had eaten had been the Mars bar in the booking hall at Portsmouth. His stomach and throat were tight with nauseous hunger, and although he was not actually seasick, the ferry's violent heaving intensified the dizzying discomfort. He had tried begging money from other passengers, but had had to stop when one of them complained to a steward, who gave him a severe warning.

He smoked the cigarette right down, until the edge of the speckled yellow filter crinkled and singed, then he flicked the stub over the side. The gale blew it back against the dark, teetering hull, where it shattered in a cloud of dull red sparks before spinning down into the swelling, troughing wash of foam.

He turned around just in time to see the bloke who had given him the ticket walking unsteadily towards him along the deck. 'About bleedin time,' Kevin said irritably, his words slurred by the cold numbness in his chin and lips. 'I'm fuckin freezin me bollocks off.'

Michael smiled. 'Sorry. Got that docket?' he asked, clinging onto the rail and putting his free hand in his coat pocket.

'Yeah. Ang on a minute.' He turned and bent over to open his kit-bag, where he had secreted the remaining half of the ticket.

Michael's hand emerged from his pocket and his body twisted, arm raised. Something black flailed downwards. The dull, heavy crunch as it connected was lost amidst the howling wind.

Michael worked quickly. Once he had hauled the nameless boy's limp, lightweight, feebly breathing body into the shadows beside the nearby lifeboat locker, it only took a few moments to complete what he had to

276

do. Putting on a pair of gloves, he unzipped the boy's thin bomber jacket and tucked the tail of his red football shirt deep inside the waistband of his jeans, tightening the belt hard. Then he opened the first carrier bag. He took out six unopened cans of Guinness and stuffed them, one by one, down the shirt's vee-neck, arranging them under the fabric around the boy's waist. When they were in position and he was sure they were secure, he zipped the jacket up again and placed one more heavy can in each of its deep pockets. He removed the ticket docket from the kit-bag, slipped the last two full cans under the flap and closed it. Ten cans in all – it should be just about enough. Now, all that remained in the first carrier bag were two empty cans and the half-bottle of whisky. He laid the cans on the deck, opened the whisky bottle and laid it beside them, shifting position to avoid the sharp-smelling liquid as it glugged from the neck and formed an erratically spreading puddle on the pitching deck. The second carrier bag was fat with a rolled-up jumper, socks and underpants, to which he added his wallet, the docket and a passport, leaving the bag propped in the corner against the bulkhead. He hesitated, then took the docket out again. He wiped it thoroughly on his trouser leg, then took off a glove and pinched the glossy paper several times with his bare fingers. Satisfied, he put it back in the carrier bag.

The last task was harder. After one final check to make sure it contained nothing to identify him (there was only a passport, which Michael pocketed), he secured the boy's kit-bag to his shoulders, then – with a quick glance along the desk – lifted him up by one hand, pushed his arm between his thighs and hefted him awkwardly on to his shoulder. Teetering, top-heavy, he staggered across the tipping deck, slammed grunting into the rail and toppled the limp weight over the side.

He saw the lumpily misshapen body fall, arcing outwards with flailing, windmilling limbs. A sudden gust caught it and swung it back. It hit the towering hull with a loud thump, careened off and slithered into the boiling foam with a violent splash that was instantly swallowed by the ferry's scything wash as the body and kit-bag vanished beneath the froth-webbed black surface.

As he turned, Michael's toe bumped against something. He glanced down and picked it up; it was the thick woollen sock containing the last full can of Guinness, now dented and seeping. He flung it out into the hollow, wind-rushing night, then walked slowly along the deck to the nearest lifebelt stand.

Detective Sergeant Comber paced quickly along the corridor. At the end, he turned right and flung open the door to the Incident Room. It was buzzing with activity: three uniformed constables were unloading boxes and files from a trolley onto the vast central table, where six CID officers were unpacking them and laying out the contents in systematic order. Another officer was stapling photographs to a large pinboard on the wall. DI Spearman was supervising the unpacking. He looked up as Comber crashed in through the door.

'Any luck?' he asked.

Comber pulled a disgusted face. 'You must be joking. Talk about Mickey fucking Mouse. Any news on who we've got?'

Spearman restrained a smirk. 'Detective Chief Superintendent Kenneth Hazlitt, no less,' he said.

Comber glanced at the constables and lowered his voice: 'Shit! I thought you said we'd get Frazer.'

'We would have, but he's been called up to Newcastle

on the Gordon Barrow case.'

'But *Hazlitt* . . .'

'We didn't have any choice, Graham. The Super requested Lang as a second choice, but what could he do? It was a rush job.'

'But—'

'Look, don't give me any grief over this. We've got enough on our fucking plates as it is.'

The door opened again and a tall, cadaverous man walked in. He had dark, sunken eyes and heavy jowls, and an air of gravitas which inspired an ill-founded respect amongst those who didn't know him or his reputation. It was said about him in CID that his resemblance to a bloodhound was about as close as he came to being a detective.

'Afternoon, sir,' said Spearman. 'I don't believe you've met DS Comber. He's been on the Invisible Man case since the start; done most of the leg work on it, in fact.'

Superintendent Hazlitt smiled shrewdly at Comber and peered at his face as though taking aim at it. 'Graham,' he said. 'Am I right?'

'Yes, sir.'

'Thought so,' said Hazlitt smugly. 'Good start; names and faces, gentlemen, names and faces. Bedrock of good detection.'

Comber and Spearman glanced at each other. 'Yes, sir,' said Spearman, scowling forbiddingly at Comber while Hazlitt was looking the other way. 'Perhaps we could make a start over here, sir. I'll fill you in on the basics, and then we can work from there.'

Spearman led Hazlitt to the far end of the room, where a flip-chart had been set up. On the top page, a chronological summary had been set out. 'Yesterday evening; the twenty-seventh,' Spearman began, paraphrasing from the chart. 'Ten fifty-three p.m: DS

Comber and myself call at Chief Inspector Gorvin's flat. No response, so entry is forced. Search conducted. Evidence recovered which is filed in ... er, Box 421A ... Eleven forty-eight p.m: Alert issued to all ports and airports ... Twelve fifty-one a.m: An A. Gorvin found to have set sail on the cross-channel ferry *Esprit de Cotentin*, eighteen minutes before issue of alert.'

'Near miss,' sighed Hazlitt.

'Exactly, sir. Twelve fifty-five a.m: French police notified at Ou ... Oost ...'

'Ouistreham,' said Hazlitt.

'Ouistreham. Meanwhile, alert also passed to Captain of *Esprit de Cotentin*, along with warning to ferry company to preserve all boarding passes, passenger list and used tickets. Description and mugshot faxed to French police.'

Hazlitt frowned. 'You're not going to tell me they missed him?'

'Not exactly ... Five thirteen a.m: Ferry's Man Overboard alarm sounds. Captain orders lifeboat lowered and commences circling pattern until arrival of French Coastguard launch at five forty-one a.m., then continues on course for port ... six thirty a.m: Ferry docks at Ouistreham. French police conduct stop-searches and passport checks on all vehicles and foot-passengers disembarking. No result. Only listed passengers unaccounted for are a couple called Smith, a party of schoolchildren, and one *Alan Gorvin* ... Seven forty a.m: Ferry cleared and searched. Ship's steward finds *this* behind a lifeboat locker on deck.' Spearman led the Superintendent over to the table and opened a large box which was overflowing with plastic evidence bags. 'This lot was flown in this morning. One carrier bag containing items of clothing – enough for one complete change – one ticket docket and one passport, both in the name of Alan Gorvin. Also, several cans of

Guinness and one half-bottle of whisky, all empty, all found alongside the carrier bag. The Captain also informs us that the lifebelt station from which the alarm was raised was close to where these items were found.'

'So,' said Hazlitt, picking up the polythene-bound whisky bottle and peering with distaste at its label. 'Seems pretty simple to me. Gorvin, consumed by remorse, drinks himself into a stupor and commits suicide.'

'Or it could have been an accident,' suggested Spearman. 'The sea was very rough. He could've been drunk and fallen over the side.'

Sergeant Comber, who was standing behind them, cleared his throat. 'There's only one problem, though, sir. I've been on to the French Coastguard, and there's still no sign of a body.'

Hazlitt looked at Spearman. 'Would we necessarily expect one this soon?'

'Difficult to say, sir. Depends on what he was wearing, whether he sunk or floated, what the tides and currents were doing, etcetera etcetera . . .' He waved a hand vaguely as if to suggest limitless possibilities.

'It's possible he faked it, sir,' said Comber.

'Faked it?' said Hazlitt. 'A man in the state of mind he must have been in? I doubt it, Sergeant.' He folded his arms and surveyed the forlorn array of bagged items on the table. 'What a legacy, eh. I worked with Alan once. Did you know that? Hmm. He was a DS when I was DCI over at Poole Street. Good thief-taker, one of the best. Never quite the same after that secondment to Special Branch, though. Bit strange, bit of a mystery man. Still, I'd never have believed he could have . . . well, done what he did. Not if I hadn't seen the evidence with my own eyes . . .' He looked at his watch. 'Listen, I've really got to dash, gentlemen. Press conference

281

about the hunt, you know. Now, which one of you wants to come and be my prompt?'

'Come on in,' said Spearman. 'Close the door and sit down.'

Comber sat in front of the desk and tossed a thick manilla folder onto it. 'It's all in there,' he said.

'What have you got?' Spearman opened the folder and skimmed through the papers inside.

'Not a lot. Statement from the Captain giving further details about the emergency procedures he took. Interesting point: They were unable to find out who raised the alarm. They put out an announcement over the tannoy system for the person to come forward, but nobody did. Interesting, that . . . There's also a statement from a Mrs Dawson. She was in her cabin at the time and claims to have heard a loud thumping noise followed by something falling past her porthole shortly before the alarm was raised.'

Spearman nodded. 'So he did go over.'

Comber pursed his lips. 'Well, someone did. Or something.'

Spearman sat back and sighed. 'You're still sticking by his theory that he faked it, then? Got any evidence?'

'Well, I had the items found on the deck dusted.'

'And?'

'Gorvin's prints were all over them. *But –*' he leaned forward excitedly '– they *weren't on his boarding card*.'

Spearman looked blank. 'Is that it? Shit, Graham, I've been on holiday to France. Those things are handled by loads of people. The bloke who gives it to you, the bloke who takes it off you, fuck knows who else besides. His prints could've been obliterated.'

'Yeah, maybe, but we could get these people's prints and eliminate them. Find out if there's any prints left not accounted for.'

Spearman shook his head firmly. 'It's too thin, Graham. Face it – Gorvin's dead, and good riddance.'

'I'll believe it when I see his corpse. *Some*one's body's gonna wash up sooner or later, and I bet you it won't be his.'

Spearman sighed. 'I'm warning you, Graham – just leave it.'

Comber glowered at him. 'This is Hazlitt, isn't it?'

'Listen, I've known you a long time, so I'll spare you the bullshit. Hazlitt wants a quick result on this one, and he's not the only one. It's not just about the opportunity to close the Invisible Man case, it's also a potential embarrassment for the whole Force. To tell you the truth, Hazlitt's pleased as punch. Saves him a lot of time, and saves everyone a very humiliating trial. This way, it's all over in a few days, and next week the press can get back to which MP's shafting whose secretary.'

'So we let this sick fucker escape just to save a few brain-dead senior officers a bit of embarrassment.'

'If there's one thing he was, he wasn't a fucker,' grinned Spearman. '. . . Sorry. Bit sick.'

'Don't piss me about, sir. This is a fucking cover-up.'

'No, Graham, it isn't.' Spearman stood up and walked around the desk. 'Look, be realistic,' he said, sitting on the edge of the desk. 'Gorvin's gone, and every scrap of evidence we've got says he's dead. Everyone's happy. What I'm saying is we're stretched enough without wasting time and resources chasing ghosts. The case is *closed*. Got that?'

Comber glared up at him, but nodded reluctantly. 'If you say so, sir.'

'Good. Now, there's plenty more villains out there who could benefit from your attentions. I suggest you get out after them.'

15

J udy Krepps finished checking the last page of the
annual Acquisitions (Periodicals) printout and looked
up over the top of the Information counter. Across the
room, a woman was loitering between the photocopier
and the double door which led to the Lending Library. It
was the third time Judy had looked up in the last five
minutes, and each time the woman had still been there,
looking abstractedly at the posters pinned to the notice
board, advertising local drama groups, evening classes,
museums in Bradford and Leeds, the Yorkshire Sculpture Park, lunchtime concerts and a variety of self-help
and therapy groups. Judy watched her with interest.
The notice board was a common place for people to
stand and wait for spouses, children, parents or whoever to finish browsing or checking out their books, as
well as for people just keeping out of the rain, so there
were usually at least one or two people hanging around
there at most times of the day. This particular woman,
though, had tugged at Judy's curiosity: there was nothing unusual in her appearance – early middle age, dark
hair cut in a longish bob, utilitarian dress, a bulky
shoulder-bag and a rolled-up umbrella twitching restlessly from hand to hand – but her manner was oddly
agitated, almost furtive. Every so often, she darted
nervous little glances around the room, at people passing by, at the shelves of dictionaries and directories, and
at Judy herself. Her face wore a taut, nauseated expression that hinted at depression or despair, and a number
of speculative scenarios were flickering across Judy's
mind (battered wife, single mother at the end of her

tether, victim of a sexual assault perhaps) when their eyes met. Suddenly, the woman was clinched into making a decision to either approach the counter or turn and flee. She hesitated for a moment, then walked towards the counter.

Judy stood up, composing her features into a sympathetic half-smile, and quickly rehearsed the directions to the Women's Crisis Centre on the third floor. 'Can I help you?' she asked.

The woman hefted the strap of her bag into a more comfortable position, giving Judy the fleeting impression that she was cranking her voice out manually. 'Do you have newspapers here?' she asked.

Her interpretations confounded, Judy was nonplussed for a moment, and had to deliberately pull back the puzzled expression she felt pinching her face and stop herself from dumbly repeating the request as if she had been asked if they sold fresh maggots. 'Yes,' she said, clearing her throat and leaning forward to point along the aisle between the bookstacks. 'Down there at the end on the right. Newspapers and magazines.'

'Thank you,' the woman murmured vaguely.

Judy watched her go, then sat down again and went back to her files and forms. A few minutes later, she sensed a shadow hovering above her, and looked up. The woman was back.

'Excuse me,' she said. 'Sorry. I meant old newspapers. Do you keep old ones?'

Judy smiled. 'Oh, I see. It depends how old you mean. We've got *The Times* and the *Yorkshire Post* on microfilm. What sort of thing were you after?'

The woman frowned and pursed her lips. '*The Times* would probably do. About three or four years ago?'

'That's no problem. Have you ever used a microfilm reader?' The woman looked blank. 'I'll show you,' said Judy, standing up and coming round from behind her desk. She led the woman around the corner into the main part of the library and along to the end, where there was a glass-partitioned room with microfiche- and microfilm-reading machines on tables around the walls. She showed her where the newspaper reels were shelved and how to load them on to the reader, then left her to it and went back to her desk.

It was a quiet day, and Judy worked without interruption for nearly an hour. She was looking at her watch (only fifteen minutes to lunch) when the same woman – looking, if possible, even more agitated than before – came around the corner. Her face was white and her eyes were wild. Without even glancing at Judy, she hurried across the foyer, slammed out through the main door and was gone, leaving the door swinging violently on its springs behind her.

Judy stared at the door for a few moments, then made a jocularly grimacing face to herself and the empty room, and went back to her work.

It was not until later that afternoon, after she returned from her lunch break, that Judy happened to be passing the micro-reading room and found that the woman had left her umbrella lying on the floor under the chair. She had also left the reader switched on, its cooling fan whirring noisily in the empty room. On the table beside the machine lay several reels of film, some in their brown cardboard boxes, a few others scattered about and beginning to unroll. One was still loaded on the spindle, and the last page the woman had been looking at was still illuminating the large, grainy plastic screen. Intrigued, Judy pulled up the chair and sat down. The focus had been zoomed in on one quarter of a double-page spread containing bits of three different stories; a piece continued from the front page about some murder investigation in London, a headlining item about local protests against plans for a wind farm somewhere in

North Yorkshire, and the top half of an article about A-Level standards. She glanced at the nearest empty box: it was labelled 'TIMES: JAN–MAR 94'. A bit late to be getting so upset about the wind farm, she thought. Turning the handle, she reeled back to the front page to look at the rest of the murder story. She found it at the head of the page, under the headline she now remembered having read at the time: 'Invisible Man: Murder-Hunt Detective was Killer,' it said. She read the article with a mixture of reminiscent interest and bewilderment before packing away the reels of film and switching off the machine. Then she gathered up the umbrella and took it up to Lost Property.

Carole had walked the whole length of the main shopping street and found herself in the middle of the market square before even noticing that it was raining. It was splattering down, drumming on the tarpaulin canopies of the stalls, running in rivulets from their edges and splashing onto the cobbles. Her coat was dark with water over the shoulders, and her fringe was plastered to her forehead in a row of irregular, dripping kiss-curls, but it barely registered on her numbed senses. She felt as though she were under great, dark depths of water, trudging with leaden feet, all the babble and roar of sound surrounding her seeming muffled and distant; disconnected; her confused mind trailing behind her body like an anguished child.

Suddenly, she felt an overwhelming desire to sit down – anywhere; even on the wet, glistening marble steps of the war memorial, or right where she was now, on the grimed edge of the kerb. Out of the haze around her, the signboard of the Market Tea Rooms shivered unsteadily into focus. She gazed at it for a moment, then headed towards it, walking slowly and with unstable deliberation on the uneven cobbles.

Inside, in the humid, tinkling, cup-clattering atmosphere, her giddiness redoubled. Fortunately, there was a small table vacant right beside the door, and she sat down quickly at it, just as she felt her knees begin to buckle. A spindly teenage waitress in a short black skirt and a white pinafore materialised in front of her, took her mumbled order and vanished. Carole stared dismally at the remains of the previous occupants' snacks: the crumbled corner of a whipped-cream scone, a red skidmark of jam beside it on the plate, a teacup with filmy dregs in the bottom, and a paper napkin crumpled and stuffed into a cappuccino cup which had a skin of drying, brown-stained milk foam clinging to its lip. As she looked at it, the nausea which had been hovering threateningly at the fringe of the crowd of sensations clamouring dully inside her began to burgeon and swamp the rest.

She only just made it to the toilets in time, slamming open the cubicle door and stooping forward as the first convulsion ejected a stream of vomit that pattered on the plastic seat then clattered and splashed in the bowl. Resting her hands on the cistern, sweat beading on her forehead and mingling with the dripping rainwater, she emptied her stomach in two cramping, aching, liquid heaves, then continued retching dryly and gasping through the strings of acid saliva swinging from her mouth and nose. When the cramps had subsided, she wiped her face with a wad of toilet paper and flushed it down, then went to the basin to wash herself. As she held her fingers under the comforting flood of hot water, she stared, unseeing at first, into the mirror. After a while, her face settled into focus like a reflection in a slowly stilling pond. The image it showed her, she knew, was her own face, but she struggled to recognise herself in the soaked hair, the haggard lines and the hollow eyes. How could it be her face, the same face she had worn last week, yesterday, or even that very morning, when she had been a different person, before she had staggered across the stage, stumbling through the proscenium and dragging the elaborate make-believe scenery down around her. *Murder-hunt detective was killer*, the face whispered to her, repeating the words over and over: *Murder-hunt detective was killer* . . . Her skin prickled where his fingers had touched her: her neck, her breasts, between her thighs – a hundred blood-tainted caresses. She lifted the front of her jumper and looked at her belly and breasts, expecting to see slimy snail-trails of corruption criss-crossing the skin . . . Her gullet griped, and she had to rush back to the toilet to vomit again.

When she had regained sufficient composure to return to the tea room, she found that her table had been cleared and wiped, and her predecessors' messy detritus replaced by a clean, empty cup and a chrome-headed cafetière of coffee she couldn't remember ordering. She poured it out mechanically, milking and sugaring the brown liquid before remembering that she no longer took either milk or sugar; hadn't done for a couple of years. She stirred it anyway. As she looked at the spinning ochre vortex, the front page came revolving out of it like a cheap special effect from an old movie and jerked to a stop in front of her eyes: *Murder-hunt detective was killer*. She could see the layout of the page as clearly as if it were really there; although the columns of text were just grey and amorphous, she could see the headline and, most importantly, the photograph beside it.

He had changed quite a lot. The photograph was poor – it was taken in half-profile as he was ducking to get into a car, and the low-grade half-tone of newsprint had combined with the degradation of microfilm reproduction and the grainy screen of the reading machine to make the features blurred and vague – but he was still recognisable. Despite the poor quality and the changes (he had been a lot heavier about the face then, and clean-shaven) which would make him almost unrecognisable to a casual acquaintance, she, who knew every crook and contour of his face, knew him instantly. The name captioned under the picture – Detective Chief Inspector Alan Gorvin – meant little to her beyond a faint, distant tug of indistinct memory. She could only ever think of him as Steven.

16

You think I'm evil . . . Pulling all the pain down on her own head. God, he thought, if only she knew. If only she knew just how wrong she was.

Steven sat on the grass on the hilltop above the farm and gazed at the horizon. He had been standing until a few moments ago, but had been overcome by a tingling-edged, numb dizziness which had forced him to slump down onto the turf. He had eaten virtually nothing for two days. The thought of food had made him gag, but this morning he had woken feeling suddenly ravenous, as though his body were no longer willing to tolerate the vicissitudes of his mind. He went to the house, but Carole had gone and the doors were locked. He was so hungry he could almost have munched the straw of his bed or even sampled the sacks of locust feed which were stored at the far end of the barn. In the end, he had dug up some half-grown carrots from the kitchen garden and eaten them, squatting on his haunches on the tilled black soil. The carrots were small and pale and clumped with mud, but he brushed them down and ate them, his teeth grinding on the clinging grit. He had felt slightly better after that, and he walked up the hill to survey the landscape and plan his leaving.

It was harder than the last time, when he had stood on top of the cairn all those months ago. Not only did he still have no clear idea of where to go; not only did he now have no money at all (he had given the handful of notes he had brought with him to Carole to pay for some new clothes), not only all that: now, the vague tug of guilt he had felt before had swollen to a desperate longing to stay, an overwhelming feeling of love for Carole, a feeling he would never have dreamt himself capable of until now. And it was that very affection that meant he *must* go, knowing what he knew now. Had Carole been any of the other women he had known – however superficially or however intimately – he was sure he could have stayed and brazened it out, lived out the pretence until forced to leave by the inevitable exigence of the chase or until she discovered who he was (which was surely impossible). With Carole, though, it would be futile. He couldn't even bring himself to look at her.

Then, as he had done on that previous afternoon, he came to the same sudden decision: to leave quickly and improvise his path of flight; and to do it now, before Carole returned. His dizziness had abated while he sat on the grass, and gave way now to a swelling rush of adrenalin. He stood up and strode down the hill, vaulted over the gate into the kitchen garden and went to the barn.

That was when he heard it: a distinctive, familiar sound, just as he put his hand on the barn door; the descending, rasping, farting overrun of the Morris's engine as it slowed to turn in to the lane.

He hauled at the door, and it groaned open. Suddenly,

as he darted inside, his panic brought the nausea and giddiness back, and he almost blacked out. He wavered unsteadily on his feet and put his hands to the wall for support. The fuzziness passed after a few moments, but left him weak and disorientated. He heard the car grumble across the yard and squeal to a stop – Pause – Door slamming – Pause – Front door opening – All heard through a hissing wash of blood pumping in his ears.

This was futile. Getting away without being seen might be no problem, but in this state, he wouldn't get more than a couple of miles: he had to have food. Bracing himself, he left the barn and walked across to the house. The front door had been left open. He stepped through and called out: 'Carole?' There was a pause, then her voice came indistinctly from the parlour: 'In here . . .' He went along the hallway, his heart thumping, his neck and scalp sweating with sickness and apprehension. He stepped into the parlour, then halted suddenly.

At first, in a fleeting, momentary delirium, he thought he saw a pair of eyes: two hollow, close-set, deep-sunk eyes staring into his, floating just a few inches in front of him. Eyes without a face, extending towards him on long, smooth stalks. Far, far beyond them was Carole's face, dark eyes also hollow and cold; below, her knuckles were white where they gripped the stock, one finger extended and resting on the trigger. He tried to speak, but nothing would come out. His first thought, which almost made him laugh and choke at the same time, was what desperate measures she had resorted to to keep him here. Through the haze, he could see her lips moving, but there seemed to be a delay between the movement and the emergence of sound in his brain. Then the voice cut in:

'In a minute,' she said, her voice cracking and hoarse.

292

She swallowed and started again: 'In a minute, I'm going to call the police. First, I want to know two things: How you found me and what you want from me.'

Hypnotised by the barrels hovering in front of his eyes, he opened his mouth to speak, but found he had no power to shape the sounds that came out: 'Whawav-lagl . . .' He stopped and tried again. This time, the forms came, but no sound. 'What?' he whispered.

Her ashen face was starting to suffuse with colour. 'I'm going to ask you one more time, you bastard. How did you find me, and what do you want from me?'

'I don't know what you mean,' he choked.

The black eyes vanished, and there was a blur of brown as the butt of the gun swung round and slammed into the side of his head. He teetered and sank to his knees as the shotgun resumed its steady aim at his face.

'I said I'd only ask you once,' said Carole. 'Now fucking answer me.'

He gazed up at her: her face, red with rage, was bobbing about unsteadily, fading in and out of focus in unison with the pulsing throb in his skull, fading behind a seeping smear of darkness. His body swayed, his muscles melted, and he collapsed forward onto the carpet.

Gail picked up the phone on the second ring and clamped the receiver in the crook of her shoulder. 'WDC Higgins,' she said, pulling folders out of a pile on her desk.

It was the switchboard operator. 'I've got a woman on the line from Yorkshire,' she said. 'She's asking to speak to someone in CID.'

'Yorkshire? What about?'

'She wouldn't say. Says she's spoken to enough switchboards already and wants a proper police officer.'

'Okay, put her through.' There was a pause filled

with bleeps and whirring sounds, then a click. 'WDC Higgins,' she repeated.

'Hello,' said a woman's voice. 'I'd like to speak to someone about the Invisible Man.'

Gail frowned. 'Invisible Man?'

'The murder case. The nurses.'

'Oh, I see. That case was closed several years ago. Do you have new information?'

'Yes. Can I speak to someone?'

'Well, I'm afraid the officers in charge of that case have either retired or moved on.' She glanced around the office. 'Could you hold on a moment . . .' She muted the mouthpiece and called across the room: 'Sarge, you worked on the Invisible Man, didn't you?'

He looked up. 'What, Gorvin? Yeah, I did.'

'I've got a woman here'd like a word with you. I'll put her through.'

He nodded and picked up his phone. 'DS Comber,' he said. 'How can I help you?'

'I've got some information,' said the woman. 'About the Invisible Man.'

'Okay,' he said, opening his notebook. 'Why don't you give me your name and I'll take down the details.'

Gail watched his face. 'Anything useful?' she asked when Comber had put the phone down.

'Dunno,' he said, peering at his notes. 'Librarian. Sounded a bit batty to me, but it could be something. Claims to've seen a woman acting strangely over some old news reports about the case.'

'Acting *strangely*?'

'In a sort of panic, apparently. Been sitting on it and worrying about it all day and finally decides to call us.'

'Did she know this woman?'

'No. Said she'd seen her in the library before, though.'

'Any action, d'you think?'

Comber shook his head. 'Not much I can do, is there?

Pass it on to the local CID, I suppose, and wait and see.' He tossed the notebook onto his desk and stood up. 'Anyway, I'm off up to the canteen. Fancy a coffee?'

'Okay.' She gathered up her jacket and purse. 'D'you think this woman was a crank?' she asked as they walked up the stairs.

He shrugged. 'Dunno. Any other case, I'd say yes, but not this one.' He stopped on the top step and turned to Gail. 'You know, I *never* believed Gorvin was dead. They never did find a body, but the DI and the Super and all the rest just closed ranks.' He grinned. 'Christ, they'll look ten kinds of idiot if the slippery bastard really does show up now.'

Carole stood over the crumpled rag-doll body lying face-down at her feet, the shotgun hanging limply from her hands, muzzles hovering over his head.

She had thought for one moment, as his eyes turned up and he toppled forward, that he was dead. Half of her had even hoped he was. His collapse had taken her by surprise; she didn't think she had hit him that hard. The boiling hatred in her stomach had overcome her self-control and forced her to lash out, urging her to swing the gun and smash his head to a pulp, but she hadn't been able to do it. It was still *his* face, after all, *his* eyes looking at her, and all she had managed was a feeble tap above the ear; not enough to knock him over, let alone out cold. At least, that was how it had felt to her. Why he had gone down like that she couldn't imagine. The shock of realising that at long last he had been found out, perhaps.

Steven . . . no, *not* Steven. She tried thinking the name she had read in the newspaper report: *Alan. Alan Gorvin.* Her mouth moved silently around the syllables, but they didn't connect with the man lying at her feet. She tried *Invisible Man* instead, repeating it over and over:

Invisible Man, Invisible Man, Invisible Man . . . *Gorvin* . . .
Alan . . . *Al-lan* . . . None of the sounds resonated: they
all seemed hollow, meaningless, even absurd. At last,
she tried *Steven* again: *Ste-ven*, and felt an instantaneous
tug in her chest and saw a momentary flicker of a face.
She swept the sensations aside and tried *Alan* again.
This time, she felt a slight catch, just the thinnest, tiniest
thud like a muffled clapper in a small bell. She tried
again: *Alan*, saying it aloud this time, *Alan Gorvin* . . .
murderer . . . *Invisible Man* . . ., repeating it like a mantra
until the anger and hatred which had been blunted the
moment she hit him with the gun butt was whipped up
again, sore and livid. The confusion she had felt yesterday was gone; she had been right all along about the
pattern, and the purpose of the pattern. All she had got
wrong was how the pattern would unfold: he was not
here to provide her with redemption through atonement, but through retribution. In her mind, she at last
relinquished the role as culpable betrayer and recast
herself as Beverley's agent of vengeance.

She could see the place on his head where her blow
had connected. She pushed back the hair with the tip of
the gun. Her first impression had been right: there
wasn't even a mark . . . She could make one, though; a
light squeeze of the trigger, just one cartridge, one
explosive *boom* and it would all be over . . . Her finger
moved to the trigger and drew it back against the spring
– an infinitesimal movement – until she felt it catch. One
more tiny, millimetric squeeze was all it would take; less
muscular effort than flicking away a fallen eyelash . . .

She released the trigger and let the gun swing back to
her side, away from his head. What good would it do to
shoot him when she hadn't had any answers to her
questions yet? Perhaps something less final would suf-
fice to let out the painful anger; perhaps one or two
really good kicks in the ribs. She could imagine the

deep, satisfying thump of her shoe ramming into his body. She reached out experimentally with her foot, measuring the range. As she nudged his side, he groaned. *Shut up*, she muttered as the sound of his voice elicited that confusing little tug again. She swung her leg back and poised herself to launch it at him with every ounce of her strength. He groaned again and moved. 'Shut *up!*' she screamed, her eyes filling with tears.

She kicked him. Her foot shunted into his side with a dull, heavy *whump*, forcing a blast of breath from his mouth, somewhere between a gasp and a cough, and she felt a triumphant wash of euphoria flood through her. She kicked him again. He groaned and rolled onto his side, clawing at the arm of the sofa, struggling to get to his knees. 'Carole . . .' he wheezed. '*Shut UP!*' she yelled. Why did he have to speak? His voice was confusing her, tainting the pure fire of her rage. She seized the gun by its barrels and swung it up over her head like a club, taking half a step back to correct the distance, so that the full weight of the arcing swipe would crush his head. He looked up at her, his back against the sofa. His face looked calm and resigned, as if inviting her, *wanting* her to do it. She gazed through a blur of tears, then tightened her grip and swung. There was a thrumming whisper as the gun scythed down through the air. He closed his eyes and waited for oblivion. There was a loud, violent thump, and his head was jarred to one side.

When he opened his eyes again, Carole was kneeling on the floor, head bowed, hands covering her face, sobbing wretchedly. The shotgun lay across his legs, and the cushion it had slammed into was wedged up against his head.

'I can't do it,' she wept, her voice broken with sobs and muffled by her hands. 'I can't – fucking – do it.'

He pushed the gun aside. 'Carole,' he wheezed, reaching out towards her and wincing at the pain from his ribs. '*Carole . . .*' He touched her arm with his fingertips.

'*Don't touch me!*' she shouted, slapping his arm away and staring furiously at him. 'Don't you dare fucking touch me, you bastard . . .' She scrambled to her feet and backed away from him. 'You evil, murdering bastard. *Why*? Tell me why!'

He was staring at her, then he glanced at the gun lying on the floor beside him.

She noticed the glance. 'Do you want it?' she whispered. 'Is that it? I can't kill you, but you could kill me, couldn't you? Well, go on then – do it! That's what you came for – why'd'you wait so long, hn? Go on, shoot me if you're going to!' She picked up the gun and thrust it into his hands. 'Go on! I can't take it any more – just fucking do it, like you did to Beverley. Well, what are you waiting for?' He was gazing at her with frightened eyes, and she laughed contemptuously. 'Oh, don't you like guns? Would you rather a knife?'

Her whole body was shaking as she shouted into his face. Unable to bear it, he pushed her away. He seized the gun and flung it across the floor. It slammed against the wall and both barrels detonated with a huge, concussive *BA-BOOM.*

There was dead silence as their hearing recovered from the jarring blast. They looked at each other through the diffusing pall of smoke. He glanced to his left. A huge, raggedly blackened hole had been blasted in the side of the sofa, only a foot away from his shoulder. He stared at the smouldering crater in the upholstery, then looked at Carole again. Her face was white. 'Are you all right?' she asked in a tiny voice.

He nodded. Silence fell again. Steven struggled to find words to say, fearful of breaking the uneasy lull and sending her into another frenzy. 'I'm not him,' he whispered at last. 'It wasn't me who did that to Beverley.'

The sneer returned to her face. 'I've already listened to enough lies from you. How I could be stupid enough to believe in you, I'll never know.'

'I swear,' he said urgently. 'I swear it wasn't me. I know who you think I am, but I didn't do it.'

'I'm warning you, Ste— I'm warning you – don't you fucking lie to me.'

'I'm not . . .'

'You are!' she shouted. 'You're not Steven bloody Goldcliff. You never were! You're *Alan Gorvin*. You—'

'I know,' he said. 'I admit it. But I didn't kill Beverley. I didn't kill any of them! I was stitched up, framed.' He rose to his knees and pleaded with her: 'You've got to believe me, Carole. Please listen . . . It wasn't me, I wasn't the Invisible Man. The Strand Scourer was the Invisible Man . . .'

'The *what*?' she said. The wretched man was babbling now.

'The Strand Scourer. He calls himself the Strand Scourer. *He* was the Invisible Man. He set me up, and he's been after me ever since. He won't let me rest. Everywhere I go, he finds me. Why the hell do you think I've been running for the past three years?'

'*Why?*' she repeated incredulously. '*Why?* Because you're a murderer! The police are after you! And I hope they fucking castrate you.'

He shook his head impatiently. 'Don't you listen to the news?' He paused. 'No, you didn't, did you . . . Listen to me: As far as the police are concerned, Alan Gorvin is *dead*. You walk into any station in the land and ask about the Invisible Man, and they'll tell you: the case is closed. The prime suspect died in the English Channel three years ago.'

She was about to retort, but hesitated. It was true:

299

they had all told her – her father, mother, brother, Rosalind – they all said he was dead and gone. This information was intended to make her feel better, give her a sense of closure, but it hadn't worked. What was more, it was evidently not true.

'So what?' she demanded, even though her newly constructed certainties were already wavering. 'So they think you're dead. What does that prove?'

'It *proves*,' he said, trying to be patient. 'It proves that . . . that I'm not running from the police. There's someone out there, Carole, and he's been hunting me down everywhere I go. I get somewhere, I make a new life, and after a few months there he is again.'

'But who *is* he?' she insisted. 'Assuming you're telling the truth, which I doubt.'

'I don't know,' he said miserably. 'He's the Invisible Man – I don't *know* who he is. Most of all, I don't know why he's done this to *me*.'

She gazed at him. 'You're a liar,' she said. 'You've lied to me ever since you got here. And that's another thing – you still haven't told me why you came here, how you found me.'

He shook his head. 'I don't know that either.'

'*What*? There is no way you're going to tell me it was a coincidence . . . I don't be*lieve* this . . .'

'It *is*! I promise you, until the other night, I had no idea who you were. Even when you first mentioned Beverley I didn't connect. Why do you think I reacted like that when I realised?'

'*I* don't know!' she shouted. 'Maybe you . . . maybe . . . I don't know. I can't think straight. You *must* be lying.'

'No, Carole. The only lie I've told you since I first met you was the amnesia, and even that started feeling real after a while. Christ, even the things I told you about my childhood, all those things I wrote down, even that was

300

all true. For God's sake, I used to be a policeman, Carole – I've never told so few lies in my life!'

In spite of herself, she couldn't restrain a smile from briefly twitching across her lips. Annoyed with herself, she turned the expression into a deep scowl, but not before he had noticed the smile.

'Listen,' he said. 'Since I've been running from this . . . this *psychopath*, I've had three attempts at a new life with a new identity.' He gestured at his surroundings. 'This is the fourth. Every time, I've lived a lie, one hundred per cent: false name, false history, false documents whenever I could get them, and an invented character. I never realised I had such a talent for it until I started. Christ, I was even *French* for a whole year. I was a walking lie everywhere. Except here. And d'you want to know why? Because of you. As soon as I set eyes on you – Christ, before that, when I could only hear your voice, I . . . I just couldn't do it any more, couldn't make the lies come. I couldn't tell you the truth, so I just played an amnesic version of myself. But that was the point; it was *me*. Or as close as I can get to myself after all this time. God knows, I *wanted* to forget. And I didn't even supply my own false name – you did that. I don't know who the hell Steven Goldcliff is. I bought that jacket in a charity shop in Birmingham. I didn't even know it *had* a name in it. Everything else was me. You know more about my childhood than anyone I've ever met, including my parents.'

Carole stood up and retrieved the shotgun. She broke the breech and ejected the two spent cartridges. Steven watched anxiously as she took two fresh ones from the cupboard and slotted them in.

'What are you doing?' he asked nervously.

'I'm going to call the police,' she said, snapping the breech closed again and pointing the gun at him. She looked down at him, into his frightened eyes, and felt reassured by her power. 'Eventually,' she added. 'First, you're going to tell me everything. And I mean *every-thing*. Right from the beginning.'

'I will,' he said. 'Anything you want.'

'*Then* I'll decide whether I believe you or not.'

He nodded. 'Can I ask one question first?'

'What?'

'Can I have some food? I'll pass out if I don't eat anything soon.'

Carole shepherded him cautiously to the kitchen. Under the steady gaze of the shotgun's twin muzzles, he cut and buttered bread for both of them, piling it onto plates, along with cheese and honey and apples. Carole watched him closely, making sure that any cutlery he touched was put back where she could see it. Then, still at gunpoint, he carried the plates back to the parlour.

They sat opposite each other, he on the damaged sofa, she in the armchair, and talked and ate. Or rather, he talked and ate, tearing ravenously at the buttered bread, chewing lumps off the cheese, his words often mangled as he tried to eat and talk simultaneously. Carole simply listened, the gun resting across her knees, her hand on the stock, her plate of food untouched. From time to time, she stopped him and cross-questioned him, making him elaborate, fill gaps in the narrative, or backtrack and repeat passages. After the first hour of halting, disjointed telling, he struck his stride, and the speech flowed as every suppressed detail of the past three years returned to him.

He told her about how Alan Gorvin had changed into Michael Spring, who had evolved into Michel Viveau, who had become Paul Chapel and then Nigel Inkpen; he told her about Cressida and her Twins, about Christine and about Tessa; he described le Temple and his house in the village, Southampton and

302

Morris Minor Restorations, the Caldicot Level and the porn video industry; and he told her about the Strand Scourer. He described all of his persecutor's cryptic signs and messages, and he recounted the letters, almost verbatim, recalling vividly their mocking, ironic and covertly threatening words. He paraded the gallery of enemies he had made in his life – including several clever and monstrous individuals he had encountered in his time with Special Branch – but all seemed desperately inadequate as suspects for the Strand Scourer's real identity. Finally, he talked about his decision to try and bury it all in the mud and sand of the Severn Estuary, and described his flight from Wales. He told her about his arrival in Birmingham, his failure to find work, and his descent into begging in the city's streets as a desperate means of conserving his dwindling reserve of cash. And he recalled the moment he knew it was finally over: he was crouching against a shop window in the Bullring near the end of a long day, staring into the milling forest of hurrying legs, when a small piece of paper fluttered from a passing hand and settled on top of the spartan accretion of coins scattered on the piece of cloth at his feet. He picked it up. There was writing on it. *We have fallen into the very pit. Who shall save us now nor where will we flee when all around us are watching eyes and the prying claws of the dead . . . ?* It was over. He fled into the night without guidance or plan, tacking this way and that across the north country, sleeping in doorways and ditches, walking by day, hitching rides where he could, scavenging for food amongst the refuse of towns and in the woods and fields of the country, drawing on the last of his money whenever the yield was too thin to sustain him, until one rain-filled night, the last desperate dregs of exertion brought him to an isolated lane and a farm and a bed amongst the dust and straw.

When he had finished his story, his eyes were vacant, his mouth was dry and his senses numb. He had talked for hours: when he began, the sun had been arcing slowly down towards dusk, which had grown and deepened to darkness; now, as he finished, the blackness beyond the window was fading to grey and the colours of dawn were beginning to seep back into the world.

Carole had not moved, except to lay the shotgun down on the floor at her feet. Somehow, it had felt increasingly absurd to keep the weapon hovering in readiness. She listened intently to every word, and the more she listened, the more she knew that it was the truth. Nobody could improvise or invent such a story in such circumstances. More than that, she understood the truth of who he was: as he spoke, the names and characters – Alan, Michael, Michel, Paul, Nigel – eddied into his body, his face and his speech, while in the interstices, Steven himself peered through, consistent and familiar ... Steven ... She knew and felt the consonance of Steven and Alan, but he was still Steven to her; he always would be. More than this, she knew the truth at the core of him; the truth of his innocence and persecution; that the Steven she knew and loved was not capable of killing.

There was silence for several minutes while Carole digested his words and drifted inexorably towards these truths. Steven, turning out from his interior vision, floated slowly to the surface and gazed at her.

Never taking her eyes from his, she rose from the chair and walked across to him. Stooping, she closed her eyes and placed a single, slow kiss like a benediction on his forehead, a kiss that communicated forgiveness, love and contrition in one gentle ligation. He reached out to her, and she fell into his arms.

They were too talked-out to speak, too dry to weep, too exhausted to make love, so they simply clung to each other as though clinging to life itself, limpet-tight limbs coiled together, muscles squeezing away every last fraction of unfilled space between them.

After a while, Steven felt Carole's body shift slightly against his, a tiny grunt escaping from her throat.

'Uncomfortable?' he asked, relaxing his arms to let her move.

'Hmm. No, I'm okay,' she breathed, settling down again. She was quiet for a while, then: 'Steven?'

'Mm?'

'There's one thing I still don't quite understand.'

'I was about to say that.'

She looked up at him. 'What?'

'Something I'm not sure about. What were you going to say?'

She smiled. 'Ask me yours first.'

'Okay. How did you guess who I was? I mean, we never met, did we?'

'No. I was interviewed by some sergeant. No, I had this dream. This really vivid dream like a vision. I remembered seeing you at Beverley's funeral.'

He frowned. 'Oh. Oh, I see.'

'You were there, weren't you? I didn't imagine it?'

'No. You're right, I was there.'

'With two of your colleagues.'

'Mm,' he grunted. 'What was it you wanted to ask me?'

'Well,' she said. 'Something I still can't quite grasp is the fake suicide. Or accident or whatever.'

He hesitated, hoping she didn't notice the tiny catch in his breathing or the slight acceleration of his heartbeat beneath her cheek. 'What about it?' he asked.

'I understand the false passport and the disguise and the two tickets, but surely they'd know only one person got on, cause you could only actually *use* one ticket, and you'd only get one boarding card.'

Steven paused. Every word of what he had told her had been true except this. But what good would it do to come clean now? None at all. It could only do damage; how could anyone believe that the man who would do *that* could not possibly commit those other demonic acts?

'It wasn't easy,' he said. 'As I remember it, I handed both tickets in at the kiosk and said my mate had gone off to the toilet. They gave me two boarding cards. I handed one in and dropped the other one on the ground by the guy's feet. That way, it'd get noticed later. He'd think he'd dropped it.'

'Oh,' she said. 'I see. Wasn't that an awfully big risk? What if the ticket man had remembered you?'

'I couldn't help it. Anyway, he didn't. I read in the papers that Alan Gorvin was dead and the case was closed.'

Satisfied at last, all doubts gone, Carole settled down again and closed her eyes. As daylight grew outside, diluting and then annihilating the artificial yellow glow of the lamp, their heartbeats slowed and their breathing shallowed, and they slept.

Invisible Man

A black Rover hissed along the dark street and purred to a stop at the kerbside, under the drizzle-glittering cone of orange light from one of the few unbroken streetlamps. Alan walked quickly across the road and tapped on the Rover's window. There was a sibilant whir as the window lowered, and he leaned towards the opening, folding up his jacket collar against the prickling drizzle.

'Evening, sir,' he said. 'Wasn't expecting to see you.'

'Just passing,' said Superintendent Frazer. 'All set?'

Alan nodded. 'Yeah. Four cars covering the area, eight plainclothes PCs, plus my crew. We're set all right.'

Frazer shook his head. 'Well, I just hope you get a result to justify all this overtime. And I'm still not entirely happy about using this probationer.'

'She'll be well looked after, sir. Anyway, she's the best lookalike we've got. Matches Kirsty Marsden to a tee.'

'Hmm. Think he'll show? I mean, the weather . . .'

'If it's any night it'll be tonight. Every other one's been between ten and twelve on the twenty-first of the month. We can only do our best.'

Frazer sighed. 'Well, Alan, it's your case. I just hope this bugger isn't quite as clever as I think he is. Good luck.'

'Thank you, sir.'

The window rolled up and the Rover pulled away. Alan turned and ran back to his own car, which was parked on the other side of the street. He climbed into the passenger seat and slammed the door. 'Shit,' he muttered. 'Bastard weather.'

'Looks to me like it's easing off,' said DS Comber. 'What'd Frazer want?'

'Just sniffing around.'

Alan looked at his watch and twisted around in his seat. In the back of the car, DI Spearman was sitting with the young WPC who had volunteered for the operation. She seemed uncomfortable in the short skirt and leather jacket that had been supplied for her; out of place, like a little girl in her mother's clothes. She did look remarkably like Kirsty Marsden, though: tall and slimly built with long dark hair and strikingly beautiful features.

'Okay,' said Alan. 'We go in . . . three minutes. You're sure you're okay about this, Chrissie?' She nodded. 'You know you can pull out any time,' he added.

'No, sir,' she said confidently. 'I'm fine.'

'Good girl. How's your wire? Comfortable?'

'Yes, sir.' She put a hand to her ear and patted her chest with the other.

'Right. Now, you know the score: you'll be in contact with us constantly and one of us or one of the PCs will be within ten seconds' radius if you get into any difficulties.' He checked his watch. 'Okay, let's go.'

Chrissie got out of the car and began to walk slowly along the pavement.

'Good-looking girl,' said Sergeant Comber, watching her go. 'I'd turn out for her if I was him.'

'Hmm,' murmured Alan, concentrating on adjusting the frequency on the receiver, pushing buttons and watching the LCD digits flicker.

Comber put his hands on the wheel and stretched, groaning and pushing his hips forward. 'Yeah,' he said. 'Wouldn't mind letting her mount up and gallop a few furlongs on my face.'

He and Spearman laughed. Alan glanced at him and seemed about to speak when the receiver crackled: 'Not tempting, Sarge,' said Chrissie's voice from the speaker. 'The only bit of me that's like to come in contact with your face is my boot.'

Alan grinned. 'Well, the wire's working ... Chrissie, you can walk a bit faster than that, love. You're supposed to be on your way home, not touting for business.'

'Sorry, sir.'

Alan turned to Spearman. 'Right, Glyn, be ready when she reaches the corner ... And ... go!'

Spearman got out and started walking, tracing Chrissie's steps. When he reached the corner of the street, Comber started the engine and the car pulled away, cruising smoothly past the line of parked cars.

'Come in!' Alan called. His office door swung open and DS Comber walked in. 'Oh, hi Graham. Well?'

Comber sat down in front of the desk. 'She's upstairs, having another go with the photo-fits.'

Alan sighed and threw his pen down on the desk. 'Waste of time,' he said. 'They were all just blokes. None of em came anywhere near her ... Not exactly the most successful op in CID history, was it?'

Comber smiled complacently. 'Oh, I wouldn't say that, sir. We did get this.' He took a plastic bag containing a single slip of paper from his pocket and passed it across the desk. 'It's him, sir.'

Alan stared at it. 'Where the fuck did this come from?'

'It was in her jacket pocket – her *inside* jacket pocket. She didn't find it till she got home last night.'

'*What?*'

Comber shrugged, still looking smug. 'I know, and no one came near her.' He watched Alan turning the slip over, peering at it through the clear plastic. 'What d'you think?'

309

Alan read the words, written in lopsided capitals in blue fountain pen:

NICE TRY, GENTLEMEN, BUT NO <u>FINESSE</u>. THIS GIRL IS A FAKE: VERY APPEALING, REALLY QUITE TEMPTING BAIT, BUT UNFORTUNATELY A <u>GLARING</u> FAKE. I FEEL QUITE INSULTED.

'Get this handwriting looked at,' he ordered.

'Already have,' said Comber. 'Written left-handed by a right-handed person. Exactly the same as the others. Nothing new.'

Alan gazed thoughtfully at the writing. 'Not bad for left-handed, is it?'

'It's not as hard as you'd think, actually, sir.' Comber paused. 'No disrespect, sir, but have you missed the point a bit here?'

Alan looked up. 'What?'

'Well, none of these blokes came near her. The note was *inside* her jacket. That means it was put there *before* she put it on.'

'What? Yes, I suppose it does . . . Where did the jacket come from?'

'Stores. He was *here*, sir. He was *in* the station at some time. Not only that, he knew about the op in advance – who was on it, who the decoy was, what she'd be wearing, everything.'

Alan stared at him. 'What exactly are you suggesting?'

Comber's complacency started to weaken, and he actually looked fearful. 'Sir,' he said quietly. 'I think it could be someone on the Force.'

After the sergeant had left, Alan sat at his desk for a while, his head in his hands. *Someone on the Force? In this building?* The thought made the back of his neck prickle.

He stared at the note. Comber was right; even if it wasn't someone here, it had to be someone who could gain access. Of course, that was why the papers had coined that ridiculous name; he had proven himself quite capable of getting anywhere, without being seen or leaving a trace of his presence behind. Except, of course, the grotesque, ghoulish items he chose to leave, and these yielded no hints of his identity.

Only one person claimed to have seen the Invisible Man. A security guard called Albert Rowe had been doing the rounds of some of the Bond Street shops on the night of the Beverley Cunningham murder. Albert was nearing retirement and his eyesight was of doubtful reliability, but he swore he had seen a man emerging from a side-street near the shop where the woman's face was later found. The man, Albert claimed when he was interviewed by Spearman and Comber, had been caught for a moment in the light of a streetlamp, and Albert had seen his face. It was the first of the Invisible Man murders, and Alan had immediately gone out and hauled in Gilbert Dacey. Dacey was known to be living in the area, having been recently released after a sixteen-year sentence for a string of sexual assaults. He had never actually murdered any of his victims, but he had cropped and shaved their heads and bodies in the same way as the Invisible Man. At the hastily organised identity parade, they had been one man short for the line-up, so Alan himself filled the empty space. Behind the two-way mirror, there was excited tension as Albert hesitated, peering alternately at Dacey and a gas-fitter called Wayne. He shook his head, then walked on. Suddenly, he stopped and pointed. *It's him!* He said excitedly. *Number One – that's him!* Number One was Alan. Albert was thanked – quite politely considering the circumstances – and sent home. Since then, as the notoriety of the perpetrator grew, there had been any number of claimed sightings, but all gave utterly disparate descriptions. As the case dragged on, the investigating team's spirits flagged.

Feeling desperate, Alan stood up and went downstairs to the Incident Room. Along one wall was a vast pinboard, in the centre of which was a map of London, patchily speckled with colour-coded pins: yellow for victim sightings, green for claimed suspect sightings, red for scenes of crime, and so on. Red ribbons fanned out from the red pins, terminating in mosaics of photographs, one group for each victim.

There were three of them: Beverley Cunningham, the first, nine months ago; Angie Diffield, six months ago; and Kirsty Marsden, the latest, a little over eight weeks ago. All nurses, all from different hospitals, but all working in Casualty departments. Nothing else in common except a vague similarity of build (tall and slim), facial features (attractive and graceful) and hairstyle (glossy hair worn long and straight). Every possible common element, past and present – boyfriends, patients, co-workers, families, social habits, domestic circumstances, medical records, even estate agents, car dealers and driving instructors – had been thoroughly investigated, but no connections had been found. Even the details of what was done to them varied in subtle ways. All stripped. None raped. No signs of struggle, so probably killed quickly and painlessly by someone they knew or believed they could trust. All nevertheless perversely violated after death. Hair shaved and removed from the scene. Bodies partially excoriated: Beverley's face, Angie's breasts and buttocks, Kirsty's genitalia and thighs. And each body accompanied by a different, laconically written note.

Alan looked closely at the photographs. Each group contained one pre-mortem picture. Angie's and Kirsty's were nursing graduation photos: clear, clean and pristine features and crisp uniforms in fine-grained colour; smiles hovering between pride and self-consciousness. Beverley's photograph, on the other hand, appeared to have been taken at a party: the background was domestic; her face was relaxed and grinning, her pupils red from the flash. Each of these pictures stood at the centre of a hideous montage of scene-of-crime photographs: naked, pallid skin streaked with dirt and brown-black congealed blood, the cursory formality of multiple angles turning the lifeless array of bellies, breasts, shoulders, backs and limbs into disorientating, disconnected fleshy masses, the powerfully visceral and the pathetically poignant in stark, antagonistic contrast to the vibrant life of the pre-death portraits.

Paradox seemed to be the touchstone of this case. How had he done it? At first, it had seemed as though it must be somebody the women knew and trusted, but the investigation had turned up no friends they had in common. Given this fact, how had he persuaded these women – alone and vulnerable as they were – that he was trustworthy; so much so that they accompanied him quietly and presumably willingly to their place of death. And there lay the other paradox: The manner in which he had killed them contradicted everything Alan knew about what motivated a person to kill; they were put to death quietly, quickly and painlessly, without any apparent trauma. And then their lifeless bodies had been mutilated in a manner which suggested a level of calculated viciousness that could signify nothing but the most venomous animal hatred and contempt.

Or did it? That would certainly be the reaction of any sane person, but if he looked carefully and insinuated himself reluctantly into the mind of this man, it seemed to Alan that these atrocities were done with the care and skill of an artisan. He groped for a parallel: not quite like a taxidermist, nor a surgeon; perhaps more like a vivisectionist. Yes, that was it: the attention to detail showed clearly to him now that the horror of the mutilations was not a factor to this man. It was like comparing the fox-hunter to the laboratory dissector: for one the pleasure lay in the sweat of the chase and the red-throated violence of the kill, whereas for the other, the thrill was the serendipitous probing of boundaries with blank disregard for the heat and life of the organism.

But why? What was the goal of this person's painstaking researches? Alan scrutinised each portrait with desperate futility, interrogating the eyes: *Who has done this to you? Who could do such things?* There had been a theory in the Nineteenth Century that microscopic examination of a murder victim's retinas would reveal a burned-in image of the last sight seen – hopefully, the killer's face. Perhaps searching the face of the victim before death might give an insight into who, what kind of person, might want to kill and mutilate her ... He caught himself in time: why the hell was he thinking like this? The truth was that he had been severely shaken by Comber's suggestion that the Invisible Man might be a police officer, perhaps even one of his own. Cod psychology and ludicrous mystical fantasies were not going to help him. What he needed was sleep; a good night's sleep and a clear head in the morning. He tore himself away from his frantic scrutiny of the photographs, left the Incident Room and headed towards the car park.

Three days after the failed entrapment operation, DI Spearman was walking along the corridor towards the

Station's rear entrance when his attention was caught by a hoarse *pssst!* From the doorway of the men's locker room. He paused and looked around. 'Sir,' hissed DS Comber. 'In here, quick!'

Spearman glanced up and down the corridor, then followed him in. 'What is it?' he demanded. 'I was on my way home.'

Comber closed the door and leaned against it. His face was grey and anxious. 'I've got him,' he whispered.

'Who?'

'The Invisible Man.'

Spearman stared at him. '*What?*'

'I've got him!' Comber repeated.

'Got him? What the fuck are you on about? If this is a joke, Graham . . .'

'I was right! You know I told you I thought it was someone in here? A copper? *I know who it is!*'

'Well, *who?*'

'You're not gonna believe this, but I think it's Gorvin.'

Spearman stared. '*DCI* Gorvin?'

'Yes.'

'*Alan* Gorvin?'

'Yes.'

Suddenly, Spearman laughed. 'You sick cunt. You *are* joking.'

'I'm not . . .'

'Excuse me, Graham, are we living on the same fucking planet here? For Christ's sake, you'd better not repeat that to anyone else if you val—'

'Look at this.' Comber took the note they had found on Chrissie out of his pocket. 'This was the key. This gave it away. I went into the DCI's office the other evening to get it back from him. He wasn't there, and I found *this* on the desk.' He took out a sheet of notepaper and held it up next to the plastic-encased note. 'Look at it: it's the same handwriting!'

315

Spearman examined the two samples. They did look strikingly similar. 'So what?' he objected. 'It's not much to charge a bloke on, is it.'

'There's more. I was thinking: remember that ID line-up? Maybe old Albert Rowe's eyesight wasn't as bad as we thought. And that's not all. I mean, I thought the same as you at first: I've been sitting on this for a couple of days cause I couldn't believe it. Then, this morning I dug out Gorvin's time-sheets for the past nine months. Every one of the murders was done when he was off-duty or away from the Station on his own!'

'Naah,' said Spearman, waving the slip of paper like a fan. 'I'm not buying this. Why would he incriminate himself like this?'

Comber shrugged. 'Don't ask me. Experimenting with writing cack-handed or something. They match, though, you can't deny it. Maybe he wants to get caught – they do sometimes, psychos.'

Spearman looked at the pieces of paper again. 'Where is he now?'

'Gone. You know he called in sick yesterday morning – well, he didn't turn in today, either.'

'Shit . . . Okay, we'll run with it for a bit.' He gripped Comber by the arm. 'Graham, we have got to be *so* fucking careful with this. I mean, kid gloves are gonna be too rough, know what I mean? Right, here's what you do: Who is there in CID you'd trust with your life? Sound as a bell, preferably not on this case . . .'

Comber frowned. 'Jack Allan, I suppose,' he said.

'Right – you collar Jack and tell him what you've told me, and you get him to sniff around, see what he can find out about the DCI's movements on those dates and report it straight back to me. And he's to do it so no one gets suspicious. Got that? Then you meet me in the car park in one hour.'

★ ★ ★

'He's in,' said Comber, taking the sledgehammer out of the car boot. 'The blue Carlton there, and the old Bristol next to it – they're both his.'

'Well, let's hope he's ready for visitors,' said Spearman, turning and walking along the path towards the block of flats.

'Sir,' said Comber hesitantly.

Spearman turned back. 'What?'

'You do think we're right, don't you? We haven't got carried away?'

Spearman walked back to him. 'Carried away? This was your idea.'

'Yeah, well, I dunno. I'm not so sure. I mean, like this business of him being off-duty; it was always at night – he probably *would* be off, wouldn't he? Maybe it doesn't mean anything.'

'Ah-ah. Jack got back to me on that. Angie was killed right in the middle of the Walton Road obbo. Gorvin was on that most nights, but not that one. Nah, I think we're on to something. I thought of something else, too: Remember the note we found with the first one?'

' "My name's Beverley", you mean?'

'Yeah. Remember we got Gorvin's thumbprint off it? We all ignored it at the time, didn't we, assumed he'd handled it at the scene or something, even though SOCO swore blind he couldn't have. I mean, we would ignore something like that, wouldn't we? The DCI in charge of the case?'

Comber nodded and glanced up at the building. 'I know. I just . . . I dunno. I don't like it.'

Spearman placed a hand on his shoulder and spoke confidently, even though he felt doubtful and fearful himself. 'Don't get cold feet now, Graham. Look, we'll handle it carefully. You keep an eye on him and I'll do the talking. I'll keep it friendly, ask if we can look

317

around, tell him *we* don't think it's him, we've just got to check. He'll understand. If he doesn't, if he turns nasty, then we nick him and use the warrant.'

Comber sighed. 'Okay ... Fuck, I hope we're right, or our careers are fucked. He'll have our knackers on a plate.'

There was no answer when they knocked on the door of Alan's flat. They made inquiries amongst the neighbours, but none of them had seen him for at least a couple of days. Deciding to err cautiously, they waited for half an hour before knocking again. Still receiving no reply, Comber gritted his teeth and swung the sledgehammer, battering the lock free in two blows.

'Sir?' Spearman called as he walked into the hallway. 'Alan? Anyone home?' He switched the light on. 'Okay, Graham, you take the kitchen and the lounge. I'll do the rest.'

Comber went to the living room and switched the light on. The room showed signs of having been unoccupied for at least a day or two. The remains of a half-eaten Chinese takeaway mouldering on the dining table smelt rancid, and the copy of the *Telegraph* lying on the sofa was three days old. Comber had barely registered these observations, however, when there was a shout from Spearman.

'Graham! Come here!'

He found him standing on the threshold of the bedroom. He had just turned the light on, and was frozen there, his hand still on the switch. Comber looked over his shoulder; the look turned to a stare, then gaping disbelief. He pushed past Spearman and walked into the room.

'Jesus,' he whispered. 'Oh, Jesus fucking Christ ...'

Behind him, he heard the beeping of Spearman's mobile phone. 'Hello, Mrs Frazer. DI Spearman here. I'd

318

like to speak to the Superintendent, please . . . Yes, it's urgent.'

Alan let himself into the building and trudged up the stairs to his flat. He was feeling depressed, preoccupied and more than a little inadequate. It barely registered in his brain that the hall light was on when he walked in. The living-room light was on, too. He frowned, but then dismissed it. He put his carrier bag on the table and began unpacking it: Foil box, 29 scrawled on the lid, chicken chow mein; polystyrene pot of vivid red sweet and sour sauce; brown paper bag blotched with grease, containing pork balls; and two more aluminium boxes, 61, curried noodles, and a fried rice. Far more than he could eat by himself, but he could always microwave what was left for breakfast.

He ate straight from the containers, using a fork and spoon he had put out for breakfast that morning but not used. As he ate, he thought. Or rather, he tried to think. He tried to think about anything other than the case. He put the television on and sat at the table with the remote in one hand and his fork in the other, hopping from channel to channel while he picked at his food. Everything he saw reminded him of the case: The news (story about a boy abducted from his home in Wiltshire); a detective drama on ITV (serial killer storyline); an opera on BBC2 (fleeting image of a woman in the chorus line who was the spitting image of Kirsty Marsden); wildlife documentary on Channel 4 (hyenas eviscerating the corpse of some unrecognisable animal).

This was becoming altogether too strange for Alan. He had reached a state in his feelings about the investigation that he had witnessed in other officers but had always believed he would never succumb to himself: he was becoming obsessed. Obsessed with the victims, obsessed with his own frustrated attempts to trap the killer, obsessed with the nature of the mutilations inflicted on the bodies. Why didn't this man rape his victims like so many of them did? Why the removal of skin, why the shaving? The montage on the Incident-Room wall kept replaying itself behind his eyes, and he recalled the scenes of the crimes; horrific as the photographs might be, there was something clinical and clean and anodyne about them – the systematic coverage, and the perfect gloss of the paper – which masked the reality of cold, damp air blanketing the dank ground, drizzle settling on the dead, naked skin . . . and the smell: a mixture of wet earth and air pollution mingling with the odour of flesh in incipient decay.

His spoon hovered over the dish of chow mein for a moment, then he dropped it into the tangle of noodles and beansprouts and lumps of grey chicken, and pushed the dish away. He had to stop thinking like this; his job was to detect, not dwell morbidly on images of the dead. Only detect . . . Things in that department were coming adrift, too. Comber's theory about it being someone at the Station, for instance. It just seemed too outrageous. Of course, he had a point: how else could the note have got into the WPC's pocket? But no, it didn't add up. Expert analysis of the style of all the notes they had found so far indicated someone with a bit of education, or perhaps a taste for literature, or both. None of the current crop of officers (at least those he knew of) fitted that description, except maybe himself (a little) or Superintendent Frazer (a lot). There was Chrissie the WPC, of course. She'd had a good university education, but . . . He paused, his mouth hanging open – the note in her pocket, the victims not being raped . . . The notion danced around in his mind for a few frantic moments, then collapsed. He was just being stupid now . . . No, he decided, returning to his original line of thought, none of the officers he could think of seemed capable of that kind of crime. Some of them had definite sadistic tendencies – indeed, he himself was not exactly known for the restrained politeness of his interview technique – but none were likely killers.

The constant, unrelenting tension was giving him a headache. Between his shoulder blades, the muscles were plaited taut in a hard band, all the way up the back of his neck to the base of his skull, where they pumped insistent pain into his head. He snapped open his brief-case and rummaged inside for the strip of aspirin he always kept there. He couldn't find it, but he did find a thick hardback book wedged in between some folders and envelopes. He took it out and looked at it: it had a blank green cover and bore a University of London stamp on the fly-leaf. Strange; he had no recollection of ever having been in that library, let alone borrowed any books. He looked at the title page: *A Handbook of Clinical Psychopathology*, edited by Ezra Schatz. A page near the back of the book had been marked with a yellow Post-It note, and two paragraphs under the heading 'Multiple Personality' had been outlined in pencil.

. . . Undoubtedly the most reliably documented (but nevertheless contentious) case of this syndrome is that of Donald Cicciani, the so-called 'Boonton Wolf' (Weisbaum *et al.* 1979; cf. Schwartz 1981). In 1975, Cicciani, a 41-year-old builder from Mountain Lakes, New Jersey, was arrested and charged with the rape and murder of five adolescent boys in the Boonton/Lake Hiawatha/ Parsippany area. The evidence linking him with the crimes was overwhelming: His fingerprints matched those taken from the crime scenes; he fitted the description given by the only surviving victim; items of the victims' effects and clothing were found in a trunk in the basement of his house; and he was unable to provide alibis for any of the dates in question. Despite this, when questioned by the Morris County Sheriff's Department and later by the FBI, Cicciani persistently denied any knowledge of the crimes, even with administration of sodium pentothal. When a polygraph test failed to reveal any flaws in his wall of denial (for example, the polygraph recorded no response to photographs of the victims), federal investigators resorted to hypnosis, which yielded a surprising result: A secondary personality called Lorenzo was revealed. 'Lorenzo' freely claimed responsibility for the murders and described in detail how he had conducted them. After the interview, Donald had no memory of the hypnosis, nor of Lorenzo, and continued to protest his innocence.

The pathogenesis of multiple personality (which should more accurately be labelled Selective Psychogenic Amnesia or SPA – see Krantz 1986) is uncertain, but may indicate a degree of compartmentalization in LTS which allows selective repression of unpleasant memories, a disorder observed in many combat veterans and others who have undergone severe psychological trauma (Stoval *et al.* 1982). This disorder also raises an interesting ethical and legal question: Should Donald Cicciani be held culpable for crimes committed by Lorenzo? The law found that he could, refusing to accept the psychiatric report either in evidence or mitigation. Cicciani was found guilty on all counts and later executed . . .

Alan put the book down, more puzzled than ever. He got up from the table and went to the bathroom in search of aspirin. There were none there, so he went to try the drawer of his bedside table.

Strangely, the bedroom light was on as well. He hadn't noticed it earlier. Guided by autopilot, he flicked the switch as he walked into the room, throwing it into darkness. A moment's confusion, then he tutted and turned the light back on again. For several long seconds, he thought he was dreaming. He had had paradoxical dreams like this before; being somewhere that he knew was familiar – his flat, his parents' house, the Station, his old school – all in flat contradiction of the evidence of his eyes. The familiar transformed, but still familiar. The bed was still in the same place, still half-covered by the mountainously rumpled duvet he had crawled out from underneath that morning. But that was all: everything else yelled strangeness at him; bizarre, unreal, horrible strangeness . . .

He wandered around the room in a daze of disbelief. The wardrobe, laundry basket and chest of drawers had all been moved to one corner of the room, next to the bed. The three remaining walls, now unobstructed by furniture, had been turned into an enormous triptych of collaged images: an obscenely evolved version of the montage he had been looking at earlier that evening in the Incident Room. Half of each wall was devoted to one of the Invisible Man's victims: Beverley, Angie and Kirsty. As in the Incident Room, each woman's collage was arranged in an annular pattern, with post-mortem photographs ranged around pictures of the victim alive. There were differences, however. The first difference was that the latter pictures had all been taken without the subject's knowledge: in profile against a blur of pedestrians on a busy street; stepping out through the front door of a house; sitting at a table outside a pub. The second difference was that each collage was speck-led with images apparently cut from pornographic

323

magazines: comminuted female and male bodies, limbs cut away from torsos, scattered like the pieces of a jigsaw. The third difference was the boxes. About a year ago, Alan had bought a set of six little antique boxes at an auction. They were made from polished mahogany with bright brass hinges and clasps. He had never found a use for them, and they had sat ever since at the back of the wardrobe. Now, they had been set out like six little altars, two in front of each wall, with pieces of coloured cloth draped over them. Three altars – the ones below the collages – had objects placed on them: Three long, thick cords of hair bound with thread – burnished corngold, dark chestnut and ash blonde – and three small china bowls containing what looked like little rats' nests of dark, fluffy down. The fourth difference was what really spun Alan's brain from erratically rotating confusion into an insanely whirling panic: In the centre of one of the bare sections of wall, above an empty altar, a new collage had been begun: a small arrangement of monochrome prints waiting for the brutal colour of post-mortem mutilation. And here the pattern had shifted: the nurse's uniform was still there, the antici- pated victim was again tall and slim, but this time he was a man. Three women, one man and two empty spaces.

Suddenly, as though a switch had been thrown, it all slotted into place with diabolical, inexplicable logic: the notes, Chrissie's jacket, the experiment in left-handed writing that looked so similar to the original, the ID parade, the thumbprint; details falling crystal-clear from the tangled mess of his mind.

He turned and fled from the room. An acid bile was burning the back of his throat. He went to the bathroom and crouched in front of the toilet, thinking he was going to be sick, but nothing would come out. The acid was creeping on to his tongue and insinuating itself into every crevice of his mouth. Unable to vomit, he went to the kitchen and drank some water from the tap. Thinking was out of the question: his mind had been blasted into insensibility, and all he was aware of was the bilious taste in his mouth. The water failed to wash it away, so he went to the fridge in search of something stronger. He opened the door and looked inside. As usual, there was very little in there; just a carton of orange juice, half a pint of milk, some cheese, and . . . strange, he didn't remember *that*. He suddenly had an image of the fridge at home, when he was a child. On sausage-and-mash night (Tuesdays, without fail), his mother always cooked more sausages than could be eaten. The survivors could always be found the next day, chilled and pale on a china plate in the fridge, cocooned in webs of stiff white fat. He hated cold sausages, so what was this one doing here? It was short and fat, slightly lumpy and pale brown, the end pointing towards him puckered and wrinkled like a little cauliflower floret. His fingers were heading instinctively towards it when, at last, he realised what it was.

He slammed the fridge door and backed away from it, trembling and turning white. *Ohjesusohfuckohchristohfuckfuckfuckohgodohgod . . .* He ran back to the bathroom. This time, his stomach convulsed and he vomited profoundly into the toilet.

. . . Okay, try this one out. You're being set up; someone has put all this here, someone who wants *you* to go down for it, someone with one hell of a grudge against you. It stands to reason . . . Well, all right, maybe you *did* do it. Without knowing? In some sort of altered state of consciousness? You really believe that can happen? Okay, okay, let's go back to the beginning: You're being set up . . .

He sat on the sofa, staring across the room at the

stunted Sansevieria he was always forgetting to feed. He felt bizarrely calm and numb, as though part of him was detached from the furious argument going on in his head, just hoping that a conclusion could be reached before he finally toppled over the edge into insanity . . .

The decision came. Twenty-four hours later, he was in the back room of a pub in Lewisham. He was not known there, but he knew from the grapevine that it was believed to be a staging point for IRA operatives entering London. After long, delicate negotiations, he had been introduced to a man called Sean, who they said could help him. Alan had cleared out his bank accounts that morning, and two-thirds of the money covered a ten-year passport with five years left to run on it.

Twenty-four hours after that, he was drawing away from England for what he felt sure would be the last time.

At six o'clock that morning, the naked, shaven, mutilated body of Robbie Daniels had been found lying between the rails just inside the tunnel at Piccadilly tube station. The police pathologist who examined the corpse estimated that it had lain there for between twenty-four and forty-eight hours. Despite the similar manner in which the young man had been killed and mutilated, the police remained sceptical about any direct connection with the Invisible Man, except perhaps the possibility of imitation. Only when Inspector Spearman, Sergeant Comber and scene-of-crime specialists thoroughly searched Alan Gorvin's flat the following day and discovered the photographs and the severed penis, was the connection firmly established. By that time, of course, Alan Gorvin was dead, tumbling through the darkness beneath the waves of the English Channel, and the two blank spaces in the giant triptych were never filled.

For more than a year he lived in fear of himself, believing that somewhere inside his head lived his very own Lorenzo, an entity over which he had no control. He regularly scanned the pages of the *Charente Libre*, looking for local crimes he might have committed. His suspicion of himself also turned outwards: he avoided the company of other people, and was grim and hostile to those he could not avoid. As the first months of his exile passed, he began to relax, settling into his new identity with an ease that surprised him. The year he had spent training as a carpenter between an abortive first term at university and joining the police determined his new trade, and the store of French gathered between school and college eased the transition. However, the taciturnity which he had adopted for protection endured and, socially, he kept himself to himself. It was not until he received the Strand Scourer's first cryptic communication that the scales were lifted from his eyes and he knew for sure that the killer did not live inside him. Now he had the freedom to run. What he still did not understand, however, and would continue not to understand for a long time yet, was that there were more ways than just the merely literal for one being to live inside the head of another.

Part III

Mutato Nomine

17

The rain was still falling outside. She could hear it whispering in the grass, pattering and trickling in rivulets on the rocks above. A cool tickle of droplets balmed her stockinged feet, protruding from the mouth of the shelter into the cool, moist air. And, deliciously, delightfully, his weight was upon her, bearing her down on the dusty surface of the rock; and within her was an even heavier weight, a weight of love so pressing she could scarcely breathe. She stroked him, cupping the backs of his calves in the arches of her feet, cradling his head in her hands. And she raised him up, drawing his head from her shoulder, a face framed in ivory hands, luminescent golden curtains hanging down and brushing her cheeks. She smiled up, but different, familiar eyes smiled back at her: Beverley. Beverley's eyes closed, and she grew heavier, heavier, heavier. No longer smiling; crushing. She felt her bones breaking; shoulder blades cracking, ribs snapping, spine grinding on the rock. She closed her tear-filled eyes and opened her mouth to scream,

—and woke. Her eyes opened suddenly, then closed again slowly. Steven's weight was against her, his head on her shoulder. They were still sitting on the sofa where they had slipped into sleep in the growing light of dawn. Carole's eyes had opened just long enough to notice that the daylight was still bright outside, still slanting across the parlour window, so they couldn't have been asleep for more than a few hours. She sighed and leaned against him, settling her cheek against the soft cushion of his hair. He grunted, and she smiled. 'Wake?' she slurred drowsily. There was no reply. He seemed to be getting heavier, leaning on her until the bracing of her own body was insufficient to support him. She shoved him gently with her shoulder. Still no response, so she shoved him again, slightly harder. *'Steven,'* she complained groggily. *'Heavy. Stop it. Budge over . . .'* She opened her eyes,

—and there he was: all blurry, sitting opposite her in the armchair. She closed her eyes again. This wasn't right. Open again, sticky and sleepy. Rub . . . He was still there, gazing at her from the armchair, but she could feel his weight propped limply against her, here on the sofa. She smiled to herself; she was dreaming, and she relished the rare sense of awareness of dreaming. It was not unknown to her, but it was unusual, this knowledge that a dream is a dream while it is still being dreamt. She wondered what would happen next. Just so long as the Steven opposite didn't turn into Beverley again. She couldn't bear that. She closed her eyes again and opened them, but the second Steven was still there. He smiled at her. Aaaah, that was the source of the dream: this Steven looked quite different. He was smartly dressed and heavier about the face, more like the old Steven, the one in the newspaper photograph. He smiled at her again, and this time she smiled back. What was he called? He wasn't Steven then; he was . . . who?

'Good morning,' he said pleasantly.

At the sound of his voice, the delirious spell shattered. The details of the room rushed in on her, much too dense for dreaming. It *was* Steven sitting in the armchair. This wasn't right at all. Her body tensed, and she tried to sit upright, but the weight on her was too heavy. *Whose weight?* In that moment, everything around her slowed down; she gazed at Steven sitting opposite, then there was a long, slow, blurred saccade as her body twisted and her eyes swivelled round to the person beside her, levering up his head, looking into his closed eyes, his open mouth – *Steven* – then another long saccade, eyes widening now, sweeping across the room, back to Steven in the armchair, skating across the barrels of the shotgun slanted on his knee, changing direction, moving up to his face. Still smiling at her. It *must* be a dream: the details of the night before drifted back to her; she judging him a murderer, standing guard over him with the gun; him cleared of all charges, so that she was once again the only guilty party, and now *he* was sitting in judgement on *her*. She struggled to remember *why* he had been innocent. The Steven opposite, the one who looked like his old photograph, was opening his mouth in slow motion, about to speak. *Then* she remembered. There was a rising, rushing sound in her ears as his voice emerged and real time cut back in:

'Good morning,' he repeated. 'The door was open, so I . . .' He shrugged.

She stared at him in horror, all confusion gone, knowing at last who he was. 'Oh God,' she whispered. Her hand went to Steven's shoulder and shook it. 'It's him, Steven, it's him. Oh Christ, it's him!' But Steven wouldn't wake up. She shook him violently, with all her strength, hurling his weight off her. He slumped over and came to rest against the arm of the sofa, his eyes still closed, his mouth hanging open. '*Steven!*' she screamed.

'Calm down,' said the stranger.

'*Steven!* Wake up!' She shook him again, knowing it was futile, knowing he was dead. '*STEVEN!*'

'Be quiet,' said the stranger, his voice louder and sterner.

Sick with horror, she looked at him and at the shotgun on his lap.

333

'Good,' he said. 'That's better. Now perhaps we can—'

'What have you done to him? You . . .' She rose, ready to attack, but the gun swung up and pointed at her, and she froze.

'He's fine,' said the man. 'He's just sleeping. I couldn't take any chances, you see.' He held up a tiny hypodermic syringe between his fingers like a cigarette.

Carole stared at him while her mind rushed frantically, estimating the distance to the door, whether she could reach it before he had time to bring the gun to bear and squeeze off a shot; could she get to the car in time, or the Suzuki . . .

'One important question,' he said calmly. 'Just now, you said, "It's him" . . . *Who*, precisely, did you mean?'

'Him,' she whispered weakly, her voice harrowed out and hollow, her body shrinking back into the sofa.

'Yes,' he said. 'Yes, I am. *A* him, obviously, but what particular him did you have in mind?'

She searched her memory for it . . . something strange, something . . . 'Strand Scourer,' she murmured. 'The Strand Scourer, the Invisible Man.' Her voice rose: 'You're the—'

'No,' he said. Suddenly, the smile was gone and there was a look in his eyes, almost of fear, a look which confounded her own terror. 'No, I'm not the . . . I'm not him. You've got it all wrong.' He pointed at Steven. 'Who do you think *he* is?'

Disorientated, wondering if she was still dreaming after all, Carole glanced at Steven's face as if to check. 'He's Steven,' she said. 'How can you look like him? How can you—'

'Steven?' he interrupted.

'Alan, I mean. His real name's Alan: you know perfectly well who he is. And I know who you are. What do you want from us?'

334

The man looked disarmingly bewildered. 'What do I *want*? I don't want anything from you; I just want *him*.' He sat forward in the chair. 'Listen . . . Carole, isn't it? Listen, Carole, I don't know what he's told you, but he isn't Alan Gorvin.' He paused and shook his head. 'Sorry, look, this isn't quite what I was expecting.' He looked her in the eyes and pointed at himself. '*I'm* Alan Gorvin,' he said quietly.

Carole stared at him for a long time in a silence breached only by the dull tocking of the mantel clock. Later, she found it difficult to account for her sudden rush of instantaneous comprehension and absolute knowledge, but in that moment she knew it to be true. As hard as she might fight against it, the inexorable sense of it forced its way into her brain.

He gazed back at her with an expression whose ghost she had sometimes seen in Steven's face. This, though, was the real thing: a look of calm – not stunned, but calm – bewilderment; almost of disappointment at this last unfair card his life had dealt him; to have come through all this and then have his name, his whole identity, usurped by the man who had so diligently persecuted him. Perhaps it was this, or perhaps it was his face: there was no gainsaying the fact that he did look so much more like the newspaper face; the true face. Whatever it was, she believed him; immediately and utterly. But the conclusion she reached was not so simple: there must be *two* Alan Gorvins, both persecuted, both innocent, and somewhere out there was their tormentor. Feeling once more that she was sliding into a dream state, she turned her gaze on Steven again. He was still the same Steven, still the Steven she had loved and cared for . . .

The stranger, the man who called himself Alan – no, *was* Alan – was speaking to her again, his voice seeming to come from a long way away. 'I know what you're thinking,' he was saying.

'What?' she heard herself ask, still not taking her eyes off Steven.

'You're thinking, if *I'm* Alan, then who is *he* . . .'

Carole shook her head slowly, although it was true that a part of her was thinking that; not wondering, but knowing, dragging up the same feelings of sick horror she had felt in the library yesterday . . . God, only yesterday? In that short time, Steven had been charged, tried, acquitted, forgiven, and now he was charged again. All the same crimes were once more laid at his feet, along with a new one; stealing another man's identity, another man's history, stealing his whole life. She felt the dizzying sensation of seeing all his words, his evoked images, his stolen stories crowd under the surface and burst out of him in a cacophonous rush, hovering in the air above his evacuated soul for a few uncertain moments, then swirl across the room and charge into the body of their rightful owner.

'He never dreamt it could come to this,' Alan was saying. 'Never in his wildest nightmares. After what he's done to me. He destroyed my life, almost drove me mad, almost drove me to death. He never imagined this happening. He thought he was immune. I think he even thought he was immortal, but I got him in the end, and now I've got him again.'

'No,' Carole whispered. 'No, this isn't right. It's not him, not the person you say. He's *my Steven*. I'd have known, I'd have guessed. It's not fair! You can't come here and do this to us!'

'You did guess, Carole. Didn't you?'

In spite of herself, she nodded. Tears were starting to form in her tired eyes. 'Yes,' she said weakly. 'But I was wrong!'

He shook his head. 'You were right. You *know* you

were right . . . Just as a matter of interest, Carole, *how* did you guess, exactly?'

She hesitated. 'I remembered seeing him . . . I mean, seeing you. Or him. I remembered his face at the funeral.'

'Funeral?'

'Beverley's . . . He admitted it then, that he was Alan Gorvin.'

He sighed. 'And he told you how Alan had been framed for all those killings. Which was true, except that he wasn't Alan Gorvin. If he had been, he'd have known that Alan Gorvin wasn't at Beverley Cunningham's funeral. I was busy at the Station that day. I sent two of my officers. You must have remembered me from somewhere else. I did do a couple of TV appeals – you must've seen those.' He paused, gazing steadily at her face. 'You're Carole Perceval, aren't you? I thought so. We never met, but I saw you once, and I read your statement. You know, I think that was the one thing he had a trace of bad feeling about: the fact that you blamed yourself for him killing Beverley. Oh yes, his knowledge is incredible: he knew all about you. I suppose it was that little speck of humanity in him that made him come looking for you after I'd finally broken him.'

'*Looking* for me?' she asked. Her skin was beginning to prickle.

'Of course. Did you think it was a coincidence?'

Carole looked at Steven again. 'What do you mean, *broken*?'

Alan stood up. Seeing Carole look at him with a resurgence of fright, he laid the shotgun down on the armchair and held up his hands in a peaceful gesture. 'It's all right,' he said gently. 'You're safe now. I think we ought to do something about him, though. He won't stay asleep forever, and I only brought one dose with

337

me. If he wakes up and finds me here, then you'll really see his true colours.'

Carole edged away from Steven as though expecting him to wake at any moment and transform into a frenzied raptor. 'What are you going to do to him?'

'Lock him up somewhere while you call the police.' He took hold of Steven's limp arm and hauled him upright. 'I've looked forward to this moment for a hell of a long time,' he grunted, crouching and heaving the unconscious body onto his shoulders. 'Where are your keys? I'll put him outside.'

Carole took her jangling bundle of keys from the mantelpiece and pushed them into Alan's free hand. He grunted and shifted Steven's weight into a more manageable position, then staggered unsteadily towards the front door.

As soon as he was gone, she ran to the phone and dialled 999. As she waited for the dial to whir itself to rest after each digit, she cursed herself for her sentimentality in not replacing this ancient article with a push-button model. At last, she was through. 'Which service do you require?' asked a woman's voice. 'Police,' said Carole breathlessly. There was a pause, then the voice repeated, 'Which service do you require?' slightly louder. 'Police!' she shouted. 'Is there anyone there?' said the voice querulously. 'YES!' she bawled. 'Oh, not *now*, for God's sake!' This plea was directed at the phone itself. It had been switching its speaking function moodily on and off like this for the past few days. 'Why now, you bastard?' she demanded of it. The operator's warning that making hoax emergency calls was a punishable offence went unheard as Carole bashed the receiver furiously on the desk: *thump-thump-thump*, 'Hello?' she said, holding it to her ear again, but the operator had cut her off. She slammed the receiver back onto its cradle and stared frantically around the room, her eyes finally falling on the shotgun. She picked it up and hefted it in her hands, but it didn't make her feel any better. She had learned the hard way that it was useless unless she was prepared to use it; she wasn't about to tiptoe out to the end of that precarious limb again until she was absolutely, incontrovertibly certain of who was who and what was what. On the other hand, she couldn't put herself at the wrong end of it. She broke the breech and took out the cartridges, slipping them into her pocket, then scrabbled around the floor, searching for the spent cases from yesterday's accident. She found them under the sideboard and stuffed them into the breech. She went to close it up, but hesitated; the little dents made by the firing pins in the centres of the brass discs were glaringly obvious. If he turned out to be lying, she wanted him to keep feeling powerful, guessing that he would be most dangerous if he felt vulnerable. She took the spent cases out again and threw them away, then took two fresh cartridges from the gun cupboard and hid the rest behind a stack of plates in the sideboard. Using a pair of scissors, she hastily picked open the ends of the orange plastic tubes and gutted them, tipping the wadding and lead balls into the waste paper bin. At last, she slid them into the gun's breech, slapped it closed and laid the gun back on the armchair. He still wasn't back, so she ran to the kitchen. In the cutlery drawer, she found a sharp-pointed vegetable knife with a hefty plastic handle and a four-inch blade. It wouldn't sit comfortably in the waistband of her jeans, so she ran back to the parlour and rifled through the desk until she found a roll of sellotape. Rolling up the baggy sleeve of her jumper, she secured the knife to her inner forearm with two straps of tape, butt-down so that the point would not catch on her sleeve if she needed to get at it in a hurry. With the sleeve rolled down again, the knife was undetectable.

339

She had just sprinted and dived back onto the sofa, and was trying to control her breathing, when she heard the back door open.

He smiled at her from the doorway. 'Did they say how long they'd be?' he asked.

'What? Oh, er . . .' For a moment, she toyed with the idea of lying: *Oh, about twenty minutes . . .* 'No,' she said. 'The phone's not working.'

'Not working?' He picked it up and dialled, but could get no response to his request for the police. 'Strange,' he said. 'You don't think he could have tampered with it, do you?'

'I don't know.' She hadn't thought of this. 'What have you done with him?' she asked.

He went back to the armchair. Carole tensed as he picked up the gun, then relaxed a little when he laid it on the floor and sat down. 'Locked him up,' he said. 'We'll be safe for the time being.'

She looked doubtfully at him. 'Are you really Alan Gorvin?' she asked.

He seemed more saddened than affronted by her doubt, and she felt reassured. 'Yes,' he said quietly. 'Surely you must have seen pictures of me. We're quite easy to tell apart, really. Not nearly as alike as identical twins usually are. But then, he did have a much harsher upbringing than me. It's bound to take its toll. I didn't even know I *had* a twin until a few months ago. It explained a lot of things. Like the fact that I was picked out of an identity parade once as the Invisible Man. Did he tell you about that when he was busy stealing my life?' He gazed sadly at her. 'He really took you in, didn't he. You still don't really believe me. Not that I blame you – I mean, he must be very convincing. He's got incredible talents.' He paused and gave a little laugh. 'You really took me by surprise, you know, thinking I was him. Before you woke up, I'd actually been wondering if you might be in league with him.'

'In *league* with him?' said Carole.

'I know. *In league* – what a melodramatic term. But it's not impossible, is it – I mean, Ian Brady had his Myra, Fred West had his Rosemary. It's not entirely unknown for these monsters to have monstrous female accomplices.'

'But they were . . . they were—'

'Psychopaths?' he said. 'What the hell d'you think *he* is? Bloody Donald Duck?' He stared incredulously at her, then went on quietly: 'I knew I was wrong as soon as you opened your eyes. No one can fake fear like that, not spontaneously. I don't think I'll ever forget the look on your face. Now I know how it feels to have someone look at me and really believe in their soul that I'm a killer. I'll never forget that. I don't suppose he's ever experienced that – none of the people he killed had the slightest suspicion that he meant them any harm. God, if only I had a tenth of his talent for persuasion.' He leaned forward, looking gravely at her. 'I understand,' he said. 'Honestly, I do. He's taken you in, and you can't quite believe it. You're not even a gullible person, are you? But you have to understand how psychopaths' minds work. Most of them don't give off any signals, you see – that's why they're so difficult to catch, because they don't act like other murderers. Nobody suspects them, and they don't leave traces. Believe me, I know. Before the Invisible Man, I worked on quite a few murder cases, and they're usually pretty simple. Ninety-nine point nine per cent of real murders are nothing like the ones you get on TV detective shows. You see, most people commit murder when they're experiencing extremes of emotion – like rage or hatred or terror or whatever. They're not thinking straight, so they make a mess, and when they realise what they've done, they panic. They leave forensic evidence all over the place.

341

Even murderers who are relatively clear-thinking don't manage to cover up completely. It's not Inspector Morse with these things – I never raced around for days trying to puzzle it out – any murder that isn't solved within forty-eight hours usually stays unsolved.'

Now that he was driving deeper into the subject, his being seemed to become naturally suffused with the persona of the police officer, as though this was his true self floating to the surface after being buried for a long time. 'There are two exceptions,' he said. 'Two kinds of killer that don't behave like that: psychopaths and professionals, and it's my opinion that professional killers are just psychopaths who happen to have a form of psychopathology that's amenable to commercial use. The difference between the psychopath and your ordinary murderer is that the rules don't apply. There's something missing – I don't know what it is: conscience or something – so that he doesn't think he's doing anything morally wrong. He might even think he's doing good; that the victim is better off dead or the world will be a better place without this person. Of course, he knows that *society* thinks he's doing wrong, and he'll be punished if he's caught, so he covers his tracks. As policemen, that gives us two problems – One: The absence of distracting emotions means that the planning and clearing up is efficient and effective, and Two: The lack of any feeling of breaking a moral code means there's no guilt, which means you get none of the behavioural tics that tell you when someone's up to something.'

He paused again and looked at Carole. 'I know what you're thinking,' he said. 'When you realised who he was, even though you knew what he'd done, you couldn't really believe it. Not the . . . what does he call himself? Steven. Not your Steven; he couldn't be a killer. You'd have known, wouldn't you? That's exactly how

342

these freaks get away with it for so long. No one around them suspects. Of course, there are some who give signals. They *seem* weird or evil, because they're maybe lacking other things like an ability to socialise with people. That type end up as loners. It's the other type, though – the type like *him*, my *brother*, for God's sake – who are the most dangerous, because they can camouflage themselves in society. They only get caught when they eventually make a mistake. They all do make a mistake in the end. Kevin did. That's how I caught him.'

'Kevin?' said Carole. She was so hypnotised and bewildered by the twist of events that the name just bounced off her without connecting with Steven at all.

'His name's Kevin. Not very dramatic, is it? Not nearly as impressive as *the Invisible Man* or *the Strand Scourer*. He was born on 18 August 1959 at 16 Omdurman Road, Bethnal Green, about two and a half minutes before I slithered out to join him. Kevin and Alan, as fine a pair of bouncing baby boys as Mr and Mrs Gorvin could have wished for. And I never knew he existed until a couple of months ago. I still don't know the full story.' He stared down at his hands, the blunted fingernails of one picking at the skin of the other. 'I'm afraid I resorted to beating it out of him in the end. In fifteen years as a copper, I'd never done it, but he drove me to it. Evil bastard as he is, I'm not proud of what I did to him. I only managed to get a few scraps out of him before he escaped. I'm nowhere near as clever as he is; I had a bastard of a job tracking him here.'

'What happened?' asked Carole. 'Why didn't you know about each other?'

'He *did* know. He found out about me somehow. I don't know when. He was put into Care when we were about three years old. I still don't know why. Our parents must have obliterated every trace of his existence, because I never suspected anything. As for me, I think I must've blanked out my memories of him. I just wonder what it must have been that was so bad that they had to get rid of him like that, so bad that I suppressed it. I suppose you've got to feel sorry for him in a way. I mean, imagine what that could do to a child's mind – finding out you're adopted, and not only that but your parents *kept* your twin brother. I mean, *why*? You *can't* really imagine it, can you? It must be like an atom bomb going off in your skull – the rejection, the trauma, the dislocation, the jealousy. I mean, Christ, no wonder he had it in for me. Those people he killed, we were looking in the wrong direction – it wasn't about *them*, it was aimed at *me*, to implicate me, to make me feel something like the victimisation and the stigma and the anonymous persecution he thought he'd been subjected to, all repaid against me a hundredfold.'

Carole was staring into nowhere, nodding vacantly. 'Do you think he . . . with me . . . I mean . . .'

Alan gazed sympathetically at her. 'Did he intend to kill you, you mean?' He pursed his lips and shook his head. 'I don't know, I honestly don't know. He must have come looking for you for a reason, but I don't know if that was it. He was in a hell of a broken state when I last saw him. I don't know what he was capable of after that. Maybe he was planning a second phase, where he'd go after the closest friends of his other victims. Or maybe he finally found his conscience and he wanted to apologise.'

'*Apolo*gise?'

'You know what I mean – make amends, confess, atone, whatever you want to call it.'

'No,' said Carole despondently. 'No, he hid his identity until I found out for myself. But he never showed any signs of hostility or anything, either . . . Well, except maybe at first.'

'I don't know,' said Alan. 'I've been wondering – and

this is just a guess, mind – but from the look of the two of you, I reckon you had something pretty intimate going on here. Is that true?'

She coloured slightly. 'Well, yes . . .'

'Perhaps it could have been . . . well, imagine the sort of life he'd had, all the things that drove him to do all those obscene things. Then, at last, just when he's least expecting it, he meets the only person he's ever known in his life who offers him real love. Maybe you tapped into whatever little pool of human feeling still survives under all that trauma and hatred.'

Carole nodded, slowly and reluctantly. 'Maybe,' she said, and looked Alan in the eyes.

He caught the meaning of the look, and shook his head firmly. 'No, Carole, he's still the same person. Think about what he's done – think about what he did to Beverley. You haven't changed him. If we don't do something about him, he'll go on and on killing. And as soon as he realises I'm here and you've seen me, you won't be safe any more. He'll feel exposed, maybe even betrayed. It's over, Carole. I've been running from that bastard long enough. This is where it stops. We're going to turn him in.'

'No,' she said, and he stared at her. 'No,' she repeated. 'Not yet. I don't understand. I want to know what really happened. I want to know what you meant when you said you *broke* him.'

18

'I've cracked it!' said Comber triumphantly, perching on the edge of WDC Higgins's desk and slapping down a sheet of computer printout in front of her.

'Cracked what?' she asked, glancing at the piece of paper without much interest. 'I'm awful busy, Sarge.'

'Gorvin,' he said. 'I've got him!' He pushed the paper towards her. 'Go on, read it.'

Sighing, she skimmed through the printout. 'Newport CID,' she muttered. 'Blah-blah, October 17th 1996, blah-blah-blah ... Nurse.' She stopped and glanced up at him, then re-read the report properly. 'MO's a bit different, isn't it?' she suggested when she had finished.

'Close enough. Don't you get it? This was only eight months ago! I knew he couldn't keep his head down forever – he just had to kill again sooner or later. And now he's popped up in Yorkshire.'

'Sarge, it could just be a copycat. I mean, it is a bit different.'

'He's off his home patch, Gail. He hasn't got access to the same resources as before.'

'Hmm. You've still got the tiny problem of him being dead, though, haven't you.'

Comber smiled. 'I've been through every record I can get my hands on. Ever heard of a place called Ile d'Ouessant? Thought you wouldn't. It's a little island off the tip of Brittany. About two years ago, some fishermen from there trawled something up in their net that wasn't haddock. It was so decomposed, the clothes were virtually all that was holding it together. The pathologist reckoned it had been in the water for over a year. Weighted down with Guinness cans. Can you believe it – fucking Guinness! The French police couldn't make anything of it, so they passed it over to the British authorities. In the end, they got possible matches with five missing persons.'

'And Gorvin was one of them?'

'No, of course not – we'd've heard if he was. Oh, they checked against him all right, but there was no match.' He snorted. 'Dozy cunts didn't twig that that was the whole fucking *point*.' He took another piece of paper from his pocket and handed it to Gail. 'That's a list of the five possibles. Look at number three. Kevin McKenzie, aged eighteen. Went missing on or about the twenty-fifth of February 1994. He was expected in France to meet friends, but never showed up.' He tapped the piece of paper. 'That's our baby, Gail.'

'Why wasn't this brought up at the time?'

He shrugged. 'You don't know what it was like in this nick that week. Upstairs wanted it closed, so we went through what we had and closed it. Now, though, Christ – this is enough to reopen the case!' He snatched up the pieces of paper and stood up. 'I'm off to see Reynolds. We should be able to get inquiries going by tomorrow.' He slapped his hand on the desktop excitedly. 'I've got the bastard, Gail. I've got him at last!'

Alan sat and silently picked at a threadbare patch on the arm of the chair, pulling and twisting the frayed edges. After a few minutes, he seemed to realise what he was doing, and stopped, smoothing the patch down with his fingers and glancing sheepishly at Carole. She hadn't noticed, and continued to gaze at his face, waiting for him to begin explaining.

'When I left Wales,' he said. 'The day I left, I almost died. Did he tell you that?'

'Yes. You nearly drowned.'

Alan nodded. 'That's right, I nearly drowned. He certainly got that right. But I bet he didn't tell you I nearly died *twice* that day. The second time was his doing, even though he probably didn't know at the time ... Didn't you think it was strange that I managed to survive in the water for so long and then just toddle off happily afterwards?'

'I hadn't really thought about it.'

'No. Well, you've probably never seen the Severn

347

Levels foreshore on a cold day. By the time I'd swum back to shore, I was so cold and exhausted I could hardly crawl up the sea-wall. When I finally managed it, I had to walk nearly a mile to the culvert where I'd left clean clothes and my money. When I got there, they'd gone. *He* took them. He'd been watching me all the time. As soon as I went over the wall, he took my stuff and legged it. So there I was, soaked, freezing cold, exhausted. I almost died. This farmer found me a few hours later, curled up by the edge of a ditch, unconscious. To cut it short, I got a bed for a couple of nights and some fresh clothes, but still no money. I, er, well, when him and his wife were out, I stole some cash from the house and took off. I ended up in Bristol and caught a train to Birmingham. I ended up—'

'Begging,' Carole interrupted. 'I know. He told me.'

'I'll bet he did. Do you know what it feels like to have your identity stolen like that?'

'Maybe that was how he felt about you,' Carole said, more in the tone of an observation than a suggestion. 'Maybe that was why he persecuted you.'

'Maybe. Yeah, I suppose so. You know what's really galling, I bet you anything he told my story much better than I ever could. More convincing by a mile. That's the secret, isn't it, telling a story well. That's one of the first things I learnt as a copper. I've seen real villains walk because they had their storytelling really sorted – not just their facts, but the *way* they told it – and I've seen men I suspected were innocent banged up for a quick result because they were crap liars and they ended up incriminating themselves. That's all it takes – no alibi, usually, or an alibi that's too embarrassing to put up until their brief forces it out of them, and already the lies have piled up. Makes a bad impression on a jury, that sort of thing. After that, with a clever prosecuting counsel, it's like shooting fish in a barrel. Get hold of the emotional weak spot, the hole in the story, and you've got your man.'

'Your *innocent* man,' said Carole.

Alan shrugged. 'Sometimes. Like me. That's why I had to run when all that evidence turned up. I couldn't front it out, because I'm not good enough at telling stories. If it'd been reversed, I think Kevin could have talked his way out of it. I mean, he made *you* believe in him, didn't he. And you probably got closer to him than anybody ever has. If he could achieve *that* . . .'

'How did you catch him?' she asked. She had no desire to pick over the putrefying carcass of her relationship with Steven. Or Kevin. Steven – Alan – Kevin – Michael – Paul – Nigel – the carousel of christian names revolved dizzily, and she had to struggle to keep track of which ones belonged with which of the two subtly variant twin faces. She noticed that he was looking at her oddly.

'Is something the matter?' he asked, looking at her left arm.

She realised with a start that, while he had been talking, she had been fingering the knife through the sleeve of her jumper. She quickly converted the movement to scratching. 'Just an insect bite,' she said. 'Been bothering me for days. You were saying? About catching him?'

He frowned at her for a moment. 'Why don't you put something on it? Here, let me have a look . . .'

'No, leave it. It's fine. Just tell me what happened.'

He sat back in the chair, still glancing doubtfully at her arm. 'Okay. Where was I?'

'Birmingham. Begging.'

'Yeah,' he sighed. 'I've never been so low in my life. It was the only time I've ever known what it was like to feel really dirty, really despised, really ashamed. It was like people made me invisible, blanked me out. At least

349

if people think you're a psychopathic killer, they're frightened of you, they give you a sort of twisted respect. I mean, even people's fear and hatred has got to be better than that feeling of being dirt. What sort of society do we live in where a beggar is more despicable than a killer?'

'I don't think that's true.'

'No? Well, just go and try it. Find yourself your very own piss-puddle shop doorway to sit in and find out what people think of you. They don't hate you or anything, they just hate the sight of you. They just wish they could blank you right out of existence. And worst of all, you agree with them sometimes, on nights when the hostels are full up and it's raining and the winos have got together and they're chewing lumps off each other while you're trying to sleep, but you can't because you're freezing your bollocks off and pissing yourself with fear that they'll start on *you* next.' He stopped and collected himself. His cheeks were going red and his breathing was laboured. 'When that note came,' he went on when he had calmed down. 'When he dropped that note on me, that was the last straw. I went after him. I could *see* him, disappearing through the crowd. It was the second time I'd tried to chase him, but this time he didn't get away. I kept him in sight all the way out of the Bullring and into the streets. I almost got run down a couple of times, but I just kept going, and all the time I could see him up ahead, sometimes a long way off, sometimes closer. When I knew I had him was when we were out of the city centre and there were no people about for him to hide behind. He started running. In the end, I caught up with him in this deserted factory by a canal. That was the first time I'd seen his face. I almost passed out from the shock . . . I fought him, there on that filthy floor, rolling in the oily puddles and the dirt. He nearly killed me. He was on top of me, strangling the life out of me, but somehow I managed to get the better of him. I tied him up against a pillar and kept him there for five days. I never tortured anyone in my life before, but by God I tortured him then. I starved him and rationed his water to one squeeze from a wet rag every six hours. He broke at the end of the fourth day. Admitted what he'd done to me, and why he did it. I would've got more out of him, but I came back on the fifth evening with some food and there he was, gone. But I'd seen the look on his face. He was beaten. Broken, like I said. You see, all his power over me came from my fear and his anonymity. Once we'd looked each other in the eyes and he saw I wasn't afraid of him any more, he was finished. Now he was *my* prey. It's taken me months to track him down, but now it's finally over.'

As he came to the end of his story, an uneasy silence settled over the room.

'Over,' Carole repeated absently.

Alan leaned towards her, searching her face. 'Can I trust you, Carole?' he asked imploringly.

The intensity of his gaze was so great that she felt as though her soul was being scoured; that any hint of a lie would be as visible to him as a bloodstain on a white sheet. 'Yes,' she whispered. 'Yes, of course you can.'

'And do you trust me?'

She hesitated, and he looked anxious. 'Yes,' she said. 'Yes, I think I do . . . No, I'm sure I do.'

He smiled. 'Good girl. What I need you to do is—' He glanced up. 'What was that? I heard something.' He stood up suddenly and stalked silently to the window, peering out cautiously. 'Carole,' he whispered, coming back and seizing her arm. 'We've got to move!'

'What's the matter? I didn't hear anything.' He had dragged her to her feet and was hustling her towards the door. 'Where did you put him?' she demanded.

'No time,' he said urgently. He took her hands in his.

'Go upstairs. Have you got a lock on your bedroom door? Good. Lock yourself in, and don't open the door. Now I'm here, you're not safe until he's dealt with. Please, Carole, I've got to do this on my own. You'll be safe soon. I won't harm him. Now *go!*'

Carole ran from the room. Alan listened to her footsteps on the stairs. When he heard the bedroom door close, he went to the foot of the stairs and listened for a moment, then went to the kitchen. He quickly and quietly rifled the drawers until he found a medium-sized carving knife with a razor-sharp edge, then he went cautiously to the back door and stepped out into the yard.

Through the Mirror

Deep . . . deeper . . . deepest . . .

An ordinary house in an ordinary street. It is nearing dusk, and stillness reigns inside 22 Cleevis Terrace. The late sun slanting through half-drawn curtains falls on still, silent rooms. The house which, at this time of day, should be filled with the noise and impatience of nearly-teatime feels as though sound and movement have been evacuated from it like a blown egg. An experiment has been conducted here, and its designer has yet to reach a conclusion about its results.

Mrs Jean Goodmanson, thirty-two years old, adoptive mother of one sweet-looking small child and – until a few months ago – devoted and harassed wife of one unexpectedly unreliable husband, has been the subject of the experiment. She is renowned locally as a formidable source of sound and movement, but on this fading afternoon, she is as still and silent as the bricks, plaster, paper and paint that make up her little, spartanly furnished house. If we examine the results of the experiment, we find Jean in the hall. Or at least half in the hall, half still on the foot of the stairs she never quite finished descending. Her left foot, bare and with toenails still shell-pink with the varnish applied for Sunday's day-trip to Southend, is caught between the third and fourth banister railings, the Dulux-glossed white wood gouging deep, bloodless welts in the skin of her ankle. Her right leg, splayed against the wall, is bent at the knee, the calf resting across the narrow band of worn pink nylon stair-carpet, on the third step. Her inclined posture has caused the skirts of the lemon-yellow flannelette dressing gown she put on this morning to ride to her waist, exposing (and her fastidious sensibilities would be appalled by this if only she were aware of it) yesterday's underwear, soiled by the sudden, involuntary evacuation of bodily fluids in the first few teetering moments of the experiment. Her hands lie limply by her sides, one pointing up, one pointing down, the normally cosseted fingernails scarred and broken in a pattern which matches the scrapes and scratches in the wallpaper further up the stairs. Her stringy, early-morning hair lies like octopus tentacles around her head, which is twisted to one side, a thread of blood tracing the contour of her white cheek, wide-open hazel eyes gazing steadily and sightlessly across the surface of the hall carpet and through the open door of the darkening front room.

And there, sitting small and coiled on the floor, almost as still, almost as silent as his mother, is Kevin, swaddled in the soft red wool of his Ladybird dressing gown. In front of him, the record-player drawer of the Pye radiogram is open, and an LP is rotating on the turntable, the needle stuck indefinitely in the record's terminal groove. Kevin's body is inclined forward, his head tilted towards the dulled brass mesh of the radiogram's speaker cabinet, listening intently to the persistent, sibilant *sssssssssssssssssssssss-tch-sssssssssssssssssssssss-tch*. His *Snow White and the Seven Dwarfs Colouring and Puzzle Book* and his pristine *Thomas the Tank Engine* lie disregarded on the carpet beside him as he concentrates on the whispering Pye. His experiment is nearing its conclusion, or so he hopes – even though he doesn't know quite why he began it or what its purpose is. Still, he is enjoying himself, so what does it matter? The record is his mother's favourite – a Music For Pleasure collection called *Piano Romance* – and Kevin has chosen it quite deliberately. He has hatched and nurtured a theory (it came to him while he was sitting on the stairs, studying her broken, twisted body) that her Last Message to him would be found in the hissing last groove of her favourite LP. Now that her soul has gone to a higher world, she must have access to knowledge he can barely contemplate: her Message will contain the Answer; the key knowledge which will unlock the whole world of things he doesn't understand. This, he reasons, must be the ultimate purpose of the experiment . . . Nothing yet, though: He thinks he can hear whispering voices in there, but he cannot discern any words. He reaches up and twists the right-hand bakelite disc, turning the volume up full: *SSSSSSSSSSSSSSSSSSSSSS-TCH-SSSSSSSSSSSSSSSSSSSSSS-TCH* . . . Now he can hear something, faint and indistinct.

BANG-BANG-BANG!

The sudden percussion of the door knocker would make any other child flinch, but not Kevin. He is so absorbed in his scrutiny of the crackling white noise from the towering Pye that he barely notices it. It is the third time this afternoon that the knocker has hammered like this. The letter-box squeaks open. 'Jean?' says a woman's voice. 'Jean? Anybody home?' There is a pause, then the flap clatters shut again, followed by a flurry of muted, urgent voices. Kevin doesn't even look up; his gaze is still fixed on the hissing brass mesh.

21 Cleevis Terrace is in many ways identical to its neighbour, Kevin observes: The same layout of rooms, the same staircase, the same wooden banister. The stair-carpet, down which his slippers are padding, is a rich horse-chestnut russet rather than fuchsia pink, and the wallpaper against which his outstretched fingers brush is printed with bold yellow roses rather than the speckle of pale blue forget-me-nots, but otherwise it is the same.

Even the whispering hosts of spectres embedded in the house's fabric seem the same: forgotten, nameless generations babbling seamlessly about their own private, banal tragedies. As Kevin nears the foot of the stairs, the whisper of ghosts gives way to the murmur of voices from the front room:

'—the boy I feel sorry for,' a woman's high-pitched, nasal whine is saying as he presses his ear to the closed door. 'Imagine being alone all day with . . .' She trails off helplessly. 'No wonder he seems a bit touched.' Kevin recognises the voice as that of Doreen, the vicariously blonde and blowsy woman who turned up this morning attached to the arm of his estranged father. At her insistence, the two of them will be spending the night at the B & B in Gordon Road, because she will not set foot in 'that place', as she refers to her lover's former home. 'Rubbish,' says Kevin's father's truculent voice. 'He's always been like that. I never wanted to have the little bleeder in the first place. It was Jean who insisted.' 'God rest her poor soul,' interjects the rolling contralto of Mrs Septimus, the pillow-bosomed matriarch of Number 21. There is a long lull filled with the genteel tinkle of best china cups rising and falling in their saucers. 'I suppose you'll be taking the boy with you after the funeral,' says Mrs Septimus. 'I've seen to it that all his things are laundered and packed.' This supposition is followed by a silence pregnant with almost tangible embarrassment, shame and resentment, which Kevin can sense even through the solid wood of the door. There are some mumbled words (his father's voice) which he can't make out, interspersed with a few truncated exclamations from Doreen. At one point, belying her earlier concern, she shrills: 'It wouldn't surprise *me* if it was him done it to her.' There is another painful silence. 'Perhaps his mother and father will take him back,' says Mrs Septimus confusingly. Kevin frowns to himself; how can they, now that one is gone and the other is as good as gone? There is more mumbling, during which the portentous words *Social Services* keep recurring. This sounds familiar: he has read these words on a piece of paper he found at the back of his parents' bureau. He has no idea what it means. His name – Kevin Anthony Goodmanson – appeared on the paper, above the unfamiliar word *withheld* in the box marked *Parents' Names and Address(es)*. Why have his parents withheld (he has looked the word up in his *Concise Oxford Dictionary*) their names from this mysterious entity called *Social Services*? Have they been in hiding from someone? If so, why did they let *his* name be revealed? 'Couldn't you take him in just for a little while?' asks Mrs Septimus. 'I've been very happy to look after him, but there's a limit to what I can do at my age.' 'We're very grateful, too,' says Kevin's father hastily. 'We can't take him, though.' He sounds more resentful than regretful; more *won't* than *can't*. 'Me and George are getting married,' announces Doreen proudly and defiantly. 'We was gonna have to wait for the divorce to come through, but, well, we thought we might as well as tie the knot now.' Another silence. 'I see,' says Mrs Septimus. Kevin can sense the tightness of her lips as she says this. 'We might want to have children of our own,' says his father. 'Anyhow, like I said, it was always Jean as wanted him, not me.'

Kevin has heard enough. He turns away and climbs the stairs. It does not occur to him to regret his experiment (even though he never got to hear the Message), but he does feel a growing apprehension about what will become of him.

'Alan! Will you come *on*.' Pauline Gorvin hauls on her son's hand. She is tired and exasperated; it is Christmas

Eve, and she has already had to trail around all four floors of Hamley's after him (she and her now emaciated purse would have preferred Woolworth's), squeezing through the screeching, giggling congestion while he examined every Dinky and Corgi car, Keil-Kraft aeroplane kit and Action Man outfit. Now, they have barely covered fifty yards of Regent Street and he is already dragging behind. 'Come *on*!' she shouts, and gives his hand one more tug. At last, he comes unstuck like a rubber sucker from a pane of glass and follows her, casting curious glances over his shoulder and repeatedly colliding with people's legs and his mother's shopping bags.

He is distracted; so distracted that he has forgotten all about the exciting assortment of toys nestling in the stout paper carrier bag bumping along at his elbow. He has just had an extraordinary experience: They were caught in a bottleneck where the press of shoppers filed between the shop-fronts and a bus-queue standing two-deep at the kerb, and he was looking at his reflection in the window of a café, when he had the sudden dizzying impression of seeing *two* reflections of his face, superimposed and slightly offset. What was more, the deeper of the two reflections didn't seem to quite follow his movements. He winked, the first reflection winked, but the second reflection just stared blankly. He nodded and grimaced, the first reflection mimicked him, but the second tilted its head to the side and frowned. He was trying to puzzle out how the effect was done when his mother, with a Herculean strength born of desperation, hauled him away.

All the way up Regent Street, he keeps looking back, but the mysterious café window is soon lost to view beyond the mill of pedestrians, then they are descending the steps to Oxford Circus. Apart from Hamley's, the tube ride is always the most exciting part of a trip up

West, and before long, his thoughts of the strange double reflection are swamped by the thrilling vertigo of gargantuan escalators and the clatter and hum of the trains in the echoing tunnels.

'Are you going to order anything or not, son?'

Kevin doesn't hear the waiter's voice. He has just had an extraordinary experience, like gazing into a distorting mirror, and he is still staring at the blurred space where the other boy's face was.

'Well?' the waiter insists. Kevin's eyes turn reluctantly away from the window and look up coldly at the waiter, who is studying him with narrowed eyes. Suddenly, the waiter leans forward and whispers angrily: 'Get out. We don't want your sort in ere. Gahn, git!' Kevin stares calmly at him for a few moments before standing up, giving the waiter the discomfiting impression that his face is being recorded and logged for future reference. He has never felt threatened by a nine-year-old before, and he is relieved when the boy leaves.

Kevin walks down towards Piccadilly in a delirium. He knows well enough what the vision meant: he has seen himself as he might have been in another life. Not that he is in any doubt that the boy's face was real: since his removal from Cleevis Terrace, nobody has taken any pains to conceal the circumstances of his origins from him. The staff at his first Home, then Mrs Murchie, the old Aberdonian harridan to whom he was fostered out for a year (his continued research in thanatological divination soon made that accommodation untenable), then the staff at the second Home (the first refused to take him back); none have made any attempt to keep secret from him his rejection by two families. This puts him in a league of his own compared with the other children, none of whom have been turned out by more than one set of parents (not *proper* ones, anyway).

Enough information has been imparted for him to guess that the boy he has just seen was neither an illusion nor an accidental doppel-gänger. Tomorrow morning, he knows, the other boy will wake to a family and a house filled with decorations and warmth and presents and turkey and cake, while Kevin has to make do with his metal bed in a barely heated room, with the bruises of fumbling hands on his body and the bitter taste of his tricks lingering in his mouth.

Not that there has been much trade today. Nevertheless, he makes his way to the concourse at Piccadilly Circus and stands with his back to a pillar, expertly eyeing the passing commuters, picking out the nervous, the sick, the apprehensive, the ones who may be in the mood for one last treat before the circus strikes its tents for the Christmas holiday. It was Tom who taught him this living. He met Tom the second time he went into Care. They shared a room, and Tom told him about the money that was to be made down here. He taught Kevin all the skills of observation, enticement, entrapment and technique, how much to charge for what services, and how to tread the line between uncomfortable safety and lethal danger. Kevin took to the trade immediately, fascinated by the vile filthiness of hasty, hot-breathed liaisons transacted in toilet cubicles. He does not share the undertow of shame and self-loathing which Tom expresses transparently as aggressive defiance: on the contrary, he feels he has stumbled across one of the very deepest and dirtiest of gutters, and is pleased that he has experienced it so early in life. He also suspects that this is merely a prelude; that this gutter leads into a real sewer. He knows he will have to stay alert, ready to disengage himself before the flow tips him over the edge, so that he can be preserved. He wants to know what things swim in that sewer, but at a controlled proximity rather than a helpless flounder.

He is so preoccupied with his thoughts that he doesn't realise that the floor of the gutter is about to open beneath him and plunge him into the very deepest tracts of that sewer. This is the harshest lesson he will ever learn; that the sewer is not signposted.

'It's not getting any better, is it?' Pauline watches anxiously as Dr Gerard palpates the long, ragged scar on Alan's smooth, pink cheek. Livid purple and spotted with yellow pus-filled blisters, it runs from the corner of his eye to the top of his lip. It looks painful, but Alan barely winces under the touch of the doctor's fingers. He is clutching his knitted rabbit to his chest, its pink woollen arms draped limply over his, its head lolling to one side. Kevin used to call it Dead Rabbit, and its neck seam bears the blue stitches where Pauline had to sew it up after he had conducted a makeshift tracheotomy with the kitchen scissors.

The doctor finishes his examination and rummages in his Gladstone. 'It's just a little infection,' he said. 'I'm putting him on a course of penicillin. That should clear it up.'

After the doctor has left, Pauline comes back into the living room. Alan is still sitting on the settee where she left him, still holding on to his rabbit. 'Does it hurt, darling?' she asks, kneeling in front of him and looking at his scar. He isn't listening; he is looking past her. Suddenly, his face clouds over with anxiety and he points a chubby finger. 'Kebbin!' he exclaims. His mother twists around in alarm, but there is nobody there. 'Kebbin!' he shouts again. She searches for the source of his fright. Eventually, she notices that the two of them are reflected in the blank screen of the television set; her rear end distorted and bulbous in the convex screen, Alan's little body a minute blob beyond her shoulder. She sighs. 'There's nobody there, darling. It's just a reflection, can you see? Look, there's Mummy waving. See?' He nods, and she strokes his hair. 'Kebbin?' he says. 'Kevin's gone, sweetheart.' She kisses the top of his head. 'Gone away now, all gone.'

She is almost right. Kevin has gone, but his traces will take some time to disappear. Over the next few months, Alan will develop an obsessive fear of mirrors. Whenever he sees his reflection, he will freeze in terror and need to be patiently coaxed away. This will pass eventually, especially after the family moves from the house in Bethnal Green to a new home in Lewisham, and Alan will forget all about Kevin, the fear of him passing away like the fading line of the scar on his growing face. In a few short years, he will not even remember that Kevin existed. Even the mention of his name (it will happen accidentally from time to time) will elicit no flicker of recognition.

Sergeant Alfred Butterman has been a police officer for a long time; he was a constable all through the Blitz, and he saw some terrible things then, and quite a few since, but even he has never seen anything quite like this. He is almost as shocked as nineteen-year-old PC Frazer, who has only been in the job for nine months. They were on their beat around Piccadilly when an hysterical commuter rushed out of the underground station and almost collided with them, pleading incoherently for their help. They followed him down the steps into the station and across the concourse to the gents' lavatories, where they were confronted by the sight they are now staring at. They are standing just inside the door, on one of the few patches of tiling that isn't coated with the thick film of blood spreading out from the body that lies half-in, half-out of the nearest cubicle, wedged under the locked door, the white face staring up at the ceiling.

Alfred cranes his neck and peers at the face. 'I know him,' he says. 'Gerry Cotterell. Collared him a couple of times last year for gross indecency with a minor. Never got charged, mind.' He glances at PC Frazer. 'Shall we take a closer look?' Frazer turns his wide eyes on the Sergeant, his face almost as pallid as the bled corpse. 'All right, son, leave it to me.' In order to see the lower half of the man's body, Alfred has to walk across the pool of blood, which sticks and skids under his boots like thick oil, and climb onto the toilet seat in the next-door cubicle. 'Has he been stabbed, Sarge?' asks PC Frazer as Alfred's helmeted head appears above the partition and peers over. Alfred takes some time to reply; he is so appalled by what he sees that only his strong sense of personal dignity prevents him from quailing in front of the young constable. The man's trousers are pulled down and tangled around his ankles, and... 'No,' he says weakly. 'No, son, I don't think he's been stabbed. Not exactly.' A little unsteady on his feet, he steps down and rejoins Frazer near the door. 'You stay here,' he says. 'Make sure nobody comes in. I've got to go and telephone the Station.'

In the dank darkness deep inside the northbound tunnel of the Bakerloo Line, Kevin crouches against the dusty bricks of the tunnel wall as a train screams and clatters past, the carriage lights strobing on his face and the live rail sparking intermittent blue flashes. He does not know it, but the place he has chosen to squat down and collect his senses is deep beneath Regent Street; directly below the precise spot, in fact, where his mirror-image stood on the pavement and gaped at him through the plate glass of the café window. Another thing he doesn't know is why he did what he has just done; all he was conscious of was an uncontrollable urge to close his jaws until his teeth met in the middle and the blood pumped over his face and chest like hot water from a tap. He didn't feel the frenzied blows to his head, nor did he hear the screams. The next thing he was conscious of was running along the deserted platform and spitting out the lump of softened flesh as he jumped down into the rail trench, heading blindly into the hot draught of the tunnel.

The bruises are beginning to throb now, and the blood is congealing on his skin, gumming his eyelids. He spits on his hands and wiped away the worst of the blood, then he stands and starts walking onwards, deeper and deeper into the underground.

He only intends to hide for a short while, but it will in fact be three years before Kevin sees daylight again. He will live underground, penetrating the deepest tunnels, crawling through ducts, discovering long-disused passages, living like Sméagol amongst the rats and the soot and the fumes and the darkness, only emerging above ground at night to forage for food and water. His eyes will become adapted to the faint glimmer of service lights and chinks from the tall ventilation ducts, and his ears will grow sensitive to the slightest vibrations in the air, the bricks, the stones and the steel that make up his world. He will become adept at insinuating himself into the awkwardest places, both underground and in the night above, and he will mix with people that even he does not yet know exist. After three years, his emergence into the blinding daylight will feel like a second birth, and he will be ready to educate himself, to assimilate the things he has learnt and put them to good use. In all his seamless days and nights in the dark, he will not have forgotten the face of the boy who peered at him through the glass; he will hug the image to himself and, one distant day, he will find a way of stepping through the mirror.

19

He parted the rushes and stooped over the stilling surface of the water. When it had settled, his reflection appeared, haloed by a ring of blue sky and silver-silk clouds. Something was moving under the surface. He peered closer and, to his surprise, found that there was a second reflection lying under the first: another reflection of his face, deeper in the water. He gazed at it through the glassy shallows, hypnotised. The lower reflection began to rise towards the surface, becoming clearer all the time until, with a quiet rippling, it breached the top reflection and floated, beaded and dripping, on the water. The face smiled at him and, as he stared, transfixed, a hand rose out of the water. The emerald green triangle of curved glass clasped between its fingers glittered momentarily in the sunlight, then blurred and dashed across his cheek, laying open a bleeding furrow from eye to lip. He gasped as the blood ran into his mouth and dripped off his chin into the water. He toppled forward, splashing and floundering at first, then lay still and let the water mingle with the blood in his mouth. Everything turned black and muted, then he heard trampling feet amongst the rushes and felt hands scrabbling at his collar, hauling him up—

—a murmur of voices as he lay on his back on the soft grass, one voice rising melodically: *Monsieur Vi-veauuu* . . . echoing as if from a deep cave. 'I think he's dead,' said another voice, much closer. 'Nonsense, he's just sleeping, poor lamb,' said the first. 'Look, he's waking up . . .' He opened his eyes to a haze of faces bobbing on either side of him, silhouetted against the sun. 'We thought we'd lost you,' said Cressida. 'You shouldn't have gone so close to the water, you silly Monsieur.' She stroked his face with her cool fingertips, humming and cooing softly in his ear. 'I still say he's dead,' said the other voice. 'Let me check.' He felt more fingers stroking his chest and neck. 'I can't find a pulse.' '*I* know what'll bring him round,' said a third voice (he couldn't attach a name to it, but he had a mental image of a washing machine and a satin dressing gown). 'He likes this. I used to do this all the time; it never fails.' He tried to focus on the faces, but the only discernible one was Cressida's, shaded against the glare of the sun by the wide brim of her hat. There were hands all over him now: on his face, his neck, his chest, his groin, his legs, all gently stroking him. He groaned with pleasure. Cressida's humming was joined by Tessa (Tessa! That was the name) and Christine, all their voices buzzing with different tunes, their fingers skittering and stroking all over his body and face . . .

—'What the hell is going on, Steven?' His eyes snapped open, staring up at Carole's furious face. 'That does it,' she said. 'I'm going to have to shoot you now.' He watched in helpless horror, the probing hands holding him down as the shotgun was brought to bear on his face. There was a blinding billow of smoke and flame as his head exploded,

—and he woke, gasping and sweating. The light in his eyes was intense, blinding. The floor was stone-hard under his aching back, and he could still feel the stroking fingers all over his face and hear the humming voices while he struggled to tease apart the seam between dreaming and waking. He teetered uncertainly for a single moment . . .

—and screamed, a hoarse, guttural scream dredged from the pit of his stomach. The fibrillating mask leapt up from his face, dissolving into the air and swarming in a cloud of alarm around his head. He sat up and screamed again, his arms and legs windmilling in panic, sending the thick blanket of locusts flying up towards the ceiling. His whole body was shuddering convulsively; he put his hands up to cover his face, but the tenacious insects were still clinging to his fingers. He shook them off, but more appeared, some careening off his skin, some clinging with twitching legs, as the dense, circling swarm battered against him. The more he struggled, the thicker they became, the swarm growing to a whirlwind as more and more of them rose from the thick, undulating carpet. They bounced off him, landing and crawling up his sleeves and trouser-legs, tangling themselves in his hair and scurrying down the back of his neck. His screams turned to desperate, hyperventilating sobs as he thrashed his limbs wildly about.

He wondered afterwards if he might have utterly lost his mind in that maelstrom of horror if he hadn't, in the space of one tiny chink of clear sight, noticed the glass cubicle on the far side of the room. Still flailing against the locusts, he rose to a crouch and ran, feeling the little tubular exoskeletons crunch under his feet. He hauled the glass door open and slipped through, slamming it behind him. He tried to open the wooden outer door, but it was locked fast. He tugged and pushed frantically at it, rammed it with his shoulder again and again, tears of desperation rolling down his face, but it wouldn't budge. His body was still crawling with the locusts he had brought with him into the cubicle, and he danced desperately, brushing and shaking them out of his clothes and hair. They fell to the floor, stunned, and he trampled and stamped on them until they were reduced to a thin mat of pulped bodies under his feet and he was finally free of their creeping, crawling touch.

He fell into a crouch and covered his face with his hands. Only when his panic had abated and the painful, dizzying hyperventilation had subsided did he begin to wonder how he had come to be in there. Surely not Carole? How could she move him without waking him? Could he have wandered in here in a sleepwalking delirium, perhaps? More urgent, though, was the question of how he would get out; however he had got in, somebody had *locked* him in. He stood up and had one more futile go at the door, then gave up. He looked all around the cubicle, searching for anything that might help him. On the floor beside the feed bucket, he found a flat-bladed screwdriver which Carole had been using to repair the timer; now all he needed was something to undo. The door was still useless; it had no exposed hinges or catches. The only means of exit appeared to be the two ventilation panels, each about two feet square, let into the wall at chest height. It ought to be possible to remove the steel meshes and crawl through. The only problem was that both were on the far wall; to get to either of them, he would have to enter the locust-room again.

He couldn't afford to let himself dwell on his horror; it was fiercely hot in here, and the air in the little glass cubicle would not last forever. His only hope would be to clear the locusts from his path somehow ... He took a handful of feed from the bucket and, bracing himself, opened the glass door. He tossed the feed into the near corner of the room – away from the vents – and quickly shut the door again. The locusts nearby dived on the food, and a pattern like a shock-wave spread through the rest. The humming rose in pitch, and the mass began to swarm. He hoisted up the bucket and threw more food in, this time emptying the entire contents into the corner. As he watched through the glass, his skin crawling and his gorge tightening with revulsion, the locusts homed in on the mountain of food, buzzing furiously, accreting in a great seething, coagulating cloud in the corner of the room. This was his chance. He flung open the door and ran across the room. The air was still buzzing with insects, but much less dense than before. His profoundest horror was of them touching his face, so he kept his hands up and his shoulders hunched as he ran, every muscle tense and flinching as the careering locusts collided with him from all directions. He could feel the panic welling up again as he fumbled with the screwdriver, but he eventually had all the screws out and was able to lever the mesh panel away. Behind it was a square hole in the double-skinned blockwork and another mesh attached to the outer face. With a desperate rush of strength, he punched the panel with both fists; it buckled and, on the second blow, flew out into the open air. Feet scrabbling against the wall, he squeezed through the hole, hanging precariously for a moment before slithering out and tumbling onto the grass in the field behind the barn.

He lay on his back for a few moments, eyes closed, savouring the cool, fresh air. Something tickled his cheek, and he brushed it away; looking up, he found that some of the locusts were beginning to follow him out through the open vent. He jumped up and retrieved the panel, but it was bent and the screws had been ripped from their sockets. He found a bundle of black silage plastic in the hedge, and stuffed that into the hole instead.

Now he could begin trying to find out what was going on. His mind was swimming with speculation, mostly involving Carole knocking him out and dragging him into the locust-house. But why? Had she changed her mind about his story? Perhaps she had never believed him at all; the police might be here at this very moment.

He crept around the corner of the building and peeped into the yard. There were no police cars, and the Morris Minor was still parked in front of the house where she had left it the day before. Keeping an eye on the windows, he walked cautiously across the yard to the house and crouched down against the wall, keeping his head below window-level. Edging carefully along, he peeped through each window in turn. There was nobody in the kitchen, nor in the dining room. Holding his breath, he stretched up and stole a glance through the bottom corner of the parlour window, then ducked down again hurriedly. There were two people in there: Carole he recognised instantly, sitting in half-profile, but the man sitting opposite her, although familiar, was harder to identify. Then he remembered: he was the man from the graveyard in Haworth. The hat was missing, but he was certainly the same man. Steven took another peek, trying to see the face. He was talking to Carole, and his head moved from time to time as he spoke; suddenly, he was caught almost full-face in the light . . .

Steven dropped down again and leaned heavily against the wall, his heart pounding, then he jumped up and ran across the yard to the barn. An avalanche was tumbling through his brain; frozen snows that had accreted year after year slid away, crushing everything in their path and leaving the stark, obvious truth exposed in the glaring sunlight. From the deepest, darkest, most ancient recess of his memory came understanding. Looking at that face through the reflection-sheened glass had triggered it. He recalled his mother's impatient voice and a familiar face gazing out at him from the depths of a mirror-glass.

He went into the barn and shut the door. Suddenly, everything was clear and focused: what had been done to him, how it had been achieved, and, most of all, *why*. And he knew what he had to do. He went to his straw cot and stripped away the bedding, hurling the blankets, sheets and pillows into a heap on the floor. Then he dug down into the straw, burrowing, hauling and scattering clumps of it until he uncovered the tobacco tin. His fingers shaking, he sat down and opened it. Inside were three compressed wads of oiled cloth. He took out the first and unrolled it, the glittering contents tumbling into his hand; two four-inch lengths of steel tubing, machined and perforated, and two steel rods. The two tubes screwed together to make a single seven-inch tube, and the rods screwed into holes in its sides, making an asymmetric cruciform. The remaining cloth packages were smaller. One yielded a flattened, moulded block of steel slightly larger than a cigarette lighter, which slotted and clipped firmly into the underside of the tube, and a steel cup like a long thimble with two short, thick cords of heavy-duty elastic attached. He hooked the ends of the elastic onto the rods and opened the third cloth bundle. This contained three short, stubby, polished .38 calibre bullets. He inserted one into the open butt of the tube and, pulling the elastic taut like the strings of a crossbow, placed the cup over it and let it slide slowly, gently into position. He put the two remaining bullets in his trouser pocket and stood up, holding the gun at arm's length. It demanded cautious handling; the firing pin inside the cup was resting directly on the bullet's firing button; one sudden jolt and it could go off.

He stepped lightly over to the door and opened it; just a crack, just enough to let him peep out at the house and the yard: there were no signs of life. He tried to analyse the situation rationally. He had only caught the briefest glimpse, but it had looked as though Carole was under the impression that this man (Steven scrabbled about for

372

a name, couldn't find one) was trustworthy, which meant she thought he was him – the true him, that was; Alan Gorvin . . . Maybe. Now, assuming that was the case, so long as she continued to believe him and he didn't become excited, she ought to be safe; just so long as she didn't express doubt or – even worse – challenge him. Steven dwelt on this with a certain degree of confidence for a few minutes before realising how wrong he was; this was the Invisible Man, and Steven should know better than anyone that it was when he had achieved their absolute trust that his victims succumbed. If Carole really did believe that this man was Alan Gorvin, and showed evidence of trusting him, then she was in the utterest, most lethal danger.

This realisation was just unfolding in his mind, and he was on the brink of making a dash for the house, when he saw Carole's face appear in the window of the spare bedroom; the one with the lockable door. He was half-expecting to see a second face behind her when he heard the back door open, and the visitor came round the corner of the house and set out across the yard towards the locust-house. Up above, Carole was peering out of the window, trying to see what was going on, but from that bedroom only the corner of the yard and the end of the barn would be visible. As the man walked past the barn door, Steven saw something metallic glint in his right hand before he disappeared from view. There were sounds of keys jangling and the locust-house door opening. Steven stepped out into the daylight. He glanced up at the window and saw Carole's hand go to her mouth in alarm. At that moment, the man burst out of the locust-house at a run. Steven aimed the gun and drew a brief, grim pleasure from the fact that the man's consternation was so great that he almost ran past before noticing the figure standing silently by the barn door and the shining gun barrel aimed at his body. He skidded to a halt in the wet mud, his kitchen knife raised in futile resistance.

The look of fright passed away almost instantly, though, and he stood up straight, his face relaxed and confident. 'Well, well, well,' he smiled, gazing calmly at the gun, with its strange structure of rods and tensed elastic, bearing on him like a mutated catapult. 'How extraordinary, a zip-gun. I haven't seen one of those in over twenty years.' He took a step forward. 'May I take a look?'

'Stay right where you are,' Steven growled. 'Don't think I won't blow your fucking brains out, you bastard.' The man's voice had disorientated him; like the bizarre mingling of familiarity and alienness in hearing a recording of one's own voice for the first time.

The man stopped still, but continued beaming good-naturedly. 'Of course,' he said. 'How presumptuous of me.'

'And get rid of the knife – no, don't drop it, throw it. Over there.' He gestured with the gun. 'Good. Now put your hands on your head and kneel down.'

'My goodness, is this to be an execution?'

'Shut up and do it!'

The man shook his head pitifully. 'You know, you really should keep your flanks covered in a situation like this,' he said, looking to Steven's left.

'What?' Steven demanded, not taking his eyes off his target.

'I said—'

'Put the gun down, Steven,' said Carole.

He glanced to his left and, for the second time in as many days, found himself looking into the unwavering barrels of the shotgun. The man – his brother, he thought reluctantly (*what was his name?*) – raised his eyebrows. 'This situation is getting more interesting by the minute,' he said. 'Good job I haven't got a weapon

374

to complete the triangle: we could be stalemated into eternity.'

'Stop it, Alan,' said Carole irritably.

'*Alan?*' Steven cried, trying to coordinate outrage and a steady aim. 'For Christ's sake, Carole, he isn't—'

'*Shut UP!*' she shouted furiously. 'Just shut up! I've listened to enough of your lies, you bastard. I don't want to hear any more, okay?' She breathed deeply (out of the corner of his eye, Steven saw the gun barrels rise and fall slightly), and brought her voice under control. 'It's over Kevin,' she said firmly. 'Face it, you can't run forever. It's all over.'

Kevin ... Yes, that was it! *Kevin* ... *gone, sweetheart, gone away now, all gone* ... He remembered a mirror, a garden swing drifting back and forth above him, and an excruciating pain below his eye ... 'Kevin,' he murmured. 'Kevin ...'

As the name reverberated inside his skull, he knew what he had to do; time seemed to slow to a crawl, and several things began to happen simultaneously: His grip on the pistol tightened and his left forearm tensed, drawing back the firing cup as his eye refined the aim on his brother's head – the man's arms began to rise towards his face, which was tightening with alarm, and his body inclined to one side as if preparing to dive – to Steven's left, he sensed Carole's grip on the shotgun firming up, the barrels dipping, their line of aim declining from his head to his body – he released the firing cup and, in the fractured instant between release and detonation, both shotgun barrels belched out fountains of bright sparks and smoke, the thunderous roar swamping the feeble crack of the pistol – the force of the blast rammed him full in the side of his body, and he felt his feet being wrenched from the ground as it hurled him sideways – and, as he flew, he seemed to see the pistol bullet as a ghostly line searing past his enemy's head – after just a few short feet of flight, the muddy ground tilted and rushed up to meet him, slamming against him and rolling him onto his back. He was conscious of Kevin looking down at him, his expression evolving slowly from alarm to unrestrained glee. Then, as his life drained out of him, he saw Carole flip the shotgun over in her hands – Kevin, still gazing down at Steven, was unaware of the weapon as its heavy butt swept down in a blurred arc, connecting with the side of his head with such force that, like Steven before him, he was swept off his feet and crashed to the ground.

That was the last image he saw: the side of his chest and abdomen screaming with coruscating agony, Steven closed his eyes and gave up the struggle for life.

20

By the time the second body had rolled to a stop, Carole had flipped the shotgun round again and broken the breech. She took two fresh cartridges from her pocket and loaded them. Both men were lying motionless; crumpled and twisted and smeared with mud. Keeping a safe distance, she approached and stood over them. She kicked the soles of Steven's feet. 'Steven,' she said loudly. There was no response, so she kicked him again. 'Steven!' This time, he groaned faintly and moved. 'Wake up,' she ordered.

'I'm dying,' he wheezed, fumbling feebly at his side. His jacket and sweater were blackened and holed, and the exposed skin was livid.

'Don't be stupid,' she said tersely. 'You're just a bit singed. Get up.' She watched as he raised himself on one arm, wincing and hugging his side as though expecting his innards to tumble out on to the ground. He looked up at her in bewilderment. 'They were just blanks,' she said. 'You're a bit burnt and winded, that's all. By the way,' she added, gesturing with the shotgun, 'I've reloaded, and these *aren't* blanks. Now, being very, very careful and very slow, you're going to pick him up and carry him.'

He looked at the crumpled body lying beside him. In spite of himself, he was impressed; this time, she had obviously held nothing in reserve. There was a wet, trickling, hair-matted graze on the side of his brother's head and a bright red patch on the skin of the temple and cheek, waiting to blossom into a magnificent rainbow bruise. Steven glanced up at her. '*Carry* him?' he said. 'I don't think I can even stand . . .'

'Shut up and get on with it,' she ordered impatiently, emphasising the point with a wave of the gun. He obeyed. Raising himself onto his knees, he gritted his teeth against the pain in his side and heaved the body on to his shoulders.

'Is he alive?' she asked, sounding more curious than concerned.

'Yes,' said Steven. 'He's breathing. Where d'you want me to put him? Don't let it be far, for fuck's sake.'

'In there,' she said, indicating the barn. She swung the doors wide and followed him in, keeping well back. When he had staggered to the middle of the floor, she ordered him to stop. 'Put him down there . . . Right, now tie him up – there's rope over there.' She watched as he uncoiled several lengths of blue nylon rope from a rusty hook on the wall. 'Tie his feet together and his hands behind his back . . . When you've finished, sit him up against that bale. I want him upright.'

As he tightened the knots, Steven glanced up at her and smiled. 'God, Carole, for a minute back there I really thought he'd taken you in.' He hauled the unconscious man into a sitting position and propped him against a bale as he had been directed, then stood back. 'I was right, you know. You should have been an actress.'

She stared coolly back at him. Looking at herself from the inside, she could scarcely believe that this was actually her, so calm and cold.

'Now you,' she said quietly.

'What?'

'Ankles first, and I want to see real knots. Tight ones.'

'I don't understand,' he gabbled. 'It's *him*. Carole – he's the—'

'Be quiet! I don't want to hear another word out of you unless I ask for it. Get tying.'

He flushed, and shook his head defiantly. 'No fucking way! I haven't done anything!' He glanced at the gun. 'What are you going to do, shoot me?' he said sarcastically.

This was not a good approach under the circumstances. Carole settled the stock against her shoulder and took aim at his head. 'Try me,' she said, and the sheer contempt in her voice astonished even her. 'What would you say it was? Manslaughter? Self-defence? I probably wouldn't even get a custodial sentence.' She could see the uncertainty in his eyes as he weighed up the situation: she was out on that limb again, and she could feel it buckle and sway precariously beneath her feet. This time, he was too far away for her to strike him with the butt, and anyway, he would be bound to anticipate that form of attack by now; she would have to either shoot or submit. The air between them was thick with tension as they stared into each other's eyes. After several taut, straining seconds, Steven wavered and sat down sullenly. Carole began to breathe again as she watched him bind and tie his ankles. 'Tighter than that,' she said. 'Good. Now lie on your face and put your hands behind your back.'

He made no attempt to resist as she tied his wrists: he was morally and physically beaten. When she had finished, he sat up, scrabbling and swinging his body clumsily until he too was propped against a straw bale. 'What now?' he asked.

She dragged up a third bale and sat down on it, facing her two prisoners like a judge. 'Now we wait,' she said.

'What for?'

'Him to wake up. Now, be quiet or be gagged.'

He stared resentfully at her, but said nothing. And so they waited . . .

. . . And waited. For hours they sat in silence. Carole got up once to examine the unconscious man for signs of coma, but he seemed all right. The side of his head looked atrocious, though: the blood was crusting, and the bruised skin was developing a rich purple bloom tinged with yellow and indigo. Seeing the injury close-up for the first time gave her a strange, morbid thrill; a shiver of exhilaration at her power, at the violence she had never imagined herself capable of. As she examined him, it occurred to her that he might be shamming unconsciousness, so she tried pinching him hard with her fingernails in a few sensitive places – earlobe, under one eye, the soft skin of his throat – but there was no reaction; not even the slightest flinch. Perhaps it hadn't been wise to hit him so hard after all; then again, she wasn't particularly experienced in administering concussive blows, and had had no choice but to err on the side of excess.

She sat down again, and they carried on waiting; tiresome as it might be, she had decided that the only way to judge which one of them was guilty and which one innocent would be to cross-examine them simultaneously, reasoning that this would make it harder for them to lie and easier for her to observe their differences of personality.

As the afternoon wore on into evening, Steven began to tire. His eyelids drooped and his head lolled until, as the sinking sun was pouring the last of its warmth through the barn door, his chin sank forward on to his chest and he started snoring quietly. Carole herself was beginning to feel her grip on consciousness loosening: watching the two sleeping figures in front of her, listening to the soft rasp of Steven's snores, and feeling the gentle warmth of gathering dusk; all combined to drag a blanket of drowsiness over her. She had to keep jerking her head back and shaking it to stop her brain sliding over the lip of sleep.

Finally, deciding that she could trust to their bindings, she left her charges in the barn and went to the house in search of artificial stimuli. The first thing she did was find her cigarettes (they were still on the floor in the parlour where she had left them) and light one up, closing her eyes and shivering as she drew the smoke down into her lungs; she hadn't had a cigarette all day, and her mouth was watering and her cheeks aching from withdrawal. When she had consumed half the cigarette, she set about making a large pot of extremely strong coffee.

Steven woke with a start, his neck cricking as his head jerked back. He had dreamt that he was back in the mud of the Levels, only this time he was bound tightly and couldn't even struggle as the salt water lapped and trickled into his mouth . . .

It was almost dark now, and a light breeze was wafting in through the barn door. Carole was gone, and he felt a tremor of alarm, but relaxed again when he realised that his fellow prisoner was still tied up beside him, awake at last. Steven studied him silently: he was gazing glassily towards the open door, his face expressionless and his body absolutely still. Steven's mind was seething with things he wanted to say: questions, curses, demands, remonstrations, and a deep black well of knowledge which he could scarcely begin to plumb. Nearly forty years of life separated the two of them, but they were conjoined by a condensed century's worth of torment. Mutual torment, Steven supposed, even though he felt impotent to imagine the degree of vengeful loathing which must have driven such a campaign of murder and persecution.

In the end, all he managed to say was, 'Where's she gone?' There was no response; not even a flicker to indicate that the question had been heard, so he tried again: 'Where's Carole gone?' This time, the question elicited the tiniest shrug of the shoulders. Steven gazed at his profile. 'Why, Kevin?' he whispered. 'Why have you done this to me? I know you must hate me, but it wasn't my fault, what happened to you. And what about all those people, those nurses, what had they ever done to you? Why didn't you just come and get me if you wanted to destroy me?'

Kevin didn't answer. He turned his gaze away from the doorway and looked at his brother: instead of the anticipated expression of loathing, there were tears running from his eyes and a faint, bitter smile on his lips. 'Poor old Alan,' he murmured, giving Steven a jolt at hearing himself addressed by his real name for the first time in so many years. 'As oafish and obtuse as ever. How could anyone hate such wide-eyed puppy-dog foolishness? I'm disappointed, dear brother – I thought I'd made myself much clearer than that. Didn't you read my letters? Do you really think I'd go to all that trouble just for a little cheap revenge? Now the two of you have ruined it all with your wretched mistrust. Don't you

381

realise who I am – *what* I am?'

Kevin's smile grew to a broad grin of maniacal glee and, to Steven's horror, he stood up and raised his arms, the ropes falling loosely to the floor. Then he knelt down beside Steven and held up a crooked, shining object in front of his eyes. Steven opened his mouth to cry out, but before he could even gasp, a large wad of cloth was stuffed into his mouth. He gazed in mute terror at the open razor. Kevin laughed. 'What a woman,' he said. 'I don't think she trusts me any more, do you? But I think even you would have been intelligent enough to search me.' He gently thumbed the edge of the blade. 'They were all just as stupid as her, you see, with their silly little diminutive names – *Beverley, Angie, Kirsty, Robbie*, and their pathetic, trusting little hearts. I mean, would *you* believe I was a police officer? Would anyone with a functioning brain? *They* believed. So who'd miss them, apart from other equally moronic fools? The world's no worse off without them, you know.' He laid the razor flat against Steven's throat. 'You had a run-in with one of these once before, didn't you?' He smiled and pressed harder, until Steven could feel the edge biting into his skin. Kevin laughed at his bulging, terrified eyes. 'You've never been able to work out why I chose nurses, have you? Oh, I dare say the estimable Sergeant Comber got there in the end. His slow brain must have thrashed around and eventually hit upon Cindy McCutcheon . . . Yes, I know it was a long time ago, but it was bound to leave a scar. Imagine, the happy couple – the rising young detective and his pretty nurse. You had such promise, and she jilted you for that foetid little radiographer. I can't think why you did nothing about it at the time . . . Oh, don't worry – I remedied that little omission on your behalf. Remember her little yellow Datsun? The one with your semen stains on the back seat? Well, a little snip here, a little saw there . . . I understand she's coping quite well with the prosthesis now, but only having three-quarters of a face is still something of a problem . . .' He frowned. 'Now now, Alan, there's no need to look at me like that. You should be grateful. Loyalty, brother, is a commodity we can never value too highly. Oh, I'm sure yours weren't the only stains on that cheap upholstery. She wasn't loyal to you, and neither will this one be.' He nodded in the direction of the house and shook his head. 'Not in the end. Not when it really matters.'

He stroked the razor slowly, delicately across Steven's throat, then suddenly whipped it away and folded the blade back into the handle. 'I have to leave you now,' he said pleasantly. 'We'll meet again, so don't miss me too much now, will you.' He stood up and, with one last amiable smile, he turned and walked out through the door.

Carole filled the Thermos with coffee and screwed on the lid, then poured the remainder of the pot into a mug and sipped it. It was scalding, so she lit up a third cigarette and stood by the kitchen window, looking out at the darkening yard. From here, if she craned her neck and put her cheek to the glass, she could just about keep an eye on the barn door.

How on earth could this possibly be so difficult? Until a few days ago, had she been asked, she would have had not the slightest doubt about her ability to tell a man from a monster; surely there would be signs that any intelligent person's instincts would be able to read. She remembered how, in *The Lord Of The Rings*, Frodo knew that Strider was the real Aragorn because, had he been an agent of Sauron, he would 'seem fairer but feel fouler.' If only it were so simple. Yesterday, when she knew without a doubt that Steven was a murderer, her feelings about him had militated against that knowledge and caused her to believe his story. Then, without warning, this new, entirely unexpected piece had materialised on the board. This man who claimed to be the real Alan Gorvin certainly seemed fairer: he looked more like the newspaper photograph, he talked more convincingly like a policeman, and his version of the story – blunter and veined with a shamefaced honesty about morally dubious acts – seemed truer. On the other hand, he did *feel* wrong, but that might be because her sentimental feelings for Steven had obfuscated her analytical feelings. There was certainly no specific wrong-feeling trait in this man that she could put her finger on, no glint of evil in his eye, no trace of cold monstrosity in his voice, nothing implicitly threatening in his manner. One thing he had said was evidently true: seeing them both together proved that the most dangerous psychopaths offered no clues, no signals. She had tried to think of some simple, Solomonish act which would quickly prove them, such as taking a knife and opening her wrists in front of them (at the moment, this was insidiously attractive) and observing their reactions: the real monster might reveal himself by seeming aroused or coolly indifferent as she bled before them . . .

Her train of thought was derailed by a gentle clunking sound from the hall. She turned away from the window and listened. There was silence for a few moments, then another soft clunk. She picked up the shotgun and went warily into the hall. The front door had been left ajar, and was swinging slowly back and forth against the latch gathering breeze. She peered querulously at it for a moment, then pushed it closed.

Steven struggled against the grip of the ropes until his wrists and ankles burned and sharp pains shot through his twisted joints. He tried to spit out the gag, but it was wedged in too tightly. In the end, with a desperate effort of will, he flung himself forward and began slowly and painfully snaking across the floor, kicking his legs and writhing his body inch by inch towards the open door, grunting and squeaking, sirens screaming in his nerves as the rough floor scraped the tender, burnt skin of his side. Halfway to the door, he paused to regain his breath. His panting and gasping kept dragging the trailing edges of the cloth against the back of his throat, making him retch violently.

Suddenly, he stopped breathing altogether, and his eyes widened with anxiety: he had just heard the door of the house slam. He listened, and out of the silence came the sound of steady footsteps padding across the yard towards him. He jerked his body sideways and rolled over and over, away from the door and into the black shadows by the wall. The footsteps came closer, and a swaying wash of lantern light cut into the cavernous space of the barn and danced with the leaping shadows. The light grew, and a figure stepped in through the door, silhouetted against the glare of the lantern.

With a flood of relief, he recognised Carole. She had the shotgun tilted over one arm and a flask tucked under the other, the loop of the lantern hooked over her wrist. She stopped and stared at the bales where the two men should have been. *'Mm-hmm-mnff-hnn!'* he squealed, almost choking on the clot of soggy cloth. Carole started and whipped round to face him. *'Mm-mmmm!'* he pleaded.

She held the lantern up and peered at his face. 'Oh no,' she murmured. 'Oh shit . . . the *door!*' She dropped the flask and the lantern, gripped the gun in both hands and ran back out into the yard.

The lantern flickered out and plunged the barn back

into darkness. *'HNNN-NNH!'* he screamed as her foot-steps receded. *'CHMM-BMMN!'*

He levered himself strenuously to his knees, then to his feet and, wobbling precariously, hopped to the door-way. By the time he got there, Carole had vanished from sight. One by one, the windows of the house were lighting up, and he could hear the sounds of doors slamming and Carole's voice shouting. He hopped fran-tically out across the yard, but his balance was uncertain and the mud slippery; he lost his footing on the third leap and crashed headlong to the ground. He lay there, stunned and winded and choking, helplessly watching the frantic son-et-lumière unfolding in the house. Soon, all the windows were lit up and from time to time he saw her silhouette flit past them as she ran from room to room. Eventually, silence and stillness settled over the house. He waited nervously for several minutes, his ears straining and his eyes darting from window to window. He was about to try and struggle to his feet again when a shadow moved by the far corner of the house and Carole's shape walked towards him, minus the shotgun. A torch flicked on in her hand and its beam swept round the yard several times before settling on him and closing in.

'There you are,' she said, crouching down beside him. She lifted his chin and reached into his mouth, dragging out the soggy ball of rag. 'Are you okay?'

He retched and gasped for breath. *'Un—'* he splut-tered. *'Un-tie-me . . .'*

'What?' she said. 'Oh, right, of course.' She rolled him onto his side and began picking at the tight knots.

'Where is he?' he wheezed, sitting up and massaging his wrists as they came free.

'Gone,' she said, loosening the knots at his ankles and tossing the rope away.

He stared at her. 'What d'you mean, *gone*?'

386

'I mean gone,' she said, standing up and holding a hand out to him. 'Vanished, left, disappeared . . . *gone.* Come on, we'd better get you indoors.'

He stayed where he was, gazing up at her doubtfully. 'You do realise which of us is which now, don't you?' he asked.

She sighed and nodded. 'He left something for you,' she said, taking hold of his hand. 'Come on, Alan.'

21

Rosalind picked up the tray and carried her supper through to the sitting room. Two Shredded Wheat with hot milk and a blanket of sugar; her favourite supper, prepared especially to accompany a late showing of *Camille Claudel*, one of her favourite films. She settled down on the sofa with her bowl and switched on the television. Perfect timing; the adverts were just finishing. Then, instead of going straight into the film, there was a *Crimestoppers* slot. As the programme brandished its tacky little synthetic fanfare, Rosalind put her Shredded Wheat to one side and consulted the listings page of the *Guardian*. 'You're overrunning, you arseholes,' she muttered. 'Can't you leave this till tomorrow?' She picked up her bowl again and chopped irritably at the stringy pads of sugary wheat as a trail of local crimes too mediocre for *Crimewatch UK* were paraded on the screen: a ram-raid on a department store in Bradford, a series of pensioners conned out of their savings in the Oxenhope area. Artists' impressions of the man and woman responsible for the cons flashed up. 'Well, *I'd* bloody know them if I saw them,' she scoffed. 'How many alien mutants are there in Oxenhope?' How much easier police work would be if criminals actually looked like police-artists' drawings, she thought: *Yes, officer, I saw the man. He had mad staring eyes, no ears, and a chin like the top of Gordale Scar. Oh, and his head was wider than it was tall*. After the two star items, there was some foggy video footage of credit card fraud in a Leeds bank, then, tacked on as an afterthought, a *have-you-seen-this-man* accompanied by a passport photograph taken against a vivid orange background. Thoroughly annoyed by this time (her Shredded Wheat was clearly not going to last even into the opening titles of *Camille Claudel*), Rosalind barely glanced at the picture. Then, picking up on the words *extremely dangerous*, she looked again. *He should on no account be approached*, said the voiceover. *If you have any information, please call this number* ... Rosalind stared at the screen, her laden spoon frozen halfway to her open mouth, trembling and dripping warm milk down the front of her shirt. 'Oh shit,' she whispered, 'oh shit oh shit oh Jesus fucking shit ...' *I told him about Beverley* ... *He couldn't bring himself to look at me* ... *He thinks I'm evil* ...

'Come *on*,' said Rosalind impatiently as the ringing tone chirruped in her ear. '*Come ooon*, pick up the phone, Carole, for Christ's sake ...' The ringing went on and on, but there was no answer. She slammed the receiver down, then picked it up and dialled again, *tap-tap-tap* ... 'Police!' she shouted, not giving the operator a chance to speak. 'Please, get me the police!'

Carole sat down heavily in the armchair and cradled her forehead on her fingertips. 'I can't believe I've been so bloody stupid,' she muttered. 'I *knew* I should've gone to the police. Yesterday, straight from the library.' She sat back and looked at Alan. 'Oh, I don't know, maybe not,' she reflected. 'I suppose they'd have just hauled you off, wouldn't they?'

He nodded. 'Yes, they would. The wrong man.'

'The wrong man,' she repeated absently.

He read the note again. Unlike the others he had received over the years, which had all been neatly inscribed on expensive writing paper, this brief message was hastily scrawled in pencil on a torn-off scrap of paper.

> *Dear Steven,*
> *You know I always respect your chosen names. No time for verbiage. I have to leave you now, so there's no point wasting time on writing when I could be putting distance between us. I can't depart, though, with you thinking that I hate you or wish vengeance upon you. You are my twin, my double in every respect. I didn't do it all out of hate, but out of love. I am sure you will come to understand that in time. We are indivisible, brother, you and I. The two of you may believe you are one, but in reality it is only the two of us who are so conjoined. If I cannot have your trust, I shall have the next best thing.*
> *Anyway, time skitters, so I shall leave you.*
> *With love (believe me),*
> ~~*Stran*~~ *(what's the point of hiding now?) – Kevin*

'Where did you find it?' he asked.

'Up there,' she said, nodding at the mantelpiece.

'And you're absolutely sure he's gone?'

She shrugged. 'I've looked everywhere – all the cupboards, under the beds, behind the curtains. There's no sign of him.'

'What about the loft?'

'Nothing.'

'And the cellar?'

She shook her head. 'There isn't one.' She gazed at the slip of paper in his hand. 'What do you think that last bit means?'

He skimmed through it again. 'Which bit?'

'The bit about the next best thing to trust.'

He shrugged. 'Well, trust is important to him – he can only kill when his victims trust him.'

'So, what's the next best thing?'

Alan read the line several times, but could make no sense of it . . . It did ring a very distant bell, though – hadn't there been something in one of the Strand Scourer's letters about trust? . . . *second best to trust* . . . 'I don't know,' he concluded lamely, unable to recall the words.

Carole frowned. 'What could be the next best thing to trust?'

'I don't know,' he repeated, shaking his head. He sighed and sat down on the arm of her chair. He went to stroke her hair, but to his surprise, she flinched and shrank away from him. 'It's all right now,' he said gently. 'It's *me*.'

She looked up at him with a mixture of irritation and suspicion. 'No it isn't,' she said. 'It *isn't* you.'

He laughed. 'Of course it's me. I'm still the same.'

She stood up and moved away from him. 'No,' she said. 'No you're not; you're not *Steven* any more.'

His face fell. 'Yes I am . . . I *am* still Steven . . . Alan, Steven, it doesn't make any difference: they're both the same person.'

'And are they the same person as Kevin? *He* seems to think so.' She waved a hand at the note.

'I don't give a toss what he thinks! He's insane, Carole, he's not rational . . . I thought you loved me.'

'I do . . . I mean, I did . . . I don't know.' She rubbed her eyes. 'I don't know how I feel any more. You were Steven when I loved you, not Alan. It doesn't make any difference if you think you're the same person; you're

390

different to *me*.' She slumped down dejectedly on the sofa. 'Anyway, can't this wait? I can't think right now. It hasn't exactly been the easiest day I've ever lived through.'

Alan nodded and fell silent. He picked up the poker and prodded listlessly at the loose ashes in the fireplace. It had been a warm day, but the subsiding stress had left him shivering and aching with cold, and he toyed lethargically with the idea of building up a fire.

'What happened to him?' Carole asked.

'Pardon?'

'Kevin,' she said. 'Why were you separated?'

Alan put the poker down and sighed. 'It came back to me today,' he said. 'I didn't even remember he existed until now, then it all came back when I saw him.' He shifted uncomfortably. 'When we were three years old, our mother found him in the garden, trying to cut my face off with a piece of broken glass.' He touched his cheek, tracing a line from his eye to his lip. 'From here to here. You can still see the scar when I get a tan. My mother always told me I was attacked in my pushchair by an Alsatian.'

Carole stared at him in horror. 'Why?' she asked.

He shrugged. 'He'd gone, I suppose, and the family were trying to convince themselves he'd never existed.'

'No,' she said. 'I meant why did he do that to you?'

'Oh. Does someone like that need a reason? I think that was what really freaked Mum and Dad out. I remember screaming and blood everywhere and Mum going hysterical, but Kevin just stood there smiling. He was smiling when he was carving up my face, too. He wasn't angry or anything like that; just smiling calmly like he was playing Fuzzy Felts or something. I think he did other things as well, but either I wasn't there or I've blanked them out. He was sent into Care, and that was the last we heard of him.'

'Jesus,' Carole murmured. 'Your poor parents. Imagine having to get rid of your own child . . . Hold on a minute,' she said, frowning. 'When all this started – you know, when you were in the papers and everything – surely your parents could've guessed who was behind it. Why didn't they come forward?'

'Dead,' said Alan dully. 'They're all dead. Mum and Dad died in a house fire on Christmas Eve, 1977. My big brother Tim was there as well, with his wife and their little girl. They all died.'

Carole put a hand over her mouth. 'Oh God, I'm so sorry . . .'

'I would've been there too, but I got snowed in in Liège.'

'What were you doing in Liège?' she asked. Now his amnesia was exposed as false and the history of the last twenty years of his life was there for the asking, she was struck by the sheer breadth of the void of ignorance that separated her from him.

'I was working on a building site,' he said. 'I didn't find out what happened until I got back in January . . . You know, I've often wondered if that was the real reason I joined up – a need to belong to something again when I didn't have a family any more.'

Carole nodded thoughtfully, then suddenly looked at him in alarm. 'Wait a minute. This fire – you don't think . . .' She hesitated: no, it was too awful . . .

Alan gazed at her calmly. 'Kevin? It wouldn't surprise me.'

She shuddered. 'You know,' she said. 'There's something else – you realise this means it *was* coincidence, after all. You coming here, I mean.'

He was silent for a long while. 'Stranger things have happened,' he said at last. 'I once knew a bloke called Ken Hereford. He was famous in his day. I nicked him in 1988 for running a string of illegal gambling clubs all over the East End. Back in the Sixties, when he was a lad, Ken walked into a casino in Monte Carlo with fifty quid in his pocket. He went to the nearest roulette and put the lot on Black Six. It came up. Instead of walking away, he left the whole lot – stake and winnings – on the same square. Would you believe it, it came up again. By now, he thought he was invincible, so he left it there again. According to the newspaper stories, nearly fifty people saw Black Six come up a third time. When he left the casino, he was a millionaire. Used his winnings to bankroll his new empire, but he never gambled again himself. Reckoned he'd used up a whole lifetime's worth of luck in that one night.' Alan paused and looked at Carole. 'If you tried to work out the odds against it, you couldn't fit the numbers on the page. Compared with that, well, you and I meeting seems almost inevitable.' He leaned forward and stirred the ashes around the fireplace again. 'I'm freezing. Shall we get a fire going?'

'Okay. I'll have to get some coal in.' She stood up and picked up the scuttle, then looked sheepishly at him. 'Will you come with me?'

'Sure.' He picked up his zip-gun from the sideboard and inserted a bullet. 'Purely psychological,' he said, noticing her anxious expression.

'You don't suppose he'll come back, do you?'

He shook his head. 'I've given up trying to fathom how his mind works. I think we've seen the last of him for a while, though. He's lost a lot of his power now his mask's gone. Trust, remember – he hasn't got our trust. We're safe.'

Carole nodded uncertainly. 'Mmm,' she murmured, opening the door and going out into the hall. 'I just wish we knew what ... What's that smell?' she frowned, stopping abruptly and sniffing the air. Suddenly, her eyes widened. 'Oil!' she gasped, rushing to the kitchen

393

door. As she flung it open, a thick fug of sour petroleum stench rolled out, making them both gag. The fluorescent light flickered on, revealing a dark slick of fuel oil on the floor. It had already covered the flagstones and was starting to seep under the doors. 'Shit!' Carole shouted, slithering across to the Aga. The feed pipe at the back of the stove had fractured, and the oil was dribbling steadily onto the floor. 'I can't turn it off!' she wailed. 'The pipe's broken!'

'Is there a mains tap?'

'Yes, it's—' She stopped, and they stared at each other, listening to a deep rumbling sound that seemed to come from out of the very stones of the walls.

'What the *fuck* was that?' he said. The noise came again, apparently from the direction of the parlour. Alan held a finger to his lips. 'Try and fix that,' he whispered. 'I'll go and have a look.' He crept out into the hall and along to the parlour door. He pushed it open with the muzzle of the pistol and stepped inside.

. . . Second best to trust . . .

There was a powerful reek of carbon in the room, and a dense cloud of soot was settling on the carpet in a wide semicircle around the fireplace, where it lay in a thick, grey bank studded with pieces of broken brick. As soon as he set eyes on it, he understood:

Ignorance. Ignorance is second best to trust.

The tiny voice that had been whispering to him from a muffled recess inside his skull ever since he first read the note suddenly burst into a deafening shriek: *He's here! He's here! He's here!*

'HE'S HERE!' he shouted, but the words had barely had time to travel from his brain to his tongue when he sensed a sudden movement behind him and he spun round, the shout coming out as a mangled yelp. The parlour door swung closed and a figure stepped out from behind it. Alan registered a brief glimpse of a

394

ravaged, soot-blackened face, then something small and metallic scythed through the air towards him. He threw up his left arm and staggered back, and the razor which had been arcing towards his throat slashed through the fabric of his jacket and sweater and tore a deep gouge across the skin of his forearm. As he stumbled back and fell against the bookcase, he brought the gun up and stretched back the elastic, but the figure was already halfway out of the door and heading for the kitchen. He loosed the firing cup, the muzzled flared and banged, and the bullet passed over Kevin's receding shoulder and smashed a shower of splinters from the edge of the banister rail. *'CAROLE!'* he bellowed, scrambling to his feet and clutching his bleeding arm. *'CAROLE! IT'S HIM!'*

There was no time to reload the gun, so he dropped it and grabbed the poker from the fireplace. As he reached the hall, he heard Carole scream; a short, high-pitched yelp, suddenly cut off. He charged at the open kitchen door but at he hit the threshold, his feet skidded on the oil and flew out from under him, sending him crashing to the floor, arms flailing wildly. As he went down, the scene blurred and tilted before his eyes: Kevin standing above him, the red-smeared razor held up in his right hand; and Carole, backed up against the kitchen table, both hands raised to her face, eyes wide and mouth hanging open in horror. He struggled to get up, but Kevin took a step back and trod on his leg, lost his balance and went over backwards, landing with a thrashing *whump* on the hall carpet. The razor flew from his hand and clattered against the skirting board. Alan stared at him in astonishment; there was a dense patch of dark, wet red spreading across his shirt-front and, from its centre, the black plastic butt of a knife protruded, trailing tangled ribbons of sellotape, its blade rammed deep into his stomach just below the ribs. His fingers clawed on it and, as Alan and Carole watched in appalled, breathless silence, he climbed slowly to his feet, clutching the edge of the hall table for support. Then, looking them both in the eyes, he wrapped his fingers around the handle of the knife and drew it out. He stood gasping for a moment, then let it fall to the floor.

'Good,' he whispered hoarsely. 'Very, very good, but I'm not that easily discouraged.' And he smiled a thin, sardonic smile as he gazed at their faces.

It was this smile that breached the dam inside Alan and set the floodwater of vengeful hatred pouring out. He seized the poker and leapt up. He feinted to the left and, as Kevin raised his arms to cover his head, he swung downwards and smashed the steel rod across his shins. Kevin gasped and clutched at the table, his fractured legs buckling under him. Alan raised the poker again and brought it down on his hunched shoulders with a heavy, crunching thump, knocking Kevin off his feet and toppling him to the floor. Then, all aim and calculation gone, Alan set about the writhing, flinching body with a frenzy of crashing blows.

'No!' Carole yelled. 'NO! Stop it, stop it!' She leapt on his back and grappled with his arm, trying to wrench the poker from his hand. 'Stop it! Leave him, you'll kill him!'

'Good!' he shouted. He raised the poker for another swipe, but Carole managed to grasp his wrist and with all her strength, pulled him away.

'This isn't the way!' she shouted as he turned to face her, his eyes burning with fury.

'Not the way?' he yelled into her face. 'Have you forgotten what this *cunt* has done? Never mind what he's done to me, remember what he did to Beverley. Have you forgotten about that? Have you? *You* never saw the photographs of what he—'

'*Shut up!*' she yelled back, gripping his sweater and tugging. 'You can't *do* this! He's half dead already. If you kill him, you'll be no better than he is!'

Alan stepped away from her and leaned back against the wall, his face red, his hoarse breathing mingling with Kevin's desperate, burbling gasps.

'He isn't,' Kevin whispered, choking painfully. They stared down at him. The smoothly turned-out almost-duplicate of Alan who had materialised out of nowhere that morning was now a crumpled, broken mess. Blood was seeping from the scatter of cuts and grazes and mingling with the patches of black soot on his clothes and skin. The knife wound in his belly was oozing profusely, and the whole of his shirt-front was now bright, shining red. 'He isn't,' he slurred, his hoarse voice straining to escape from his throat. 'No better than . . . me . . . Killer . . . just as much.'

Carole glanced at Alan. 'What's he saying?'

'Kevin,' said Kevin. 'Ask him . . . about . . . Kevin.'

'What does he mean?' Carole demanded, but Alan didn't reply: he was staring at his brother, his face dissolving from furious red to a ghastly pallor.

'My namesake,' Kevin whispered, and looked up at Alan. 'Was that deliberate? No, I don't suppose you'd have the . . . imagination, would you . . .' His eyes rolled in his head, searching for Carole's face. 'How did you think he . . . staged his own . . . death so successfully? *Some*body had to stand in for him.' His eyes struggled back to Alan. 'How . . . how old would you say? Seventeen? Maybe younger . . . I wonder if . . . anyone . . . misses him . . . Did it make you feel good . . . when he . . . when he went over the side?'

'*Alan,*' Carole insisted desperately. 'What does he *mean*?'

'I had no choice,' Alan said, addressing Kevin. '*You*

put me in that position, you bastard. *You* had a choice – you didn't have to do any of it. How many, Kevin? How many before all this?'

Carole tugged at his sleeve, which was wet with blood from the razor wound. '*Steven,*' she said. '*Tell* me!'

He turned to her. 'I'm not Steven,' he said. 'You were right, I'm not Steven.'

'I don't under*stand*,' she pleaded, even though she did. 'Tell me what's going on,' she insisted, even though she dreaded hearing it.

'I had no choice, Carole, I had to do it. It wasn't me, not myself, I was out of my mind, it was—'

'You killed someone . . .'

'No! I mean, yes. I—'

'That's how you covered yourself . . .' She started backing away towards the parlour door. 'You lied to me . . .'

'I could hardly tell you the truth about *that*, could I . . .' Suddenly, he looked down at the floor. 'Where is he?' he gasped. There was a patch of blood on the carpet where Kevin had been lying, but he was gone.

'Not far,' rasped a voice from behind them.

Alan spun round. While he and Carole had been concentrating on each other, Kevin had crawled across the hall and was slumped against the frame of the kitchen door, lying in the slick of oil. Alan stood there, frozen and dumbstruck, staring down at Kevin as he reached out an oily, bloody hand and grasped the razor. 'Take it,' he said, pushing it into Alan's hand. 'You know how . . . easy it is.' He glanced at Carole. 'She's not for you . . . We're One Soul, one brother . . . End her!' Alan gazed at the open razor in his hand. 'Go on,' Kevin urged. 'I *know* you can do it.'

Alan looked at Carole, who stared back at him, glancing nervously at the open blade.

'Do it,' said Kevin. 'We can be together at last.' There

was a hollow rattle as he took a box of matches from his pocket. 'It's your choice,' he said, poising the head of a match over the box's sandpaper strip. 'Flames or fraternity, my brother . . . it's all the . . . same to me . . . End her or . . . end . . . us all.'

Alan, his eyes blank and dead, looked from Kevin to the razor, then at Carole's face. He raised the blade and held it aloft for several moments, then turned and hurled it at Kevin's head. The handle glanced off his cheek and went spinning away onto the floor.

Kevin shook his head sadly. There were tears gathering in his eyes. 'Why not?' he gasped. 'All I ever wanted was . . . to be in . . . you,' he whispered. 'That's all I ever desired . . . And I *shall* have it . . . Elsewhere, perhaps . . .'

Before Alan could move, the match scraped on the box and everything before him – Kevin, Carole, the walls, floor and staircase – disappeared behind a blinding, whooshing sheet of flame.

'Come on,' said Rosalind through gritted teeth as the Renault's engine churned on the starter. 'Come *on* . . .' On the fourth attempt, it fired: she rammed it into gear and accelerated away down the hill towards the Keighley road.

She had given the police the address and directions to the farm, and they had told her to stay where she was, but after several minutes of anxiously pacing up and down and chewing her nails, she hadn't been able to bear the tension any longer. Now, as she sped through the dark, late-night streets and out onto the black country roads, she hastily formulated plans to get Carole out of there without arousing Steven's suspicions, and prayed last-ditch atheistic prayers that nothing had happened to her yet. Her prayers grew more and more intense and desperate as she drove up on to the moor and saw the orange glow of fire in the distance.

★ ★ ★

The air in the kitchen was thick with fumes from the oil and, as it ignited, the massive blast blew out the kitchen windows and wrenched the back door from its hinges. Carole, who had been standing on the threshold of the parlour, was shielded from the force of the explosion, but Alan was swept up and hurled the full length of the hall, his body slamming against the front door and collapsing on the floor. As the fireball imploded and subsided to a rushing, roaring blaze edged with the plangent tinkle of shattered, crumbling window panes, Carole hurtled from the parlour and ran to him.

'Steven!' she cried, falling to her knees in front of him. She put her hand behind his neck and raised his singed, blackened head. 'Steven!' she sobbed. 'Speak to me . . . please . . .'

He groaned and opened his eyes. He was stunned and battered, but otherwise unharmed, and Carole hauled him to his feet, stroking his face and sobbing with relief. The hall was filling with thick black smoke; the whole of the far end had vanished behind a wall of flame which was creeping and flaring across the walls and ceiling towards them.

'Get out!' he yelled, choking on the smoke.

She tried frantically to open the front door, but the knob wouldn't turn. 'It's double-locked!' she shouted in horrified disbelief. 'We're trapped!'

'Come on!' He seized her wrist and, pulling the neck of his sweater up over his face, dragged her back down the hall towards the fire. The flames were lapping around the frame of the parlour door, shivering on the painted wood and pouring thick smoke across the opening. Gripping Carole's wrist, he braced himself and dashed through the flaming curtain into the room, dragging her behind him. 'Smash the window!' he ordered, letting go of her.

She grabbed the stereo from its shelf, sending ornaments, books and potted plants scattering and smashing as the nest of wires trailed out. She took aim and hurled it through the pane of the lower sash, then tore down the curtains and hastily draped them over the jagged glass teeth still clinging to the lower edge of the frame. She was straddling the ledge, just about to duck out, when she realised he wasn't behind her. Her eyes stinging and watering, she peered into the gloom of smoke. 'Steven?' she called above the roar of the blaze, feeling herself starting to slide into panic. 'Where are you?'

She was about to go back and look for him when he emerged from the smoke. 'Here,' he croaked. 'I'm okay – go on.'

She ducked under the frame and slid out on to the ground, crawling away quickly on her hands and knees as he landed heavily behind her. 'What the hell were you doing?' she demanded when he had caught up with her.

He lay on his side, coughing wretchedly. 'This,' he gasped, holding up the zip-gun.

'What the hell d'you want that for? You could've *died* in there!'

He shrugged, still coughing and wheezing painfully. He didn't know why he had gone back for it; he had glimpsed it while Carole was making good their escape route and, acting on an inexplicable impulse, he had stepped back through the advancing flames to retrieve it. The steel had been searing hot when he picked it up, but he had held on to it determinedly. It was cooling quickly now in the chill night air. The elastic cords had escaped the flames, and it was still in working order. He dug his last bullet out of his trouser pocket and loaded it. Again, he didn't know why he did it, except that he could hear that tiny voice whispering inside his head again. He noticed Carole watching him. 'It's not over yet,' he said.

'He's dead, Steven. It's finished, he's gone now.'

'*All gone now* . . .' he murmured absently, then he shook his head. 'No, I won't believe that bastard's dead until I've seen his body.' He looked at her. 'And stop calling me Steven. How can I still be Steven now you know what you know?' She gazed back at him in silence, and for the first time since he had known her, he had the feeling that he was utterly transparent to her eyes, that everything inside his brain was laid open to her. He averted his eyes and touched her arm. 'Come on,' he said. 'We've got to get you away from here. Have you got your car keys?'

She rummaged in her pockets and produced the leather fob with its single, diminutive key. She helped him to his feet and, supporting each other, they began to trudge around to the front of the house. The fire had spread to the front and upstairs rooms now; the glass had shattered and the flames were bellying out and licking at the lintels. The little Morris, however, was standing just far enough from the front door to be out of danger, its red paintwork seeming to shiver and glow from within in the reflected firelight. Carole climbed into the driver's seat and turned the key in the ignition. The engine burst into life and the headlamps flooded white light across the red-glowing yard. She leaned across and flung open the passenger door, but he didn't get in; he just stood, shoulders hunched, leaning on the bonnet. She climbed out again. '*Get in!*' she shouted. 'Come on, *quickly!*'

He raised his head and gazed sadly at her, then shook his head. 'I can't,' he said. 'I have to stay.'

'What are you talking about? Just get *in*, for God's sake!'

'No, Carole. It's for the best, believe me. Go to Ros, or

your parents, *any*where. He's still here. I can feel him. You've got to get out of here.'

She stared at him. 'No!' she insisted. 'If you stay, I stay. If I go, you're coming with me. I didn't mean any of what I said back there. I don't *care* what you've done, I still love you – Now get in the fucking car, for Christ's sake!' he seemed to waver then, and she held up her hands. 'Wait a minute,' she said. 'I've got to get something first.'

She turned and ran across to the barn. Just inside the door, lying in the dust by the dead lantern and the broken, leaking flask, lay the little blue notebook. She had brought it out earlier in the hope that it might provide a means of testing the two men. Now, if she had to take only one thing away with her from this place, it would be this little book. She picked it up and ran back out to the yard. He was standing by the open door of the car, watching her with bewilderment, and she raised the book in the air as she ran. 'Get in!' she shouted. 'We're off!' That was when she saw it; just a glimpse in the corner of her eye, a sudden, slight movement on the periphery of the headlamp beam, and there it was: a blackened figure standing crooked and tattered by the corner of the house. As she turned her head in mid-stride, she saw the figure raise something in the air. At first she thought it was a stick, but as it rose to his shoulder, she recognised the shotgun. Her foot slammed down on the ground, and she skidded to a halt, her eyes following the line of aim across to Steven's body. He was still looking at her, even more puzzled than before. She opened her mouth and screamed: '*STEVEN!*' In that instant, he seemed to sense what was happening, and he swivelled on the spot, bringing the pistol up towards the illuminated figure. At the same moment, the shotgun turned like a compass pointer, seeking out the magnet of her screamed warning. The two guns fired simultaneously. She saw Kevin's head jerk to one side, the back of his skull exploding and showering fragments into the white light, then everything before her seemed to blur and skid and stretch as a massive weight like a speeding truck slammed into her chest. The fountain of orange flame dancing around her house froze for a fraction of a second, then rushed sideways, and she felt herself leave the ground and go soaring upwards, flying, tearing through the black night sky, upwards and upwards, expecting to tilt over the peak of her trajectory at any moment and slide down to land with an almighty, bone-smashing crash. But it never came. As she flew onwards and upwards, the stars faded and the sky closed over her, black and silent and dead . . .

. . . From out of the blackness, she thought she glimpsed Steven's face gazing down at her. There were tears in his eyes, and he seemed to be shouting at her, but she couldn't hear him. Then he faded to black, and she seemed to see Ros's face, also gazing down at her, also with tears in her eyes, also speaking words that she couldn't hear. *I was right*, she tried to say, *right about him*, but instead of the words came a convulsive pain in her body and a flood of hot, sour fluid in her mouth. She closed her eyes, and the pain began to ebb away. She felt a cool, familiar touch enfold her hand and, as soon as the soft skin brushed against hers, the pain vanished and a brilliant, blinding halo of corngold light surrounded her and suffused her with warmth. She gripped the hand, took a step forward and flew into the light.

'Well,' said a gentle voice in her ear. 'I'm back.'

After

Afterwards, life went on. There was a hospital, of course; a corridor deep inside the building, away from the pulse of repaired life, and off that corridor was a tiny room, unfurnished except for a small monochrome video monitor mounted on the wall, and on that monitor was an insidiously familiar image . . .

'Could you look at the screen please, Miss Barton . . .'

Rosalind kept her eyes averted. She had already glimpsed it. Her arms were folded tightly across her chest, the fingers of one hand splayed over her nose and mouth.

'Please?' the Detective Sergeant repeated.

'Why?' she asked. 'I've given you a statement.'

'I know, but we have to have a formal identification. Now, I realise it's painful for you, but could you please take a look.'

Reluctantly, she turned her eyes towards the face shown in oblique half-profile on the screen. They had done their best to clean it up, but the ravages of burns and bruises and God knew what besides were still hideously evident.

'Very good,' said the Sergeant encouragingly. 'Can you identify this as the man you knew as Steven Goldcliff?'

She nodded. 'Yes, that's him.'

'Thank you.' The Sergeant nodded to the attendant, who switched off the monitor. He led Rosalind out into the corridor. 'Let's see if we can get you a cuppa,' he said kindly.

She didn't hear him: she was gazing down the corridor. A grey, elderly-looking couple were standing some distance away, talking to another policeman. 'Who are they?' she asked.

As she spoke, the couple looked in her direction as though they had heard her, even though they were much too far away.

'Mr and Mrs Perceval,' he said quietly. 'They're here to identify their daughter. I thought they'd've been gone by now.'

Rosalind's mind went blank for a moment. 'Perceval?' she asked. 'Carole's parents? God, of course. I didn't recognise them ... They look so *old*.' They were still gazing at her. 'I think they blame me,' she whispered.

The Sergeant took her by the arm. 'No they don't,' he said. 'They're in shock, that's all. Come away now.'

'It wasn't my fault,' she murmured, allowing herself to be led away. 'I never liked him. I tried to warn her, but she wouldn't listen.'

'I know.'

As he led her through a swing door into another corridor, she still couldn't tear her eyes away from Mr and Mrs Perceval; her gaze remained tied to theirs until the door swung closed and severed the thread forever.

Receding, piercing the far horizon ...

He had made this crossing once before. This time, though, it was uneventful. Afterwards, the man with the shaven head and the inward-looking eyes stood on the quay for a while, gazing up at the red bulk of the ferry's hull, his eyes squinting against the brilliant sunlight and scanning the deck rail. He noticed a man looking down at him and a faint, ghostly smile swam slowly across his face. He held the gaze for a few moments, then shouldered his rucksack and turned away, joining the milling crowd of foot-passengers heading for the gates.

As they funnelled through and slowly dispersed towards Ouistreham, his pale scalp bobbed and wove intermittently amongst the dapple of distant heads, then gradually receded until, at last, it vanished as completely as if it had never existed.